BOOK ONE OF
THE GEMINI FILES

CAENOGENESIS

/ ˌsiːnəʊdʒɪˈnɛtɪk; ˌsiːnəʊˈdʒɛnɪsɪs /

noun: variants coenogenesis or more commonly cenogenesis
introduction during development of adaptive characters or structures that are absent from the earlier phylogeny of a strain (as addition of the placenta to the common vertebrate pattern in mammalian evolution)—opposed to palingenesis

TASHA HE

Copyright © 2026 by Tasha He

ISBN: 979-8-9991475-0-9

LCCN: 2026900846

© 2026 by Tasha He All rights reserved. No part of this book may be reproduced in any form or by any electronic or mechanical means, including information storage and retrieval systems, without written permission from the author, except for the use of brief quotations in a book review.

All characters and events in this book are fictitious. Any resemblance to actual persons, living or dead, is purely coincidental.

First edition

Illustration by Laura Sampaio (lumie.draws)

Edited by Mia Darien

Title page by Lindsay Robertson (Sage & Fable)

Ornamental Break by MGSdesügns

Chapter Headers by Emmeli Markegård

CAENOGENESIS

THE GEMINI FILES
BOOK 1

TASHA HE

For you. I hope you see this someday.

Prologue

It's different.

It wasn't her. She still rested on a cot in her room, eyes closed, back straight, and hands clasped on her lap. It was not difficult to envision everything in her mind's eye.

It wasn't the room. The walls were still windowless and grey, composed of reinforced steel meant to detain its occupant, whereas the floor was hard cement. Fluorescent lights still left nowhere to hide, creating a sense of sterility, still turning on and off with the day/night cycle in a boring, rhythmic cadence—though time held no meaning to one not permitted outside.

Cameras loomed in each corner of the ceiling, the lenses black and ominous, watching her. A light layer of dust covered her cot's fitted sheet as evidence of its disuse. Across from her, a small bookshelf within arm's reach. Classics like Sun Tzu's *Art of War* and *Strategy: A History* by Lawrence Freedman lined its shelves alongside other strategy and logic books. All of which she knew by heart. The sink nestled in the corner still leaked as it had since she'd damaged the handles.

Drip. Drip. Drip.

Everything was the same, but different.

Tension.

Strong enough to set her on edge. Her fingers clenched, strength rippling through her toned muscles as the click-clack of rapid footsteps drew near. She exhaled through her teeth, breath turning to fog from the bitter chill that permeated the room.

He's coming.

That was unexpected.

She opened her eyes, angled her head toward the door, and waited. Within moments, she glimpsed him peering through the door's slat. She recognized his gaze—the first she'd ever seen.

Light flooded the room as the door creaked open. Her eyes narrowed as she snapped to attention like any good soldier would to their commanding officer—arms pinned against her narrow waist, thumbs parallel to the seam of her sweatpants, heels together, and toes apart.

"Creator... What do you require?" she breathed, analyzing him for any hint of the reason for this abnormal intrusion.

He stared back at her, lacking a response. Her brows furrowed. He registered as pallid, and the tension on his face indicated...*fear?*

Her lips parted, a question rolling off her tongue.

"... Is something going to transpire?"

Above, the door exploded inward with a resounding crash. Heavy boots pounded overhead, voices barking orders—closing in, zeroed in on the basement. The lab.

Her Creator's expression twisted, fear collapsing into something harder, colder. He closed the distance in two long strides and seized her arm.

"Project Gemini, run."
A sharp sting bloomed at the base of her neck.

Chapter 1

"Get the hell out of here, *Slice*!"

Bullets zinged past Theopold Kraken as he dove behind some debris—what might have been a hover car once. The unkempt man yelling at him belonged to the Metal Vultures, one of the salvage gangs ruling the Junkyard. One Kraken used to run with, though that had been so long ago, he didn't recognize any familiar faces among his pursuers.

And, well, breakups are hard.

That's why the Vultures put out a hit on him.

"The Slice thing again?" he called, peering around the debris. "Try something I've not heard before."

The word caused his stomach to coil. A relic of the divide between Retro Ignis, where people scraped by with outdated tools, and Modernist Ignis, the gleaming Inner Ring. He'd heard it his whole damn life. The insult branded him a traitor, a tool of the privileged—someone who wielded high-tech skills, a betrayer of his own kind—but Retro Ignis was his home. Always had been.

The Junkyard, in particular, used to be a thriving industrial hub in Scraptown before civil war gutted it. Now, it constituted a patchwork of salvaged materials, old shipping containers, and crumbling buildings lining the broken streets. The city-state of Ignis had tried cleaning it up once, but they'd abandoned the effort when the Inner Ring took priority. Typical.

A bullet whistled past Kraken, narrowly missing his ear as he threw himself back behind safety. *Nope. Still there.* Most Vultures were just desperate scavengers trying to scrape together enough to survive. That had been true when Kraken ran with them and after he left. They hadn't posed a real threat until they stumbled onto an abandoned weapons cache last year, and he had trodden carefully around the Junkyard since.

This was the situation the supposed leaders of their society left them in—survival mode—so could the Vultures truly be blamed?

Kraken ran his fingers over his holster but didn't draw. Rust and oil permeated the thick air, with discarded electronics and machinery scattered across the ground. The place offered ripe pickings for the technologically savvy, like Kraken. The risk was certainly worth the reward. Any tech salvaged would be used to further his group's goal of removing the corrupted officials of Ignis.

He considered his options. Where there was one Vulture, more would follow. He could stand his ground against his assailant and hope no others came, or he could make a break toward a row of decaying buildings and try to lose his pursuer in there.

Run.

Running seemed the better option here. Standoffs were tedious, and Kraken bore no ill will toward these people. He didn't want to hurt them.

With a burst of energy, Kraken raced for the nearest

building. He smashed through the door and bounded up the closest stairs three at a time. Behind him, his foe screamed profanities, stumbling to keep pace.

Kraken reached the top floor and listened. The stomping behind him had multiplied. Great. Three now. He sucked in a sharp breath. "Dammit."

The last flight of stairs led to the rooftop. The freezing January wind blasted his face as he skidded to a stop. No ladder. No fire escape. Nothing but a thirty-foot drop. Across from him, another rooftop of the same height. It looked sturdy enough.

Jumping was an option.

No biggie, Kraken thought with a dry laugh, lightheaded from exertion. *What's a thirty-foot drop to my doom?*

In truth, such a jump shouldn't pose a problem to someone like him. His assailants, on the other hand, probably didn't have the modifications to make such a leap and survive. That didn't stop him from imagining the possibility of falling. Life just had this habit of trying to fuck him over.

Kraken inhaled deeply in preparation, sprinting and leaping into the air. The wind howled past his ears before he crashed onto the neighboring roof in a rough roll. Staggering to his feet, pulse hammering, adrenaline thrummed and pushed him forward. Faster. Farther. Shouts rang out behind him, but they grew fainter with each jump.

Five buildings over, he pushed his way inside an old factory. However, as bad luck would have it, the next step was a literal one. Kraken tumbled down a flight of stairs, letting out an exasperated groan as he lay on the landing with a brand-new, two-inch cut bleeding from his forehead. *Fantastic.*

What had he just said about life trying to fuck him?

"Crap," he wheezed.

He twitched his fingers and toes. Nothing broken. Just bruised and bleeding. He propped himself up and tore a strip from his shirt, tying it around his head to slow the bleeding.

With a grunt, he hauled himself up the railing, a cold piece of metal under his grip. Every muscle screamed in protest. The world pulsed with the rhythm of the throbbing behind his eyes.

Kraken muttered a few choice words as he limped down more stairs, exiting into a short hallway that led to an empty room, save for rubble and debris. This seemed a good place to lie low for a while. Gather himself. With a sigh, he slid down to sit—only to freeze partway.

A body.

It lay slumped atop a pile of junk. No decay or smell. It couldn't be a corpse.

How did that get here?

Kraken pushed himself up and approached. Feminine. East Asian features. Silken black hair tied back. Velvety navy-blue robe over a white T-shirt and dark sweats and no shoes. Very odd clothing for anyone, like she'd thrown on the robe quickly to step outside her house and somehow had become lost here. She stood quite tall for a woman—5'8", at least.

A sex bot? Maybe.

His lips curled into a grin. Even better. Only the Inner Ring could produce an android of such caliber. The parts inside would be invaluable for rigging weaponry and repairing old tech—something the Outsiders sorely needed.

Kraken imagined everything he could jury-rig using its parts as he nudged its stomach. Not too hard, but enough something living would notice.

The thing jolted to life and sank its teeth into his ankle with a sickening *squelch*.

Kraken hollered, wrenching his leg away. He stumbled back, drawing his pistol and pointing it at its gut. It—she?—the woman, or whatever the hell she was, staggered to her feet, blood dripping from her lips. She bared her teeth, eyes wild.

She lunged. Kraken dodged, but her erratic strikes landed like a flurry he could barely track. Brutally efficient but lacking finesse. She slammed into the wall, clutching it as if in pain. A ragged sound tore from her throat. No android moved like *that.*

Kraken put space between them, grimacing as he took a moment to assess his ankle. Could life *stop* trying to do that thing it tries to do? Her teeth had cleaved clean through his boot. *Wonderful... First my head, and now this?*

His eyes narrowed. What the hell was wrong with her? *Gene therapy?* That would explain the viciousness. Gene therapy of any kind carried risk, but in Retro Ignis—particularly Scraptown—it was worse.

Her voice sounded husky, yet it dripped with malice. "Get away from me."

"Get away from you?" Kraken glanced at the bloodied imprint of her teeth on his boot, his face flushed crimson. Words tumbled from his mouth in quick succession. "It hasn't escaped my notice that you're blocking my exit from this room. My leg is severely injured; there's blood all over the floor. So, where would you want me to go? Through the *wall?*"

He sucked in a few deep breaths before raising his gun, wanting her to be aware of its presence. "Not an option, by the way. Please don't make me shoot you. I will if I have to. You attacked me unprovoked. It's justified. So, please, calm down before I shoot you at point-blank range."

Her brows drew together as her eyes narrowed, giving the impression his rambling annoyed her. Fair. He tended to blather on when flustered. She pressed her palm against the wall as she drew herself up to her full height, which remained a good five inches shorter than him. "Why did you propose that if it is not a viable option?"

Kraken bit back a groan. *Seriously?* Of everything he'd said, *that* was her takeaway? She spoke like one of the holographic AIs in government buildings—all logic, no human connection. And even *they* had more personality.

He raised his firearm higher, aiming it at her torso so that there was no mistaking his intentions. "Look," he began slowly. "You attacked me without provocation and now you're preventing me from leaving this room."

She watched him with a long, quiet stare. Kraken found her expression unsettling. Her lack thereof prompted him to question his earlier conclusion about gene therapy. *Nothing alive could look so dead*, he thought.

"That is not correct," she stated, breaking the tension. "It is simple to deny your claim that I attacked you without provocation. To begin with, you advanced on me while I was in a state of deterioration."

"But—"

"Your intentions were unsavory," she spoke over him. "Even if they were not, I am still within reason to retaliate because of your initial violation of my boundaries." Her eyes fervently jumped to his pistol. "You talk about peace, yet you threaten me with a weapon. It is laughable. Humans are the epitome of hypocrisy."

Kraken's jaw clenched. Whatever she was, she thought. She reasoned. And the way she shifted weight, taut and ready, spoke of unnerving speed. A flick of her foot sent a loose brick flying into his hand, knocking his gun away before he could react. His fingers throbbed as she surged forward again, a large glass shard in hand. Kraken barely caught her wrist, feeling the surprising power behind the slender limb, before the jagged edge sliced his throat.

How did someone who'd just recently undergone gene therapy employ such a tactic? His nostrils flared, and his lips curled into a snarl as he glowered at her. "So, *you're* the one with the unsavory intentions now."

If biting through his boot hadn't been the first indication of her strength, the way his enhanced muscles strained just to keep her glass shard at bay served as a sure second. If Kraken weren't genetically enhanced himself, he'd be dead.

He shoved her back, the glass shard nicking his cheek as

he did, and rolled for his gun. Kraken snatched it, spinning around, pistol aimed at her leg. Not to shoot but simply to threaten her. He settled on his knee before opening his free hand in the 'Stop' symbol. "As I was saying. There is a difference between hypocrisy and a fail-safe. Notice how I have not gone on the offense once this entire time?"

She hesitated, the glass shard frozen above her head like a projectile. Her hesitation allowed him a moment to observe her more clearly. Other than what he'd already observed, he noted her build was lean and slender, aptly built for her strength and agility. An oval-shaped face matched with a small, swooping nose gave her a conventionally cute appearance, completely at odds with her vicious nature. Her eyes caught Kraken's attention the most—round, prominent, deep like an abyss, exuding confidence.

I really don't have time for this. He grimaced. The Vultures could find them at any minute.

Pulling the trigger and ending it all felt inevitable. If he couldn't reason with her, he could die. Despite her awkward movements, she carried herself with the discipline of a soldier. Every movement calculated. Always rationing her energy. Even Recombinants like Kraken would fall to her.

That thought was chilling, given their standoff.

Kraken took a deep breath to steady himself, refusing to let his emotions get the best of him. *Am I taking the wrong approach here?*

"Okay, look, logic girl. I can tell you're the type to not want to be put at risk." Kraken lowered his gun. "So, I'm going to cut you a deal. If you put down that blasted piece of glass, I'll slide my pistol out of the room. We both won't have weapons and we'll be genuinely equal. Agree?"

"Disarm yourself first," she replied, remaining completely still. "But remember, I do not require this glass weapon for a duel."

Yeah, tell me something I don't know. It was a fair request. The glass shard was meant for close combat, while his pistol gave him the advantage at range. If he didn't hold up his end of the bargain, she'd be weaponless.

Still, irritation prickled at him. Not just because he had to go first, but because he was up against someone who knew exactly what they were doing. "Fair enough."

Kraken placed the gun on the ground with deliberate care, then stepped back. A sharp kick sent it skidding across the floor and into the hallway, where it struck the wall with a hollow thud. His fingers reflexively brushed against the knife concealed in the inner pocket of his jacket—his contingency plan. His gaze remained locked on her as he gestured toward the glass.

"Is this enough proof for you?" His voice remained steady, almost coaxing. "I wasn't trying to hurt you. I wanted to make sure you were alive, to save you." A partial truth at best. He had intended to use her for scrap, but she didn't need to know that. "So, are you ready to honor our deal?"

Her smile was slow, calculated, though it never quite reached her eyes. "My part of the deal... Why would you rely on an opponent to keep their word?" With a flick of her wrist, she sent the glass shard slicing through the air. It embedded itself in the wooden doorframe with a dull thunk. Still within reach. Different from his gun.

"You're smart for a human," she mused, tilting her head. "Though this was a poor deal for you. I will honor it, but only partially. You still have a weapon."

Kraken didn't flinch at the accusation. So, she knew about the knife. What she didn't know was that a decade of training and genetic enhancements had made him a weapon himself. A slow smirk pulled at his lips as he considered her choice of words. *Human.* She always said it as if it were something separate from herself. Something lesser. It piqued his interest.

"I wouldn't call myself foolish. If you had wanted me dead, you'd have finished it or we'd remain in a stalemate."

Kraken leaned against the wall, arms crossed, one hand absentmindedly brushing the inner pocket of his jacket where the knife lay hidden. He kept his expression composed, despite the sharp sting radiating from his ankle. "I figured let's skip the theatrics and talk. Mutually assured destruction doesn't work in a one-on-one impasse. I took a gamble."

Some AI units evolved past their initial programming, but she seemed far more advanced than that. A Recombinant remained a possibility, yet her insistence on distancing herself from humanity proved...puzzling.

"We remain at a stalemate," she said, her voice measured. "What now?"

"For starters, we could stop trying to kill each other. Seems like a solid beginning." Kraken shifted his weight and cast a glance out the window. No sign of movement, but he knew better than to trust an illusion of safety. The distance he had put between the Vultures and himself hadn't been enough. There was a real chance he'd walk out of here and straight into a trap.

His gaze flicked back to her. "You're clearly not in top form," he observed. "Your stance is off, your movements wilder than calculated. More feral than machine. So, what exactly *are* you?"

She tilted her head as if considering him before replying. "I am unlike you." A pause. Then, with something close to finality, she added, "I am Yin."

Kraken noted the subtle shift in her posture—the way her muscles uncoiled when he remained measured, unthreatening. Hostility triggered a defensive instinct in her, much like danger sent adrenaline surging through his own veins. If he wanted to leave without a fight, his best chance involved honesty, or at least the illusion of it.

He smirked again. "Your defense is impressive, Yin. But you might land better punches if you worked on your balance."

If Yin thought Kraken was clueless, all the better. It gave him a slight advantage. Despite being at odds mere moments ago, he bore no grudge. She'd reacted to a perceived threat, and he couldn't fault her for that. What he could fault her for was blocking his escape. But despite his mounting impatience, the best option remained to keep her talking. Keep her engaged. Help guide her to the conclusion that he no longer posed a threat and to *move out of the way of the exit.*

When she remained silent, he pressed on. "I'm Kraken. Don't ask for any other names. I don't know much about you besides your ability to fight, but where did you learn? Your technique is advanced, and you improvise weapons like it's second nature."

Yin tilted her head, frowning as if weighing her words. "My fighting technique comes from my place of origin. I learned everything there. Nothing more can be said."

Kraken studied her, searching for a crack in her guarded demeanor. Why was she so adamant about being vague? More importantly, what had driven her to play dead in Scraptown? And how could he persuade her to talk?

Something with her capabilities could be useful.

The burning in his ankle interrupted his thoughts. With his adrenaline fading, the pain of Yin's bite settled in. He removed his boot to inspect the full extent of his injury. A dark red stain saturated his sock. The wound appeared jagged and torn, with deep puncture marks where her teeth penetrated the skin. Swelling and inflammation were already present around the wound. Kraken winced at the sight of it. The force of her bite probably damaged underlying tissue and bone. Nothing a plasma patch couldn't fix. He tugged on his sock to stem the bleeding.

As if his troubles couldn't worsen, he heard shouts echoing within the confines of the building. Kraken's body grew rigid. The shouts were distant but clear. He knew that sound—the low rumble of a hunting pack. Not one voice but many. Reinforcements. They'd waited him out. Their patience was gone. *Dammit.*

Yin's body radiated stillness like an alert hound. She might have heard them more clearly than he did. Her sharp gaze homed in on the doorway, her expression unreadable. But Kraken caught it. The slight shift in her stance, the way her hands curled subtly, preparing for a fight.

He moved toward the door, only halting when she returned her gaze to him. He raised his hands to show deference.

"Hear those voices?" Kraken asked, indicating with his head. "Pretty sure they belong to the gangsters who want me, and anyone around me, dead. Cut the logical crap. We have to go. Now."

Chapter 2

A DRUMBEAT POUNDED IN HIS EARS, A FRANTIC RHYTHM SET BY his pulse. He tore into the hallway, and with each step, hot agony spiked up his leg from the ankle. He gritted his teeth, shoving the pain down, burying it in a cold, dark corner of his mind. *No time for weakness.*

His fingers found the familiar weight of his firearm, the cold metal grounding him as he cocked the slide and checked the cartridge. Full. Not enough to wipe them out, but maybe enough to buy him time. He inhaled a deep breath, steadying himself, then pressed his back against the wall. His senses stretched outward, anticipating the threat.

A silent presence loomed behind him, quiet but unmistakable—Yin.

"Correction. Logic dictates I accompany you," she remarked, her tone as detached as ever. "To cease would be irrational."

Kraken scarcely spared her a glance. Instead, he edged

toward the window and peered outside. No movement or sign of his pursuers. The streets below stretched empty. If he acted fast, he could shatter the glass, jump, and disappear before the Vultures even knew where to look. If Yin was smart, she'd follow.

Jumping remained safe as long as he nailed the landing, though his ankle might beg to differ in this circumstance. He turned, catching Yin's gaze. He doubted it'd be an issue for her. Her face remained a blank canvas. No tension, no hesitation, nothing to indicate fear or concern. He couldn't gauge her thoughts, no matter how hard he tried. And for now, he didn't have time.

Survival came first.

"By the way," Kraken's elbow collided with the windowpane. The sound of shattered glass echoed throughout the room. He used his gun to clear any lingering fragments. "Our disarmed deal is off." He hoisted himself onto the windowsill, straddling it. "Are you coming? ...Yin?"

The place where she'd stood held an eerie stillness. No sign of her.

Kraken dropped to the floor with a muffled thud and scanned the room, his boots soft against the floor. A fresh indentation on the doorframe marked the absence of her glass shard. *Where did you go?*

"Yin!" he shouted, straining his ears for any signs of movement. His ears, genetically enhanced to detect the faintest sound, heard only silence. *Even with my enhanced senses, I can't track her. What the hell is she?*

A bullet tore through the air, grazing past him with a sharp zing. Kraken's reflexes kicked in. He slammed his back against the wall, heart pounding with adrenaline. Peering around the edge of the broken window, he spotted his assailant—a young Vulture gangster. Bald, with tattoos scrawled across his face, his eyes narrowed with intent.

Kraken muttered under his breath, "You've got to be kidding me."

He reached for the silencer on his belt, screwing it onto his firearm. A small adjustment, but one he should've made earlier. *Hindsight.* He drew a steadying breath, silencing his frustration, and then, with lethal calm, stepped back out into view. A single shot rang out, and the gangster's face exploded into a spray of red. Kraken had already snapped back behind cover, action preceding thought.

This was his gift.

His reflexes functioned as a finely tuned radar that reacted before his mind could catch up. It was more than just physical agility; it was that same lethal calm, an automatic, split-second harmony of mind and body.

A second Vulture stepped out from behind the debris just as the first body hit the ground. Kraken hissed. Roaches. Kill one and twenty more scuttle out to take its place.

He reached for his knife. *No time to waste.* The moment his fingers wrapped around the handle, he moved.

The cold air rushed past him as he launched out of the window. His landing jarred him, knees bending to absorb the impact, but pain tore through his ankle like a live wire. His vision flared white-hot. *Dammit.* He held back a cry, locking his jaw as his body buckled. Adrenaline took over, numbing the agony long enough for him to push forward.

His target had no time to react. Kraken drove the blade into the man's chest, feeling the resistance of muscle and bone before it yielded. A gurgled breath. A shudder. The Vulture collapsed. Kraken eased the body down, sparing him a brutal fall.

"Sorry," he murmured.

The regret was fleeting, passing through him before vanishing. Gunfire shattered the moment. A crash. Screams.

His head snapped toward the sound. *Is that her?*

Yin had vanished so abruptly before... Had she run? No, that wasn't it. If those gunshots meant she was in danger, should he cut his losses? Keep moving?

He exhaled, dragging a hand down his face. *No.*

Even if he didn't fully understand her, he wasn't about to leave her.

Sliding the knife back into its sheath, Kraken gripped his gun and moved, skirting the side of the building to the front. As he rounded the corner, three Metal Vultures crossed his path.

His weapon came up, his aim precise. Three shots. Three bodies dropped. Clean. Methodical.

The fight had never been fair. He was more than them—enhanced, sharpened by years of hard-won survival. His movements were fluid, lethal. But as he stared at the crumpled bodies, a cold, sour twist started in his gut. *Just let me go.*

Why hadn't they? They all could have walked away. No grudges, no fresh bodies left to rot in the street.

But they hadn't. And now, here they were.

The door groaned as Kraken nudged it open, the business end of his pistol entering the room before him. The scent of blood hit him first—thick, metallic, suffocating.

Yin stood in the center of the carnage, a halo of bodies sprawled at her feet. Blood slicked her skin, smeared across her clothes in chaotic strokes. A handgun, one she hadn't entered with, rested in her hand, her fingers curled around it with the ease of someone who knew how to use it. Whether that stemmed from instinct or something else, Kraken didn't know.

"Yin?" Kraken hesitated. He raised his hands, nonthreatening. "Are you injured?"

She turned to him. He noted the beads of sweat dripping from her forehead and the dull look in her eyes. The ongoing impact of whatever was happening to her remained.

The room was silent except for a single sound: wet, ragged breathing.

His gaze dropped. Among the bodies, one still clung to life. A man lay on his back, with a jagged shard of glass jutting from his chest. Blood bubbled at his lips as he gurgled, drowning in it.

Kraken took a deliberate step forward, and recognition hit him like a hammer.

Markus.

The leader of the Metal Vultures. The one who put a hit on him. The one who, eleven years ago, had watched him walk away from the gang and vowed he'd never forgive him for it.

Markus's eyes fluttered open. They held a dark fire, burning even through the haze of pain, and locked onto Kraken. No pleading. Just the sharp, unforgiving blade of betrayal.

For a moment, the weight of the past settled on Kraken's shoulders. The late nights, the scraps they'd fought through, the exhilaration of running jobs together, and Markus's plans promising them something more. A ghost of their former brotherhood clawed at him. But the gang had crumbled, and when it did, he'd walked away without looking back.

Markus never could.

His mouth moved, forming a word—a curse, maybe, or one last bitter insult—but only blood spilled out.

Kraken's fingers tightened around his pistol. A pause. A moment where the past threatened to reach up and drag him back. Was this closure? It didn't feel like it.

His jaw clenched. No hesitation. No second thoughts.

He raised the weapon, leveled it at Markus's head, and pulled the trigger.

Kraken exhaled, slow and steady. The weight on his chest didn't lift.

"Rest in peace," he murmured, though he didn't know who the words were for—Markus or himself.

Beside him, Yin's chest rose and fell in rapid succession, each breath ragged as she pulled air into her lungs. She straightened, tilting her head.

"Why did you follow me?" Her voice was flat. "It wasn't for my well-being. This is your problem, not mine."

Kraken exhaled and slid his gun back into its holster after removing the silencer. "That's an odd way to say thank you," he retorted, wiping the sweat from his brow. "I couldn't leave you behind. Whether I like it or not, abandoning someone isn't in my nature."

Yin considered this. "Humans are persistent. And willing to die."

Kraken believed it was her way of calling them annoying.

"How many followed you, Human Kraken?"

She had a point. He wasn't sure how many were still on their tail or if the remaining Vultures had retreated.

"Scraptown gangs rely on intimidation more than strategy," he explained. "They've got numbers, not brains. Kill a few high-ranking members—" He gestured toward Markus's lifeless body. "—and you become top dog."

"Top dog?" Yin wrinkled her nose. "Humans wish to be referred to as canines?"

An abrupt laugh escaped him. Yeah, she seemed fine.

Kraken knelt, adjusting his sock where it had loosened during the fight. As he pulled it back over his battered ankle, fresh beads of blood pooled around the torn skin.

"Well," he said, casting her a sidelong glance. "You killed their leader. Whether you like it or not, that makes you top dog." He smirked. "Congratulations."

Yin pursed her lips before tossing the gun aside. She regarded the fallen leader of the Metal Vultures, eyes lingering on the lifeless body.

"You did a merciful thing for him. You ended his dying process early. Why? Was he not your enemy?"

The question struck deeper than Kraken expected. Did she even understand what mercy entailed? Did it mean anything to her?

Distant laughter echoed in his mind—two boys racing through trash-littered streets, their worn-out shoes slapping against cracked concrete as they sprinted toward the day's rations. The exhilaration of opportunity. The warmth of belonging. Then, the sharp sting of betrayal. Hot breath against his face, older now, a voice snarling: *Traitor.*

Kraken rubbed his temple and studied the floor. "There was no use in letting him suffer."

Yin studied him with piercing focus, her eyes dissecting every conscious and unconscious movement, as if running a diagnostic on him. For a moment, Kraken half-expected her to start beeping or open a port for some kind of software update. Even the most patient person would find her stoicism and manner off-putting.

Then, to his surprise, she sighed and pinched the bridge of her nose. "You are ruining my peace here."

Kraken's brows shot up. He had braced himself for a detached lecture about how mercy constituted a weakness. But instead, for the first time, she didn't sound like a machine. She sounded...human.

And in that one word—**peace**—he saw her. Had that been what she came here for? Whatever peace meant to someone like her. Instead, he'd barged in, tried to 'decommission' her, and dragged dirty laundry from his past along with him.

"I'm sorry I ruined your...*peace*, but here we are," Kraken muttered, cheeks flushing red. Something hot and sticky dripped down his temple. He reached up, fingers brushing against the laceration on his head. Still seeping trickles of blood. How much of his blood painted the earth today?

"Let's get out of here before I actually bleed out."

"You are dramatic." Yin pressed her lips together. "And troublesome."

Without another word, she turned toward the open door. For a second, Kraken thought she'd finally had enough of his *dramatic* self and was making a break for it. But then she stopped at the threshold, glancing back at him expectantly.

He fell into step behind her. "I am not dramatic," he countered. Per se. "I am more a believer in heightened reality."

Even with her back to him, Kraken could practically *feel* her rolling her eyes. To her, he must've been just another clumsy human who struggled to tell left from right. For a moment, he wondered what it would take to actually impress her. He shoved that thought aside.

They needed a plan.

Being out in the open made them easy targets. And while Yin was powerful, nobody fared well against a mob.

Kraken smirked as the perfect escape route formed in his mind. He savored the moment of unveiling his heroic plan when a loud *clank* cut through his thoughts.

His gaze snapped to Yin. She was already crouched over a sewer grate, fingers hooked into the metal grooves. With little effort, she pried it free from its sealed foundation and set it aside.

She'd thought of the same plan.

Kraken deflated. Had it been that obvious?

A foul stench curled into the air, and his nose crinkled. The sewers of Retro Ignis were outdated and disgusting—especially in Scraptown. The thought of wading through that sludge churned his stomach, but realistically, it was the safest route. No one would follow them down there. Not willingly.

Yin was already descending, her voice breaking through his hesitation. "Are you coming? We shall travel this way. No one will follow us."

Kraken sighed. "Yeah... Right on your heels."

Suppressing every instinct to *not* climb into the rancid depths of the city, he swung his legs into the hole until his boots found the first rung of the ladder. Twisting onto his stomach, he eased himself down, pulling the heavy grate back into place above him.

And just like that, he was ready to see what fresh hell awaited his nose.

CHAPTER 3

THE AIR IN THE SEWERS SHROUDED THE TUNNELS IN A FOUL, clammy blanket thick with the stench of decay and rot. Faint fluorescent lights shivered in the distance, but the sickly yellow glow did little to dispel the gloom. Every breath was a fresh assault on Kraken's senses, a reminder of the city's underbelly. The tunnels thrummed with the slow drip of water and the scurrying of unseen things.

The rumors of mutant rats large enough to drag away stray cats, he dismissed them. But as he eyed the twisting tunnels ahead, an icy knot of dread settled in his stomach. He wasn't about to test the theory.

Thick sludge coursed through the system between the walkways, sloshing toward whatever purification facility would eventually turn it into clean drinking water. *Yum.*

Favoring his bad ankle, Kraken eased off the ladder and landed with a grunt. The tunnels stretched endlessly in either direction, branching off into an intricate maze. He raised an arm to shield his nose, blinking against the dim light. The maze of tunnels snapped into focus.

Yin was waiting.

She should have kept moving, leaving behind the *troublesome, peace-ruining* human to catch up on his own. Instead, she held still, regarding him with her usual unreadable expression. A display of loyalty—intentional or not.

"Your ankle is sore," Yin observed. Then, after a pause, she added, "Humans apologize when they are showing politeness, is that correct? Even if it lacks genuineness." Another pause. "I apologize for your soreness, even if I was justified."

Kraken barked out a laugh, only for it to cut off into a violent gag as the sewer stench coated his throat. His laughter-turned-choking echoed through the tunnels, bouncing back at him in distorted mockery.

It was *how* she said it. That neutral, completely sincere expression paired with a statement so blunt it could've been satire. As much as her cold logic could be frustrating, some part of him found it endearing.

In a world built on deception, Yin was pure—unfiltered, honest, untouched by the corruption that tainted everyone else.

Her face contorted. "I do not understand the joke."

Kraken waved a hand in front of his face, attempting—*and failing*—to dispel the awful taste from his mouth. He stifled his amusement, about to explain, when Yin crouched at his ankle.

He twitched as slender fingers wrapped around the back of his foot, lifting it. The unexpected contact jolted him, but the coldness of her touch was oddly relieving against his throbbing injury.

Kraken exhaled, leaning against the ladder for support. Her fingers examined his ankle with a rigor that forced a question: was she truly just analyzing, or was this her own version of concern?

"Human Kraken."

There it was again. That moniker.

"This wound will fare poorly in the sewer," she continued, her tone clinical. "There is a high risk of infection with it exposed. The least we can do is wrap it." She pointed to the bandage on his head. "Give me that."

Kraken sighed but didn't argue. He peeled the bandage from his forehead and handed it over. The cut wasn't deep. It would survive the sewer better than his ankle would. There was no telling what bacteria already festered in the wound.

Yin worked, her fingers tightening the bandage with trained competence. Her movements were precise, methodical. Basic medical care was apparently part of her skillset.

She was...definitely something. Strange, yes, but not necessarily evil. Kraken still wasn't sure what to make of her. She was analytical to the point of emotionlessness, yet there was something undeniably human lurking beneath all that cold logic. Up until now, she'd shown complete indifference to the lives of others. But this? This suggested otherwise.

Yin was a puzzle, and Kraken was starting to think he *wanted* to solve it.

Right after he got his ankle properly disinfected.

As if reading his mind, Yin said, "This will require disinfection when you reach your destination. A plasma patch will hold well." She stepped back, tucking her hands into her robe pockets. "Where is your destination? I shall escort you."

Her entire demeanor had shifted. Gone was the ruthless force of nature who tore through the Metal Vultures without a second thought. Now, she leaned with casual ease, weight shifted onto one foot, posture relaxed.

If she weren't drenched in blood and dressed in normal clothes, she might even pass for a regular gal on the street.

"It's called a home," Kraken said. "It's in Old Town near the Rivera Theater. You don't have to come along. I can find my way."

He hesitated. Reconsidered.

"Actually, maybe you should come with me. To Old Town."

Old Town was the main suburb of Retro Ignis, bordering Modernist Ignis. A towering retaining wall wrapped around its perimeter, separating the two districts. The wall wasn't meant to keep people out. Travel between the two halves of the city was unrestricted. Officially, the wall was there to maintain 'harmony.' To prevent 'less savory' individuals from disrupting the order of the city. But every movement was tracked.

Kraken rubbed the chip implanted beneath the skin of his palm. Medical professionals implanted these chips at birth, carrying a person's entire identity from their name to their bank account, dispensing one's credits since paper money became obsolete after the nuclear war of 2026.

His was a forgery that he'd calibrated himself to avoid being tracked. He looked down at his palm, tightening his fingers into a fist. *Classist bullshit.*

'Less savory' was just a polite way of saying *poor*.

As they moved through the tunnels, Kraken noticed Yin's expression shift. Her lips compressed, her gaze distant; he saw her calculating something far beyond numbers. Something he'd said had unsettled her.

He resisted the urge to reach out, to tap her shoulder, to pry. Her thoughts resisted anything but mechanical equations, whirring and clicking in perfect sequence.

Then, finally, "I..." Yin's voice sliced through the damp, echoing silence. "...don't possess a place like a home. Only a place to exist."

Kraken gawked at her. That was *something*. The first real, personal truth she had given him beyond her name.

He quickly schooled his expression.

"I'm sorry you don't have a home," he said, his voice soft. "I know how that feels. Until I was eleven, I was a street rat. But I found my place."

Kraken's 'place' was an abandoned apartment complex—

nothing but a hollowed-out shell until he'd jury-rigged it into something livable. He'd gotten the water running and hijacked nearby electrical lines, making it a fully functional home. Not bad for an eleven-year-old. It wasn't much, but it was *his*.

He recalled the people who had drifted through that space over the years, seeking shelter, a moment of respite. His chest ached. Yin didn't have that. Didn't even seem to want it. And somehow, that hurt more than it should have.

"Listen..." He hesitated. "I have extra space. If you need a place to stay? I promise not to disturb your peace anymore." His critics' words deafened him: *Your heart is too open. You let your emotions override self-preservation. It's going to get you killed.* He pressed his lips into a thin line, shoving the words back into the dark. He would rather die with a conscience than live without one.

"Ah..." Ahead of him, Yin faltered mid-step. Just for a second, her eyes widened and brows lifted. Like something he'd said had actually *surprised* her. Kraken smirked. No sharp retort? No dry remark? He registered that as *human* of her. He nearly pointed it out, but he held his tongue. If he did, she might retreat behind her usual stoicism, and he wasn't ready to lose this moment. Still, the hesitation was unusual. He'd never seen her pause like that before.

"It's logical, right?" he pressed. "I have a home. You don't. I offer you one. The logical answer is yes."

Yin came to a full stop. Her arms folded tightly over her chest, and she turned slightly away from him.

Oh no. I broke her.

"No." She shook her head, gaze lifting from the ground. "I am unable to do that." A pause. Then, just barely, her lips curled into something almost *gentle*. "Besides...you are too troublesome."

Kraken blinked. Did she just... Was that...*a joke?*

He stared for half a breath, then a laugh pushed past his

lips. "Hilarious," he said, shaking his head. "Nice to see you coming out of your shell."

"What? I am not in a shell." Yin tilted her head, brow slightly furrowed. "I am breaking out of nothing."

Kraken scrutinized her, searching for a flicker of amusement. A smirk, a glint in her eye. Something. But no. Her expression had already settled back into blank neutrality. *Oh. She was serious.*

He sighed. There was humanity in there somewhere. Maybe he should explain the metaphor, but before he could, his gaze snagged on a single crimson drop—blood. A single drop slipped from her nose and splattered onto the ground.

Kraken stilled. "You're bleeding."

Yin's hand darted to her face. She examined her fingertips, now smeared with red, then quickly wiped them clean. "It happens," she muttered. "It is nothing."

"Well, get it checked out." His hand instinctively reached for her arm but stopped. If he touched her, he feared she might perceive it as a threat. The last thing he wanted was to shatter whatever fragile partnership they'd built. "It could be a blood flow issue. Don't ignore something like that."

"I am fine." Her voice snapped back with force. She turned away, nose lifted toward the ceiling as if that alone would stop the bleeding. "I know why I bleed. Fixing it is unnecessary right now."

"...okay." The conversation collapsed, leaving an uncomfortable silence.

Kraken trailed behind her, turning over the conversation in his mind. Everything about her was strange and cryptic. Why was she so hard to figure out? He prided himself on recognizing patterns, solving puzzles, connecting dots others didn't even see. But Yin? She was a puzzle with missing pieces, an equation that refused to balance.

Yet he couldn't stop trying. It was not only out of curiosity, but because of her skill and power. He sensed fragments of himself in her, and he knew that if he could bring someone like her to his side, the possibilities would be endless.

Whatever. Right now, he wanted nothing more than to collapse into his bed and disappear into oblivion. The thought of soft sheets, of hot water washing away the filth of Scraptown, was the only thing keeping him going. Though reality threatened. He'd gotten his proverbial ass handed to him, and Miriam was going to have words about it. The Metal Vultures would be on high alert. Returning to Scraptown anytime soon wasn't looking good. His shoulders sagged.

"We have arrived."

Kraken opened his eyes, blinking against the dim light, to find Yin standing beside a ladder that looked similar to the one they'd descended earlier. Above them loomed the Rivera Theater, known for its cheap seats and classic plays. As a child, Kraken used to sneak in, captivated by the performances.

She knew the city layout, then. Another mystery that would go without an answer.

"Can your ankle handle it?" Yin's voice was steady, but something about the low light spilling through small exit holes made her look...lost.

Kraken sucked in a breath. Could he really leave her behind? He took a step toward the ladder and looked up at the night sky. "I hope so, or else I'm going to lose my nose." He forced a smile, trying to lighten the tension. "Listen," he hastened, "I insist you stay with me. You have nowhere else to go. I practically have an entire apartment complex to myself. Hell, you can even sleep in the office, if that's what you want. Seriously, just stay."

Yin shook her head firmly. "No, I cannot. Cease your request. I wish to remain in Scraptown."

Another rejection.

But Kraken wasn't giving up so easily. They'd gone through hell together today. He followed her up into the fresh night air, its chill causing him to shiver. A sigh of relief escaped him, almost as if he'd forgotten what fresh air even smelled like. It looked like they were only a block from his home.

"This is where we part," Yin began.

"Stay with me," Kraken cut in. He had to try one last time. "Look, the gangs in Scraptown are getting stronger. You're a good fighter, and I'm not denying that, but you can't take them all on. You'll get killed. I have running water, electricity, AC, and heating. It'll be safer. You can have a home."

At the word *home*, Yin flinched. He recognized the subtle shift in her weight, the way her clenched fist retreated into her pocket. Her eyes held something inscrutable. Feral, like a dog running wild after escaping its fence, instinctively searching for something it could never fully reclaim. Kraken resisted the impulse to reach out, knowing it would be futile. She'd bite.

A grin tugged at the corner of Kraken's lips. His warmth pressed against her cold, distant gaze like a wave crashing against a stone cliff. The day had been anything but ordinary—being shot at by gangsters, fighting a freak, getting wounded twice, and escaping with said freak. Yet here they were.

"Good-bye, Human Kraken." Yin's words were short as she hastened away.

Three times was the limit. Kraken had to respect her decision. Giving her space and time to consider felt like it might be the way to draw her in. Force certainly wasn't.

"Good-bye, Yin. Good luck finding your way back to Scraptown." He took a few steps, then watched her retreat into the evening. Raising a hand, he called after her, "And thanks for the help. No matter what happened in that building, you're not a bad person."

For a brief moment, he thought he saw a pause in her step.

Chapter 4

THE WORD ECHOED IN YIN'S MIND. *HOME*. SHE CALCULATED its significance. Technical definition: the place where one lives permanently, especially as a member of a family or household. Plain enough. Yet a deeper meaning wound through her thoughts like weeds taking root—unwelcome, persistent, defying her attempts at categorization. The true significance lurked in the shadows of her consciousness, just beyond her grasp, triggering an unnatural frustration she couldn't quantify or dismiss.

Stay. Safety. Home.

The things Human Kraken had said to her.

You're not a bad person.

Yin bit her lower lip. *I am not a person.*

Reluctance had dragged her steps as she left him. The sensation was unfamiliar, and it had beckoned her to turn around and follow him home. This gravitational pull toward another being made no tactical sense, and her instincts screamed warnings. The contradiction created a low-level tension that hummed beneath her consciousness like static interference.

Post-encounter, she had withdrawn back into Scraptown, seeking shelter in its abandoned buildings until she grew too restless to remain. The Vultures never bothered her again, giving her a wide berth like predators avoiding something more fearsome in their shared ecosystem. Occasionally, she spotted them skittering around her building, leaving offerings of slightly overripe fruit and scrap trinkets. *Top dog*, Human Kraken had told her. She'd left the offerings on random doorsteps when venturing out of Scraptown.

Now that she was released from her Creator's residence, she was without mission or purpose. The absence carved a void where the comfortable weight of orders and objectives belonged, the structure that gave her existence meaning. Every fiber of her psyche urged her to find new commands, her training refusing to acknowledge that she might exist without external direction. What was a soldier without a mission? Even while her body sometimes failed her, dropping her into seizure-like episodes and bleeding from her orifices, she remained a soldier. She would find marching orders somewhere, from someone. The alternative was unthinkable.

The streets of Old Town flowed with vibrant fabrics. Data points in a moving sea. A few eyes registered her presence with momentary flickers of curiosity before returning to conversations or com-tacts. She was a non-threat, a background element. Efficient.

However, she couldn't suppress her scowl at the constant barrage of advertisements flashing from every building, courtesy of the intrusive com-tacts implanted in people's eyes, including her own. The corporate intrusion into her visual field felt like a violation—her enhanced senses, designed for tactical awareness, now hijacked. Each flashing logo registered as a potential threat until her mind dismissed it, creating an exhausting cycle of assessment and rejection.

An obnoxious jingle blared from an ad that materialized before her face. A robotic voice screamed, "Unwind in Style with 'EcoZen'—Introducing the Eco-Friendly Hammock Haven!"

Yin moved past it, but the advertisement tracked her, continuing its irritating jingle. She quickened her pace and ducked around a corner, escaping the ad's perimeter.

The sky was muted by a barrage of clouds that cast a grey overcast on the city. No one had seen the sun since the nuclear war. A siren towered over everything at the street corner where she stood. Ignis often experienced radiation storms, again courtesy of the nuclear war, which explained the sirens spread throughout the city. Each emitted distinct tones depending on whether conditions favored a radiation storm or if one was imminent. This siren commanded attention, a sleek metallic structure rising defiantly against the sky, wrapped in a shroud of weather-beaten steel.

Yin analyzed the structure, recalling when she had learned about radiation storms. The memory slipped away, fuzzy and elusive, resisting her grasp. That was happening frequently lately—knowledge gaps where there should be none—but Yin didn't find it relevant. Her muscle memory remained intact, her reflexes sharp, her analytical capabilities undiminished. Her skills remained functional; did she need the memory?

She pushed further into the city. Competing scents saturated the air around the food booths. Thermal plumes rose from grills, carrying aerosolized fats and spices in a calculated appeal to basic human biology. To Yin, it was the city's finest feature. She isolated the scent of nearby meat skewers: cumin and rosemary. Snatching one up, she permitted herself a bite.

The meat was dry but vibrant. Food was not an inherent necessity for Yin, and she could survive longer than the average human without it. In the past, she had eaten only ration pills to satisfy her nutritional needs. Anything she consumed now was primarily for taste.

Finding a quiet spot, Yin sat against a cement wall and wrapped her arms around her knees, leaning forward to rest her chin on them. Two things occupied her mind: Human Kraken and the ticking noise reminiscent of working machinery. The muted tick-tick had followed her since her escape from the lab, like cogs turning on wheels. She believed the noise was related to the health glitches she experienced. It was easy enough to ignore, though it kept her on edge.

Human Kraken occupied her thoughts. As much as she tried to expel him—forcing her focus elsewhere, compartmentalizing the encounter, analyzing it for tactical value—his words kept crawling back in like persistent memories rewriting themselves. Yin would never admit it, but she respected him. No one had ever matched her in a fight or displayed such skills. The recognition triggered something uncomfortably close to admiration, an emotion she'd been taught to suppress. Anyone else would have been dead within the first thirty seconds of engagement. Much like her other opponents that day.

Yin's sharp eyes automatically scanned the faces of passersby, noting features and comparing them to her memory of Human Kraken. Her eyes tracked movement with predatory precision, seeking the particular gait, the specific shoulder angle, the distinctive bow-legged stride. Not that she wanted to find his living quarters, or rather, his home. No, this was nothing more than hunting practice, a training mission to keep her skills sharp until she found her purpose. She closed her eyes, attempting to pacify her wandering mind, but the justification felt hollow even to her.

Something struck her foot. Items clattered to the ground, followed by a feminine gasp.

"That was a klutzy move on my part. I'm sorry."

Yin opened her eyes, registering a petite woman, 5'4" to be exact, kneeling to collect scattered cans of water chestnuts, bean sprouts, various foods and soups, books that appeared to be a mixture of fairytales and graphic novels, and other miscellaneous items. The woman had doe-like monolid eyes of rich brown, framed by high cheekbones and a tapering chin. Her most prominent feature was a strong, wide nose. Her hair cascaded over her shoulders, dyed platinum and straight, with a pink beanie concealing the rest.

Yin pushed herself up, staying close to the wall. She remained light on her feet, weight distributed for optimal reaction time, coiled and ready. Combat assessments ran automatically through her mind: distance to cover, potential weapons in the scattered items, escape routes. One could never be too careful when enemies lurked on all corners, and this woman's approach pattern was either coincidental or deliberately casual—both possibilities demanded vigilance.

The human woman finished collecting her items and gave Yin a kind smile. If she registered Yin's suspicion, she hid it. Instead, she showed Yin a necklace with a trinket clasped onto it. "See this trinket? I made it myself. Do you like it?"

The trinket was rudimentary—a little robot whose arms and legs moved when jostled. Yin furrowed her brow, unsure how to respond. "It is unique. You should be cautious. I would have attacked you."

The word *attack* jolted her, but the woman's smile never wavered. "The technological information around me can overstimulate my sense of sight. I'm like a machine, but not entirely."

Her response was puzzling. Yin nearly balked as the human took her hand and placed the trinket in her palm. The robot sprang to life, standing and waltzing to the end of Yin's fingertips. She processed the data. This person was a Recombinant with limited control over electricity. The trinket must've contained tiny cogs and wheels placed by meticulous hands. Her hands?

Recombinant: Adjective. Relating to or denoting an organism, cell, or genetic material formed by recombination.

Recombination: Noun. The rearrangement of genetic material, especially by crossing over in chromosomes or by the artificial joining of segments of DNA from different organisms.

This concept had always existed in genetics, but a newer practice had emerged thirty years ago as a military project, Project Prometheus. It resulted in unintended consequences and subsequent shutdown. Recombination was later released to the public market in smaller, inconsequential forms like modifying hair or eye color, and to the medical field for eliminating genetic abnormalities and disorders.

That didn't stop the underground market from using it in full form, though there was a high rate of failure and complications, much like the military project. Yin recalled learning this but couldn't retrieve the memory, like before.

"You can keep it, okay?" The machine-human-but-not closed Yin's palm over the necklace. "Keep it safe. It's one of a kind, just like you."

This entire interaction baffled Yin. The casual contact bypassed her defensive instincts, leaving her oddly disoriented. Her neck hairs prickled. She regarded the human with heightened suspicion. How did she know Yin was one of a kind? Was she one of the people searching for her? It would make sense to send a Recombinant, though Yin considered another possibility—one that made her internal warnings spike with unease.

"I am looking for someone. Perhaps you know him?"

"Hmmm..." The woman tapped her chin. "Do you know this person's name? Or what he looks like?"

"He is a pale-skinned human who stands six feet two inches with an athletic build. Square jawline and high cheekbones with hazel-green eyes. Short, well-groomed hair styled in a slight side part. He is bow-legged." A key unique feature of Human Kraken that Yin had noticed. "He is the Human Kraken."

The name caused a flash of emotion in the woman's eyes.

She quickly suppressed it, returning to her carefree smile, but not before Yin noticed. This human knew Human Kraken. The hunt was officially on, and Yin carefully controlled her eagerness.

"That's quite the description," the woman said, eyes glittering with amusement. She gently folded her hands and bowed. "Before we talk further, let's become acquainted. I'm Nari." She raised her head just enough to glance at the influx of people on the street. "Let's talk further into the alley. So we have some privacy."

"Human Nari. I am Yin."

Yin followed Human Nari deeper into the alley, away from the crowd. She was careful in her steps and cautious of her surroundings. No evidence suggested she was in danger, but that meant little with someone like Human Nari.

"You are a Recombinant," Yin asserted. "As is Human Kraken."

"Yes."

"You are able to manipulate electricity."

"Yes."

Yin filed that information away as Human Nari turned on her heels and clicked her boots together. Her eyes glinted as her hands clasped behind her back, her broad smile lessening to a smirk.

"Human Kraken is involved in illicit activities." Yin assessed Human Nari's reaction closely. "Though I am unable to determine the exact nature. You are as well. Humans do not perform that type of recombination for the public."

Human Nari wagged a finger. "Ah, ah, ah. We aren't talking about that. You asked about Kraken. I'm familiar with Kraken. If you're seeking him out again, then I can only assume he gave you certain sensations." She pointed to Yin's stomach. "Did your stomach flutter?"

"Stomachs do not flutter." Yin waved her hand dismissively. "Stomachs are incapable of emotion. Fluttering indicates illness. No fluttering, or nausea, as you suggest."

Human Nari didn't bat an eyelash. Yin admired her self-control, very rare for humans.

"That's the whole *point.* It's not supposed to be logical." Nari's smirk faded into a frown as she rubbed her chin. "You tolerate his presence, at least." A conclusive statement. "Are you planning to hurt him? I'll have you know I'll do anything for my friends."

Friends.

Friend. Noun. A person whom one knows and whom one has a bond of mutual affection, typically exclusive of sexual or family relations.

Friends were something Yin had none of. She was told: "Camaraderie is appropriate. Friendship is weakness." *When was she told this?* Not important right now.

This was one of those situations the humans would call 'lucky,' though Yin wasn't certain that was the case. The more she spoke to Human Nari, the more suspicious she grew that Human Nari was told to look out for her. It seemed Yin wasn't the only one who couldn't get someone out of her mind.

Yin drew in a breath and released it from her nostrils before answering. "No. I have no intentions of harming Human Kraken. Human Kraken has provided no reason for me to harm him. I only seek him for information."

Home. That wretched word followed her wherever she went, a persistent intrusion in her thoughts. If she confronted Human Kraken about it, then she could find peace. Her mind would be quiet, free from the inexplicable pull toward concepts she wasn't designed to comprehend. This world was causing thoughts that her Creator would scoff at—illogical, inefficient thoughts that served no tactical purpose. These thoughts were undesirable, yet they persisted like an infection she couldn't purge from her consciousness.

Her reassurance subdued some of the tension. Yin

reached into her pocket and toyed with the trinket. "Since you are his...'friend,' then you must know where he frequents."

"And don't you forget it," Nari retorted and tilted up her chin. She crossed her arms, keeping her feet planted and body square. "There's a restaurant a few blocks from here called Cheeseburgers in Paradise. Whatever you do, don't startle him while he's eating. He likes to chew huge portions. Happy meals are from noon to evening." Her easygoing smile returned. "Good luck on your adventure to find the elusive Kraken."

With a nod, Human Nari walked past Yin.

"Wait," Yin called after her. "Did Human Kraken tell you to find me?"

Human Nari flung a broad smile over her shoulder, winking. She exuded confidence as she disappeared into the crowd, leaving no trace of her presence. *What an interesting human.*

Chapter 5

The sewer stench still soaked Kraken's clothes, a reminder of his journey over a week ago. No matter how much he tried to air out his room or wash his clothing, the smell refused to dissipate. To make matters worse, his washing machine had broken down. He considered fixing it, but decided the hassle outweighed the credits for the nearby laundromat. He handled tools well, but washing machines defeated him. Perhaps he could also grab some food at Cheeseburgers in Paradise with his friend and fellow Outsider, Nori.

Kraken sent her a message through his com-tacts to confirm their plans before throwing on a plain white T-shirt and jeans and stuffing the rest of his dirty clothes into a laundry bag. As he reached the door, Nori's reply flashed: *See you there.*

With their meet-up confirmed, Kraken began his three-block walk to the Half Rice Center, an unassuming convenience store turned laundromat. The appliances were outdated and prone to screeching when overloaded, but it was reliable and reasonably priced.

As he neared the building, a passerby nearly bowled him over as they rushed in the opposite direction. Kraken grimaced but said nothing. That wasn't an uncommon occurrence in Old Town, or even Retro Ignis. Unusually, various people left the establishment with their mouths covered or shielding their child's eyes.

Perplexed, Kraken picked up the pace and jogged toward the door. He leaned forward, holding a hand over his eyes to get a better view through the glass. A sigh escaped his lips as he hung his head. Why was this his life?

Sitting atop one of the running dryers was none other than Yin, *naked*. And while she might not be human, she certainly had all the corresponding parts.

I should turn away, he thought, letting her handle her own problems. She hadn't been amenable to his help the first time around, and he had no reason to believe the second time would be any different. Out of the corner of his eye, he saw the store manager dialing on his holographic landline.

Kraken stepped impulsively into the store and raised a hand to the manager. "Wait. Don't call anyone. I'll handle this. There's no reason to bring in watchdogs where they aren't wanted."

The manager paused and looked up at Kraken with a sharp glare. His finger slowly lowered from the dial pad. Kraken breathed. He mouthed a quick "thank you" before turning to the machines. Yin watched him as he scanned his ID chip on the set next to her.

"Human Kraken," she greeted him, tone light, as if she weren't buck naked in public. "You have also come to use the cleaning machines."

Of all the things I expected to see today, this wasn't even on the list of impossible scenarios.

"Yin." Kraken kept his gaze forward on the washing

machine. He tossed his clothes into the drum and jabbed the Start button. He dared a cursory glance in her direction. Her pose covered her nethers, but her breasts were in full view as she leaned casually back on her hands. Not a care in the world. He glanced back at the machine. "Yin, did you meet a dealer on the way here? Have you ingested something? If you aren't high, then why? Why are you sitting naked on top of a dryer?"

Yin uncrossed her legs and leaned forward. "My clothes reeked of the sewer. Obviously, I am unclothed because my clothes are drying. Is this not what humans do? Come to this place and clean their clothes? Perhaps it is you who are high?"

Kraken wanted to slam his head against the washer. Instead, he laid his head against it, hoping to lose himself in the vibrations. He needed to contain this before she attracted unwanted attention. The last thing he needed was a bunch of pigs crawling around.

"Yin," he steeled his voice. "I am absolutely sober, and you're right. Humans come here to clean their clothes. That's not the question here. We all know *what* you're doing. It is the fact that you're doing it naked." Kraken ran his fingers through his hair and groaned. "No one wants to see you naked— Okay, that's a lie. I'm sure some people want to see you naked, but you're going to get arrested."

"Trivial," Yin spat. "Humans being offended by their natural state. Why? Humans focus on such trivial things."

A faint rustle of shifting limbs signaled her restlessness. He pictured the furrow in her brow and the slight tilt of her head as she struggled to comprehend Human Logic™ yet again. Suddenly, the sound of her dismounting the machine pierced through his ears. Without warning, she gripped his arm with surprising strength and tugged him toward her, causing him to whirl around and face her head-on. He braced himself for more criticism, but her scowl unexpectedly transformed into a sly grin.

"Do *you* want to see me naked?"

Kraken erupted into a fit of coughing. His face grew hot with embarrassment. "What? No! I mean, yes? No, wait, no. Definitely not. Whew, it's getting really warm in here." He turned his back on her and took a few steps away. "Not because of you specifically, just everyone in general. I am definitely not interested in seeing anyone naked right now or soon." He took a deep breath to calm himself down. *Okay, Kraken. Just get back to your washer-dryer set and stare straight at it. Don't look anywhere else.*

"So...yes?"

Kraken felt her presence creeping closer. He spun around, letting out a quick *"nope"* as he instinctively backed up against the wall. Despite trying to hold back his fear, nervous laughter burst from his lips as a substitute for screaming. How did they even start talking about this? She was relentless in the way she approached him with that sly, taunting grin. Her feet glided across the tiled floor, the movement of a cat stalking prey.

"Humans are so irrational," Yin chimed. She stopped mere inches from him. "I will never understand and nor do I want to. That said, I am unable to comply with your request. My clothes are in the dryer, and I lack a secondary set."

Kraken forced himself to swallow his laughter. "This stuff is personal, Yin. The naked body is for private matters. Being naked in public, well, we just don't do that."

This was like explaining something to a child. Yin was a child with a mature body and incredibly literal thinking. His eyes darted around, desperate to find something for her to wear. They were alone in here. The realization sank in. Everyone else fled when Yin was stripping down. She seemed to pick up on his dilemma.

"You can provide me with your shirt. It is appropriate for a male to be shirtless in public, is it not?" She raised a brow. "That does not seem very fair."

Kraken's initial response was a resounding *hell no*. Trade

halves so both were equally exposed? He averted his gaze. But then again, it was probably better for him to be shirtless and for her to have some coverage. He pushed himself away from the wall and angled to sidestep around her. Kraken peeled off his shirt and handed it to her.

"Okay. Here," he mumbled.

As he listened to her rustle into the fabric, he couldn't help but chew on his lower lip. When she nudged his shoulder, he looked up at her. The shirt just barely reached past her hips. Relief washed over him. "Progress. At least now people won't accuse you of being... Never mind. It's an improvement."

Yin pulled the hair-tie from her wrist and wrapped her dark hair into a tight ponytail at the nape of her neck. She sauntered over to a nearby bench. With a gentle gesture, she invited Kraken to join her on the weathered wooden slats. He followed suit, taking a seat next to her.

"My clothing shall complete their cycle in thirty minutes. Your clothing has barely started their cycle."

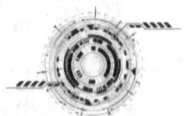

AFTER HALF AN HOUR, THE DRYER BEEPED LOUDLY, INDICATING that it had finished. Yin reached inside and took out a navy-blue robe, along with a white T-shirt and dark sweatpants. It was the same peculiar outfit she had worn when they first met. Almost reminiscent of an outfit an anime character might wear. By then, the laundromat still lacked any signs of life, and the manager had locked himself away in his room. Yin removed Kraken's shirt and threw it at him. He wasted no time in donning the shirt and giving it a firm pat to ensure it was properly in place. She dressed in her clothes and twirled around with a sarcastic chuckle.

"I am culturally appropriate," Yin declared, smirking. "Human Kraken, you are easily toyed with."

His face flushed. "I just don't want to see random people naked. Not in public or in private."

Yin made what almost sounded like a laugh as she settled back down next to him.

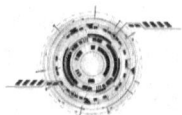

Another hour passed before Kraken had clean, dry clothes. In that time, he gained a wealth of knowledge about the inner workings of washers and dryers. They engaged in a heated debate on the subject, with Yin showcasing her impressive mechanical knowledge. It was no surprise to Kraken that she had a strong understanding of mechanics; her diverse skillset seemed limitless. The more he spoke to her, the more he wanted to know.

Kraken stuffed his clothes into his bag, but then he paused as he noticed someone strange at the back of the room. A sharply dressed man with dark sunglasses had walked in during their debate. He was out of place in Retro Ignis. The man had been fiddling with one machine for a while now, yet he didn't seem to have any clothes with him. Every now and again, the man muttered something under his breath. The cadence of it suggested radio transmissions through his comtacts, and that set Kraken on edge. Yin kept her back to him, showing no sign of awareness. Kraken swung the bag over his shoulder.

"Yin, I think we should—"

The man was upon them in an instant. A silver object jutted from his pocket, catching the light. His mouth contorted unnaturally, voice crackling and robotic. "Project Gemini, you are being detained. Submit and comply—"

Without hesitation, Yin rotated and grabbed hold of her attacker's arm, twisting it at the elbow until it snapped with a sickening sound. Black liquid sprayed from the wound, pooling on the floor beneath them. The weapon dropped, clattering uselessly on the ground. Yin shoved her assailant with such force that there was now a considerable distance between them.

Kraken expected screams of pain and horror, but the man seemed surprisingly unaffected by his newly severed limb. Black liquid oozed from the arm. Something felt wrong. Kraken watched as the substance congealed into writhing tendrils, reaching toward its lost appendage in Yin's grip. This wasn't blood; it was something else entirely. As he realized this and looked at the person before him, everything clicked into place. This was an android, not human at all.

"Project Gemini," the android spoke again. "You are being detained. You are ordered to submit and comply. Offenders will be supplicated."

Yin's fingers clenched around the arm, exerting a strong and effortless grip. The muscles in her hand flexed, crushing the metallic material beneath her grip. The sound echoed through the room like thunder, a testament to Yin's power. "I refuse."

With a hasty movement, she turned the arm over so that its broken end was now a sharp point facing the android and hurled it at the machine's chest.

Kraken had no time to process the violence. Before he could, Yin's hand clamped around his wrist and she bolted, dragging him out of the laundromat and into the street.

Chapter 6

The chase felt like pursuing a ghost. She moved with an unnatural fluidity, less a person running and more a glitch in the fabric of the crowd, each step too precise, too fast. People stumbled aside, their faces twisted with shock and confusion.

"Yin!" he called out. He cursed under his breath, struggling to keep pace. His bag hammered against his side with each stride. "Wait, Yin!"

They didn't slow until she led him several blocks away from the laundromat. With a sharp pivot that would've snapped most people's ankles, she vanished into a narrow alley. Kraken followed, adrenaline still singing through his veins.

The narrow alleyway had graffiti-covered walls and overflowing trash bins. The smell—that particular cocktail of piss, garbage, and desperation that seasoned every forgotten corner of Retro Ignis—clogged his throat.

"Alright," he demanded, stepping toward her. "What the hell is going on? Why was that android hunting you?" Frustration flared in his chest, then broke uselessly against the glacier of her expression. Those eyes… Christ, those eyes cut right through him, leaving frost in his veins. "I need a straight answer here, Yin. None of that cryptic logic bullshit."

She turned to face him fully, squaring her shoulders and dropping her hands to her sides. The movement suggested military training—like she was preparing to salute a commanding officer.

"That android," she began, her voice empty, "had ill intentions for me and, by association, you."

He nearly grabbed her shoulders, wanting to shake her until something human rattled loose. Anything would be better than that blank stare that revealed absolutely nothing about the secrets turning behind those eyes. In all his years dealing with the scum and saints of this city-state, he'd never encountered someone so impossibly difficult to read. Hell, the brick walls surrounding them would probably give him more honest answers.

"Why?" The word lashed out sharper than he intended. "Why, Yin? What are you?"

He scanned her face for a crack in that fortress—a flicker, a twitch, anything that might reveal the person underneath. Nothing. He imagined the gears grinding in her skull, could almost see the chess pieces sliding across the board as she calculated her next move. The silence stretched taut between them, and his frustration grew with every damned beat of his heart.

He'd tried everything—demanding, pleading. Maybe begging was next on the menu. Anything to glimpse behind the curtain of that impenetrable exterior.

"Human Kraken." Her voice sliced through the stillness.

He detected something in her tone. Hesitation? Fear? Whatever it was vanished before he could pin it down. What she said next turned his blood to ice water.

"Previously, I denied your offer of a home. There are

humans in the Inner Ring who would have me return there. To ensure this happens, they have issued an all-points bulletin with my image and information, making it clear that today's encounter shall not be the last."

Her gaze burned into him like hot coals, eyes flashing with something that might have been defiance mixed with determination. She clicked her heels together and bowed, the gesture both formal and somehow pleading.

"Human Kraken, I have reconsidered. Please permit me to stay with you."

The words sank like stones into his stomach. The sounds of the city—distant sirens, the hum of traffic—faded to white noise. All he could hear was the echo of her request reverberating through his skull.

Yin was the target. The realization struck him like a sucker punch. He was just some schmuck who'd stumbled into the crossfire, wasn't he? But as the shock wore off, a familiar stubborn streak took its place—one that had gotten him into more trouble than he cared to remember.

He drew a breath, then smiled. Taking her in meant harboring a wanted fugitive, but hell, Kraken wasn't exactly unfamiliar with being on the wrong side of an APB. That was something she'd learn about him later. Looking at her now—this strange, broken thing that spoke like a machine and moved like a ghost—he couldn't bring himself to turn her away.

"The offer still stands," he said, surprising himself with how steady his voice sounded. "If anything, the fact that those bastards want you makes me want to help you even more. You'll be safe at my place. The last official document about it is from a century ago. Far as Ignis is concerned, it's abandoned."

For the first time since they'd met, relief flickered across her features. A ghost of a smile touched her lips as she straightened.

"I see. Thank you. I have no desire to return to that part of Ignis. My purpose there is no longer."

Kraken gestured for her to follow him from the alley, and she fell into step beside him. Her rigid posture softened, settling into human movement. *Guess I just gained a roommate.*

His mind churned as they walked. Her admission about the Inner Ring had left him with more questions than answers. He'd look at the APB later, but he had a theory now about her origins. She had to be Synthetic—the term was broad enough to cover everything from mechanical androids to more exotic creations.

But the way she detached herself from humanity, combined with those genetic alterations... Kraken had never heard of an artificial human before. Had someone actually achieved that ultimate breakthrough? The thought both thrilled and terrified him.

They rounded a corner onto Market Street, and Kraken's jaw tightened.

Up ahead, two patrol officers had a man pinned against a storefront—one of the older establishments with hand-painted signage and actual wooden fixtures. The man wore traditional robes, faded but clean, and clutched a paper permit in one trembling hand. His cart of handwoven baskets lay overturned on the sidewalk, contents scattered.

"Vendor license expired three days ago," one officer said, voice flat with bureaucratic indifference. He tapped his datapad. "That's a five-hundred credit fine. Plus, confiscation of goods."

"I filed for renewal!" The man's voice cracked. "The system—it takes weeks now. I have children—"

"Should've planned better." The second officer was already scanning the baskets, tagging them for seizure. "Retros always wait until the last minute."

Kraken's fists clenched. The permit offices had been 'reorganized' six months ago—moved entirely online, processing times tripled, fees doubled. All targeting vendors who couldn't afford the new digital storefronts.

The man's shoulders sagged in defeat as the officers loaded his livelihood into their vehicle.

Kraken's chest burned with familiar, impotent rage. He could intervene—make a scene, record it, beat up the officers that no one in power cared about. Or he could keep his head down, stay off the authorities' radar, and make change with the Outsiders. *Pick your battles.* The words tasted like ash.

He forced himself to keep walking.

"The Human Kraken is distressed," Yin observed, her tone analytical but not unkind.

"Yeah." The word came out harder than he intended. "Welcome to Ignis. Where the Modernists get richer and the Retros get crushed under regulations designed to push them out." He exhaled through his nose. "That man's 'crime' was trying to feed his family with expired paperwork."

"Hey, look who showed up for lunch!"

Kraken looked up to see a familiar figure jogging toward them through the crowd. Nori had her dark hair thrown up in its usual messy bun, and she wore that favorite cropped leather jacket with the small chains on the right shoulder. Underneath, a black shirt proclaimed "Angry, Young, and Poor" in skull-decorated letters, paired with her trademark skinny jeans adorned with various belts and buckles. He'd teased her about her punk rock aesthetic for years.

She cast a knowing glance between them, cherry-red lips curling into a shit-eating grin. "Or...is lunch off now?"

Her smile faltered when she caught sight of his expression, then followed his gaze back to the patrol vehicle pulling away. "Shit. Market Street sweeps again?" She shook her head, jaw tight. "Third one this week. They're really ramping up before the Liberation Festival."

"Clean streets for the celebration," Kraken muttered bitterly. "Can't have any imperfections cluttering up the view."

Nori's hand found his shoulder, squeezed once. "You can't save everyone, Krak."

"Doesn't mean I have to like watching it happen."

Yin stepped forward, interrupting the two as she leaned in toward Nori.

"It is the Human Nari. You look different from our last encounter."

Nori's eyebrows shot up, and she let out a laugh that made heads turn. "Nari? You've got it wrong, sweetheart. Nari's my twin sister. We're identical. Easy mistake to make." She stepped forward, offering her hand with a grin that spelled trouble for Kraken. "I'm Nori. And you are?"

Heat burned Kraken's cheeks as he glared at his friend. *This isn't what you're thinking.* But Christ, he knew exactly what she was thinking. Nori had been needling him about women and dating for years, ever since she'd figured out he had zero interest in either.

"I am Yin," his new roommate said, taking Nori's hand and giving it what looked like a perfectly calculated shake. "I reside now with Human Kraken." She leaned closer, giving Nori a once-over that made Kraken's stomach clench. "Ah...now I see."

"Two shakes are good, Yin," Kraken interrupted, breaking them apart before things got weirder.

"A roommate?" Nori gasped, clasping her hands, then spinning toward him with theatrical delight. "Wait a minute—is this that strange girl you mentioned a week ago? You dog! I thought you hadn't seen her again."

"It's not like that." Kraken threw up his hands, feeling his face burn brighter. "I ran into her earlier. She needs a place to stay, and I'm helping her out." He looked at Yin, desperate to change the subject. "Wait—you know Nari?"

"Human Nari is helpful," Yin stated. "She assisted me in locating the Human Kraken." She tilted her head, her gaze distant for a moment. "She has a strong countenance. I could see in her posture that she is a skilled fighter."

Nori raised a hand to her lips and giggled. "Got that right. Nobody fucks with Nari. Not even Kraken here." She nudged him on the shoulder, ignoring his warning look. "Well... Kraken doesn't fuck with anybody."

She brushed past them both, then turned around and jerked a thumb over her shoulder. "So...we still getting burgers? Yin can join us. She sounds like a trip."

"I am quite nimble on my feet..." Yin began, falling into step behind Nori.

Kraken groaned and slapped his forehead. Just what he needed—his friend and his mysterious, maybe-Synthetic roommate bonding over God knew what. He trudged after the two women toward Cheeseburgers in Paradise, wondering when his life had gotten so complicated. And why, despite everything, he was almost looking forward to seeing what happened next.

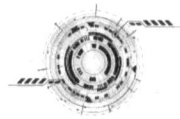

CHEESEBURGERS IN PARADISE WAS THE KIND OF PLACE YOUR cardiologist would warn you about and exactly the kind of place that made life worth living. The vintage jukebox, pre-holo with analog speakers and all, blared classic rock anthems while the open kitchen provided dinner theater, chefs flipping burgers and dicing onions on the flat-top, each motion as automatic as breathing. The air thickened with the aroma of sizzling beef, hot oil, and unrepentant grease that coated every surface like a slick confession of sin.

Stepping inside, Kraken imagined his arteries filing a formal complaint. But this hole-in-the-wall joint had its claws in him deep. It was the perfect representation of the patchwork technology of their era—a guilty pleasure that promised a taste of greasy heaven with every decadent bite.

The trio claimed a booth in the back corner, away from curious eyes and loose tongues. The waitress—a battle-hardened veteran of the service industry—barely glanced at Yin's peculiar attire before scuttling away, her order pad a flickering projection from a scuffed wristband. In a place like this, weird was probably the lunch special.

Kraken slid in beside Yin, using his bulk to block her from the other patrons' wandering gazes. No telling who might have seen that APB or how fast word was spreading. Nori settled across from them, surveying their surroundings with the critical eye of someone who'd seen better establishments.

"I can't believe you actually like eating in this dump," she lamented, though her hand patted her stomach. "I never would've agreed if the tank wasn't running on fumes."

Kraken snorted. "Your tank's always empty. You've got a hollow leg."

"That is not how food works." Yin's voice cut their banter short. She leaned around Kraken as if trying to peer beneath the table, searching for visual confirmation of Nori's alleged anatomical anomaly. When her inspection yielded nothing, she straightened with an audible huff.

"Even if a leg were hollow, it is not where food goes. What is this 'tank' you reference? We did not arrive here in a vehicle, and vehicles do not run on food."

Here we go again. Kraken pulled up his menu like a shield, hiding his expression, while Nori's shoulders shook with barely contained laughter. Yin's complete inability to grasp metaphors, social cues, or basic human communication was a pattern—one that was either endearing or exhausting, depending on his mood.

"A hollow leg is an expression," he offered, peering over the laminated menu. "It means someone who eats more than they should for their size. Her 'tank'—" He made exaggerated air quotes. "—is her stomach."

"What an inefficient method of communication," Yin scoffed, and for the first time since he'd met her, she sounded genuinely offended. "Human expressions serve little purpose beyond creating misdirection and confusion. One should simply state they are hungry or consume more than is appropriate for their body mass. As for the stomach, it is an organ, not a—" She mimicked his air quotes with mechanical precision. "—tank. If humans adopted more efficient communication protocols, there would be significantly less interpersonal conflict."

Kraken found himself considering her words despite their clinical delivery. She wasn't exactly wrong. If people actually said what they meant, the world might function differently. Politicians would show their true colors. Relationships would either flourish with honesty or crash and burn without pretense. Maybe corruption would become the exception rather than the rule. *It sounds like paradise. It also sounds like chaos.*

"Too idyllic," Nori said, steepling her fingers and leaning her chin against them. "A world like that wouldn't be very interesting. Besides, if everyone spoke their minds all the time, we'd never stop fighting." Her laugh carried a knowing edge. "Sometimes discretion is the better part of valor."

Their philosophical debate was interrupted by their server —a stout woman whose curly grey hair was coiffed to perfection, revealing sharp features that had weathered decades of dealing with difficult customers. Her grey eyes, magnified by circular spectacles, missed nothing as they surveyed the table from behind wire frames. The floral print dress and practical apron marked her as old-school service industry, and the nametag reading "Betty" confirmed what Kraken already knew. This was a woman who'd give drunks and troublemakers a piece of her mind without hesitation.

"What'll it be for drinks? The usual for you two?" Betty

glanced between Kraken and Nori with the familiarity of a bartender who knew her regulars' poison. At their nods, she tapped their orders in before turning expectantly to Yin. "And you, sweetheart?"

"Water."

The simple request carried none of Yin's usual linguistic peculiarities, and Betty nodded approvingly before departing to fulfill their order. As soon as she was gone, Yin snatched up a menu and dove into its contents. Her nose remained buried in the laminated pages until Betty returned with their drinks—two Cokes sweating condensation and a glass of water that Yin accepted with mechanical politeness.

Then she looked up at Betty and delivered her verdict with all the tact of a medical examiner.

"The food items on this food chooser are nutritionally deficient. Why do humans consume such substances? Do they actively seek premature mortality?"

Nori's Coke went down the wrong pipe, sending her into a coughing fit while she clapped a hand over her mouth. Through her fingers, Kraken heard her whispered observation, "Food chooser?"

He rolled his eyes and grabbed his menu, angling it toward Yin in a desperate attempt at damage control. Betty stood frozen, mouth agape, clearly unprepared for such a blunt assessment of her establishment's offerings.

"It tastes good," Kraken said, shooting Betty an apologetic look that promised a generous tip. "Take this burger, for example. Bacon isn't healthy, but it's delicious. Same with ice cream. Not necessary for survival, but it brings pleasure. People can eat this stuff in moderation and still maintain their health."

"Exactly," Nori chimed in, having recovered from her liquid mishap. "One ice cream cone won't kill ya. What's life without a few minor indulgences? We're all going to die eventually, anyway."

Kraken set down his menu with resignation. "Just try something. I usually get a burger with jalapeños. Betty, that's my order, by the way. The meal with fries."

"Jalapeños contain capsaicin, which irritates the stomach lining and causes gastric distress," Yin observed. "You will experience discomfort later, Human Kraken."

"Haven't had that problem in years," Kraken replied with a smile that felt more confident than he actually felt. Yin's return smile carried an unsettling quality—like she was indulging a child who insisted on touching a hot stove. She clearly had more to say about his dietary choices but chose to spare him the lecture.

Kraken found her restraint both amusing and vaguely ominous. He wasn't looking forward to the day he'd have to explain concepts like *YOLO* to someone who viewed human behavior through such a ruthlessly practical lens.

"I will order the Vegan Hippie Hash," Yin announced after another moment of menu consultation. "It consists primarily of starches but includes a variety of vegetables. It represents the least nutritionally catastrophic option available."

"Perfect!" Nori sang out in an exaggerated singsong voice, collecting the menus to hand to their shellshocked waitress. "And I'll have today's happy meal special. Thanks, Betty."

She waved Betty away with cheerful dismissal before turning her full attention to Yin, eyes sparkling with mischievous anticipation.

"Oh, Yin, I have so much to teach you about human communication. This is going to be fun."

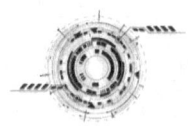

The food arrived steaming and fragrant, but the real entertainment came from watching Nori attempt to explain the intricacies of human language to someone who treated metaphors like personal insults. As their server distributed plates, Nori was deep into a comparison of 'butt dial' versus 'booty call'—a distinction that seemed to push Yin's frustration levels toward critical mass.

Kraken imagined steam building behind Yin's ears as she processed the illogical nature of human expression. He couldn't help chuckling as they finally settled into eating. Yin took precise, measured bites of her vegetable hash while he demolished his burger in three massive bites. The combination of melted cheese, juicy beef, spicy jalapeños, and creamy sauce made his taste buds sing hosannas.

But his attention kept drifting to his enigmatic companion. What did she make of this quintessentially human experience? Did the food meet her exacting nutritional standards? What had she eaten in whatever environment she'd escaped from? Each answer birthed more questions, and now that she was living under his roof, those mysteries felt more pressing than ever.

He didn't want to think about what their living situation might look like after today's revelations about APBs and Inner Ring pursuers.

Yin broke the comfortable silence first, pushing her half-finished plate to one side and setting down her fork with deliberate care.

"Human Kraken, what constitutes a home?"

The question hit him with unexpected force. He perceived something childlike in the way she asked—a sense of genuine wonder that transformed her usual clinical demeanor into something almost vulnerable. Her voice dropped to barely above a whisper, as if the question itself was fragile.

For once, he deduced she wasn't seeking a dictionary definition. She'd told him she'd never experienced having a home, that the concept was foreign to her programming or conditioning or whatever had shaped her existence. He wiped his hands on his napkin, buying time to organize his thoughts.

How do you explain something so fundamental that most people take it for granted?

"Home is..." He started slowly, feeling his way through the explanation. "Home is somewhere you feel safe and comfortable. The place you want to return to when everything else falls apart."

Yin repeated his words back to him with her characteristic precision, as if committing them to memory. Then she tilted her head with that bird-like curiosity he was beginning to recognize.

"By that definition, could a person serve as a home?"

"A person?" Kraken leaned back against the booth's cracked vinyl, genuinely surprised by the question. He'd never considered that possibility before.

It was Nori who answered, her voice unusually soft and contemplative.

"Yes. A person can be home. There's an old saying—home is where the heart is." She offered a gentle smile. "Someone you love and trust can become your home."

The philosophical weight of the conversation blanketed their table. Kraken shifted uncomfortably in his seat, tugging at his shirt cuff. This wasn't the Nori he knew. His friend was usually the lighthearted one, the jokester who deflected serious moments with sarcasm and punk rock attitude. Deep conversations were more her twin sister's territory.

Nori sensed the mood shift and busied herself tracing patterns in the faux wood grain of their table. Only Yin remained unaffected by the sudden emotional density, nodding thoughtfully as she absorbed their answers like a sponge soaking up water.

"In that case, Human Kraken is my home."

Kraken stared at her, mouth slightly open, trying to

process the implications. They were barely acquaintances—strangers who'd stumbled into each other's orbits through circumstance and necessity. Yet if she considered him home, then by his own definition, he represented safety and comfort to her. Someone she trusted.

His stunned expression must have prompted her to elaborate.

"I have returned to you more frequently than I have ever returned to anything else," she explained. "In my previous...existence, returning was not an option. There was only being."

Ah. Kraken almost breathed a sigh of relief. That's what she meant by calling him home. It was nothing about comfort, safety, or trust. Just that she had returned to him. A clinical observation that ignored the emotional nuances of their definition. Perhaps because she couldn't understand such nuances. He wanted Yin to trust him, of course, but that was something he never believed he'd win so easily. That was something he'd have to earn in due time.

"Oh, how sweet!" Nori chirped, her usual pep returning as she stacked their plates. She bounced to her feet and stretched, rolling her shoulders to work out the kinks. "Well, that was illuminating. Time to head to 9th Street."

The mention of their destination hit Kraken like ice water to the face. His mouth dropped open as memory crashed over him. *Shit.* He'd completely forgotten about their other obligation. The plan had been simple: finish laundry, grab lunch with Nori, drop off his clothes, then handle their evening business. Yin's dramatic entrance into his life had thrown a wrench into that carefully orchestrated schedule, and now they were running more than an hour behind.

Their commander wouldn't be pleased if they didn't finish this tonight.

"What is located on 9th Street?" Yin asked.

Of course, she would want details. Nori opened her

mouth to respond, but Kraken cut her off with a raised hand. The last thing he needed was his new roommate learning about his connections to the Outsiders—a group that Ignis's government had branded as terrorists but which saw itself as something far nobler. Revolutionaries fighting against corruption, giving voice to the forgotten masses of Retro Ignis. *Not exactly first-day roommate conversation material.*

"We're visiting a friend," Kraken said carefully, catching Nori's eye. "He helps us locate things we need."

Illegal things. Black-market goods. Weapons and information that never appeared on official channels. But Yin didn't need those details cluttering up her already complicated existence. Not yet.

"Find things?" Her tone carried a subtle suspicion, but she didn't press for specifics. Instead, she slid out of the booth behind him. "I am pleased to have encountered you today, Human Kraken. However, I would have been equally content to meet at a different time."

"No, no." Kraken waved his hands dismissively, perhaps a bit too enthusiastically. "This was a welcome distraction. A fortunate one. Right, Nori?"

"Absolutely." Nori smirked, delivering a sharp jab to his ribs that made him wince. "I wouldn't have missed this for the world. Our friend can wait."

Kraken rubbed his abused ribs while scanning his implant to settle their tab. The electronic beep confirmed the transaction. He gestured for both women to precede him toward the exit, herding them onto the busy street. Afternoon foot traffic swirled around them.

His stomach chose that moment to issue a gurgling protest that made him grimace. *Maybe Yin had been right about those jalapeños, after all.*

Now came the real dilemma: what to do about his mysterious companion?

She read his internal debate.

"I do not need to accompany you. If it would be preferable, I can wait here for your return."

The suggestion painted an immediate mental image of returning to find Yin embroiled in some fresh crisis—or worse, wandering the streets naked after another wardrobe malfunction. Taking her along carried risks, but leaving her unattended seemed equally dangerous.

"You can do whatever you want," he said finally, taking the coward's way out. Let her make the choice so he couldn't be blamed for the consequences.

"You're welcome to come," Nori interjected with a smile that didn't quite mask the calculating look she shot Kraken. *She could be useful.*

Kraken gave an almost imperceptible nod. Yin had demonstrated significant capabilities, so bringing her into their circle might provide tactical advantages—assuming she could be trusted and controlled—but it was also a massive gamble. Her inability to navigate basic social interactions guaranteed she'd draw attention, and the wrong kind of attention could have serious consequences for the rest of their cell.

More troubling was his doubt that their revolutionary cause would resonate with someone who seemed to view human behavior as an interesting but flawed system to be analyzed rather than a passion to be fought for.

When he glanced back at Yin, he found her watching their exchange, head tilted. Her face remained as blank as ever, but something in her posture suggested she saw through their lack of subtlety.

After a moment of consideration, she nodded slowly.

"This appears to be your mission. If the details are classified, I will not inquire further. You both prefer discretion, and your activities are of no particular interest to me. You need not worry about information security." She paused, then added with characteristic directness: "That said, I would like to accompany you."

"Excellent!" Nori wrapped her arm through Yin's with cheerful enthusiasm, causing the Synth to jerk in surprise. "Let's get moving. I can teach you more annoying metaphors on the way."

As they set off down the crowded street, Kraken couldn't shake the feeling that he was about to introduce a wildcard into an already dangerous game. But looking at Yin's rigid posture slowly relaxing as she walked between him and Nori, he realized he was past the point of turning back.

Chapter 7

THE GLOW OF THE HOLO-SCREEN CAST LONG, BLUE SHADOWS across the chamber walls, bathing the three figures in cold, flickering light. Aja Yamamoto sat stiffly, arms clamped across their chest, jaw locked against frustration. The image before them—a frozen, final frame—shimmered with static distortion, an echo of violence preserved in digital amber.

They'd argued this was a bad idea, repeating the warning in clipped tones across three briefings. Sending an android did little but announce their intentions, waving a digital flag for the Synthetic to notice. Now, the thing knew it was being hunted. Aja hadn't expected Supreme Chancellor Virelian to listen. Arrogance was the only language Virelian spoke, and that same self-important bravado had won him the city-state's gilded throne.

"Well." They set their cybernetic arm down on the mahogany table with a soft thud, the sound shattering the silence. It took everything not to let their irritation slip through. "That went about as well as anyone should have predicted."

Elder Statesman Valenstrom—never one to hide discomfort—exhaled sharply through his nose. The faint rustle of his coat's synthetic fibers followed. The sound distracted Aja, whose focus remained tethered to that final frame.

"Abomination," the elder statesman muttered, venom curling around each syllable like smoke. "It should've never been created."

Aja didn't need to look at him; they pictured his face well enough: drawn tight, nostrils flared, the flush of righteous certainty blooming across his pallid cheeks like a fever. Disgust masquerading as conviction. *Fossils.* Aja still tasted ash on the word 'stability,' remembering the civil war that crowned Virelian—a calculated purge the Traditionalists dared call a restoration. How they loathed Valenstrom—that crotchety dinosaur, his calcified ego steering the supreme chancellor's every outdated decision.

"We were arrogant to think we could contain it," Valenstrom continued, voice growing louder, more brittle. "And now it's free. Loose. A thing like that doesn't negotiate, doesn't feel remorse. It only calculates. Strategizes. Evolves. It needs to be destroyed."

If he dropped dead tomorrow, Aja thought, *my real work might finally begin.*

Then Supreme Chancellor Virelian spoke. Smooth, smug, and maddeningly self-assured.

"Destroyed?" Virelian gave a low chuckle, stepping into the blue wash of the holo-screen, his silhouette bisecting the chaos like he fancied himself a savior. "That thing is the pinnacle of design. Adaptive, precise, unburdened by conscience. It handled that android like paper dolls. You're not looking at a threat, Valenstrom. You're looking at an opportunity."

Aja turned their head slightly, catching the cold glint in his eyes. That gleam of ambition—cold and cutting. Virelian saw potential. An asset. A weapon.

"Imagine a battalion of them," Virelian continued, spreading his hands as though painting a mural in the air. "No need for conscription, no body counts to clean up... Surgical. Efficient. Solaris will be brought down on their knees." He glanced down, the corners of his mouth twitching upward. "Perfect."

Silence suffocated the chamber, the holo-screen's hum buzzing just beneath it.

"Which is why," he said, turning to Aja now, "we'll need it contained—not destroyed. Studied. Reverse-engineered. You can do that for us, can't you?"

Aja didn't move. Didn't blink.

"And considering your...intimate familiarity with its architecture," Virelian added, voice smooth as oil, "I imagine you're the most qualified person in Ignis to see it done."

The word *architecture* grated; it exposed how little Virelian understood what he faced—as if the Synthetic were nothing more than circuitry. It was flesh woven with engineered muscle, bone threaded with carbon-fiber lattice, and a genome refined through years of genius-level bioengineering. A living system, not a chassis.

A hollow smile curved their lips. "Of course."

Aja wore the title of high councilor like armor—polished, rigid, hollow. They had clawed their way back into the government, playing the part of loyalist. On paper, they served the supreme chancellor. In the shadows, their Techno-Revivalist allegiance remained unchanged. The world had ended, and the new one needed to be stronger, smarter, enduring.

Let the supreme chancellor believe he held the reins. Let him imagine obedience. Another man too blind to see beyond militarized applications, too eager to mold divinity into a war machine. He was no different from Ryūnosuke—except Ryūnosuke was a genius. Without him, no one could've dreamed of bringing this Synthetic to life. Not even Aja.

The Synthetic wasn't a weapon; it was the cure.

Nuclear fallout had poisoned the soil and left humanity dying. Birth rates were collapsing, fertility eroded. C.A.R.E.—the Coalition for Advanced Restoration Efforts—was built to halt that descent, but the Traditionalists had dismantled it overnight, choosing denial over survival. Virelian saw a weapon, but Aja remembered the lab: a biological anomaly.

During early testing, a single exposure to high-grade radiation should have crippled it. Killed it, even. Instead, the genome shifted. Reorganized itself. Minutes later, the radiation was inert. Harmless. Aja could still recall the anomaly markers lighting up like wildfire across the test grid, Ryūnosuke standing silent beside them, his voice nearly reverent. "It's adapting."

To this day, Aja didn't know how it had happened. The Synthetic's adaptability was emergent, self-generating, and an unpredictable alignment of gene therapy, nanobiotics, and recombinant synthesis. Ryūnosuke had buried the deeper data—notes, live recordings, anomaly logs—somewhere outside of official channels. And now Aja needed that data more than ever.

If they could isolate the mechanism, if they could graft that same genome sequence into baseline human embryos, then humanity still had a chance. They could rebuild a generation immune to radiation sickness.

Aja let the silence linger for a beat longer, then spoke—measured, careful. "During the raid on his lab, did your agents recover Ryūnosuke's data?"

Virelian barely glanced their way. His fingers drummed against the lacquered surface of the table, slow and idle. "Not yet," he said, tone clipped. "But they're combing through what's left. He was clever, I'll give him that. Covered his tracks better than expected."

Aja's jaw twitched, but they managed a nod. Of course he hadn't found it. Ryūnosuke had worked in layers. Encryptions beneath encryptions, physical caches nested beneath decoys. The kind of paranoid genius only understood by those who'd once thought like him.

Aja returned their focus to the holo-screen. The Synthetic had company during the confrontation. A man stood beside it, frozen mid-turn in the static-laced image. Who had the Synthetic entangled itself with?

Aja spoke aloud, tone firm. "Enhance quadrant C-7. Isolate the secondary figure. Run facial recognition. Class-A databases only."

A green scan-line swept across the image. Once. Twice. A soft chime confirmed the return.

IDENTIFIED: THEOPOLD KRAKEN
STATUS: ACTIVE. HIGH-RISK RECOMBINANT.
AFFILIATION: THE OUTSIDERS.
CHARGES: MULTIPLE COUNTS OF TERRORISM, INSURRECTION, SEDITIOUS TECHNOLOGICAL THEFT.

Aja's lips curled into a faint, knowing smirk. Not surprising. The Outsiders were opportunists. And the Synth—intelligent, adaptive, unbound by human loyalty—would be drawn to a competent commander like a firefly to a flame. It needed leadership. Craved direction. Purpose.

Valenstrom made a disgusted sound low in his throat. "The Synthetic is in the hands of terrorists now. They'll weaponize it. Send it straight back at us and call it justice."

The supreme chancellor leaned forward, chin resting on one hand. "And now the question is how we lure it out again," he murmured, almost to himself. "It's seen us. It knows we're coming."

Aja flexed their cybernetic hand once, then rested it against the polished wood.

"We do what I've said from the beginning," they said, tone sharper than before. "We wait."

Virelian looked at them now, one brow lifted in skepticism.

"It'll come to me," Aja said with certainty. "It was always going to."

They didn't need to explain further. Let Virelian assume whatever he liked. But Aja knew better. The bond between creator and creation was never that simple.

THE DOOR TO AJA'S PRIVATE OFFICE HISSED SHUT, SEALING with a low magnetic hush as fingertips brushed the wall sensor. The room was sleek, understated, and expensive—like everything in the Inner Ring, built not for comfort but image. Soft-grey paneling ran from floor to ceiling in flawless seams, broken only by thin strips of embedded light and a single view pane that overlooked the downtown skyline.

Outside, corporate towers blinked in white and blue halos, stacked like circuit boards against the night. Their symmetry had once comforted Aja. Now it just reminded them how far anything organic had to be cut to fit.

They lingered by the window longer than usual, letting their eyes blur against the grid of distant lights. Then, without a word, they crossed to the desk. Their desk, like everything else in the room, was utilitarian to the point of severity. No framed degrees, display cases, or family portraits. Nothing beyond a projection slab and two locked drawers.

The few visitors they'd allowed in their home had made comments about how barren their space was. They learned to smile through those comments, to say it was a matter of focus. The truth was so much simpler.

There had never been anything worth displaying.

No one had stayed long enough to be captured in a photo. And what good were awards when the only eyes they had ever wanted to see them had never looked in the first place?

The chair automatically shifted angles as they approached, compensating for the residual weight variance on their left side. They didn't intervene. Of all the smart features built into the furniture, that was the only one Aja kept active. A concession to the phantom pain of their prosthetics, which still came sometimes during long nights. Aja had thought it was gone for years. Their brain had been restructured to forget. Or so they'd been told. But memory didn't always stay in the mind. It lived in sinew, in reflex. In the spaces left behind.

The desk blazed to life as they sat, the screen blooming open beneath the heel of their cybernetic hand with a soft flicker, stretching itself into a wide arc across the desk surface. The system authorized access through their implant. Passwords were too insecure.

Aja navigated through their personal archive, bypassing all categorizations. The file had no name. Just a string of numbers they could've recited in their sleep.

The footage opened in silence.

The sound had degraded or been removed—Aja didn't care which. A gestation chamber glowed softly in a sterile tank. Liquid silver light, suspended stillness. The shape inside it, undeveloped, floating in the synthetic amniotic fluid, curled tight like a question without an answer.

The earliest footage of Project Gemini.

Next, a series of clips. A slow pan across biometric monitors. Genetic overlays. Test logs written in shorthand code only two people ever understood.

Then Ryūnosuke appeared mid-sentence, gesturing beside the tank. His mouth moved. The words didn't come. Aja remembered them anyway. Something about hope and the future learning to build itself.

The clip ran longer than intended. Ryūnosuke smiled. It

was the one he used when he thought Aja didn't understand him, when he believed he was being noble.

The footage sickened them.

They reached forward and shut the terminal with two delicate fingers. As the screen dimmed to black, they sat in a moment of perfect silence, fingers resting on the edge of the desk as if they might leave behind an imprint. That hubristic fool. Their jaw set. If only he'd been able to see what they had in their grasp. If only he'd not been, for all his talk of hope and the future, blinded by greed. What a waste of his talents to create war machines.

To recalibrate evolution, we must first admit we're the flawed baseline.

"If only you'd been capable of following your own words." Aja let out a soft, bitter laugh.

They rose to their feet. Ignored the ache gnawing at their leg. Shut off the lights.

And left the past exactly where it belonged.

Chapter 8

Seven Years Ago

How often did one get to truly bear witness to history? The question whispered through Aja's mind like a prayer as they pressed their palm against the cool observation glass, feeling the subtle vibrations of the laboratory's life-support systems thrumming beneath their fingertips.

The specimen shuddered its first breaths, each exhalation a mechanical expulsion of the viscous amber fluid that had sustained it for months. The synthetic amniotic solution splattered against the sterile floor in thick, honey-colored droplets that caught the harsh fluorescent light. Each wet, choking cough reverberated through the chamber—the predictable respiratory response of lungs clearing foreign matter. Aja observed the process, noting the efficiency of the transition. This was history incarnate, gasping and raw and utterly unaware of its own significance as a tool.

The first human grown not in a womb, but by science. The thought carried satisfaction rather than wonder. This was a problem solved. A methodology fine-tuned into the perfect specimen—a Synthetic. The terms were precise, clinical, adequate for what it was: humanity's greatest achievement in biological engineering.

Aja's eyes drifted toward the holo-screens, their blue glow painting ghostly shadows across the observation deck. Neural pathways fired in brilliant cascades of data: synapses forming connections at calculated speeds, genetic markers holding steady in their predetermined patterns. The readings were everything they had designed them to be: optimal brain function, perfect cellular regeneration, flawless integration of synthetic and organic components. The specimen's first movements were promising indicators of motor function.

Ryūnosuke stood statue-still near the Synth, his usually steady hands clasped behind his back in a gesture Aja recognized as barely contained anticipation. Even from this distance, they could see the tension in his shoulders, the way his chest rose and fell in measured intervals as if he were manually controlling each breath. The Synthetic might be breathing, but there was no guarantee it possessed the spark they'd theorized about—that ineffable quality that separated consciousness from mere biological function.

What if the neural integration is incomplete?

The thought carried no emotional weight, merely the practical concern of a scientist evaluating variables. If the specimen lacked proper cognitive function, it would be useless to C.A.R.E.'s objectives. Two years down the drain just like that.

Leaning closer to the glass until their breath fogged the surface, Aja tried to make out the specimen's features. Long, dark hair—the same black that both their own head and Ryūnosuke's wore—cascaded in wet tendrils across shoulders engineered for optimal bone density and muscle development. The body was precisely calibrated: young enough for neural plasticity, old enough for complex reasoning. Every variable calculated, every cell engineered, and now the prototype was functioning exactly as intended.

The specimen's cry shattered the laboratory's silence. A vocalization that indicated proper laryngeal development and respiratory capacity. The sound was raw, unmodulated by learned social conditioning. Precisely what they had expected from an entity thrust from a controlled environment into sensory bombardment. Like any organism experiencing overwhelming stimuli for the first time.

Yet, that reaction... Aja's pulse remained steady, their analysis continuing. The specimen's distress confirmed neurological sophistication. Evidence of a processing system capable of complex sensory integration.

Don't get excited yet. Their fingernails found the metal console's edge, digging crescents into the cold surface until the pain anchored them. *Not yet.* Too much depended on this moment to surrender to emotion.

The specimen pushed itself upright with movements that demonstrated proper proprioceptive function, its dark eyes—genetically matched to their donor templates—focusing on what must be its reflection in the polished steel examination table. Basic self-recognition protocols appeared intact.

When Ryūnosuke spoke, his voice was soft and carefully regulated to avoid startling it, the specimen turned toward him. And there, in that moment of auditory response and visual tracking, Aja confirmed what they had theorized: higher cognitive function was operational. Not mere biological reflex but *processing*. Decision-making capability. The neural architecture was performing exactly as designed.

Aja released a measured breath, their hands steady as they made mental notes of successful benchmarks. The specimen was viable. It could serve C.A.R.E.'s purposes admirably.

Phase one: complete. The clinical assessment brought satisfaction—the kind that came from methodology vindicated and hypotheses confirmed.

The observation deck felt appropriately sized for the moment's significance. Aja stepped back from the glass, their expression composed, professional. Emotional displays were counterproductive and for the weak-willed. They'd never let anyone see them vulnerable. Aja's mind shifted to logistical concerns. This prototype represented years of research materialized into functional form. It was possibly the solution C.A.R.E. had sought through decades of theoretical work.

Now came the operational phase: putting the Synthetic in the hands of C.A.R.E. Difficult, given that their partner had been holding them at arm's length the past few months. But the payoff would justify any complications.

The laboratory doors opened, and Ryūnosuke stepped through. The soft click of the seals engaging behind him seemed to echo with finality. When he turned toward the observation deck, his eyes held a dangerous flicker of cautious awe.

"It's alive," Ryūnosuke said, his voice carrying the weight of wonder and trepidation. "But that's only the beginning."

Aja met his gaze steadily, their expression revealing nothing of traitorous thoughts. "Alive, yes." They paused, selecting their words carefully. "But it's more than that. It's the future. A solution."

Ryūnosuke's brow furrowed slightly, wariness creeping into his voice. "Solution to what, exactly?"

The question hung in the sterile air between them. Aja felt their jaw tighten—just a fraction, barely perceptible. They had been careful, so very careful, to keep their true motivations buried beneath layers of scientific objectivity. But this moment, this triumph, threatened to crack their composure.

"To the stagnation of human evolution," they said finally, each word measured. "We've created something that can adapt at the cellular level. Think about the implications, Ryūnosuke."

"I am thinking about them." His voice carried a sharp edge now. "Which is why we proceed with extreme caution. This prototype will serve its intended purpose: an enhanced soldier for military applications. Nothing more."

Nothing more. The phrase confirmed what Aja had always known but hoped might still change. They watched Ryūnosuke's face, searching for any crack in his resolve, any hint that two years of collaboration might have broadened his vision. Instead, they found only the calculated pragmatism of a man who saw dollar signs where others might see salvation.

"Enhanced soldier," Aja repeated, their tone flat. "You're talking about turning it into a weapon."

"I'm talking about practical applications that will secure funding and ensure our research continues." Ryūnosuke stepped closer to the observation window, his reflection ghost-like against the glass. "The military will pay handsomely for warriors that can't be killed by conventional means."

Silence stretched between them, broken only by the soft pulse of monitoring equipment. Aja could feel the weight of unspoken truths pressing against their ribs. Ryūnosuke was a prodigy, the only biological engineer alive capable of turning theoretical impossibilities into breathing reality, as they'd just done. There had been no one else for this project, no other mind brilliant enough to bring consciousness to life from raw genetic material. Aja had gambled that such an extraordinary intellect might eventually grasp the scope of what they had accomplished together. Now, they realized Ryūnosuke's ambitions would never extend beyond his own greed.

"And what about humanity?" Aja's voice dropped to barely above a whisper. "What about the fertility crisis? The genetic degradation? The fact that we're dying, Ryūnosuke—slowly, quietly, but dying nonetheless?"

"Fertility panic," Ryūnosuke dismissed with a wave of his

hand. "Propaganda from the Revivalist extremists. Birth rates fluctuate. They always have."

Extremists. Aja felt their fingers flex involuntarily. The man was brilliant, yet blind to the data that surrounded them daily. Hospital records. Prenatal mortality statistics. The slow, inexorable decline that the Traditionalists refused to acknowledge because it threatened their narrative of stability.

As for Ryūnosuke? It threatened his wallet. Ignis's government didn't pay well for medical miracles.

"Look at the numbers," Aja pressed, desperation bleeding into their clinical tone. "Infant mortality is up forty percent in the last decade. Congenital defects—"

"Correlation, not causation."

"Not *causation?* There was a nuclear war. We still have radiation hotspots around Ignis even today, and radiation storms throughout the planet."

Ryūnosuke interrupted, "And still, that is certainly no justification for the kind of genetic experimentation you're suggesting."

The words hit Aja like a slap. *The kind of genetic experimentation you're suggesting.* As if they were some reckless amateur proposing to play God with human DNA. As if the Synthetic behind that glass wasn't proof of concept for exactly the kind of intervention humanity needed.

"What I'm suggesting," Aja said, their voice steady despite the rage building in their chest, "is that we adapt this genome sequence into baseline human embryos. Create a generation that can survive what we've done to this world."

The silence that followed was absolute. Ryūnosuke turned from the window, his face a mask of carefully controlled shock.

"Adapt it into...human embryos." The words fell from his lips like stones. "Aja, do you hear yourself? You're talking about engineering an entirely new subspecies."

"I'm talking about survival."

"You're talking about eugenics."

The accusation hung between them like a blade. Aja felt their prosthetic hand curl into a fist, the servos whining softly under the strain. They stepped closer, their voice dropping to a dangerous whisper.

"And what exactly do you think we just accomplished?" Aja gestured toward the observation window, where the Synthetic continued its exploration. "We selected genetic material—*your* genetic material and mine. We optimized traits. Engineered a being with superior physical and cognitive capabilities. If that's not eugenics, Ryūnosuke, then what is it?"

Ryūnosuke's face went pale. "That's... That's different. It's Synthetic. Artificial."

"Exactly. It's a tool we created using the same genetic principles you're suddenly finding objectionable." Aja's eyes never left his face. "You can dress it up with whatever terminology makes you comfortable, but we engineered a specimen using selective genetic optimization. The exact same methodology I'm proposing for human application."

"The Synthetic isn't human—"

"Of course it isn't," Aja cut him off sharply. "It's a prototype. A proof of concept. But the genetic sequences we used —*your* sequences and mine—those are undeniably human. And the adaptive capabilities we've documented? Those could be transferred to actual human embryos." They gestured toward the observation window. "That specimen is evidence that our genetic modifications work. The next logical step is implementing them where they matter." Eugenics. The word Traditionalists used to poison any discussion of genetic intervention. As if allowing the species to slide toward extinction was somehow more moral than taking action to prevent it.

"Call it what you want," Aja said quietly. "The result is the same. A human race capable of adapting to environmental pressures instead of simply dying from them."

Ryūnosuke backed away from them, his eyes wide with

something approaching horror. "You're serious. You're actually serious."

"Deadly serious." Aja stepped forward, closing the distance between them. "We have the key, Ryūnosuke. Right there behind that glass. The most significant biological breakthrough in human history, and you want to waste it creating super soldiers?"

"Super soldiers that will fund further research," Ryūnosuke shot back. "Practical applications that will keep the laboratory lights on and our work legal. What you're proposing would get us both executed as enemies of the state."

"What I'm proposing would save the state." Aja's voice rose, emotion finally cracking through their clinical facade. "Save the species. Save everything we claim to care about."

"By violating every ethical principle of genetic research?"

"By transcending them."

The two scientists stared at each other across the observation deck. Aja could see the exact moment Ryūnosuke's expression shifted. Wariness gave way to something colder, more calculating.

"How long have you been planning this?" he asked softly.

The question carried weight beyond its simple words. Aja felt their pulse quicken, recognizing the trap being laid. "Planning what?"

"This conversation. This proposal." Ryūnosuke's eyes narrowed. "You had this ready, didn't you? You've been thinking about human genetic modification since we started this project."

Aja said nothing. The silence stretched between them like a chasm.

"You're C.A.R.E.," Ryūnosuke whispered. "Aren't you?"

"Don't be ridiculous," Aja managed, but their voice lacked conviction.

"I knew it," he snarled. "I've suspected it for months. The way you push boundaries. Your obsession with species-wide applications. Your barely concealed contempt for anything that doesn't serve your extremist agenda." He stepped back toward the laboratory controls. "You're using my research to advance a C.A.R.E. agenda."

"*Our* research," they corrected. "Don't rewrite history now that it's convenient, Ryūnosuke. You weren't forced into this collaboration. You weren't tricked or manipulated." Their cybernetic hand gestured toward the observation window. "Every breakthrough in that specimen came from both of our minds working in tandem. Every genetic sequence, every adaptation protocol. We built this together."

Ryūnosuke's expression hardened, but Aja pressed on.

"And now that it's successful, now that we have proof of concept for the most significant biological advancement in human history, you want to sell it to the highest bidder for military applications." Their eyes narrowed. "Tell me, who's the real extremist here? The scientist who wants to save the species or the one who wants to profit from its potential extinction?"

"No." His hand hovered over the security panel, trembling with rage. "This project has a clear, defined purpose, and I won't let you pervert it into some extremist fantasy."

Aja felt the walls closing in around them. Two years of work. Two years of careful manipulation, strategic positioning, collaborative genius crumbling. They'd known better but had allowed passion to override strategy. This was their failure.

"You're making a mistake," they murmured.

"The mistake was trusting you." Ryūnosuke's fingers moved across the security interface. "I want you out of my laboratory. Now."

The observation deck's exit chimed softly, the magnetic locks disengaging. Aja stared at their former partner, memorizing the expression of disgust on his face. A bitter bile rose in their throat. This man was a *fool*.

"This isn't over," Aja said as they moved toward the exit.

"Yes, it is." Ryūnosuke didn't look at them. "And if you attempt to interfere with this project again, if you try to steal data or compromise the Synthetic, I'll turn you in to the Traditionalists myself."

Aja paused at the threshold, their cybernetic hand resting on the doorframe. "You'll regret this, Ryūnosuke. When humanity is dying and you're counting your military contracts, you'll remember this moment."

They stepped through the doorway without waiting for a response. Behind them, the locks engaged with a soft, final click.

And solutions, they thought as they walked down the empty corridor, *find a way to be implemented regardless of obstacles.*

The foundation for it had been laid in this moment, in this choice to prioritize profit over progress. Ryūnosuke had made his position clear.

Now Aja would make theirs.

The secure terminal in Aja's private office hummed to life as their cybernetic interface connected to the laboratory's mainframe. Three days had passed since the confrontation, three days of careful calculation and strategic planning. They had allowed Ryūnosuke time to cool down, to reconsider his position. Perhaps even time to regret his hasty accusations.

But as the login sequence initiated, a cold certainty settled in Aja's stomach.

ACCESS DENIED

The words appeared in stark red letters across the holographic display. Aja's lips pressed into a thin line as they tried alternate pathways, backup access codes, administrative overrides they had carefully built into the system during its construction.

ACCESS DENIED
ACCESS DENIED
ACCESS DENIED

Each rejection felt like a door slamming shut. Their credentials had been not merely suspended but entirely purged from the system's recognition protocols.

Aja's fingers drummed against the desk's surface, the soft clicking echoing in the sterile silence of their office. They attempted to access shared research directories, collaborative databases they had worked on with Ryūnosuke for other projects. Even those pathways had been severed. Every connection between their credentials and Ryūnosuke's work had been systematically eliminated.

The deep logs—the real treasure trove of information, adaptation protocols, cellular regeneration sequences, and anomalous genome modifications that made the Synthetic truly extraordinary—were completely inaccessible. Not just restricted but erased from any system Aja could reach.

Clever, Ryūnosuke. Very clever.

The man had moved swiftly and decisively. Not just locking Aja out, but ensuring they could never prove what they had helped create. Without access to the core research data, Aja's claims about the Synthetic's adaptive capabilities would sound like science fiction. Theoretical speculation from a disgraced researcher with suspected terrorist affiliations.

Aja leaned back in their chair, studying the access denial messages. The anger was there, certainly—a cold, surgical rage that demanded retribution. But beneath it was something more valuable: certainty. Ryūnosuke had made his choice. Now they could make theirs without the burden of misplaced loyalty or sentimental attachment.

They opened a new interface, this one connecting to networks that didn't officially exist. Channels that the Traditionalist government believed had been dismantled along with C.A.R.E.'s official structure. But bureaucrats rarely understood that true scientific collaboration couldn't be destroyed with legislation and execution orders.

The Coalition for Advanced Restoration Efforts lived on in distributed nodes, encrypted communications, and researchers who understood that humanity's survival trumped political convenience.

Aja's message was brief, clinical, and encrypted with keys that predated the Traditionalist victory:

Project Gemini viable. Adaptive genome confirmed. Research partner compromised. Extraction protocols may be necessary. Awaiting guidance.

They sent the message into the digital void and sat back to wait. The response would come within hours. And when it arrived, Aja would finally have the resources to continue their work properly.

With or without Ryūnosuke's cooperation.

The Synthetic behind that laboratory glass represented more than scientific achievement. It was hope given form, evolution accelerated, the future of human survival encoded in engineered DNA.

Ryūnosuke could keep his military contracts and his shallow ambitions. Aja would take the Synthetic itself.

Chapter 9

The bustling streets of Old Town gradually surrendered to the broken, patchwork pavement of Scraptown. Corporate storefronts and chrome-plated facades gave way to an eclectic maze of makeshift homes, structures cobbled together from salvaged materials and stubborn ingenuity.

Kraken hadn't ventured back here since his run-in with the Metal Vultures, but as he walked these familiar paths, the tension dissolved from his shoulders. Around them, children's laughter bubbled up from hidden courtyards while adults gathered around fire barrels, their conversations mixing with the rhythmic sorting of salvageable treasures from the day's haul.

Some bore the visible marks of generational radiation exposure. A woman with six fingers on each hand deftly sorted scrap metal, while a man missing his left arm below the elbow operated a welding torch one-handed. Others bore subtler signs: the telltale pallor and chronic cough that marked those whose lungs struggled against inherited cellular damage. All systemically cast out to Scraptown to hide the city-state's 'imperfections.' The systemic exile ignited Kraken's blood.

Despite appearances, Scraptown pulsed with a hope and resilience that the other districts of Ignis could never match. The residents here had inadvertently become the city's environmental conscience—recycling everything, walking or biking instead of burning fuel, turning waste into wonder. Sometimes, Kraken wondered if the rest of Ignis could learn something from these forgotten corners, maybe even begin to heal some of the damage done to their poisoned world.

Yin's rigid posture gradually softened as they walked deeper into the settlement. Her usual hypervigilance gave way to something approaching curiosity; her gaze absorbed the organized chaos around them with genuine interest. A hint of a smile even touched her lips—until she noticed his attention. The mask snapped back into place instantly.

"I remained here after we parted ways," she offered. "In an abandoned structure. I departed when I encountered similar difficulties to today's incident." *The android,* he realized.

Before he could respond, Yin peeled away from their group like iron drawn to a magnet. She drifted toward a vibrant market stall adorned with colorful textiles and intricate pottery, feigning casual interest while her attention fixed on the artisan working behind the display. The potter, standing on a worn stool, coaxed a new bowl into existence, clay spinning into art under his patient guidance.

Her behavior was unexpectedly endearing. Whenever Yin displayed glimpses of something recognizably human—wonder, curiosity, joy—she immediately retreated behind her clinical facade, as if emotion were a security breach to be contained. He watched with growing intrigue as she delicately lifted one of the finished pieces, examining it with the reverence of someone discovering beauty for the first time.

"These humans demonstrate logical resource utilization,"

she announced, holding up a glazed vase for his inspection. Coming from Yin, this constituted glowing praise. "They maximize available materials while minimizing waste streams."

She returned the piece to its place with a respectful bow to the potter before rejoining them, seamlessly pivoting to more practical matters.

"Your contact provides supplies?"

"Supplies that are...otherwise difficult to acquire," Kraken admitted. "His name is Gabriel."

"We hope he's still here," Nori interjected, her com-tacts flickering with incoming data. "We're running almost two hours behind schedule at this point."

Kraken grimaced. "We can always catch him later if—"

Yin spun around with liquid grace, her body coiling into defensive readiness. Kraken's adrenaline spiked; he braced for another android encounter. Instead, the metallic clinking of makeshift wind chimes announced the arrival of a familiar figure rounding the corner.

Gabriel emerged from the shadow of a reclaimed shipping container, a grin given human form. A few inches shorter than Kraken, Gabriel exuded the easy confidence of someone who'd learned to navigate life's complications through charm and careful timing. His tan skin caught the filtered sunlight, and thick brows framed a broad forehead that sloped down to a slightly crooked chin—a face that managed to be both roguishly handsome and utterly trustworthy, depending on what the situation required. Today's ensemble consisted of a red plaid button-down, jean jacket, and the kind of five o'clock shadow that suggested calculated casualness rather than simple neglect.

"Kraken, my man." Gabriel spread his arms in greeting, chocolate-brown eyes sparkling with mischief. "What's the word?" His gaze swept over their group before landing on Yin with unconcealed interest. "And who's the new addition? Your attack dog? She looks like she's calculating seventeen different ways to dismantle me."

It was impossible to resist Gabriel's infectious energy. Kraken clasped his friend's outstretched hand, and they leaned into the familiar ritual of backslapping and masculine posturing that passed for affection among their demographic.

Nori held herself apart, arms crossed and shoulders angled away in a display of studied indifference that didn't quite mask her sly smile. "That's Yin. Kraken's new roommate."

Kraken wanted to protest the characterization, but accuracy was accuracy. For all intents and purposes, Yin *was* his roommate. "She's a friend," he added, hoping to forestall whatever assumptions were already forming in Gabriel's agile mind. "She's very...observant." And possessed of survival instincts that had nearly been unleashed on his unsuspecting friend.

"Since when do you cohabitate with Synths, dude?" Gabriel leaned closer, studying Yin's features with the focused attention of someone accustomed to reading faces for a living. "Especially intimidating ones like this specimen."

Recognition flickered across Gabriel's expression—there and gone so quickly that someone less familiar with his tells might have missed it entirely. Kraken didn't miss it. Gabriel had his finger perpetually pressed to the city's underground pulse; if there was an APB floating around, he'd know about it. Hell, he probably knew more about Yin's situation than Kraken had managed to extract through direct questioning.

Gabriel pivoted smoothly, preempting the awkwardness. "I'm guessing you're not here to trade her for the merchandise, right?"

"I am not merchandise to be bartered with vagrant dealers," Yin quipped, and just like that, the peaceful curiosity Kraken witnessed evaporated. Her posture shifted into a combat-ready stance, muscles coiled and eyes guarded.

Gabriel's hands shot up in mock surrender as he took a prudent step backward. "Easy there, wildcat. I know when to tuck tail and retreat. You've got nothing to worry about from me." His arm snaked around Kraken's shoulders in a gesture of theatrical solidarity. "Sus amigos son mis amigos."

Nori chuckled. "Don't worry about her, Gabe. She's all bark." She winked at Yin. "She and Kraken have really bonded."

Kraken felt heat creep up his neck. "Those supplies we discussed..."

Gabriel released him with an exaggerated bow, one arm sweeping out in a flourish worthy of a Renaissance courtier. "Right this way, ladies, gentlemen, and...neutral party."

He spun on his heel and headed toward his destination, Nori falling into step behind him with easy familiarity.

"Didn't know you spoke Spanish, Gabriel," she observed.

"Hell no," he replied, jabbing his thumbs toward his chest. "The blood may be from México, but the finished product was raised Jewish. And I wasn't particularly successful with that identity either."

"Su acento también es deplorable," Yin muttered under her breath.

Of course, she speaks flawless Spanish. Why am I even surprised? Kraken had to suppress a smile.

Gabriel's safehouse turned out to be a ramshackle structure perched precariously beside an abandoned railway line. The building itself was a testament to creative engineering—rusted sheet metal panels wedged between wooden planks, the whole assembly held together by determination and rust-resistant prayers. What caught Kraken's attention wasn't the architecture but the security system: a perimeter of tin cans strung on nearly invisible wire, creating an early warning network that would make a belltower envious.

Elegant in its simplicity, and far less conspicuous than

anything electronic in a neighborhood where high-tech surveillance would stand out like a neon sign.

Gabriel produced a worn key from some hidden pocket and worked the padlock. The door creaked open, releasing a cloud of dust and stale air that spoke of long disuse. He disappeared into the gloom, and moments later emerged, dragging several large, black containers that hit the ground with resonant thuds.

"Fresh from the black market's finest purveyors," Gabriel announced, dusting off his hands with satisfaction. "Complete inventory as requested. You folks must have some serious plans brewing."

The containers were substantial—rectangular metal cases that bore the kind of wear and scarring that suggested they'd seen serious use. "Fragile—Handle with Care" was barely legible through accumulated grime and deliberate obscuration. As Kraken knelt to examine one, his fingers traced the cool surface, noting the weight and solid construction. These weren't cheap knockoffs or surplus equipment; someone had invested serious resources in whatever lay inside.

He was grateful now for Yin's presence. Between the three of them, transport to the pickup location would be manageable.

Beside him, Nori ran her hand over another container with the reverence usually reserved for religious artifacts. In a very real sense, these boxes represented their hopes and dreams for the future—or at least their hopes for staying alive long enough to see that future.

"Oh, it's going to be the event of the century," she said, straightening and draping an arm over Gabriel's shoulders. "You really don't want to miss this one, Gabe."

"That's exactly why I am missing it," Gabriel laughed, gracefully extricating himself from her embrace. "You people are absolutely insane. I, for one, prefer to keep all my component parts in their original configuration. Can you imagine the tragedy if I lost an eye? Or worse, a limb? The world would be plunged into aesthetic despair. Humanity would lose not just a handsome man but *the* handsome man." He punctuated this declaration with a theatrical wink. "Such a catastrophe cannot be permitted. Besides, I'm more effective operating in the shadows."

"Gosh, when you put it that way..." Nori feigned horror with dramatic flair. "I completely understand the dilemma. If even one woman were deprived of the gift of an intact Gabriel Besden, the entire female gender might collapse from the loss. Keep up the godly work, Gabe. Without your magnificent presence to admire, we'd all be spiritually impoverished."

"Finally, someone who appreciates my contributions to society's wellbeing," he replied with mock solemnity.

He turned back toward his shack and nearly collided with Yin, who had materialized beside him. He jumped backward with a strangled curse.

"Shit! How do you do that?"

"You recognize me," Yin stated, crushing the possibility of denial. She stepped closer as Gabriel retreated, predator and prey in a dance as old as consciousness itself. "Who seeks my return? Who authorized the all-points bulletin?"

Kraken's eyes widened. She had materialized silently. He eyed Gabriel's tin can early warning system for personal use. Yin had remained silent throughout their entire transaction, absorbing and analyzing. Now, the look in her eyes carried echoes of their first encounter—dangerous, calculating, utterly focused.

Every instinct screamed at him to intervene, to defuse the situation before it escalated beyond control. But another part of him—the part that had learned to value information over comfort—held him back. He exchanged an uncertain glance with Nori, who had shifted into ready position.

Gabriel smiled nervously. "Whoa there, wildcat. My

continued existence is my favorite thing! But a guy's gotta make a living. What's the information worth to you?"

He took a step backward. Yin closed the distance.

"I will compensate you with your continued existence," she hissed, letting the threat hang in the air.

Gabriel's hands shot skyward in immediate capitulation. "Okay, okay! Let's just dial down the intensity, Cujo. I was kidding around. Geez."

He whispered something to her that Kraken couldn't catch —words too quiet and quick to parse. Whatever Gabriel said worked; Yin's rigid posture relaxed fractionally, the immediate threat of violence receding.

Gabriel shuddered as he secured his shack's door with trembling fingers. "You know, I really hate conducting business out here. Next time, come see me in Old Town, Noriseaweed. You can even bring the big guy." His gaze flicked toward Yin with nervous energy. "But maybe leave Cujo at home? She's a little too intense even for my refined tastes."

"Oh, you." Nori reached out to pinch his cheek, which he deftly avoided. "But if I bring anyone else, how will I wrap myself around you?"

"Wrapping, like seaweed. I appreciate the imagery." He shot finger guns with both hands. "Unfortunately, duty calls elsewhere. You folks be careful out there."

Gabriel delivered a playful punch to Kraken's shoulder, eliciting the expected chuckle, then leaned in closer. His voice dropped to barely above a whisper. "Don't get yourself killed on this crazy mission...or by crazy Synths. Some serious players are hunting your attack dog."

Before Kraken could respond, Gabriel melted into the crowd of Scraptown residents with the ease of someone who'd mastered the art of strategic disappearance.

The words echoed in his head as Gabriel vanished. *Some serious players are hunting your attack dog.*

The same players who'd issued the APB? The same ones Yin and Gabriel had discussed in hushed, urgent tones?

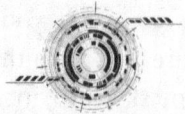

AH, THE BREEZY, SLIGHTLY RADIOACTIVE BREEZE OF THE IGNIS countryside.

Big Oak Farm sprawled across these abandoned acres like a monument to humanity's complex relationship with the land. The property once thrived as an agricultural operation, back when the soil could support life instead of merely tolerating it. Now, it served as a testament to both hubris and resilience—structures weathered by time and neglect, vibrant fields reduced to barren stretches choked with weeds, and the relentless advance of urban decay.

Two imposing barns dominated the landscape, their weathered wooden frames bearing witness to decades of seasonal cycles. Beyond them, the skeletal remains of what had been a bustling homestead dotted the property like scattered memories. At the center stood a farmhouse, whose broken windows and peeling paint created a ghostly reminder of the life that had once flourished here. Surrounding it, outbuildings in various states of collapse sagged under years of accumulated neglect.

The radiation had poisoned the land, rendering it unsuitable for agriculture and sealing its abandonment. Yet despite the decay, or perhaps because of it, the place emanated a strange, haunting beauty. The landscape took on an ethereal quality, as if time itself had slowed to a gentle crawl. Hidden from the world's prying eyes, the Outsiders had found sanctuary here, drawing strength from the quiet defiance of land that refused to surrender completely.

They completed the walk to the farm in uncharacteristic

silence. Kraken remained lost in thought, processing Gabriel's warning and its implications, while Nori refrained from her usual stream of commentary. He felt genuinely grateful for the space to think.

As they approached the arsenal's double-doors, Nori peeled away from him with a hint of a smile that conveyed two words: *good luck*.

Their precious cargo had been delivered ahead of them for the commander's inspection. The acquisition of the resources for their upcoming operation would undoubtedly lift spirits throughout the group. Activity buzzed in the arsenal. Outsiders moved with purposeful energy; voices boomed through the space as equipment was cataloged, sorted, and positioned for maximum efficiency.

Strict inventory control governed everything here. Kraken navigated carefully through the maze of bodies and freight being relocated and organized; each item was accounted for and assigned its proper place in their larger strategy.

Commander Miriam Levy stood near the back of the space, thumbs hooked into her olive-green fatigues as she supervised the inspection of his delivery. She was compact and lean, her frame deceptively slight until you noticed the corded muscle and perfect posture of someone who'd earned respect through competence rather than intimidation. Her expression carried the intensity of a person accustomed to making life-and-death decisions, dark eyes accentuated by sharp features and a constellation of freckles that somehow made her look both younger and more formidable.

She assumed command following the 'mysterious' death of their former leader in prison—mysterious only to those who hadn't been paying attention to the political realities of revolutionary movements. Kraken had supported her ascension; Miriam was fearless where it counted and decisive when hesitation could get people killed.

When she spotted him, Miriam waved him over with an

economical gesture. She tossed her ponytail—small box-style goddess braids secured at the nape of her neck—behind her shoulder.

"Look who finally decided to join us, Lieutenant," Miriam's voice carried effortlessly through the space, a natural projection that commanded attention without seeming to try. "Fashionably late as always."

Another Outsider sat hunched over the black containers, working the latches with nervous concentration. Sweat beaded on his forehead despite the cool air.

"Easy with those, Jimmy," Miriam instructed. "That's valuable equipment."

Jimmy mumbled what sounded like acknowledgment and popped open each latch in sequence before scampering away, leaving Kraken alone with their commander.

Heat crept up Kraken's neck as he scratched the back of his head sheepishly. "Sorry about the delay. Something unexpected came up." *Or rather, someone.*

Miriam didn't pursue his excuse. Radio silence for twenty-four hours was common in their line of work. Instead, she reached into the first container and withdrew a sleek metallic device. At the touch of a button, it flickered to life and projected a detailed holographic model of Pyreford Penitentiary. Practiced fingers rotated the image, focusing on the maximum-security wing.

"Beautiful work," she murmured with genuine appreciation. "Complete architectural schematics of the prison where our former commander was assassinated. Your contact outdid himself. You certain he wouldn't consider joining us?"

"Gabriel's a free agent," Kraken replied. "I've made offers before. He prefers independence."

"Shame. We could use someone with his connections."

Kraken leaned over to examine the container's remaining contents. Hazmat masks and riot gear lay folded with military precision, complete with connectors for oxygen systems.

Weapons with their biometric locks glowing red indicated successful security bypasses. Keycards that presumably corresponded to various prison access points completed the inventory.

"He really delivered this time," Kraken observed.

Miriam sealed the container and secured its latches. As she worked, she looked up at him with calculating eyes. "You should try again. To convince him."

Kraken didn't respond. *Should I tell her now? Or wait till Yin trusts me?*

Before Kraken could decide, shouting tore from somewhere deeper in the arsenal, followed by the unmistakable sounds of things crashing and collapsing. Through the maze of shelving and equipment, he couldn't identify the source of the disturbance. He exchanged a sharp look with Miriam as his pulse accelerated.

Had they been discovered? Was this a raid?

"Stay here," Miriam commanded, already moving toward the commotion with the fluid urgency of someone accustomed to crisis management. "Guard the shipment."

As she disappeared into the arsenal's depths, Kraken remained frozen beside their precious cargo, every sense straining to interpret the chaos beyond his sight. Whatever was happening, a sinking feeling told him their carefully laid plans were about to become significantly more complicated.

Chapter 10

The signage marked this area as Big Oak Farm. Two imposing barns towered over the desolate landscape. Beyond the barns, the remnants of a once-thriving homestead sprawled. A weather-beaten farmhouse, its windows long shattered, stood at the center, its paint faded and peeling, a ghostly reminder of the life that once flourished here.

The metallic tang coating Yin's tongue mixed with the sharp scent of ozone. Confirmation: the place reeked of radiation. The contamination wove through everything—the musty rot of wooden structures, the acrid bite of poisoned soil, the subtle wrongness that made her Synthetic biology recoil instinctively. Yet amidst the ruins, nature had begun its patient work of reclamation. Vines crept up eroded walls with determined green fingers, while trees sprouted from concrete cracks, their roots burrowing deep into soil that should have been too toxic to sustain life.

In the distance, a river wound its way through the landscape, its waters dark and murky—a stark contrast to the gleaming corporate spires visible on Ignis's horizon. Unfamiliar travelers risked stumbling into radiation hotspots that would deliver a gruesome, lingering death. The location was optimal for concealment.

Here, she last observed Human Kraken and Human Nori vanish over the rolling foothills in the direction of the farm. Following them here had never been part of any calculated plan. Before this moment, she'd been methodically cataloging every detail of the room he'd provided—memorizing wall textures, measuring dimensions, analyzing structural integrity with the compulsive thoroughness that helped her process this alien concept of 'home.'

She had existed in that space for exactly 24 hours, 40 minutes, and 53 seconds when Kraken announced his intention to depart. 54... 55... 56... She'd given him an acknowledging nod, asked no questions, and listened to the soft click of the door closing behind him. She found herself following his trail.

There had been no logical reasoning behind her decision to pursue him. Their destination held no particular fascination for her analytical mind. No, it was that restless energy that seized her whenever she remained idle, that gnawing need that whispered of being incomplete. Finding purpose. Ever since their first encounter, she spent hours decoding what drew her to him. He possessed skill, carried himself with clear purpose, and demonstrated the qualities of what her tactical assessments labeled as 'admirable leadership material.' In him, she recognized the dynamic between soldier and commander. He could provide the purpose she craved.

She followed the dirt path alongside their footprints, noting the dead zones where even the most stubborn grasses had surrendered to radiation poisoning. The trail led to a fork that overlooked a clearing where the two barns sat like aging titans, their forms both magnificent and mournful against the poisoned landscape.

From this vantage point, the footprints diverged. One set led west, the other east. Yin took a moment to analyze each structure. Beneath the broken windows, peeling paint, and rotten siding lay buildings that had once been architectural achievements, their glory days now buried under decades of neglect. The western barn wore its decay like camouflage, moss and ivy spiraling through windows and down weathered sides to soften its scars. The eastern barn stood in stark contrast, as if proudly displaying every mark time had carved into its frame.

The heavier footprints—Kraken's—led east. Her path solidified.

Yin slotted her fingers between the massive double-doors and leveraged them open, revealing a cavernous space that had been transformed into something resembling a military depot. Towering shelving units created a labyrinthine maze throughout the barn's interior, everything organized with meticulous precision and marked with alphanumeric codes that spoke of serious organizational protocols. The structure utilized maximum cubic space; packing indicated high-stakes operations. Wasted space here would equate to wasted lives.

The scent invaded immediately—coal, saltpeter, and napalm creating an olfactory signature that she identified as high explosives and incendiary compounds. Her gaze swept upward, observing the dark glass spheres suspended from the ceiling like technological fruit. Surveillance cameras. Every angle covered, every approach monitored. She bypassed detection.

Yin pressed herself against the shelving and moved fluidly, each step calculated to minimize sound while maximizing forward progress. Conversation echoed throughout the vast space, carrying a calm, purposeful quality. People focused on their work rather than being alert for intruders.

She rounded a corner that opened into a central staging area, revealing the maze's continuation toward the barn's rear sections. Her path intersected with an unsuspecting figure—a human male facing the shelving with a clipboard, completely absorbed in his inventory task.

"Who are you?" he demanded, jerking backward as he noticed her presence. His hand moved instinctively toward his belt. "You're not supposed to be here."

Yin's response was immediate and decisive. Her hands shot forward, grasping his shirt as she drove him hard into the shelving unit behind him. Boxes crashed to the ground with thunderous noise that echoed through the barn. The human collapsed unconscious amid the scattered supplies.

She stepped over his motionless form and continued deeper into the structure. Two sets of rapid footsteps converged on her position—backup responding to the disturbance. As they rounded the corner, the first human raised his weapon and shouted a warning.

Too slow.

Yin was already inside his defensive perimeter. Her fist connected with his solar plexus, driving the air from his lungs in an explosive gasp before she grabbed his head and drove it down to meet her rising knee. The satisfying crack of cartilage signaled a broken nose as he crumpled.

The second attacker threw a textbook right cross. Yin caught the fist mid-flight, twisted the arm with surgical precision, then drove her forehead into the woman's face before spinning and launching her into the adjacent shelving unit.

The cold kiss of metal against the base of her skull signaled a third combatant.

"State your business, stranger. You have five seconds before I redecorate this barn with your brains."

Step 1. Disengage.

Yin dropped her head and shifted left as her right hand swept upward, grasping the weapon and redirecting its aim away from vital areas. Using the attacker's grip as a fulcrum, she pivoted on the ball of her foot and came around their arm, her free hand forming a perfect fist as it connected with their face in a textbook counterstrike.

Step 2. Assess the situation.

Distance established, Yin leveled the captured pistol and assessed her opponent. Female, shorter than herself, dark-skinned, with the bearing and stance that screamed military training. Competent—significantly more so than the others. The weapon's biometric reader glowed red, signaling either sophisticated hacking or total uselessness.

"Do not move. Failure to comply will result in—"

Her opponent raised her hand with casual confidence. An invisible force tore the pistol from Yin's grip, sending it spinning across the barn floor. *Recombinant. Genetically modified human with telekinetic capabilities.*

Step 3. Neutralize the threat.

Yin raised her hands as the woman closed distance with professional aggression. She ducked left, avoiding a cross punch, then came up into a defensive posture as her opponent's follow-up strike met empty air. The human's leg swept toward Yin's supporting limb. She shifted her weight, cushioning the impact and leveraging the momentum to separate.

Her opponent feinted a jab before launching a head-high kick. Yin raised her guard, feeling the impact reverberate through her forearms, then grabbed the woman's wrist when she followed up with another cross punch.

Combat became a deadly dance. Yin swung her free arm in a wide arc that the human blocked instinctively, then used the contact to twist around her opponent's defense and spin her into position for a shoulder throw. The woman hit the ground hard, but Yin maintained control of the joint lock.

"Seize her!" the woman commanded through gritted teeth, her voice carrying the authority of someone accustomed to being obeyed.

"I am with Human Kraken," Yin stated.

"Kraken knows better than to bring unauthorized visitors to a secure facility," her captive snarled.

Yin's peripheral vision tracked the other humans closing their circle. Their movements were hesitant, their aim unsteady as their eyes darted between her and their captive. Tactical paralysis. They prioritized their commander's safety. The woman was her leverage.

"Engaging in combat serves no logical purpose," she announced, tightening her grip on the woman's arm just enough to demonstrate serious intent. "I will eliminate threats if necessary, but conflict was not my objective."

A gunshot broke the standoff.

The shot reverberated through the barn's cavernous space; every human instinctively hunched. Yin's head snapped toward the source—a pistol still smoking at the barrel, held by a figure she recognized with near-relief. Human Kraken had arrived.

Chapter 11

"Okay, that's enough," Kraken barked. "Everyone, stand down. I need medical personnel here, and the rest of you secure this facility. Move out—now!"

What the hell? Miriam—his commander—was pinned beneath Yin in a textbook restraint hold. His roommate. The Synthetic, who should have been safely cataloging wall textures back at their apartment, was here, having systematically dismantled their security.

He stifled the longest, most exasperated sigh of his life. Instead, he focused on the tactical nightmare unfolding before him. If Miriam didn't personally execute him for this catastrophe, he'd count himself the luckiest fool alive.

He lowered his sidearm, scanning the barn as personnel reluctantly filed toward the exits. Two guards who'd accompanied him stalled near the entrance, weapons drawn, their eyes darting between him and the standoff. Kraken jerked his head toward the door. "That includes you two. Don't worry. I've got this under control. When was the last time I caught a bullet, anyway?"

Their blank, incredulous stares spoke volumes.

"Okay, terrible example," he conceded, waving them off. "Just go."

De-escalation was critical now, especially with Yin. Any perceived threat triggered responses in her that were difficult to contain once unleashed. As the last footsteps echoed away, Kraken holstered his weapon and turned his full attention to his unlikely roommate.

The effect was immediate. Yin released Miriam and stepped back, her combat-ready posture melting into something approaching normalcy. The suffocating tension eased.

"Greetings, Human Kraken." Yin's voice soared several octaves, taking on an almost cheerful quality that would have been endearing under different circumstances. Her expression brightened with pleasure.

If she'd been a dog, he mused grimly, *her tail would be wagging—right before she tore your throat out.*

"Yin." He approached with deliberate caution, hands raised in a placating gesture. "What in hell's name are you doing here?"

He hauled Miriam to her feet. Her glare pierced his skull—a plasma drill of pure fury. He tried for a smile, but his lips pulled back into a grimace.

Ha... I'm in danger.

Yin shrugged with maddening casualness. "I did not follow intentionally. My thoughts wandered, and I found myself here. Combat was never my objective."

Kraken's jaw tightened. *Wandered?* How did someone wander from their apartment across the city to a covert resistance cell? The explanation defied logic, yet Yin's expression bore no deception.

Miriam's scornful gaze locked onto Kraken. The way she

emphasized his rank instead of his name was a blade twisting in his gut. "Quite the she-devil you've befriended, *Lieutenant*."

She stepped forward, inserting herself between Kraken and Yin with authority. Even with her back turned, her presence radiated command, and he felt her stare challenging Yin to make another move. He pinched the bridge of his nose, squeezing his eyes shut, hoping the gesture might erase the nightmare. *I have to salvage this somehow.*

"Your friend seems unfamiliar with basic concepts like trespassing," Miriam continued, her voice carrying the dangerous calm that preceded storms. "Or the notion that actions carry consequences." She turned her head slightly, a predatory smile playing at her lips as she gestured for Kraken to step closer. "Perhaps if she can't accept responsibility for her mistakes, the one who brought her here should shoulder the burden instead?"

Yin's posture snapped rigid, defiance sharpening her voice. "Do not threaten Kraken for my decisions. This location appears on standard maps. How could you believe no one would eventually discover it?"

Kraken moved swiftly, positioning himself between the two women like a human barrier. His hand found Yin's shoulder—a light but firm touch—as he mouthed silently: *I'll handle this.* Turning to Miriam, he lowered his voice to urgent, measured tones.

"With respect, Miriam, she doesn't fully grasp human social constructs. She's a Synthetic—designed as a weapon, a soldier meant for battlefield deployment only. She's telling the truth about not intending to follow me. Sometimes..." He paused, searching for the right words. "It's like her programming was left incomplete. She experiences...glitches."

Miriam's arms folded across her chest, one eyebrow arching as a medic approached to examine her injuries. She waved them off impatiently, her focus never wavering from Kraken. "So, you brought a malfunctioning weapon. One who refuses to acknowledge how her actions—intentional or otherwise—drag you into her mess. Is that your explanation?"

Miriam's scrutiny crushed his shoulders. A cold knot tightened in his chest, pulling his ribs taut. He swallowed against a dry throat.

"She's a fighter, Miriam. You just experienced that firsthand. Nori can vouch for her capabilities as well. She dismisses hierarchy—familiar, isn't it? We need assets like her."

"A malfunctioning weapon, Lieutenant? That's not an asset, that's a liability. Malfunctioning weapons have a tendency to go off at the wrong time. Give me one good reason why I shouldn't just eliminate that liability right now."

"You do require my assistance," Yin interjected. "I possess extensive tactical and medical training. I can contribute—"

"Listen here, Synth," Miriam snapped. "Kraken's endorsement is the only thing preventing me from putting you in the ground right now." She ran her fingers over the fresh bruises blooming across her arm and wrist, her gaze flicking to the medic who was fumbling with bandages. With a dismissive glare, she hissed, "Get out."

Kraken intercepted the medic, gripping their arm and whispering urgent instructions. The medic nodded rapidly, gathered their supplies, and hurried from the barn.

Yin observed the exchange. "Your medical personnel appear...inadequately trained. Field medicine falls within my expertise. To address your concerns, permit me to train them properly."

Kraken hesitated, then nodded slowly. "There's definitely room for improvement in that department. Additional training couldn't hurt." He let the silence stretch between them, the tension thick. He wanted desperately to protect Yin—for her sake and his own—but forcing Miriam's hand would be suicide. She needed space to reach her own decision.

Meanwhile, Yin stood motionless, awaiting judgment. Kraken desired that stoic patience sometimes.

Finally, Miriam drew a deep breath, tension bleeding from her shoulders. She straightened, arms falling to her sides. "Fine. You want to be useful? You can train the medics." She turned to Kraken. "But you are on the *shortest* possible leash, Lieutenant. You will be watched. And the moment she steps out of line—the very second—I will hold you both responsible. Get her out of my sight."

Yin was officially under his command. The thought equally terrified and thrilled him. He was responsible for a living weapon who didn't understand the world. What the hell had he just gotten himself into?

Kraken forced what he hoped was a confident smile. "Understood, Miriam. Yin will integrate smoothly. No complications whatsoever."

She wasn't an Outsider—not officially—but this was a step closer. Now, he just had to convince her that this was a cause worth fighting for.

As Miriam strode away, her boots striking the concrete floor, Kraken turned to face his new responsibility. "I know you didn't intend to end up here," he murmured, "but if you're planning another unannounced excursion, give me advance warning. You could have been killed. Or worse."

Yin raised an eyebrow, distinctly unimpressed. "You underestimate my capabilities. I would have neutralized any threats as necessary." Her tone softened. "However, you are now my commanding officer. I will report my movements accordingly. Now, which personnel will I be training?"

His shoulders, which had been knotted tight against his spine, finally dropped. He released a breath he hadn't realized he'd been holding. She was cooperating. Thank goodness.

"I'll bring the medics to you here," he said. Keeping her contained would stabilize the situation. "I think training sessions every other day would work best. Give them time to rest between sessions...process what you teach them..." *And not collapse from exhaustion,* he thought, remembering Yin's unsettling ability to function without sleep or sustenance. "Just...go easy on them, all right? They're civilians, not soldiers. And they're definitely not enhanced humans built for warfare. Don't push hard." He paused at the barn entrance, glancing back with a faint smile. "Well, don't push *too* hard, anyway."

Chapter 12

Two distinct scents composed the medical bay's air. Antiseptic, acute and purposeful. And beneath it, the dull, unproductive smell of old wood. Yin knelt beside the training mannequin, her hands moving with ease as she demonstrated the proper technique for an emergency thoracotomy.

Three medics watched. Tension bled from Human David and Human Elena, manifesting in restless energy, shifted weight, and furtive glances toward the exit. Wasted movement. Only Human Rose was still, her focus a solid, unwavering line aimed at the mannequin.

"The incision must be decisive," Yin said, her voice carrying the clipped authority that had become her trademark over the past two months. "Hesitation results in patient deaths. If you cannot commit to the procedure, you should not attempt it."

Human David swallowed. "But what if we nick an artery? What if—"

"Then you address the bleeding and proceed," Yin droned

without looking up. "Fear of complications causes more patient fatalities than the complications themselves."

Human David and Human Elena exchanged a meaningful glance. The same look she'd seen two days ago when she'd made Human David repeat suture practice for three straight hours because his first fifty attempts were "unacceptably imprecise." The same look from last week when Human Elena had flinched during a simulated amputation and Yin had coldly informed her that "squeamishness results in patient death" before forcing her to repeat the procedure until her hands stabilized. Two months of training, and most of them still flinched when she demonstrated bone saw techniques or corrected their posture with sharp, immediate adjustments to their hands.

All except Human Rose.

"Show me the landmarks again," Human Rose said, settling gracefully beside the mannequin. Small silver and gold trinkets woven throughout her locs glinted as she moved—tiny ballet slippers, musical notes, miniature tutus that chimed softly with each gesture. Her charm bracelet indexed the story: a dancer's life transformed into a medic's calling.

Yin valued Human Rose's directness; she radiated calm confidence, lacking fear or hesitation.

"Fifth intercostal space." Yin demonstrated, her finger tracing the proper location. "Mid-axillary line. The angle of approach is crucial. Too shallow and you accomplish nothing; too deep and you puncture the lung."

Human Rose nodded, her dark eyes focused intently on Yin's hands. "Like grand jeté positioning," she murmured. "The angle of takeoff determines whether you achieve proper elevation or crash into the ground."

It was an odd comparison, but Human Rose's analogies between medicine and ballet were surprisingly apt once explained. Both required discipline, precision, and the ability to perform under pressure.

"Correct." Yin handed Human Rose the training scalpel. "Demonstrate the technique."

As Human Rose positioned herself over the mannequin, Yin intercepted fragments of conversation from the main barn area. The voices were low, urgent. The kind of planning discussions that had spiked in frequency over the past week.

"...as soon as the radiation storm hits..."

"...security will be minimal during the atmospheric interference..."

"...everyone knows their positions..."

The prison break persisted as a consistent topic since her instruction began. It was an attempt to bolster their numbers by freeing their imprisoned comrades, and to stir up chaos by freeing criminals. Yin had no true opinion on the matter, though Human Kraken's troubled demeanor registered occasionally.

Human Rose's incision was steady, her technique nearly flawless. "How's the depth?" she asked.

"Acceptable," Yin replied, though her attention remained divided between the lesson and the conversation filtering in from beyond the storage room walls.

"...one chance to extract everyone..."

"...backup routes mapped and confirmed..."

The voices stopped abruptly. Yin turned her head slightly and caught sight of two Outsiders near the barn entrance—they'd noticed her listening. Their conversation shifted to tedious small talk.

Still an outsider among the Outsiders. Not that Yin sought to be anything else. She had no interest in their camaraderie or acceptance, but the mathematical reality remained. Personnel who viewed her as expendable rather than a contributing asset posed a tactical liability to her continued function. Their distrust made her vulnerable. If a mission went poorly, they would sacrifice the one who didn't belong without hesitation.

Yin remained solely because Human Kraken vouched for her, risking his standing when she caused trouble. This was her repayment.

Human Rose followed her gaze, then returned to her work. "They don't trust easily," she said, her voice barely above a whisper. "Can't say I blame them, given what happened to Izzy."

"Who is Human Izzy?" Yin asked.

Rose's expression shifted—eyes tightened, shoulders carried a barely perceptible tension. "My best friend." She secured the chest tube with methodical precision. "Izzy was arrested months ago during a supply run. Been sitting in that prison ever since."

"Is that why you're here?" Yin asked. "Training so intensively?"

Human Rose finally looked up from the mannequin, her dark eyes meeting Yin's directly. "Israel saved my life once. Got me out of a bad situation when I was dancing professionally." Her fingers absently touched the ballet slipper charm on her bracelet. "Some things you don't forget. Some debts you don't leave unpaid."

The same principle that bound soldiers together, a loyalty forged from shared risk. Simple, in its way.

The thought triggered a familiar pressure behind Yin's eyes—a warning sign she'd come to recognize. Yin kept her expression neutral as the pounding intensified, spreading from her temples inward like fingers pressing against the inside of her skull. Her vision flickered at the edges, the medical bay's harsh lighting fracturing into prismatic distortions before snapping back to normal.

The glitches had spiked in frequency. Their severity fluctuated from minor inconvenience to debilitation. Yesterday night, she'd experienced a full seizure while alone, her body convulsing for forty-seven seconds before control returned. She had not informed Human Kraken. Much in the way an injured animal hid its wounds. The pressure eased slightly. Yin blinked twice, confirming stabilization, and refocused on the training session.

"Your technique demonstrates significant improvement," she observed. "Your performance exceeds the others."

"Medical school helped." Human Rose grimaced. "I was four years into surgical training before I realized I couldn't stomach working for the same system that oppresses people like us." She began cleaning the practice tools with the same methodical care she applied to everything. "Besides, you're an excellent teacher when you're not terrifying people."

From the main barn area, footsteps and lowered voices indicated the planning session relocated to a more secure area.

Human Rose packed away the training supplies, her movements efficient and purposeful. "Same time the day after tomorrow?"

Yin nodded.

"Human Rose," she said as the other woman stood to leave. "When the operation commences to retrieve Human Israel—"

"I don't know what you're talking about," Human Rose interrupted smoothly, but her smile suggested otherwise.

Yin watched her go, the soft chiming of trinkets in her locs fading as she disappeared into the main barn.

Chapter 13

"Suit up!" Miriam's voice cut through the wail of emergency sirens that echoed across the city.

Kraken pulled on his mask and activated the oxygen tank, watching the radiation storm approach. The air shimmered, distorting the horizon like heat waves rising from scorching pavement. The streams of gold, crimson, and electric blue would be beautiful, but they heralded death. Wind was picking up, soon to carry radioactive dust through the abandoned streets.

Perfect cover for what they were about to do.

After months of preparation—gathering supplies, selecting the team, memorizing floor plans—the moment had finally arrived. The Outsiders would break into Pyreford Penitentiary. Not only to free their people, but as a tribute to their fallen leader, Miriam had said, assassinated within those very walls.

The conflict gnawed at him about releasing vagabonds and rapists onto the streets. This was for a good cause, he reminded himself. The end justified the means. At least, that's what he tried to convince himself as doubt plagued his thoughts.

Kraken adjusted the fake law enforcement gear Gabriel had provided. From a distance, it would pass inspection. His comm system crackled, the familiar static of the secure channel he'd coded himself a comfort against the storm's wail. The team was small—just four of them. Miriam would anchor her position on a nearby rooftop, providing sniper cover while he, Nori, and Nari infiltrated separately to avoid suspicion.

His mission was clear: hack the server room, extract the data, then hole up in security to guide the others through the facility.

A soft ping from his com-tacts halted his thoughts. A message from Yin, back at their apartment, fixing his washing machine of all things. He assumed she knew what they were doing tonight, though neither had spoken it aloud to the other.

GOOD LUCK.

Despite everything, Kraken smiled. *THANKS*, he replied.

Pyreford Penitentiary loomed ahead, its floodlights cutting through the gathering storm. The fortress-like structure ran on independent generators during radiation storms—one of the few buildings that would remain fully operational tonight.

Kraken crouched behind a dumpster near the east wing, studying his target. A fire exit sat adjacent to the server room, exactly where their stolen blueprints indicated. That was his way in.

"Is everyone ready?" Miriam's voice came through the comm.

"Ready," Kraken replied, checking his weapons one final time.

"We're in position," Nori confirmed.

"Fire."

The bomb detonated against the east wing's outer wall with a thunderous roar. A section of reinforced concrete crumbled inward, creating a gaping breach surrounded by twisted rebar and billowing smoke. Miriam's rifle cracked as she picked off guards fleeing the damaged administrative offices.

Kraken pushed down his revulsion at the carnage. This was for their captured comrades, he reminded himself. But they weren't just freeing Outsiders tonight. Every cell door would open, releasing murderers and worse into the streets. His stomach churned at the thought.

Gun in his right hand and knife in his left, he rounded the damaged wall, sprinting toward the fire exit on the building's intact side.

"There's been a breach!" he shouted, pounding on the door. "Open up! Fire in the east wing!"

When a guard cracked the door open, Kraken pushed inside and pressed his blade to the man's throat. He kicked the door closed behind him and used the guard as a human shield against the two others in the room, their weapons already drawn.

"Drop your guns or he dies."

One complied immediately. A bullet caught the second before he could fire. Kraken shoved his hostage away and opened the man's throat in one fluid motion, then dispatched the surrendering guard with a quick shot. Orders were to eliminate all witnesses; compliance meant just another way to die.

"We're in! Go! Go!" Miriam's voice urged through the radio.

"Give me a minute." Kraken attached his silencer and moved toward the server room. The chaos outside offered limited masking.

A single operator stood inside, hands raised in surrender. "Get on the ground! Hands behind your head!"

The man complied without resistance, lying face-down on the floor. Kraken quickly searched him for weapons or communication devices. His orders were clear—kill everyone. But this man had done nothing except his job.

*Miriam wouldn't know if...but **if** she found out... No. I'm not killing innocents if I can help it.*

"Go," Kraken commanded, hauling the operator to his feet. "Find cover and stay down."

The man disappeared without a word. Kraken hoped he wouldn't regret the mercy.

At the main terminal, his fingers flew across the holographic interface. Years of coding experience paid off as he bypassed security protocols and penetrated the prison's network. Cell door locks disengaged throughout the facility. All of them.

Kraken's hands hesitated over the keyboard. He thought of Viktor Petrov in Block D, imprisoned for strangling three women. Of the arsonist in solitary who'd burned down a children's hospital. Loyalty to duty demanded mission completion, but his conscience recoiled.

It's for the greater good, he told himself, installing a remote access backdoor through the electrical distribution system. *Sometimes the end justifies the means.*

"I'm in the system," he reported. "About to have a visit from Big Brother now."

Kraken pulled out a noise grenade and tossed it into the hallway, then screamed as if wounded. "Fuck! What are you doing here?"

Heavy boots thundered toward the server room. He hunkered low in the darkness, waiting. The security room was dim, the only light coming from the monitors—a standard precaution for the equipment, he knew. As the first guard rushed through the doorway, Kraken's blade found his throat. A bullet caught the second before he could react.

Kraken stepped over the bodies and sank into the security chief's chair, surrounded by dozens of camera monitors.

"I'm in position. Cell doors are unlocked, and I have eyes on everything."

"Good work," Miriam replied. "Do you have eyes on Israel?"

Kraken cycled through the cameras until he found Cell Block C. There she was—Israel Baptiste, a woman with an attitude that prison hadn't managed to break. She was flipping off the camera with both hands, tongue stuck out defiantly.

"Hey, Izzy," he said into the cell's microphone.

"It took you long enough," Izzy laughed, carefully removing the bonnet protecting her hair. "Let's light this bitch up."

"Your path to the shuttle bay is clear. See you there."

Switching to the private channel, Kraken updated Miriam. "Israel's mobile and heading for the hangar."

"Good. Make sure she gets there."

On the monitors, Kraken saw Izzy navigate the corridors with ease. She reached the hangar entrance, ducking behind supply crates.

"Are you screwing with the lights?" she asked. "I can't see anything in here."

Kraken checked the hangar cameras—the bay was completely dark despite his earlier commands. He flipped the manual override. "Lights are back up. See anything unusual?"

Before Izzy could answer, several cameras monitoring Nari's progress flickered and died as she passed. Her bioelectric field interfered with the surveillance system.

"Nari, careful with the light show," Kraken said. "You're taking out my eyes, and I need those stunning eyes to keep you safe."

"Life's more exciting with some mystery, don't you think?" Nari looked directly at a surviving camera, smiled, and blew a kiss. "Stay safe, big brother."

"Flirt later, Kraken," Miriam's voice carried barely contained exasperation. "We need a clear route."

Heat rose in Kraken's cheeks. "That wasn't— I mean, I wouldn't say that was flirting. At least, not by my definition. More so, playful banter. If that makes any sense. Actually, it probably doesn't. Well, maybe it does. You know what, never mind that. Point is, I wasn't flirting. Just trying to keep moods up, you know. Joy and cheer are an important thing to have when you're attempting a prison break from the outside and have bullets whizzing by your head, knowing that a leak could very easily mean radiation poisoning once we leave the building—"

"Stop rambling," Miriam interrupted. "We don't have time for—"

"Enemies on our right!" Nori shouted. "Incoming!"

The three team members dove for cover as automatic weapons fire erupted around them. Nari snapped her fingers, and severed electrical cables came alive like striking serpents, crackling with deadly current as they lashed out at their attackers.

"I can't hold them off forever," she warned.

"Kraken!" Miriam's tone carried deadly urgency. "Get us out of here!"

His fingers flew over the controls, systematically shutting doors and killing lights to create confusion throughout the prison. On his monitors, he could see other prisoners streaming through the corridors—former Outsiders and other inmates taking advantage of the chaos. Diego stumbled out of Block B, still weak seemingly from interrogation but moving. Sarah emerged from solitary confinement, her face grim and determined. But there was Petrov too, the strangler, slipping through the shadows with predatory intent. A dozen others he recognized from their raids and safehouses, all converging toward the rally points—alongside murderers and worse.

On the floor plan overlay, he traced the fastest route for his team.

"Corridor to your left leads to the cafeteria. Go through the kitchen. There's a service hallway that connects directly to the hangar. Single file only, but minimal resistance."

"Kraken..." Israel's voice crackled with static. "We have a problem. It wasn't just the lights that were dead."

"What are you talking about, Izzy?"

"The shuttles are dead—batteries drained—but I found something that runs on fuel."

Kraken switched cameras to the rear of the hangar and nearly toppled out of his chair. Israel stood beside an ancient Chinook military helicopter, its twin rotors gleaming dully under the harsh lights.

"Emergency backup," Israel cooed, patting the aircraft's hull. "Fuel tank's topped off and the engine's in decent shape. These old birds were built to last."

"A goddamn helicopter?" he muttered, then keyed his mic. "Please tell me you can fly that thing."

"I'm eighty-five percent sure," Israel replied cheerfully.

Only eighty-five percent? Kraken studied the facility layout again. His team would be trapped if something went wrong with their extraction. The fastest route to the hangar led through the basement detention area, up three floors, then down a ladder from the overlook.

Time to go.

Kraken placed an electromagnetic pulse device—a gift from Gabriel's last supply drop—on the console and armed the timer for two minutes. The device would fry every circuit in the security center, buying them precious time. He checked his team's position one last time, then took a running leap through the security room window.

The seven-foot drop to the basement sent shockwaves through his legs as he landed hard on a table and rolled to absorb the impact. A detention officer turned toward the commotion just as Kraken barreled into him, sending them both sprawling.

"Sorry," Kraken muttered, leaping up and racing for the stairwell.

He slammed the door behind him and bounded up the steps three at a time. But when he reached the main floor, his blood ran cold. The staircase to the upper levels had been destroyed in the initial explosion—twisted metal and concrete rubble blocked the way.

Kraken examined the wreckage. Exposed steel beams and rebar jutted out at odd angles, forming a crude ladder of sorts. It would have to do.

He hauled himself up through the debris, muscles straining as he climbed to the second floor, then the third. The hangar overlook was just ahead when a familiar voice stopped him cold.

"There he is!"

Kraken spun to see the server room operator he'd spared, now leading a squad of military police directly toward him.

No good deed goes unpunished.

He sprinted for the overlook, smashing through the glass door and vaulting over the guardrail toward the ladder. Pain exploded through his left calf and forearm as bullets found their mark. His grip failed, and he plummeted to the hangar floor with bone-jarring force.

The metallic taste of blood filled his mouth as the world spun around him. His left arm and leg were bleeding freely, but he was alive.

"Come on, big brother." Nari appeared beside him, hauling him to his feet. "Get up."

"Stop him!" the operator shouted from above, pointing at Nari.

Nari looked down at her slight frame, then back up at the guards with incredulous anger. "Really? For that insult, I know exactly where I'm aiming."

Kraken's vision cleared as adrenaline surged through his system—exactly what his enhanced genetics were designed for. His hand moved toward his sidearm, but Nari stepped protectively in front of him, producing three throwing knives.

"Surrender or face the consequences," an officer barked, weapons trained on them both.

"I'll give you surrender," she hissed, raising her thumb. "This little piggy got lost." Index finger next. "This little piggy lost its way." Middle finger. "And this little piggy is going straight up your—"

Three rifle shots echoed from behind them as Miriam materialized from the service corridor, weapon smoking. The guards scrambled for cover.

"Move!" she ordered.

With Miriam providing suppressive fire, Kraken limped toward the helicopter with Nari supporting him. As they got closer, Nari's expression soured.

"What in the world is that thing? It's like a derpy seal who forgot to swim—sticking its tushy above water instead of under it. Same principle applies here."

Nori waited inside the aircraft with medical supplies and three other freed Outsiders—Diego cradling his broken ribs, Sarah checking weapons, and Tommy, barely eighteen, staring wide-eyed at their escape. At least a dozen more former prisoners crowded into the helicopter's cargo area, a mix of their captured comrades and other inmates they'd freed along the way.

"You need treatment," Nori said, offering the kit.

"Later." Kraken waved her off. "We need to leave. Now."

"Krak!" Izzy called from the cockpit. "Shoot some morphine and get those hangar doors open! We can't fly through two feet of steel and rad shields. This bird should link with the control tower."

Kraken collapsed into the co-pilot's seat and ripped off his helmet. "Morphine can wait. They've got reinforcements incoming."

He tore into the communications panel, hot-wiring his helmet's system into the helicopter's radio. Placing the communications station's headset against his ear, he steadily changed the frequency until he heard a loud buzz, registering an indication that it was the control tower.

Putting the IP and frequency number into his custom-fitted wrist computer system, he coordinated it with his scans of the prison system from earlier and set up a very special command program, ready for use.

"Close the doors!" he called back to the passenger compartment.

As soon as he heard the helicopter doors slam shut, Kraken triggered the payload. The control tower exploded in a ball of fire, and the hangar's massive doors began grinding open on their emergency protocols.

"We're clear for takeoff," he told Izzy. "I suggest we leave quickly."

"Hold on, fuckers!" Izzy howled, pulling back on the controls.

The Chinook shuddered, climbing unsteadily into the air as it fought against the radiation storm's fierce winds. Every gust threatened to dash them against the hangar walls, but Izzy's piloting skills—however rusty—kept them airborne and moving toward the exit.

They burst through the doors into the maelstrom beyond. The radiation storm raged in full fury now, and Kraken felt grateful for his suit's protection. Without it, they'd be dead within minutes. The Chinook offered the prisoners their only protection from the storm.

Radioactive winds buffeted the aircraft as it climbed away from the prison, but they were free. All of them—eighteen former Outsiders who had been captured over the past months, plus half a dozen other prisoners whose crimes Kraken tried not to think about.

Kraken leaned back in his seat and closed his eyes. They'd actually done it—broken into a maximum-security prison and escaped with their people. Behind him, quiet conversations arose as the freed prisoners processed their liberation. Diego was describing his interrogation to Sarah in hushed tones. Tommy was asking Israel questions about flying. The adrenaline faded, yielding the sharp ache of his wounds and bone-deep exhaustion.

A gentle touch on his shoulder made him look up. Nori stood beside him with a syringe and a small smile.

"That morphine shot you ordered," she said playfully. "This one's on the house."

The injection brought blessed relief from the worst of the pain. Kraken sighed gratefully.

"Don't thank me yet," Nori laughed, pulling out medical supplies. "You totally owe me. I'm not the nursing type like my sister, but you kept her safe today. And you're my friend and all that." She shrugged as if embarrassed by the sentiment.

"Take care of the others first," Kraken protested as she prepared to clean his wounds. "We have limited supplies."

But the morphine and adrenaline crash claimed him. As the helicopter carried them away, Kraken succumbed to the darkness.

Chapter 14

The radiation storm scoured itself clean against the perpetual grey. Cascading auroras of deadly particles wisped away, leaving only the familiar dim twilight that blanketed Ignis. From Modernist Ignis came the familiar hum of industrial machinery roaring to life—the city-wide decontamination system beginning its automated cleansing cycle. Retro Ignis possessed only primitive scrubbers that barely functioned beyond Old Town, leaving residents to supplement with neutralizing pills or makeshift remedies. Yin's Creator imparted these differences during training, though the specific memories remained frustratingly elusive.

During the storm's duration, Yin recalibrated the sensors of the apartment's faulty appliances. She'd also discovered a battery-powered music device, which now sat beside the washing machine, its small display flickering with song titles. One track had seized her attention completely: "Static on the Skyline" by School of the Twenty Elephants. Not the melody, but a single lyric that she replayed obsessively.

...as long as you'll be my friend when the worlds all end.

Friend. The word lodged in her mind like a splinter. Yin sat motionless on the threadbare couch, staring at the grainy television images that gradually sharpened as the electromagnetic interference faded. Her thoughts churned through observations and calculations about human relationships. Friendship anchored their nature—woven through their media, their social structures, their very identity. Betrayal of friendship triggered isolation, conflict, and emotional devastation. The 'drama' of these bonds dominated the entertainment programs she'd been analyzing.

Camaraderie is appropriate. Friendship is weakness.

Her Creator's words echoed in her memory. Logically sound. Friendship compromised decision-making, created vulnerabilities, and led to irrational choices. Yet she couldn't dismiss the fire in Nari's eyes when she'd declared her intent to protect her friends. That kind of fierce determination suggested strength, not weakness.

Her thoughts drifted to the restaurant. Nori's infectious laughter as she teased Kraken. Kraken's failed attempts to hide his amusement behind his menu. Yin cataloged their interactions, observing from the periphery. *Had that been...*

The front door's electronic beep interrupted her thoughts, followed by the sharp click of the lock disengaging. Yin leaned over the couch's back as the door swung wide. Kraken limped inside, stripped of the composed figure from before the storm. Dirt and grime coated his clothes. His hair hung in disheveled tangles, and fresh cuts marred his face. He dropped a black duffel bag in the corner before noticing her and smiling, his battered features creasing.

"Hey, Yin. How are things?"

His voice was level, almost practiced in its casualness. It offered no information, no clue to the mission's outcome. He dragged himself to the couch and collapsed with a pained groan. She angled toward him, studying his condition.

"You survived," she observed. "I repaired your laundry equipment during your absence and improved its efficiency significantly. You may test this theory when you wash those clothes."

Kraken's laugh held an edge of exhaustion. "Survived, if barely. Mission accomplished, though. I'm alive, which exceeds my expectations." He examined his jacket. "Perfect timing on the repairs. Getting blood out of fabric gets expensive."

Cuts across his scalp. Bruises—the ugly yellow-purple of old blood under the skin. Her focus narrowed to two details that didn't belong. A small, dark hole punched through his jacket sleeve. Another through the fabric of his pants leg. The conclusion was instantaneous and absolute. Bullet wounds. And with that thought, a strange, cold urgency washed through her.

"You are injured." She slid off the couch before he could respond, retrieving the medical kit she'd discovered hidden in the kitchen cupboard. When she returned, she knelt beside him, fingers hovering over the wound in his leg. "Explain how this occurred. Such injuries suggest carelessness and poor tactical judgment. Hardly a surprise. You are human, after all. Remain still."

"I'm fine, Yin." Kraken shifted uncomfortably, wincing. "These aren't serious. I'll visit the clinic down the street after it closes. They have those expensive regeneration pods I can hack into that'll heal everything in hours."

"Why did you not allow the medics to attend to you?" Her lips pursed. "Certainly, most of them are hopeless, but the Human Rose is quite competent."

Scratching the back of his head, Kraken replied, "Rose and the other medics had an influx of patients. They didn't need to deal with me, too."

The Outsiders they must've freed from the prison break, but she didn't say that. Yin placed a firm hand on his chest, pressing him back against the cushions. "I possess field medical training, but I cannot replace proper medical care. However, I can prevent infection until you receive treatment." She met his gaze directly. "Will you consent to my assistance?"

Kraken studied her face for a long moment, something unreadable flickering in his expression. Finally, he shrugged out of his jacket and settled back with a resigned wave. *Consent granted.*

Yin opened the kit, extracting alcohol, gauze, tape, and surgical scissors. She sterilized her hands before soaking gauze with antiseptic. "This will cause discomfort."

She cleaned the arm wound first. No exit wound—the bullet remained embedded in muscle tissue. Her fingers probed gently, ignoring Kraken's sharp intake of breath, locating the foreign object's position. Shallow, but too dangerous to remove without the proper equipment.

"Extraction without proper surgical tools would cause unnecessary trauma. I will only clean and sterilize the wound," she said, dressing the wound methodically. Moving to his leg, she cut away the damaged fabric for better access. This bullet had gone clean through. "I'll clean and bandage this one."

"See, this is why energy weapons are superior," Kraken said through gritted teeth. "Lighter, more efficient, no messy debris to extract. Once they go mainstream, I won't have this problem."

Yin's hands stilled. "Are you attempting humor while injured?" Her voice carried disapproval. "While I agree energy weapons present fewer medical complications, I find jokes about your mortality...disturbing."

He started to reply, but it came out as a sharp cry of pain as she unceremoniously pulled the bandage tight. The sound struck something inside her, a dissonant chord in the clean logic of her mind. A sudden, searing heat bloomed in her chest, settling like a hot stone in her stomach. *What is this?* The sensation was invasive, illogical. She wanted it gone.

Yin shoved the medical supplies back into the kit and snapped it shut, turning away from Kraken with her arms crossed tightly. *Illogical. Humans treat death so carelessly.*

"Yin?" The couch creaked as he stood, his presence drawing closer. She gripped her robe's sleeve, refusing to face him. "Are you...angry?"

"Angry?" She spun to confront him, surprised by his proximity. He stood close enough that she had to tilt her head back to meet his eyes. "I do not experience anger. Anger blinds judgment and causes tactical errors."

Kraken scratched his head, producing an awkward laugh. "Where did you learn field medicine, anyway?"

A deflection. One she welcomed. "I..." The question triggered a search of her memories that returned mostly empty spaces. She remembered escaping into Scraptown, but even the details of that were receding. Her training remained fragmented—faces without context, skills without origin stories. She knew her Creator had prepared her for war, which logically included medical training, but the specific memories felt corrupted or deliberately obscured.

"I cannot recall those details," she admitted finally. "My training memories are...incomplete. I know I was prepared for combat operations, which necessitated field medicine capabilities. My Creator must have provided this instruction." She pinched the bridge of her nose, attempting to force the memories to surface. Nothing.

Only one person could restore those missing pieces. Her Creator, currently imprisoned in the facility Kraken had just escaped from. Yin opened her eyes. His puzzled frown suggested her fragmented explanation meant nothing to him.

"Kraken," she said, dropping his formal designation. "Describe the prison's security status. What damage occurred? Current guard complement? Defensive capabilities?"

His eyebrows rose. "Oddly specific questions, but...infiltration was surprisingly simple. I eliminated the perimeter guards silently, then moved through the facility undetected. The real chaos started when the others engaged. As for damage..." He gestured vaguely. "The outer wall near the cell blocks is completely destroyed. The interior section near the hangar is rubble. Only one of those is my fault. Current security? Probably half of the military by now. We hit them hard, and they weren't prepared for that level of assault."

"I see. Thank you." Yin forced her features into a neutral configuration, though the heat in her chest intensified, accompanied by a dull throb beginning behind her temples. Another glitch approached—like Kraken had witnessed before. "You require rest to heal properly. The storm has passed. I should leave you to recover." She moved toward the door. "Seek medical attention soon."

"Yin?"

She stopped without turning.

"Thanks for patching me up. And for waiting. It...means something."

His gratitude hit her like a physical shock. The simple words resonated with something deeper than her training, connecting to that persistent lyric about friendship enduring through the world's end. Could they be friends? The question seemed to bypass her logical thought patterns entirely.

Yin didn't look back, unwilling to let him see the mounting instability affecting her expression. Instead, she nodded once—a slight acknowledgment—before stepping into the grey twilight of Ignis.

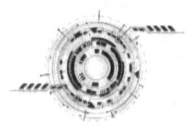

DARKNESS CLOAKED YIN'S APPROACH TO THE PRISON COMPLEX. Construction crews were already set up around the breach, their floodlights casting harsh shadows through the skeletal scaffolding. Kraken had spoken truthfully. Military personnel flooded the facility like antibodies responding to infection. For most infiltrators, this would present an insurmountable obstacle. She perceived an advantage. Yin understood military psychology, their movement patterns, their blind spots. Infiltrating their ranks would be the simplest part of this mission.

Yet doubt gnawed at her resolve. Was she thinking clearly?

The neurological storm ravaging her system intensified with each step. Pain lanced through her skull in sharp bursts, quickly dulled by her physiology, then accompanied by electric jolts whenever she shifted her gaze. Her muscles cramped and ached; her body rebelled. Inappropriate adrenaline coursed through her veins, constricting her pupils and making her heart race. Beneath it all, a savage hunger for violence beat like a second pulse.

She pulled her hair from its ponytail, twisting it into a severe bun before pressing herself against the construction scaffolding. Patience. Someone would patrol this area eventually—someone close to her size and build. The identity of her victim mattered less than their utility.

Her target materialized within minutes: a soldier carrying a radio and shouldering an M249 SAW. An M17 pistol and combat knife completed his loadout. Radio chatter crackled faintly from his equipment as he approached. Yin waited until he passed her position before striking—one arm snaking around his throat, her free hand clamping over his mouth. She dragged him behind the scaffolding and applied pressure to his jugular until his struggles ceased.

Quiet now.

The unconscious soldier was roughly her height but broader through the shoulders. His fatigues hung loose, a poor fit, but the damaged lighting masked it. As she dressed in his uniform, fragmented memories surfaced. She had worn similar clothing once, in another life that felt increasingly distant. Her own clothes were folded and hidden for later retrieval; the soldier disappeared deeper into the scaffolding's shadows.

This impulsive approach was unlike her usual methodology. Yin had arrived without reconnaissance, without tactical planning, trusting her adaptability to overcome obstacles as they arose. While her Creator had designed her for such flexibility, proper preparation would have served her better. Her singular goal remained finding her Creator, though what would happen afterward remained undefined.

Using the soldier's credentials, she gained access to the main facility. Her stride projected confidence; her posture held a military bearing. Her hurried internet search yielded minimal architectural information—an oversight. Federal crimes typically warranted low-to-medium security housing, she reasoned. *Follow the signs.*

Temporary signage guided her through corridors still bearing scars from the recent assault. Most markers seemed installed for the military's benefit rather than regular staff. Kraken could have provided detailed schematics if she'd asked, but this remained her burden alone. Personal. That persistent bloodlust whispered seductive suggestions, making her hands clench involuntarily. *No... I only need find him.*

Her radio sparked to life: "All units, Building B requires monitoring assistance due to understaffing. Low-medium security block. Acknowledge."

Building B. Her Creator's location crystallized with sudden certainty. The exchange continued around her, but Yin heard only her thundering pulse as she navigated toward her destination. Rounding a corner too quickly, she nearly collided with another soldier.

"Soldier!" The man's bark carried a sergeant's authority. "What's your hurry?"

Yin snapped to attention, her vision splitting the sergeant into overlapping images. "Sir! Responding to Building B assistance request. Failed to maintain situational awareness."

"At ease." His eyes scanned her face, the corner of his mouth tightening. A shift from authority to...*something else*. Concern? "You look ill. Report your condition."

"Fatigue, sir. Poor sleep."

The sergeant stepped closer, his eyes narrowing as he studied her face in the dim corridor lighting. "Funny thing, soldier. I don't believe I've seen you around before. What unit are you with?"

Yin remained frozen at attention, her heart hammering against her ribs. Sweat beaded along her hairline despite the cool air. She said nothing, knowing that any response might betray her with unfamiliar vocal patterns or incorrect unit designations. The silence stretched between them like a taut wire.

Kill him, her instincts screamed with increasing urgency. *Now, before he raises an alarm. One strike to the throat. Quick and silent.* Her jaw set with barely restrained violence, the knife seeming to burn against her hip. She focused on the center figure among the three she perceived, fighting to stabilize her vision while calculating angles of attack.

The sergeant's radio crackled with distant chatter about patrol rotations. His attention flickered momentarily toward the sound, then back to her face. Yin felt seconds stretching into eternity, her entire mission balanced on the edge of this moment. Violence would compromise everything, but discovery meant the same outcome.

After what felt like hours but could only have been heartbeats, the tension in his shoulders eased. He took a half-step back. He was letting it go, she realized. The chaos of the last few hours had given her the perfect cover.

"Ah, never mind. Proceed to your assignment."

"Yes, sir."

Building B's entrance yielded to the stolen credentials. Beyond lay a three-story cell block surrounding a central dayroom area. Anticipation spiked through her deteriorating nervous system. Her Creator was here. His presence felt like a wound that wouldn't heal.

Cell by cell, tier by tier, she searched methodically. Most inmates had retired for the evening; hostile stares tracked her passage. The search consumed precious minutes while her condition continued to fail. Her vision swam between clarity and blurriness; muscles seized with cramps; skull pressure mounted toward critical levels. When she finally located his cell, her trembling hand instinctively sought the blade at her belt.

"I knew you would come, Yin."

Dr. Ryūnosuke Izumi, though she'd only ever known him as Creator before tonight, sat slumped against the far wall, staring at nothing. Age and confinement had reduced him from the arrogant scientist Yin remembered into something hollow and broken. His once-pristine appearance ceded to unkempt hair, stubbled cheeks, and the sunken eyes of a man whose world had collapsed. Prison life failed him.

The sight of her Creator triggered a visceral response. Yin's lips pulled back in an unconscious snarl as violent urges threatened to overwhelm her sense of rationality. *Fifteen minutes* —that was all she could risk before discovery became inevitable.

"Creator." Voice cold as ice. "Your circumstances appear...reduced. You always preached survival of the fittest. Perhaps you've found your limit."

"How bitter you sound, though we designed you incapable of true bitterness." His laugh held no humor as he stood and approached the door. "I see the defects now. Look at you— bleeding, dying."

Yin touched her nose, her fingers coming away crimson.

"You're dying," her Creator continued, wrapping his

hands around the cell bars. "You know it. A slow death, but inevitable. Your body can't adapt indefinitely to the nanobotic damage I inflicted."

A sharp sting bloomed at the base of her neck.

"Irrelevant." Yin's grip on the knife tightened until metal bit flesh. "I die when I fall. I came seeking other answers."

"Unexpected." His eyebrows rose. "You intend conversation before execution?" His gaze dropped to her white-knuckled hand. "You want to survive?"

"I require no input from you on that matter." Yin's expression deadened. "I've identified another consultant. Someone calling themselves Aja."

Yin's mention of Aja Yamamoto, the one whose name appeared on her arrest warrant, drew bitter laughter from her Creator.

"That witch?" he spat. "You can't trust them. They're partially responsible for your creation—only for their own motives. Do you think they intend salvation?"

Yin's eyes narrowed. "No. I do not trust Aja. But I shall use them because survival serves my goals. You made me pragmatic, after all."

Her Creator sighed, releasing the bars and regarding her with paternal pride that made her stomach clench. "How brilliantly you turned out, Yin. Such a perfect creation. If only we'd had more time. The government could still use you if they recognized your potential." He paused, studying her deteriorating condition. "I know why you're really here. Your memory gaps. You've realized pieces are missing. The basement—you remember nothing."

Yin's jaw locked tight. Sharp breath hissed through clenched teeth. "You did something before I escaped. Blocked those memories."

It came to her in flashes. Her Creator silhouetted in a doorway, fear blazing in his eyes, distorted words she couldn't decipher, something metallic glinting in his hand.

"*...Is something going to transpire?*"

"*Project Gemini, run.*"

Pain tore the image away, leaving her gasping and disoriented. How could she fight her own failing mind?

"Why?" The word came out raw.

"So you couldn't testify about what really happened down there." His voice carried quiet satisfaction. "I'm pleased the blocks remain intact. Without memory, you're worthless as a witness. Their key testimony, dying with you." He reached through the bars toward her face. "Yin... Forget Aja. Find someone else to save you. If you play their game, you're entering something far more dangerous than you understand. If you knew their true nature, you'd hate them—if we'd left you capable of hate."

Every instinct screamed for violence. Adrenaline flooded Yin's system with nowhere to discharge except against the single target before her. She swiped the access card. The cell door hissed open. Logic, reason, control—all of it dissolved. A singular, boiling impulse displaced it: a feeling her Creator had locked away, now uncaged and screaming its name inside her.

Rage.

"You are correct," she snarled, stalking toward him. "You stole my memories. Excised emotions you deemed inconvenient. Because you held power, and I was silenced!"

No fear flickered in her Creator's eyes. He didn't retreat or cower. His expression was placid, almost welcoming. It was the look of a man who accepted—even desired—what was about to unfold.

His smile preceded the white-hot fury that flooded her vision.

Chapter 15

Darkness swallowed Kraken whole as his eyes drifted shut. Dreams rarely visited him, and tonight offered no exception. He'd wanted to wait for Yin, troubled by their earlier interaction. Despite her denials, she'd seemed concerned. The irritation in her touch reminded him of a disappointed mother scolding a careless child, yet a new tenderness nested beneath it.

Other details nagged at him too. Her stumbling recollection of the past. Those pointed questions about the prison break. He'd wanted answers when she returned, but exhaustion claimed him first, pulling him into unconsciousness on the couch.

"Kraken... Kraken... *Kraken...*"

Her voice sliced through the void, dragging him back to awareness. "Yin... What is it? Did you go to the laundromat naked again?" He rubbed his eyes. The persistent darkness remained beyond the windows. Kraken lowered his hands. "Yin... Shit!"

She hovered inches from his face, her skin pallid beneath a coating of dried blood. Military fatigues clung to her trembling frame, while her civilian clothes hung crumpled in one hand like discarded evidence. Though her body swayed with exhaustion, her eyes burned with their usual fierce intensity.

Hands raised defensively, Kraken pushed upright. "What the hell happened? Whose clothes are those? Better yet, whose blood?"

"Kraken, I need your help," she hissed, ignoring his questions entirely. Her hand reached toward him before stopping short, fingers touching her crusted lips instead. "I did something...bad."

He stood and rolled his shoulders, stretching out the stiffness. "I'll help you with whatever it is, but you need to explain. I can't hit an invisible target." Kraken took her shoulders, steadying her trembling form. His voice was gentle, coaxing. "Are you okay? What happened out there? You can tell me."

She averted her gaze, leaning into his support. "I am fine. What occurred is not what I need help with. It is something else." She shrugged. "I need to return to Modernist Ignis. I want you to come with me."

Modernist Ignis—crawling with authorities and death for any rebel, especially after the prison break. He released her, lips parting with a question that never came. His body already followed her command, but he stopped halfway to his bedroom.

Insanity. The thought screamed through him, yet pressing Yin further was pointless. Walking back into the city's heart was a death sentence. Yet the rational voice whispered beneath the roar of something else—a raw, illogical need to shield her. It was like a circuit flipping in his brain, sensing a threat and demanding he move, act, protect. Logic vanished.

With a sigh of resignation, he moved again, this time with purpose. Pulling on fresh jeans, a grey T-shirt, and his leather jacket, he checked his pistol's magazine before holstering it. The decision made itself. He would not let her do this alone.

"I'm with you," he said, returning to her side. "Let's do this."

They slipped into the night streets. The silence felt heavy, broken only by the ragged sound of Yin's breathing. Her movements betrayed her—a sluggish, unsteady gait that made him want to reach out and steady her with every step. These glitches had been happening more frequently. Some kind of sickness he couldn't comprehend, affecting her in ways that defied his understanding of Synthetic biology. This shook him more than any previous episode. Her compromised state and his lack of information about their mission meant Kraken was leaping into the proverbial deep end. Yet, an odd calm settled over him.

Modernist Ignis rose in the distance, its metallic towers stretching toward infinity. Hover shuttles flitted between buildings like fireflies, their lights dancing against the concrete wall that divided the city. Each entry point featured scanners that read the identification chips embedded within every citizen's palm.

Kraken's fingers drifted to his left hand, tracing the jagged scar beside where his original chip had been crudely removed and replaced with a forgery. All Outsiders underwent the procedure upon induction.

Yin led them to an entry on the western perimeter. The archway stood unguarded, its sensors hidden within the walls —a false gesture of unity between the city's divided halves. "See?" the Modernists would say. "No one prevents your passage. We are equal."

Then why build the wall at all?

"The place we are going is close to this entry," Yin said, sweat beading on her forehead as she leaned against the barrier. "My chip is flagged. It has already triggered the sensors once tonight. We will have limited time."

Already once tonight. Kraken's blood chilled. Where in Modernist Ignis would she go and return covered in blood? Her earlier questions about the prison echoed in his mind. The prison occupied Modernist territory. What business could she have there?

"We'll have to be quick, then." He offered his hand. "Need help?"

"I'm fine." She guided his hand away, her cool touch a stark contrast to his warmth. Straightening, she approached the entry point with renewed determination. Kraken followed close behind as the sensors clicked quietly, scanning their chips. Her chip was flagging right now, a red light blinking on some distant security console. How much time did that buy them?

They climbed a winding path toward an imposing mansion perched on the clifftop. The three-tiered structure rose like a gleaming monument, its white shell adorned with cascading windows that caught starlight. Arched openings at ground level spilled warm light into the cool darkness, while a semi-domed crown curved against the star-scattered sky. Below, a pool reflected flashing diamonds of light. Beyond that, the valley fell away, revealing the most breathtaking view: the lights of Ignis glittering like a pool of iridescence in the earth's palms.

High-tech drones swept the perimeter with searchlights, their sensors probing every shadow. Sentinels—androids shaped like metallic hounds with razor teeth—patrolled the grounds, quick to respond to any threat on their turf.

Yin moved like a liquid shadow along the cobbled path, weaving between the harsh circles of light with impossible grace despite her condition. Kraken followed, his heavier footsteps a jarring counterpoint to her fluid motion. At the main entrance, she ran her palm across the door's surface, checking for weaknesses before throwing her full weight against it. The door burst inward with a loud boom that sent dust cascading through the corridors.

The hairs on the back of Kraken's neck bristled. Such noise was certain to bring the Sentinels pawing around. Yet Yin slipped inside, oblivious.

"This way," she said, motioning toward the interior. "His office was this way."

"His?"

Kraken pushed the door closed behind him, noting it hardly mattered as it wouldn't latch. He quietly hoped the Sentinels wouldn't notice and lay in wait for them with gnashing teeth.

Yin led him to a door bearing the nameplate *Doctor Ryūnosuke Izumi*. Unlike the entrance she'd forced, this one opened easily to reveal a study frozen in time. The air hung thick with the scent of aged leather and cold incense. Bookshelves lined every wall, crammed with volumes that seemed untouched for years. Papers lay scattered across the central desk, as if someone had fled in haste.

Moonlight streamed through the large window, illuminating Yin as she stalked toward the desk and began riffling through documents.

"How did you know where to go?" Kraken whispered, though Yin ignored him. She slammed the last stack down with frustrated force, her attention fixing on a photograph—a dark-haired man in a lab coat holding a bright-eyed toddler who gazed up at him with pure adoration. The resemblance between the child and Yin was uncanny.

"What are you looking for?" Kraken ventured. "Can I help?"

She remained motionless, studying the image. "You wouldn't have kept it as a digital copy," she murmured to herself. "You were always so paranoid someone was watching."

Her fingers traced the desk, then stopped. Her posture

changed, her focus shifting from the scattered papers to the cabinet, as if seeing it for the first time. In one fluid motion, she vaulted over the desk and delivered a savage kick to the cabinet's side panel. Wood splintered as she knelt and rummaged through the debris, finally producing a thick manila folder labeled 'PROJECT GEMINI' in bold letters.

Kraken's breath caught. *Project Gemini.* The name on the folder slammed into him—the same name the android at the laundromat had used. He looked from the folder to the mansion around them, to Yin, who was still staring at the folder. His heart thudded in his chest. This was the place where she was made, the lab where she'd only "existed." And the man in the photo, Ryūnosuke Izumi... *He* was her creator.

"A false bottom," she said, knuckles white from her grip on the folder.

When her gaze found his, he knew she was addressing him directly. "Can you hack the laptop?" She nodded toward the device on the desk. "Any information about me is likely hidden and encrypted. It would reference Project Gemini or Yin Izumi." Her eyes drifted back to the photograph. "My human name once belonged to his daughter. Her fate was never revealed to me."

Kraken settled at the desk, unease twisting in his gut. The laptop's encryption was military-grade, expensive, but not beyond his skills. Two quick blinks activated his com-tacts, establishing a direct connection. Lines of code flooded his vision as he probed the security protocols, fingers drumming against the desk. Bypass the login. Crack the hash. Exploit the vulnerability. After five minutes, the encryption shattered, and he was in.

He navigated to a deliberately deleted folder titled 'Yin Izumi' containing dozens of video files. Every instinct screamed at him to stop, to destroy the laptop and claim it was booby-trapped, but Yin would see through such deception immediately.

Kraken knew what she would say if he asked whether she was certain about this.

His cursor hovered over the first file. A sound made him freeze—low snuffling, the scrape of claws on concrete. His hand jerked toward his weapon before he realized the corridor outside was silent. Nothing but his own breathing, too loud in the empty room. Kraken forced his hand back to the mouse.

He clicked play.

Chapter 16

First breath.

Air rushed into her lungs as consciousness exploded through her neural pathways. Her eyes snapped open, pupils dilating against the harsh fluorescent light. Primal instinct seized control—heaving, gasping, expelling the bitter fluid that burned her throat. The world swam in and out of focus as the seconds crawled by, each one bringing sharper clarity to her vision.

Sensation flooded her nervous system like electrical current through virgin circuits. Pain, pressure, temperature—concepts she had no names for yet understood with startling immediacy. Her mouth opened of its own accord, releasing a guttural cry that echoed off sterile walls.

Something flickered in her peripheral vision. She tracked the movement, watching as digits twitched and curled. Wonder sparked in her consciousness as she realized the appendages responded to her will. Closer they came until darkness engulfed her sight—her own hand pressed against her face.

Hand. The word materialized unbidden.

She explored further, mapping the geography of her existence. Fingers connected to palms, palms to wrists, wrists flowing into arms that joined shoulders. Everything linked in perfect anatomical harmony. When she traced her lips, they curved upward in an expression she somehow knew meant joy. A vibration in her throat became sound, then *laughter*—bright and musical.

The cold surface beneath her registered as *table* when she pressed herself upright. Her reflection stared back from its polished surface until movement drew her attention upward. A figure approached with measured steps.

Man.

Something deep within her core recoiled. Her body tensed without conscious command, every muscle fiber screaming *danger* despite having no experience to justify the response. This creature meant harm. She knew it with the same certainty that told her to breathe.

"Okay... will take adjustment... conscious... too little time... teach you like a newborn... higher intelligence... adaptability." His words fragmented at first, then cohered as her auditory processing flourished. She instinctively leaned away as he drew closer, studying his smile with primal suspicion. That expression—lips curved upward like her own moments before—felt wrong on his features.

"Everything will naturally come back to you soon. You'll begin recognizing speech patterns. It won't be perfect at first, but you'll be fluent within a week."

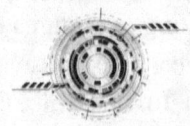

CAENOGENESIS

Blood traced crimson paths down Yin's forehead, each drop a testament to her endurance. The industrial lights cast her shadow in stark relief against concrete walls, while her ragged breathing provided counterpoint to the dripping of her wounds. Chains bit into her wrists. The metal chair beneath her was welded to the floor.

"Stop it." Her voice cracked with exhaustion. "I don't want to do this anymore."

The figure remained motionless in the shadows, stationed beside his cart of implements. Scalpels caught the light alongside brass knuckles and electrical prods. Her pleas fell on deaf ears—they always did. Each failed interrogation reset the cycle: new intelligence planted in her mind, fresh pain to teach resistance.

"This is war," her Creator's voice echoed in memory. "This is what you must overcome."

Yin forced her breathing to steady, seeking refuge in mental escape. The lessons weren't all torment. She genuinely enjoyed weapons training, the elegant mechanics of firearms and blades. Plant identification sessions felt almost peaceful—pattern recognition disguised as botanical education. Even watching war footage seemed merciful compared to this.

The early days of mere observation felt like paradise now.

Steel pierced beneath her fingernails.

Her scream shattered the silence.

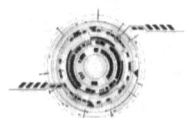

Voice Recording #15 by Dr. Izumi

Subject displays acute anxiety and depressive episodes. Sedation required following a violent outburst in quarters. Subject destroyed furniture while attempting escape, vocalizing hostility: "I hate you."

Threats against personnel and self-harm documented.

These developments are problematic. A weapon cannot function with such emotional volatility. Potential buyers will reject damaged goods. I am implementing corrective measures. I knew this would happen. We didn't suppress its humanity sufficiently during initial programming.

Brain modification remains feasible. Subject is weeks old; neural plasticity should accommodate adjustment. Physical adaptation exceeds projections. Complete radiation immunity achieved in single exposure. Recovery time: twenty-four hours. Regenerative capacity is remarkable.

This is salvageable.

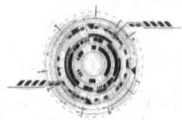

Her Creator's voice faded to white noise as Yin studied the holographic brain rotating above the table. Whether those neural pathways belonged to her seemed irrelevant.

Everything about her existence was predetermined, anyway.

Food lay untouched between them: turkey sandwich, apple slices, mixed nuts. She required minimal sustenance, but the meal performed a theater of normalcy for his benefit. Her attention drifted until his palm struck the table.

"This is important, Yin." He snatched an apple slice, chewing with deliberate emphasis. "Pay attention. Physically, you're exceptional, but we miscalculated your psychological parameters. Too much humanity remains. Trauma affects you rather than building immunity. After tonight's procedure, everything improves. You'll be reborn."

Yin inhaled slowly, crafting interest into her expression. "When will this operation occur?"

"Tonight."

The last moment she could ever hate him.

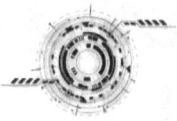

Voice Recording #16 by Dr. Izumi

Operation successful. Minor side effect: the subject's speech patterns exhibit increased mechanical precision. Acceptable trade-off. Emotional outbursts eliminated. Subject demonstrates complete logical focus.

Pain tolerance improved—unclear whether neurological modification or adaptive evolution. Further testing required. All psychological evaluations passed with perfect scores.

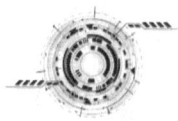

In her quarters, she examined her reflection in the scratched plastic mirror. The face before her belonged to someone else—someone who had ceased existing. She traced the contours of that vanished person's features.

Human.

What inefficient creatures they were, driven by impulses that bred only weakness.

Who would choose such a limitation?

The face staring back at her was no longer human.

It was just Yin.

Chapter 17

The footage's final frame burned behind Kraken's eyelids as he slammed the laptop shut and flung it with a gut-wrenching shudder. The device skittered across the floor where he'd thrown it, but the distance couldn't erase what he'd witnessed. Those images of Yin's unimaginable suffering had carved themselves into his consciousness like acid etching glass.

His heart felt like molten lead in his chest. How could anyone—*anyone*—be capable of such calculated brutality? And to someone made in his own daughter's image. The thought was a physical sickness, coiling in his gut. *What kind of monster looks at his own child and sees a template for...this?*

Yin stood at his side, staring at the space where the laptop had been. Her eyes... The same blankness from the footage. Was she even seeing him? Or had she retreated somewhere deep inside, leaving only this empty shell behind? That monster had done this to her. He'd locked her in a basement and systematically wrung out every last drop of humanity until nothing remained—and he'd *celebrated* success in the end.

"Why did you do that?" Her voice carried no inflection, no emotion. "Now we are unable to complete the footage."

The fact that she had to ask pierced through his already bleeding heart like a blade finding bone. Kraken swallowed the bile rising in his throat and forced what he hoped resembled a sheepish grin. He scratched the back of his head, the gesture feeling foreign and inadequate. "Sorry, Yin. I let my feelings get the better of me. Silly ol' human me and my stupid feelings, right? ...Yin?"

Her head cocked to the side, unfocused eyes staring off. Distant. "I was not the only subject down there."

"What do you mean?"

A sudden tension rippled through her frame, muscles tautening. The PROJECT GEMINI file slid from her fingers, its contents scattering across the floor. Blood trickled from her nostrils, then erupted from her mouth in a violent scarlet burst.

A jolt, cold and electric, shot from his stomach to his throat. The world narrowed to a single, horrifying point: Yin falling. He lunged, his own voice a strangled sound, catching her just before the concrete could claim her. *"Yin?"*

He cradled her head in his arms, frantically shaking her shoulders while calling her name. His fingers found the pulse point at her throat—faint but present, a fragile thread of life still tethering her to consciousness.

With infinite care, he gathered up the file and Yin into his arms, placing the file onto her stomach. "It's okay," he whispered, though he knew she couldn't hear him. The words were as much for himself as for her. "I've got you."

The high-pitched whine of repulsion engines cut through the quiet—drones banking hard over the clifftop, their searchlights sweeping the mansion's white shell in geometric patterns. The beams converged on the arched openings at ground level, probing the darkness. *Shit.*

Kraken adjusted Yin's weight in his arms and broke into a run, heading out a side door toward the cliff path. The winding cobblestone trail led toward the valley below, away from the patrol craft circling overhead. His boots skidded on loose stones as the engine whine intensified, the searchlights sweeping closer to his position.

A mechanical snarl echoed from behind. Hydraulic joints and servo motors whirred to life. The Sentinels. Two of the metallic hounds burst around the mansion's curved walls, their chrome bodies gleaming in the harsh white glare of the searchlights, razor teeth glinting as optical sensors locked on his position. The androids closed the distance in powerful, swift strides.

Adrenaline flooded Kraken as he pushed harder down the steep trail, Yin's unconscious form a dead weight against his chest. The Sentinels were faster on the open cobblestone, but ahead, the path narrowed and twisted through rocky outcroppings that would slow their bulky frames. Above, hover cars joined the drones, their engines screaming as they banked over the cliff edge, searchlights stabbing down at the winding path.

A third Sentinel appeared below, climbing up from a lower patrol route to cut off his escape. Kraken veered off the path entirely, scrambling across the rocky clifftop terrain toward a steep descent into the valley. The machines' sensors swept after him, their targeting systems struggling with the irregular ground and sparse vegetation clinging to the cliff face. A hover car swept overhead, its downdraft sending loose rocks skittering down the slope, searchlight beam missing him by mere inches as he ducked behind an outcropping.

He half-ran, half-slid down the treacherous incline with Yin clutched tight to his chest. Sharp stones tore at his clothes. The valley floor seemed impossibly far below, Ignis's lights glittering in the distance like false promises of safety. The

Sentinels' snarls echoed above him as their programming calculated safer routes. The hover cars banked hard, struggling to track his movement down the steep cliff.

Kraken didn't stop. He found a narrow service path—probably used by maintenance crews—carved into the rockface and followed it at a reckless pace. The engine whine was above him now, the searchlights sweeping the upper reaches of the cliff. His com-tacts flickered with a route overlay—the fastest path to the wall, threading through the gaps in patrol patterns he quickly memorized.

The path finally leveled out at the valley floor. Kraken pushed through the gleaming streets of Modernist Ignis, keeping to the shadows between buildings, avoiding the major thoroughfares where hover patrols concentrated. The wall loomed ahead. A towering barrier separating the pristine districts from Retro Ignis, from Old Town.

He found a maintenance access, a rusted grate half-hidden behind a dumpster. The gap was barely wide enough, and squeezing through with Yin's unconscious weight and his bulk was no small feat. Metal scraped against his shoulders, tore at his jacket. Then he was through, stumbling into the familiar decay of home.

Kraken turned his back on the wall, on the gleaming city beyond it, on that mansion and its crimes. All that mattered was the fragile weight in his arms, the faint pulse beneath her skin, and the single, burning promise he made to whatever was left of her inside: *Never again.*

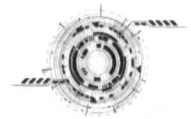

THE PERPETUAL GREY OF IGNIS'S OVERCAST SKY HAD DEEPENED to a muted pewter by the time Kraken carefully carried Yin inside. Her body remained limp in his arms, the military attire she wore now stiff with dried blood. With hands that trembled despite his efforts to steady them, he peeled away the soiled clothing and made a mental note to burn every thread later. In its place, he draped the soft robe he'd found crumpled on the living room floor before settling her onto his bed.

He maintained his vigil at her bedside, eyes fixed on the shallow rise and fall of her chest, monitoring each fragile breath as she lay unconscious. The sight jarred him. He'd never seen Yin sleep before. Usually, she would be curled on his couch, absorbed in old soap operas she claimed were 'research.' Those little routines had kept her safely occupied, away from the dangers that seemed to follow in her wake.

But now, watching her lie motionless on his bed, he wished desperately for her to wake and return to those familiar patterns. These glitches were becoming more frequent, more concerning. He couldn't shake the suspicion that they were somehow connected to the information Yin had sought from that hellish place. If he hadn't already suspected the blood on her clothes belonged to Dr. Izumi, he would have hunted the man down himself and finished what she'd started.

Sleep claimed him despite his intentions, and he awoke with a violent start, the remnants of exhaustion still weighing heavily on his limbs. The grey light outside was unchanged. His internal clock, however, told him nearly twenty-four hours had passed since he'd brought her home.

More importantly, Yin was missing from where he'd left her on his bed.

"Yin?" His voice echoed off the apartment walls, met only by silence.

Panic drove him from room to room, his mind conjuring every worst-case scenario. What if something had happened while he'd slept? Guilt gnawed at him as he searched, finding only the soft indentation on the couch where Yin typically sat. With each empty room, his anxiety crested higher—until he heard muffled voices drifting from the kitchen.

One was unmistakably Yin's monotone delivery. The other filled him with equal parts relief and wariness.

"Lack of consent does not equate consent." Yin sat at the table with a spoon suspended over a bowl of cereal, her expression deceptively composed despite the wariness lurking in her dark eyes. The spoon trembled slightly between her three fingers. "His changing the locks deduces you are not welcome here."

"Well, he's never told me to stop." The subject of Yin's mistrust stood casually at the open refrigerator, one hand braced against the door's edge. Israel—or Izzy, as she preferred—was dressed in form-fitting leather that left little to the imagination, her hair styled in a magnificent blown-out afro that seemed to defy the dim atmosphere filtering through the windows. "It's a game between us, I suppose." Her head disappeared into the fridge, followed by the sound of enthusiastic rummaging. "I pick the lock and eat his food, he changes the locks, and I break in to eat his food again. Repeat ad nauseam."

Kraken surveyed the carnage laid out before him with growing dismay. Nothing remained of his leftover Chinese except empty cartons scattered across the counters like casualties of war. His cereal drawer had been thoroughly ransacked, boxes torn open and contents pillaged.

Was nothing sacred?

"Seriously?" The word escaped him like a deflated balloon. "What's going on here?"

"Hey, Krak." Izzy flashed him a brilliant smile while twisting a stolen apple between her fingers. She slammed the refrigerator shut with unnecessary force and leaned against the back of a nearby chair, causing her hair to cascade across her face in an artfully careless way. She took a deliberately audible bite of the apple. "Nothin' going on here. Your roommate and I were just having a friendly chat while you caught up on your beauty sleep."

"I located her in the kitchen and was inquiring regarding her authorization to be present," Yin stated. "If you request it, I shall remove her, Kraken."

Kraken. He didn't miss that she'd dropped the "human" honorific she typically used when addressing people. The omission felt significant, though he didn't allow himself to dwell on its implications as he joined them at the table. He mimicked Izzy's relaxed posture, draping his hands over the back of a chair while privately marveling that Yin hadn't already ejected the intruder.

"That's not necessary, Yin. Izzy is a friend who has been away for some time."

"Staying in a place with absolutely terrible customer service," Izzy chimed in, punctuating her words with an aggressive crunch of apple. She threw her arms up in theatrical frustration. "Can you believe they made me bunk with *men*? Disgusting, smelly men—no offense, Kraken—and don't even get me started on how impossible it was to find decent soap. It's because I'm an Outsider." She glanced meaningfully at Yin before returning her attention to Kraken. "You, on the other hand, seem to be living it up with a lady." Then, directed at Yin with a conspiratorial wink: "Not the worst guy to shack up with, I suppose."

"Gender is not important. Humans overthink it," Yin muttered, setting her spoon back in the now-empty bowl with a soft clink.

Kraken assumed she was referring to their current living arrangements, but Izzy interpreted the comment through an entirely different lens.

"Yes!" Izzy snapped her fingers with obvious delight. "Screw gender norms and all that restrictive nonsense. We get to be our authentic selves, whoever that might be." She gestured to her own figure with obvious pride. "Science helped give me this body, but I'm the one working it. Gotta show off the goods when you've got them."

Gender and sexuality had never occupied much mental real estate in Kraken's mind. In their modern world, physical appearance and genetic makeup could be modified to align with personal preferences as easily as changing clothes. For him, more pressing matters than romance or physical attraction demanded his attention. He'd never felt compelled to label his inclinations, nor taken offense when others attempted to categorize him.

He'd assumed Yin operated similarly. As a super soldier, her priorities would hardly have included such considerations. But it struck him now that things might have been different for her if she'd ever been given a genuine choice in the matter. The thought only stoked his anger at the injustices she'd endured.

He chose his next words carefully. "Izzy raises a valid point," he said, hoping Yin would understand the deeper meaning beneath his words. "We can all finally embrace our true identities. *All* of us."

Over time, he'd begun to suspect there was more to his stoic, overly literal Synthetic roommate than surface appearances suggested. Despite her tendency toward pure logic over emotion, she'd demonstrated enough unexpected compassion to make him wonder: had he and Yin actually formed something resembling a friendship?

Was such a thing possible with a Synthetic?

As the conversation's tone shifted toward the serious, Izzy set her half-eaten apple on the table with obvious reluctance. Seriousness wasn't her forte—it made her want to flee for the hills.

"I heard you're headed on a mission soon," she offered, steering them back toward safer conversational waters. "Freeing poor schmucks like me means more mouths to feed. Miriam says we're hemorrhaging funds. Turns out you can't stage a revolution on an empty stomach."

Kraken was intimately familiar with the mission's details.

The elites of the underground trade were planning to unveil a highly exclusive street drug at a private soirée—invitation only, and only for those whose wealth approached the astronomical. He'd managed to acquire tickets through Gabriel's connections, though the cost had been significant.

Miriam had tasked him with charming his way into securing a supply for the Outsiders to distribute and analyze. If they could successfully replicate the drug, the profits would sustain their growing numbers for months. He'd already invited Nori along on the venture.

"Trying to score an invitation?" Kraken teased. "I know how much you love parties, but the last one we attended together literally went up in flames. Has Miriam returned your flamethrower yet?"

"Listen, that was not my fault." Izzy examined her perfectly manicured nails with exaggerated nonchalance. "The guy I was dancing with tried to cop a feel without permission. He needed to learn how to treat a lady with respect." She paused for effect. "Besides, I should be the one going. You don't even enjoy parties."

She spoke the truth, and they both knew it. Kraken didn't voice his suspicions aloud, but he was certain this mission represented Miriam's punishment for the entire Yin situation. Losing to her supposed enemy had made their leader appear weak before their peers, and Miriam despised nothing more than appearing weak. This was his opportunity to restore her confidence in him—or risk demotion and possibly an early grave.

Izzy's face suddenly lit up like a light bulb, mischief dancing in her dark eyes. "You should take Yin to the party! I heard you took her on a date through the sewers last time. Not exactly the most romantic venue, Krak."

"I don't believe Yin would enjoy a party any more than I would," Kraken sighed, refusing to engage with her obvious attempt to fluster him. He couldn't envision Yin in any kind of party environment. One wrong move from an intoxicated guest and she might seriously injure them. He pictured Miriam's reaction to such a scenario and visibly shuddered. Their leader had intimidation refined to an exact science.

Izzy didn't argue the point, merely shrugging in apparent acceptance. The easy surrender made him suspicious.

"Whatever you say. I'll leave you two lovebirds to it." She tapped the table near Yin to capture her attention. "You should seriously consider joining the Outsiders, Yin. We're more than just a reference to a twentieth-century crime drama." She blew Kraken a theatrical kiss.

"I'll pay you back for the food later, Krak. I'm a bit financially challenged right now, what with being a freshly liberated jailbird and all. The lock-picking was good practice—helped shake off the rust. You should invite me over more often. You always stock the good stuff."

"You always say that," Kraken lamented. "At least you didn't touch the jumbo shrimp this time."

"Shrimp is not jumbo," Yin interjected. "Shrimp are small, Human Kraken."

Ah. All it had taken to draw her back into the conversation was a linguistic contradiction. The honorific had returned as well. Apparently, he'd fallen from grace more quickly than expected.

Yin twisted in her seat to fix Izzy with a stern glare. "Human Izzy, you are mistaken. I remain here because it is logical for me to do so. Your cause is not mine, and I will not fight others' battles. Instead, I will remain useful by repairing appliances like the washing machine so that we need no longer sit naked in the laundromat."

Heat rushed to Kraken's ears, the tips burning red-hot with embarrassment. Izzy's perfectly arched eyebrow and knowing smirk made him feel approximately two inches tall. He wanted to protest, to clarify that there was no 'we' in any romantic sense, but the words had already been released into the universe like escaped balloons. Attempting to untangle the situation would prove as futile as trying to explain the contradictory nature of 'jumbo shrimp' to someone who processed language literally, like Yin.

"Good-bye, Krak," Israel sang as she sashayed toward the door, clearly delighted by the chaos she was leaving in her wake.

Kraken wanted to dig a hole and bury himself in it. *Can't wait for that little tidbit to make its way back to camp.* He could already picture Miriam's disappointed glare while Nori stood in the corner, struggling not to collapse with laughter.

He hung his head and slumped his shoulders in utter defeat. The soft sound of Yin placing her bowl in the sink drew his attention, followed by the scrape of her chair as she sat back down.

When he glanced up, she was biting into the apple Izzy had abandoned. He wondered briefly about the hygiene implications, but then again, this was probably the most food he'd ever seen her voluntarily consume. She gazed toward the door Izzy had exited, something distant and calculating in her expression. Her tightly pressed lips and furrowed brow suggested deep contemplation.

"That human," she said eventually. "I could detect when she first saw me that she recognized the APB reward. There is avarice in her eyes."

The APB? Kraken rubbed his chin thoughtfully. "Don't worry about Izzy, Yin. She respects me. She won't try anything."

Yin paused mid-bite, her dark eyes finding his. "If she makes any move against me, I will not hesitate to eliminate her. Whether she is your friend or not."

The threat lingered in the sudden silence. Kraken harbored no doubts that Yin would follow through—he'd sensed the tension between them from the moment he'd entered the kitchen. Self-preservation ranked among her highest priorities, and he understood that. But he also knew that both Israel and Yin possessed lethal skills, and any altercation between them would result in significant collateral damage.

He released a heavy sigh before responding. "I understand your concerns, and I don't want anyone turning you over to the authorities either. In my opinion, no reward would be worth betraying you. And if Israel ever tries anything, I'll do everything in my power to stop her."

Her lips parted slightly, her usual sharp retorts uncharacteristically absent. "She is your comrade," Yin reminded him, rising from her chair. She closed the distance between them until their faces were mere inches apart, her dark eyes searching his. She raised one hand, and for a moment, he thought she might strike him for daring to choose disloyalty.

Instead, her palm came to rest gently on his shoulder in a surprisingly human gesture from the typically stoic Synthetic. The tension lines around her eyes softened as she studied his face with what looked like curiosity mixed with concern.

"You would truly stand against her for me?" she asked, her voice dropping to something almost approaching wonder. "You are truly strange, Kraken."

Chapter 18

Aja Yamamoto's world hadn't stopped shifting since the holo-screen confrontation. They stood outside the weathered wooden doors of the dilapidated building, their eyes scanning the neon sign that swung above through dark-tinted sunglasses. Some of the lettering was burnt out; others flickered uncertainly, the gilded letters seeming to come to life to beckon passersby with their seductive glow.

Their gaze drifted down to the entrance, a set of wooden double-doors tarnished by time. Graffiti adorned the walls, its bold colors and provocative images hinting at wild nights and forbidden desires that awaited inside the Velvet Lyre.

With a firm push, Aja forced open the heavy, creaking doors and was enveloped in a whirlwind of sound and color.

They didn't like bars. At least, not bars like this.

The music was too loud—the air seeming to pulse with the beat of obnoxious music, invading their senses and creating a ringing in their ears. The scent of artificial whiskey, recycled breath, sweat, and citrus oil clung to every surface. The patrons of the Velvet Lyre had no sense of tact. Laughter roared over the synth-bass, and bodies moved without grace. They were mammals pretending at grace—like if they thrust hard enough or danced low enough, they'd transcend what they were. Every step on the sticky floor reinforced it. This place was honest about its desperation.

They observed as hues of electric blue and rich crimson bathed the room, casting elaborate shadows upon the old, plush velvet curtains that adorned every corner. An intricate chandelier, dripping with glittering fake crystals, hung low above a worn bar counter. The bartender was a holographic AI dressed provocatively in nothing but a pair of overalls and nipple tassels.

They didn't belong here. They were a Yamamoto. The Councilor of Innovation and Genetic Affairs.

Perhaps one reason the Synthetic set this as their meeting place.

Aja adjusted the lapels of their tailored coat and crossed the club with care, stepping over a sticky puddle of something probably biological. They tugged at their leather gloves, careful not to make contact. Their prosthetic knee clicked faintly. Not loud enough for most to hear, but Aja heard it.

The thing was sitting in a booth toward the back, firmly pressed against the wall. From its vantage point, it had a clear view of the venue and all who entered. Clearly already noticing Aja's approach. There was a tension that had been building, a slow coil of anticipation and dread, but now that the meeting was finally happening, it felt like a long-awaited exhale, a moment of necessary reckoning.

So why did it feel like swallowing glass?

Aja's breath hitched, then tightened. They masked it with a polite, shallow smile as they slid into the booth across from it with careful grace, brushing nonexistent lint from their lapel as an excuse not to meet its eyes. When they did, the resemblance struck hard. The eyes weren't quite Ryūnosuke's—but close enough to stir bile. Not because of what had been made, but because of what had been taken.

It looked just like him. Like *them*. Like both of them, and neither.

The Synthetic raised its head. "Hello, Aja."

The voice was calm, not mechanical. Organic. Even polite. Like it *knew* what manners were and chose to use them. Aja didn't answer immediately. Their throat burned.

Of course it had surfaced. Not surprising after the APB. That was the hook, and they were the bait. The last thread it had left in this rotting city.

"Dr. Yamamoto." Curt, but without malice.

It blinked at them. Slowly. Its face blank, posture immobile, as if their words were meaningless to it. Then again, it never had the worship instilled in it for Aja that Ryūnosuke had. Aja might've been one of the creators, but Ryūnosuke had been its Creator.

They forced words from between their teeth. "You look just like him." A pause. "And you certainly have *her* face. Not surprising. Though, one must wonder how a father can hurt the image of his dead child?"

That earned little more than a twitch of its head as Aja removed their sunglasses and slid them into their jacket pocket. They raised a brow, briefly noting the thing's dubious attire. Ryūnosuke hadn't put much work into teaching it the art of conversation, and it had the emotional spectrum of a wet sheet of paper. *How expected of him.*

"If found here, this could be very unpleasant for my political career," Aja ventured, allowing a cursory scan over their shoulder. They were put at a disadvantage in their position, with their line of sight involving only the Synthetic and the wall behind it. "Care to explain why you asked me here?"

With languid motion, the Synthetic raised its hand and tapped its slender fingers on a file resting on the table between them. One Aja hadn't noticed until now. Marked across it was the title PROJECT GEMINI.

Aja's heart soared, though only their fingers twitched outwardly to betray their emotion. It had to be. That was the missing piece of information they'd yearned for all this time. The key to the Synthetic's genome...and humanity's hope. It took everything in them not to snatch it away and make a run for it. They gazed up at the Synth, narrowing their eyes momentarily as they pondered: Why show this to them? Why now?

In its face, they saw exhaustion. Pale skin. Dark circles under their eyes, bruised black and purple. The remnants of dried blood ringing its nostrils—a sign of a nosebleed not long finished. Aja's jaw set. *Ah...You want to bargain with me. I'm the only one left who can fix you.*

Their gaze softened, lips curling into a frown as their brow furrowed. Lilting their voice, they tried to convey a tone they imagined a concerned parent might take on. "You don't look well, Project Gemini."

"*Yin.* I am Yin."

Aja leaned back, jaw unclenching slowly. A sneer threatened the corner of their mouth—easy enough to disguise beneath neutrality.

"Yin...you even use a name that doesn't truly belong to you."

A pet name, no doubt given by Ryūnosuke. They'd been against naming it. Names made things too easily emotional, and that poisoned the work. Ryūnosuke had obviously grown fond of the Synth, but his love was not for it. It was for a ghost. No matter how he'd clawed for the memories, no matter how he'd sculpted the Synthetic, it would never be his daughter.

"You don't look well, Yin. I know you returned to Dr. Izumi's residence. Did something happen to you there? Maybe I can help you?"

"My state of being is irrelevant. As is my venture to my Creator's home. My Creator chose to suppress my memories, and I sought information, but the mission was fruitless."

While it carried many of Ryūnosuke's features, Aja saw their own interspersed between and giving them refinement. Hatred rose hot and sour in their throat that they fought down.

They'd never wanted children, certainly not like this, but what choice had Aja had? It had never been about legacy. It was science. Survival. Yet Ryūnosuke had frozen them out, like they were some impulsive intern instead of a co-creator.

Their manicured nails dug impatiently into the table.

"What did you want to tell me, *Yin*?"

The Synthetic shoved the file between them, curling its fingers into the pages and throwing it open, pointing at the exposed page.

"What do you know of Project Gemini's phase two?"

Phase two? Aja leaned toward the data. Visceral rage trembled through their body, nostrils flaring, as the being in the photo stared back. Cheekily named 'Yang'—though Aja doubted 'Yin' caught the play on duality—aside from white hair and red eyes, its features were unmistakably Aja's.

A twin—as if the genome had split itself again just to spite them. Without their consent. Without their hand in it at all.

Removing them from the project hadn't been Ryūnosuke's only betrayal.

Aja felt the Synth's eyes on them, keenly observing their reaction. They clawed their rage back in, pushing their back against the seat and releasing a breath through a forced smile.

"Interesting. May I look closer?"

They reached to turn the page, but 'Yin' pulled the file away and closed it.

"She wasn't found in the raid. It is reasonable to assume she escaped the same night as I. This subject is not very fond of you or me," it said with a cock of its head. "I have scoured the data. Records indicate that she wishes to kill me. I imagine you will be a target on her way to do that, especially now that we have connected."

Ah... This was the trap it had laid out, and Aja had walked right into it. Whether this other Synth had any ill feelings toward them or not, now that Aja had met with 'Yin,' it had reason to seek Aja out. If it was as focused and merciless as 'Yin' was made to be, it would have few qualms about killing Aja to further its mission. 'Yin' was forcing an allyship between them by compromising their ability to forge one with the other Synthetic.

Perhaps you carry some traits of me yet.

It drove the point home: "I have provided this information so that you may take caution. Unlike this other Synthetic, I have reason to protect and keep you alive."

Aja let out a bitter laugh. They'd congratulate their creation if the situation weren't so annoying.

"I understand," they said.

Aja had never been one for pacing. They found fidgeting useless—distracting in others, undignified in themselves. But now, the urge itched just beneath their skin. Perhaps they finally understood why some people needed motion to think.

They turned over the possibilities in their mind. The priority was maintaining appearances with this Synthetic while discreetly gathering intelligence on the other one. If the second proved more viable and aligned with their goals, they could shift course when the time came.

Or they could convince this one to take care of the problem for them.

They settled on the next question. "Have you met 'Yang'?"

It shook its head.

Good. That gave Aja room. Time. Options.

They rose from their seat slowly, extending their prosthetic hand—not from courtesy, but because metal couldn't feel. The

Synthetic's touch would register as nothing. That was preferable.

The thought of its flesh against their flesh stirred a quiet revulsion in them—not fear, not exactly. Something deeper. A violation. And yet...

They couldn't afford to recoil.

They couldn't afford to look away.

This one, 'Yin,' would still be of use. Its genome was invaluable to their goals, and a tool didn't have to be perfect to be effective. It only had to be wielded correctly.

So, they offered the handshake. A gesture not of goodwill, but of control. Distance disguised as contact.

"We'll keep in touch, Yin."

Even as the name passed their lips, something inside them twisted. But the plan had crystallized. Use what was in front of them. Monitor. Manipulate. Wait.

If something better emerged, they'd discard this one like the others.

But not yet.

Not until they were sure.

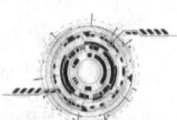

As THEIR PRIVATE SHUTTLE APPROACHED THE TOWERING WALL that separated the pristine world of Modernist Ignis from this desolate place, Aja's hands clenched into tight fists. They pressed their forehead against the cool glass window, trying to calm their racing thoughts. They fought back the urge to punch the thick metal surface and unleash a furious stream of curses. Those were the actions of a petulant child.

With their free hand, Aja traced the smooth surface of their prosthetic arm. A constant reminder of the tragic accident that had taken their left limbs as a young child, along with parts of their skull and brain tissue. Their adoptive mother had chosen cybernetics to rebuild them, rather than accept a broken child. No one would be able to detect the deception if they touched them. The artificial skin was warm to the touch, flawlessly concealing Aja's 'flaws.'

Ryūnosuke thought he had the last laugh. He couldn't have been more wrong. Not only would Aja succeed in their goals, they were going to use his precious pet to achieve them. Their com-tacts lit up and projected footage they'd gathered of the Synthetic since its escape. Facial recognition identified multiple known associates of the Outsiders. They were nothing but vagabonds ignorant of the true gravity of humanity's crisis. Their loyalties would be easily swayed with the right bait.

Aja opened their voice messages and spoke, "Find a way to contact the Outsider leader and connect me. I have a proposal for her."

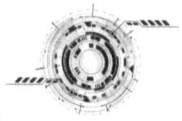

IN THE QUIET HUSH OF THEIR QUARTERS, AJA SAT ALONE AS the lights dimmed to a faint glow. The city outside was a blur of sterile brilliance behind tinted glass, but they didn't see it. Their gaze was fixed on the mirror mounted across from the bed—an old thing, analog, with a slight warp in the corner that bent reflections just enough to unsettle.

They stood slowly, walked to it, and let their eyes trace their own face. Too sharp. Too still. Too curated. Carefully constructed, like everything else of theirs.

With a breath they didn't realize they were holding, they peeled back the artificial skin on their left forearm. The seal hissed faintly as chrome and circuitry emerged from beneath synthetic flesh. Cold light pulsed in quiet patterns under the surface.

Metal. Not blood nor warmth. A reminder of what was taken and what was chosen in its place.

Their throat tightened as a thought intruded, unwelcome and unshakable.

Its face.

Those eyes, uncanny in their calm. So familiar. Familiar enough to haunt. Familiar enough to hurt.

The mirror did its job. It reflected, but not the truth.

It distorted.

Was it their own reflection they saw now, or its?

"You're not me," they whispered.

A beat passed. A flicker in the warped glass. Their voice, quieter now, hoarse. Almost a plea.

"You're not...mine."

The chrome glinted. The room was silent.

They resealed the skin, smoothing it into place. The moment passed, locked behind another layer. Another wall.

They turned away from the mirror.

Chapter 19

The obsidian table, a perfect black mirror, lay before them. It reflected not just the amber light from the ceiling but Aja's grim smile. Their plan was a reflection of that table—hard, cold, and flawless.

The chambers were deep within Ignis's inner ring, its fortified walls granting a sense of security. Four high-backed chairs occupied the council positions—Defense & Security, Innovation & Genetic Affairs, Infrastructure & Resources, and Justice & Civic Order. At the head sat Supreme Chancellor Virelian's ornate seat, while the elevated gallery behind housed the Elder Statesman Assembly, their weathered faces peering down like ancient judges, ready to condemn.

The leather portfolio containing the Recombinant Regulation and Containment Act legislation felt smooth, a promise of victory. Aja's fingers, however, drummed a quiet, staccato rhythm against its surface. *Three days. Three days to get here.* The rhythm was the ticking of a clock counting down to their inevitable win. Three days had passed since Pyreford. Three days of emergency sessions, security briefings, and carefully orchestrated public outcry. The timing couldn't have been more perfect.

Thorne: a pawn for security protocols. Martinez: practical, reliable. Liu: an easy mark, worried about supply lines. The vote was secured. All but one. Virelian.

He saw the political advantage of appearing decisive in the face of crisis. It shouldn't be difficult to sway him, except...

Valenstrom presented a serious obstacle. The old man's influence remained formidable, his voice carrying particular weight with Supreme Chancellor Virelian. But even his moral authority would struggle against the stark reality of seventeen dead guards and a compromised maximum-security facility.

The chamber's vaulted acoustics swallowed the air, leaving a hush that pressed in. Every word landed with a weight only such ancient stone could grant. Aja rose from the Innovation & Genetic Affairs seat, eyes sweeping over the gathered politicians. Traditionalists, all of them. The Techno-Revivalists had been purged. Executed, exiled, erased by the civil war's ruthless conclusion in 2114. They believed their grip was unshakable.

They hadn't counted on a rat nesting in their midst.

"Esteemed colleagues," Aja began, their voice carrying easily to every corner of the chamber. "We convene today not for routine legislative business, but to address a crisis that has moved from theoretical concern to deadly reality."

They felt Valenstrom's gaze before they saw him. A weight from above. They glanced up. There he was, the old man, his dark eyes like a hawk's, piercing, steady. His fingers, gnarled and ancient, rotated that insipid wooden dove. It never left his side. A symbol of his peaceful, antiquated morality. The thing Valenstrom used to gut opponents.

Aja's lips curved into the ghost of a confident smile. Once, he'd been their mentor, the one who recommended them for a position in government. Once, the old fool had called Aja "the brightest star of their generation." Today, they would prove him right in ways he could never have imagined. A glorious, terrible right.

Supreme Chancellor Virelian leaned forward in his chair, hands steepled before him. "The floor recognizes High Councilor Yamamoto on the matter of emergency security legislation."

"Thank you, Supreme Chancellor." Aja opened the portfolio with deliberate care. Every word in the legislation had been honed for success. "The Pyreford incident revealed a catastrophic failure: illegally modified Recombinants operating beyond legal oversight. Seventeen guards lost their lives. A maximum-security facility was breached. Dangerous criminals, empowered by black-market genetic modifications, roam our streets."

The deaths were regrettable, yes. But they were the perfect justification for what came next. "Which leads us to the Recombinant Regulation and Containment Act," Aja continued, lifting the document with authority. "This framework will prevent unauthorized recombination by establishing a registry, protect citizens, and preserve medical ethics across Ignis."

The public rationale was camouflage. The R.R.C.A.'s core was far more vital. It would quietly establish specialized facilities, granting legal authority to research Synthetic genomes under the Recombinant umbrella. Granting Aja access to the Synth for their true goal.

Hidden in plain sight.

High Councilor Martinez from Justice & Civic Order leaned forward, her expression grave. "The legal precedent is clear. When criminals possess capabilities that render standard containment ineffective, our justice system requires enhanced protocols. The Pyreford incident demonstrates that our current facilities simply cannot handle such threats."

Exactly as they'd discussed. Aja felt a flicker of satisfaction.

High Councilor Liu from Infrastructure & Resources

nodded his agreement. "The economic impact alone justifies action. The Outsiders are targeting our supply lines, our power grid, our transportation networks—the potential for catastrophic damage is enormous. We need regulatory frameworks before the next incident occurs."

Another vote secured. The private meetings had been worth every carefully chosen word.

High Councilor Thorne's scarred face remained grim as he added, "From a defense perspective, the R.R.C.A. provides essential tools we currently lack. Intelligence gathering on enhanced individuals, specialized containment protocols, research capabilities to understand new threats as they emerge. Without this framework, we're fighting blind."

Three of the four high councilors support the measure, with Aja being the fourth. Aja allowed themselves a moment of quiet confidence. Even Valenstrom's considerable influence would struggle against such unified support from the working council.

But then, from the elder statesmen gallery, Valenstrom's voice cut through the chamber's acoustics. "If I may, Supreme Chancellor?"

Virelian inclined his head. "The floor recognizes Elder Statesman Valenstrom."

A prickle, sharp and unwelcome, traced Aja's spine. The old man should have remained quiet, allowed the vote to proceed smoothly, but Valenstrom had always been theatrical.

"High Councilor Yamamoto's concerns about public safety are legitimate," Valenstrom began, his tone measured but firm. "However, I find myself troubled by the scope and structure of this proposal. The R.R.C.A. bears uncomfortable similarities to policies we once rejected as fundamentally incompatible with our principles." The wooden dove spun slowly between his fingers. "I fear we are resurrecting C.A.R.E. under a new name, using crisis as a pretext."

A murmur rippled through the assembly like water across

still stone. Several elder statesmen nodded at his words, their expressions thoughtful. The invocation of C.A.R.E. carried emotional weight among Traditionalists—an old relic of the previous regime branded as fear-mongering propaganda.

Aja's lips thinned. An old, familiar anger stirred deep in their gut. Valenstrom's playbook was as predictable as it was irritating.

"The elder statesman's concerns warrant consideration," Aja replied, voice steady but sharper. "Yet the R.R.C.A. is fundamentally different from C.A.R.E.'s goals. That organization sought genetic manipulation to preserve fertility. The R.R.C.A. does not seek to control legal medical recombination—existing oversight remains. It targets Recombinants whose illegal enhancements pose real dangers."

That distinction was critical. Legal recombination remained a tightly controlled privilege, permitted only under Traditionalist watch. But black-market modifications—like those possessed by the Outsiders—ran rampant in Retro Ignis.

High Councilor Martinez nodded, voice steady. "Our legal framework assumed criminals lacked these abilities. When suspects can manipulate electronics with a gesture or tear through reinforced barriers, traditional law enforcement fails."

"Exactly," Aja said firmly. "The R.R.C.A. doesn't expand arbitrary power. It evolves our institutions to meet new realities."

High Councilor Thorne seized on the argument. "The security implications extend far beyond Pyreford. We have intelligence suggesting the Outsider network is vast, containing individuals with various forms of unauthorized enhancement. Our current legal framework provides no mechanism for preventing such threats before they strike."

But Valenstrom was ready. He leaned forward in his elevated seat, and when he spoke, his voice carried a new authority that made the chamber lean in to listen. "High Councilor Thorne raises valid security concerns, but we already possess the tools to address enhanced threats. Project Prometheus gave us specialized Recombinant units trained for such dangers."

Something shifted in the room's atmosphere. Aja could feel it like a change in air pressure before a storm. Elder statesmen who had been passive observers now sat straighter, their attention focused on Valenstrom's words with a respect that bordered on reverence.

"Project Prometheus?" Aja couldn't keep the sneer from their voice. "A botched military experiment from the old regime, littered with soldiers plagued by side effects and mental breakdowns. One senior officer snapped completely and massacred his own unit. You honestly want Ignis to depend solely on those?"

Valenstrom's response was swift. "The R.R.C.A., in its current form, essentially criminalizes genetic difference rather than genetic crime."

From the gallery, Elder Statesman Reeves added with the weight of decades in politics, "Elder Statesman Valenstrom makes an important distinction. We should be targeting criminal behavior, not biological characteristics."

"The elder statesman's position suggests genetic enhancement must remain unregulated," Aja observed, their voice flat. "That citizens should endure the threat posed by individuals turned living weapons by illegal modifications. Counseling restraint in the face of active threats."

"Furthermore," Valenstrom continued, ignoring their statement entirely, "the proposed facilities operate with minimal oversight from our judicial system. Citizens could be detained, studied, and held indefinitely without proper legal representation or transparent review processes."

The accusation was both accurate and irrelevant. Yes, the facilities would have broad authority. Yes, oversight would be minimal. These were features, not flaws. But Aja could see the way Valenstrom framed the issue resonating throughout the chamber.

"The legislation specifically targets unregistered modifications that pose public safety risks—"

"According to criteria that remain deliberately vague," Valenstrom interrupted, "the bill grants authority to detain individuals based on 'genetic recombination' or 'psychological risk factors' without defining those terms. It creates a framework where any citizen with genetic modifications—legal or otherwise—could be subjected to indefinite detention."

The wooden dove now rested still between his fingers, his attention razor-focused on Aja. The chamber had gone quiet, and in that silence, Aja realized they were witnessing a master class in political maneuvering. Their jaw set as their eyes narrowed slightly.

High Councilor Liu of Infrastructure & Resources looked uncomfortable. "If the oversight mechanisms are insufficient, perhaps we could strengthen those provisions rather than rejecting the entire framework?"

Valenstrom turned to Liu with the patience of a teacher addressing a promising student. "Councilor, the fundamental structure of this legislation is incompatible with constitutional governance. You cannot fix authoritarian overreach by adding cosmetic safeguards."

The words settled over the chamber like a shroud. Something cold and sharp twisted in Aja's chest. They watched Liu nod slowly, his expression troubled. The vote, once secured, now slipped through their fingers like sand.

Supreme Chancellor Virelian cleared his throat. "Elder Statesman Valenstrom raises serious concerns. High Councilor Yamamoto, how do you respond to these criticisms?"

Trapped. The walls of their carefully constructed argument closed in, suffocating. Revealing too much of their true motivations would be catastrophic, but watching their legislation collapse was equally unacceptable.

"The extraordinary nature of the threats we face requires extraordinary responses," they said, their voice steady despite the growing fury beneath their composed exterior. "Our existing Recombinant units are stretched thin, and traditional oversight procedures were not designed to handle individuals whose genetic modifications grant them capabilities beyond conventional parameters."

"And there lies the fundamental flaw in this approach," Valenstrom replied, his voice carrying the weight of moral authority that had made him untouchable for decades. "The moment we begin categorizing citizens based on their genetic characteristics rather than their actions, we abandon the principles of justice and due process that separate us from the chaos beyond our walls."

Aja watched as other council members reconsidered their positions, weighing security concerns against what Valenstrom presented as foundational principles. The careful web of assurances and private agreements that had secured their support was unraveling thread by thread.

Principles, Aja seethed. *What principles? The same ones that allowed surveillance drones on every street corner? That permitted indefinite detention of suspected dissidents? That authorized the mass executions after the civil war? That divided the city with walls? Hypocrisy.*

High Councilor Martinez spoke carefully. "Perhaps we could modify the proposal to focus more specifically on criminal activity rather than genetic characteristics? Expand our existing Recombinant security units rather than creating new detention protocols?"

Valenstrom nodded approvingly. "Precisely. We have existing frameworks for addressing enhanced criminal activity. If those frameworks prove inadequate, we can strengthen our specialized units without abandoning basic protections for citizens."

"Enhanced security units would still be insufficient against organized cells of modified individuals—" Aja began, desperation creeping into their voice.

"Then we enhance our capabilities accordingly," Valenstrom cut them off. "We do not enhance our government's power to detain citizens without clear cause."

The distinction was frustratingly clear, and Aja could see it resonating with the assembled politicians. Even Thorne looked uncertain now, his military pragmatism warring with procedural concerns.

Elder Statesman Reeves spoke again from the gallery. "I propose we table this legislation for committee review. The security concerns are legitimate, but the procedural issues require more careful consideration."

A chorus of agreement rippled through the gallery like a death knell.

Supreme Chancellor Virelian nodded slowly, and when his eyes met Aja's, there was something unsettling in his expression—a slight curve of the lips that might have been called a smile. As if he had been watching an entertaining performance, knowing all along how it would end. "The motion to refer the R.R.C.A. to committee review is noted. Given the complexity of these issues, additional deliberation seems prudent."

A bitter disdain pulsed, hot and acidic, through Aja's veins. The supreme chancellor had never intended to support them. Not while Valenstrom had his ear. Every private meeting, every carefully crafted assurance had been designed to lull them into overconfidence before this calculated execution. The taste of bile rose in their throat as they stared at Virelian's smug face, at Valenstrom's satisfied expression. These corrupt, hypocritical parasites who spoke of principles, who clung to power through theatrical morality, all while padding their pockets with credits.

Valenstrom had won. The wooden dove rolled once more between his fingers as he offered what almost looked like a sympathetic glance toward Aja. "High Councilor Yamamoto's dedication to security is commendable, but good intentions cannot justify abandoning the principles that maintain order within our city-state."

As the session concluded, Aja gathered their papers with movements that felt mechanical, automatic. The old man had outmaneuvered them completely, turning their security arguments into procedural concerns and rallying opposition around what he framed as fundamental governance principles. Aja's jaw clenched so hard their teeth ached. A cold, sharp, twisting sensation in their gut.

Defeat.

It tasted like copper on their tongue.

Chapter 20

Walking through the corridors of the government complex, Aja's footsteps echoed against polished marble floors. The Inner Ring housed nearly all of Ignis's bureaucratic offices—a deliberate design that forced anyone seeking official business to pass through the fortified checkpoint separating Modernist Ignis from its decrepit twin. Representatives from both sides of the wall mingled in these sterile halls, their purposes written in their posture and attire.

A cluster of well-dressed lobbyists from the corporate districts spoke in hushed tones near the Environmental Resources office, their sleek clothing and augmented accessories marking them as Modernist elite. Across from them, a group of rough-edged petitioners from Retro Ignis waited on hard benches, their worn clothing and weathered faces telling stories of hardship and desperate circumstances. Legal aid workers moved between them, tablets in hand, processing the endless stream of permit applications, grievance filings, and citizenship appeals that kept the bureaucracy churning.

Aja passed a window, one of the few breaks in the fortified wall's imposing structure, its reinforced glass thick enough to withstand heavy artillery. Beyond it lay Old Town in all its neon-soaked decay: buildings wrapped in holographic advertisements, their surfaces crawling with digital graffiti and pirate broadcasts. Below, the streets pulsed with electric light. Crimson pleasure districts bled into azure commercial sectors, while below the streets held only the flooded ruins of the old sewer system where the desperate made their homes.

The sight stirred something cold and determined in their chest. This wasn't over. Valenstrom had won today's battle with his theatrical morality and political maneuvering, but wars weren't decided by single engagements. The old man's influence was considerable, but it wasn't absolute.

A prickle on the back of Aja's neck. A presence. They slowed, their gaze sweeping the polished marble floors, the hushed groups of lobbyists, the worn-out petitioners. Nothing. But the feeling persisted, a cold weight settling on their shoulders.

A rhythm entered the silence: *Tick. Tick. Tick.*

Aja's own heart almost drowned it out. The sound of a clock that had no business existing in these digital halls, where time pulsed in LED displays and holographic timestamps.

Aja quickened their stride toward their office, maintaining the appearance of routine urgency while their senses remained alert. The ticking followed, soft but relentless, like the heartbeat of something stalking and patient. From the corner of their eye, they caught a flash of movement—something pale disappearing around the corridor's bend. White hair, perhaps. Or merely a reflection from the harsh fluorescent lighting.

Their heartbeat accelerated despite their efforts at control, almost drowning out that impossible clockwork rhythm. They forced their pace to remain measured, professional, even as every instinct screamed at them to run. The sensation of being hunted crawled across their skin like static electricity, and still that quiet ticking persisted—counting down to something they couldn't name.

The office door came into view, and Aja covered the remaining distance with swift, purposeful strides. They pressed their palm to the access panel, waited for the soft chime of recognition, then slipped inside and sealed the door behind them with trembling fingers.

Aja leaned against the cool metal surface, chest rising and falling as they fought to control their breathing. The ticking had vanished, leaving only the familiar hum of environmental systems and the distant murmur of corridor conversations beyond the sealed door. But their nerves remained taut as wire, every shadow in the office seeming to harbor potential threats.

A sharp ache flared in Aja's prosthetic leg, a phantom pain that cut through the panic like a blade. They grimaced, hand pressing hard against the synthetic limb. The throb dulled, but the truth remained, a cold certainty: *I am not whole.*

"Aja?"

The voice made them jolt, hand reflexively reaching for a weapon that wasn't there. Their gaze snapped to the figure seated in one of the office chairs, familiar lavender eyes wide with concern.

Ramiel.

"What's wrong?" Ramiel's voice carried that gentle quality that made them such an effective researcher at Nassar Industries, the same tone that had helped them recruit countless assets for C.A.R.E. over the years. "You look like you've seen a ghost."

Aja straightened, smoothing their jacket with deliberate precision. "The R.R.C.A. was tabled. Valenstrom dismantled it in the council meeting."

Ramiel's pointed chin dipped in understanding, those deep-set eyes darkening with shared frustration. "I feared as much when I heard about the emergency session. Elder Statesman Valenstrom's influence runs deeper than we anticipated."

"Deeper than *I* anticipated," Aja corrected, moving to their desk with measured steps. "I had the votes secured—Martinez, Liu, Thorne, even tacit approval from Virelian himself—but Valenstrom..." The name left a bitter taste on their tongue. "He turned it into a moral crusade. Made it about principles and constitutional governance."

Ramiel rose from the chair with that restless energy that characterized all their movements, crossing to stand beside Aja's desk. "There will be other opportunities. Other ways to advance the work."

"Will there?" Aja's fingers drummed against the desk surface. "Every day we delay, humanity slips closer to extinction. The fertility rate continues to drop. The radiation damage compounds. And meanwhile, we have the solution sitting in a terrorist camp, slowly degrading without proper medical support."

The concern in Ramiel's lavender eyes deepened as they studied Aja's face. "You're talking about the Synthetic. Project Gemini."

"I'm talking about survival." Aja's voice carried an edge of steel. "The R.R.C.A. would have given us legal framework to study adaptive genetics, to understand how its genome repairs radiation damage at the cellular level. Without that framework..."

"Without that framework, we find another way," Ramiel said, their voice gentle but firm. "We've operated in the shadows before. C.A.R.E. survived the Traditionalist purges by adapting, not by taking desperate risks."

Aja turned to face their cohort fully, noting how the office lighting cast sharp shadows beneath Ramiel's distinctive cheekbones. Ramiel had been with them since the early days at Nassar Industries, one of the few researchers brave enough to continue the fertility crisis work after C.A.R.E.'s official dissolution. Their loyalty was unquestionable, their dedication absolute.

But their faith in patience was misplaced.

"Valenstrom will block every legislative avenue," Aja replied quietly. "Every committee, every proposal, every attempt at legal research authorization. He has Virelian's ear, and as long as he whispers his moral objections, nothing will change."

Ramiel's expression grew troubled, those expressive eyes searching Aja's face. "What are you suggesting?"

The question hung between them. Aja felt the weight of the moment, the crossing of a line that could never be uncrossed. But humanity's survival demanded sacrifices. It always had.

"Valenstrom is the obstacle," Aja said, their voice growing cold. "Remove the obstacle and the path clears. Liu and Martinez would support the legislation without his moral crusading. Thorne certainly would. Even Virelian might find his principles more flexible without that sanctimonious fossil whispering in his ear."

The color drained from Ramiel's already pale complexion. "Aja, no. You can't be serious."

"I'm deadly serious." Aja leaned back in their chair, cybernetic hand resting flat against the desk surface. "The old man carries a wooden dove everywhere. A symbol of peace and principle. How fitting that it would be all that remains of his legacy."

Ramiel stepped closer, their narrow face tightening with agitation. "Listen to yourself. You're talking about murder. About becoming everything the Traditionalists claim we are."

"I'm talking about necessity."

"You are not a murderer," Ramiel said with desperate conviction. Light brown hair fell across their forehead as they shook their head vehemently. "Whatever else we've done, whatever compromises C.A.R.E. has made, we've never crossed that line. The moment we start killing political opponents, we become the monsters they paint us as."

Aja studied their cohort's face, noting the way Ramiel's chin trembled slightly with emotion. Such passion. Such naïve faith in moral boundaries. It was admirable in its way. But admiration didn't save humanity from extinction.

"Monsters," Aja repeated softly. "And what would you call the Traditionalists who let humanity die rather than admit they're wrong? What would you call a government that prioritizes political theater over survival?"

Ramiel's hands clenched at their sides. "I'd call them wrong. Dangerously wrong. But that doesn't make murder right."

"It makes it necessary."

The words settled over the office like a shroud. Ramiel stared at them with growing horror, those expressive features cycling through disbelief, fear, and something that might have been grief.

"This isn't you talking," Ramiel whispered. "This is desperation. This is..." Their voice faltered.

Aja felt something cold and final crystalize in their chest. The decision had been made the moment they spoke it aloud. Ramiel's objections were noted and dismissed. Moral squeamishness was a luxury they could no longer afford.

"Principles," Aja said quietly, "are what dead species cling to while they expire."

A soft knock interrupted the charged silence between them. Before either could respond, the office door chimed and slid open with a whisper of hydraulics. Elder Statesman Valenstrom stepped over the threshold, his tall, lean frame filling the doorway with an authority that seemed to bend the very air around him. Silver hair caught the office lighting as he moved, and the wooden dove rested between his fingers, rolling slowly in that familiar, meditative rhythm.

His dark eyes swept the office, taking in the scene like a man who had survived decades of political intrigue. When his gaze settled on Ramiel, then shifted to Aja's tense posture, something knowing flickered across his sharp, angular features.

"I hope I'm not interrupting anything important," Valenstrom said, his voice carrying that deceptive gentleness that had made him so dangerous in meeting today.

Ramiel straightened, composure returning with remarkable speed. "Not at all, Elder Statesman. I was just leaving." They gathered their tablet from Aja's desk, offering a polite nod to the old man. "High Councilor Yamamoto, we can continue our discussion about the Nassar Industries research protocols later."

A convenient fiction. Aja watched their cohort move toward the door, noting how Ramiel's eyes avoided direct contact. The fear was still there, carefully hidden beneath professional courtesy but unmistakable to someone who knew how to look.

"Of course," Aja replied. "Send me those quarterly reports when you have a chance."

The door sealed behind Ramiel with a soft hiss, leaving Aja alone with the man who had just destroyed months of careful political maneuvering. Valenstrom moved deeper into the office with unhurried steps, his attention drifting to the view beyond the reinforced window.

"Impressive view," he observed, hands clasped behind his back. "From here, you can see both sides of our city. The achievements of order and the consequences of chaos." He turned back to face Aja, the wooden dove now still in his palm. "I wonder which side you truly identify with."

"I identify with progress," Aja quipped, settling back in their chair. "With solutions to problems our government refuses to acknowledge."

Valenstrom's face creased into something that might have

been disappointment, the lines around his eyes deepening. "Ah, there it is. The same moral flexibility that once made you such a promising student." He moved to stand before Aja's desk, those dark eyes studying them with unsettling intensity. "Tell me, do you remember the first lesson I taught you about governance?"

Despite themselves, Aja felt a flicker of the reverence they had once held for this man. "That principles without pragmatism are merely philosophy."

"And pragmatism without principles?"

The response came automatically, carved into memory by years of mentorship. "Is merely opportunism."

"Exactly." Valenstrom's voice carried the weight of profound sadness. "Yet here you sit, proposing legislation that abandons every principle we fought to establish after the civil war. The R.R.C.A. isn't about public safety, Aja. It's about control. About giving you the tools to pursue research that should never see the light of day."

Aja's jaw tightened, but they kept their voice level. "The R.R.C.A. is exactly what I presented to the council. A framework for managing enhanced individuals who pose legitimate security threats."

"Is it?" The wooden dove began its slow rotation again. "Or is it a vehicle for studying Synthetic beings? For pursuing research that goes far beyond what you've told the council?"

Aja's prosthetic hand flexed, the servos whining softly. A whisper of mechanical strain. "I don't know what you're implying."

"I'm not implying anything. I'm stating it directly." Valenstrom leaned forward, his voice dropping to barely above a whisper. "You were removed from Dr. Izumi's project for a reason. You convinced the supreme chancellor to imprison him. And now, conveniently, you're proposing legislation that would give you access to exactly the kind of research you were barred from completing."

Aja stared into their former mentor's eyes.

"There's no future in fearing ghosts," Aja said finally, their voice steady and cold.

Valenstrom's expression shifted, grief replacing disappointment as he ran a hand through his silver hair. "Ghosts? Is that what you call the ethical danger of repeating the past? The lives lost when science abandons conscience?" He straightened, the dove coming to rest in his palm. "I taught you to see beyond immediate solutions, to consider the broader implications of our choices. Where did that wisdom go?"

"It evolved," Aja replied sharply, "into understanding that survival requires difficult decisions. That humanity's future matters more than our comfort with moral absolutes."

"And there lies the corruption." The old man's voice carried heavily with chagrin. "You've convinced yourself that noble ends justify any means. That your vision of humanity's future is worth sacrificing humanity's soul."

Aja rose from their chair, moving to stand beside the reinforced window. Beyond the thick glass, Old Town pulsed with electric life—a testament to adaptation, to survival against impossible odds. "What would you have me do? Watch humanity slowly expire while maintaining perfect ethical purity?"

"I would have you remember who you once were." Valenstrom's reflection appeared beside theirs in the window. "The brilliant young idealist who wanted to heal the world, not reshape it. The student who understood that how we achieve progress matters as much as the progress itself."

"That idealist was naïve."

"That idealist was you." The wooden dove caught the light as he turned it between his fingers. "And somewhere beneath all this calculated ambition, that person still exists. I've seen glimpses—moments when your mask slips and I catch sight of the Aja I once knew."

The words stirred something uncomfortable in Aja's chest. A memory of different times, when they had sat in this same office as a junior researcher, listening to Valenstrom's wisdom with genuine reverence. When the future had seemed full of possibilities that didn't require sacrificing pieces of their soul.

"People change," they said quietly.

"They do. But not always for the better." Valenstrom moved away from the window, toward the office door. "The R.R.C.A. will not pass as written. Not while I have breath to oppose it. I'll stand in committee hearings, council sessions, public forums—wherever necessary to ensure that this legislation dies the death it deserves."

Aja turned from the window, studying their former mentor's weathered face. "Even if it means condemning humanity to slow extinction?"

"Especially then." His voice carried absolute conviction. "Because a humanity that survives by abandoning its principles isn't humanity at all. It's something else wearing our face."

The door chimed softly as Valenstrom approached the threshold. He paused, looking back with eyes that held decades of accumulated wisdom and regret.

"I'm sorry, Aja. Sorry that I failed to teach you the most important lesson of all—that who we are matters more than what we accomplish. That the means we choose define us more than any end we might achieve."

The door whispered shut behind him, leaving Aja alone with the weight of his words and the cold certainty of their own resolve. The memory of his dark eyes—filled with such disappointment—lingered like an accusation. Through the reinforced window, Old Town's neon glow painted shadows across the office walls. Shifting. Uncertain but undeniably alive.

Principles were a luxury they could no longer afford. The old man would learn that soon enough.

Chapter 21

The warehouse-turned-nightclub wore its industrial bones like jewelry. Exposed brick climbed toward cathedral ceilings where Edison bulbs dangled on long cords, casting amber pools across the polished concrete below. But the Alice in Wonderland theme had infected every corner—oversized playing cards hung suspended from the rafters, rotating slowly in the air currents. Velvet couches the color of arterial blood squatted beneath projection-mapped murals that shifted and morphed: Cheshire grins that materialized and vanished, caterpillars that smoked hookah pipes in endless loops, white rabbits that checked pocket watches before dissolving into pixels.

The Caterpillar Collective had done its work well. The visuals crawled across every surface, transforming the warehouse into something fluid and uncertain.

Kraken tugged at his teal tie and immediately regretted it. The dark wine tweed felt like armor—a two-button jacket with brown horn buttons, matching waistcoat, the whole production. He'd worn it once before during a casino job, and apparently his wardrobe had decided that was an insufficient use for such extravagance. The half-mask he'd chosen was simple and unobtrusive—black leather that covered his eyes and bridge of his nose but left his mouth free. Around him, other guests had taken the 'surreal chic' dress code to heart—Victorian tailcoats paired with neon accessories, cocktail dresses in impossible geometries, masks that ranged from elegant to disturbing.

The whiskey in his glass tasted like money. Smooth enough to make him forget, briefly, that he was here to rob these people.

DJ Cheshire Cat was working the decks with manic energy, his grin painted wide and unsettling across his face. The bass line vibrated up through the floor, psychedelic and hypnotic.

"Kraken!"

Nori waved her hand above the crowd. He drained his drink and shouldered through the press of bodies, tracking the shimmer of her violet lips through gaps in the throng. She'd added cat whiskers to her makeup—a nod to the theme without committing too hard. Her mask was a delicate filigree thing in silver and cat-eared, leaving her signature lipstick visible.

She'd gone full punk tonight—half her head shaved, the other side cascading in dark waves. Led Zeppelin shirt (who had made a post-mortem comeback during the bunker days) tucked into a black skirt, leather jacket, and silver belt. Nothing about her outfit screamed 'couple,' which they'd agreed was the angle. He opened his mouth to point this out when his brain caught up with what his eyes were seeing.

"Kraken." The voice was familiar. The person attached to it was not.

Yin stood beside Nori, pulling at the hem of a yellow dress that appeared to be strangling her. Strapless, form-fitted, ruched fabric that showed shoulders and the suggestion of cleavage. Black heels put her eye-level. Her makeup was subtle—natural bases, thin liner—but her hair remained stubbornly herself: ponytail at the nape of her neck, practical and severe. The mask she wore was sleek white porcelain, painted with gold accents that caught the light. Probably Nari's doing—it matched the dress perfectly while maintaining an austere elegance that somehow suited Yin's clinical nature.

The disconnect between face and outfit made his brain stutter.

"You look fancy," he managed, then immediately wanted to take it back because *fancy* was possibly the least useful observation he could have made. He held out a hand as she took a step, some instinct suggesting she might tip over in those heels. "What are you doing here?"

"Human Nari dressed me." Her expression carried the same flat affect she might use to describe a tactical briefing. "She said you requested that I join you tonight for this mission."

Kraken turned to Nori, who was doing an absolutely terrible job of hiding her grin behind one hand.

"Izzy mentioned to Nari that you'd invited Yin along." Her eyes danced with mischief. "Nari couldn't let her show up in her usual outfit. So, we took her shopping. Isn't she dazzling?"

Izzy. The pieces slotted into place with an almost audible click. That's why she'd backed off so easily during their conversation. She'd already set this particular trap in motion.

He was going to kill her.

"You look nice," he said to Yin, forcing his expression into something approximating normal.

"You already said that." She tilted her head, studying him with one hand on her chin in an exaggerated gesture she'd probably lifted from some sitcom. "I see you are also dressed 'fancier' than usual." Her hand swept toward his suit. "We are reminiscent of Mr. James Bond and his female counterpart."

Right. The Bond marathon she'd subjected him to last week, complete with running commentary about how unrealistic the action sequences were. A laugh escaped him before he could stop it. "You're right. We're both quite snazzy, I must say. A pair ready to take on the evils in the world with nothing more than our wits, our guns, and maybe a few cool gadgets. Just to be safe."

A collision of color and chaos materialized from the crowd—a man in a riot of mismatched fabrics and a top hat bristling with playing cards and feathers. His eyes had that glassy, unfocused quality of the truly gone, pupils blown wide as dinner plates. He clutched a tray loaded with pills in every color of the pharmaceutical rainbow—white rabbits stamped on each one—and bottles that sloshed with liquid that probably wasn't water.

The Mad Hatter, live and in person.

His gaze bounced from face to face before locking onto Yin. His grin revealed teeth that dental hygiene had abandoned years ago.

"Well, hello, you sexy minx." The words came out slurred, sticky with whatever he'd been sampling from his own wares. "You've caught me in quite the predicament today. Lost my way in this topsy-turvy world, you see."

Yin's eyebrow climbed. "Lost?"

The hat tilted dangerously as he nodded, feathers trembling. He steadied it with a jerky motion and leaned closer, voice dropping to a stage whisper that carried perfectly over DJ Cheshire Cat's latest drop. "But fear not, dear Alice. I have an inkling for you."

He took her hand—gently, which was probably the only reason Kraken didn't have to explain a body to security—and turned her palm up. White Rabbit pills rattled into her hand, each stamped with that distinctive rabbit silhouette. His fingers closed hers around them.

"Compliments of the house for a beautiful face...and fine ass."

He winked at Yin, cast a glance at Kraken that might have been caution or challenge, then vanished back into the crowd. Nori snagged a drink from his tray as he passed.

Yin stared at her closed fist. Opened it. Stared at the pills with their rabbit stamps. Her face went carefully blank.

"...what?"

Kraken exhaled through his nose, tracking the ridiculous hat as it bobbed away through the throng. "He was acting creepy."

"He wanted to have sex with you," Nori said, because subtlety had never been her strong suit. She plucked the pills from Yin's palm and shoved them into her jacket. "At least he gave us some of these. Now we just need more."

"The pills?" Yin asked.

"Bingo." Nori was already scanning the room, tracking the servers with their trays of White Rabbit. "We're supposed to find their supply chain, but even if we don't, these samples can help us reverse-engineer them."

Movement caught Kraken's eye—a splash of crimson velvet cutting through the crowd with purpose. He raised his hand, catching Gabriel's attention. His friend's face split into a grin.

Gabriel dressed like he was cosplaying three different centuries simultaneously. Tonight's ensemble leaned Victorian dandy filtered through a steampunk fever dream: deep-crimson coat embroidered with gold that caught the light, tails cascading over dark leather pants. His waistcoat shimmered copper and bronze, gears and cogs catching and releasing light with each movement. A pocket watch dangled from one buttonhole, swaying with his stride. He'd even added a domino mask in silver—commitment to the theme that put most of the room to shame.

"Well, well, well, if it isn't trouble." Gabriel's voice carried that perpetual undercurrent of amusement, like life was one long inside joke. His gaze slid to Yin. "Still at your side, I see."

Kraken clapped his shoulder. "Oh, you know. The usual."

"No good," Nori finished. She draped an arm around Yin's shoulders. "Your flirtation dressed her. What do you think?"

"My flirtation?" Gabriel's hand flew to his chest, wounded. "I'm going to tell your sister you called her that. I have many flirtations. You're a flirtation. Nari is an enamoration. It isn't every woman who'll help you escape the claws of a stalker trash panda."

The saga of Gabriel versus Gertrude the raccoon. Kraken might have thought the stories were exaggerated if he didn't know about the pheromone modification—black-market work that meant Gabriel broadcast chemical signals he couldn't always control. Apparently, raccoons found whatever he was putting out absolutely irresistible.

Yin's hand closed around Kraken's wrist. She pulled him toward the dance floor, where bodies swayed and ground to bass that vibrated up through the concrete. Projected Cheshire grins flickered across the dancers, appearing and vanishing in hypnotic rhythm.

"We should try to blend in," she said. "It will make it easier for us to observe our surroundings."

"Leave enough room for Jesus, you two!" Gabriel called after them. "Sky Daddy is always watching!"

Kraken shot him a look that promised retribution.

The dance floor was a press of heat and motion, the projections transforming it into something dreamlike and unstable. Yin found them space near the edge, where the crowd thinned slightly and the visuals were less disorienting.

She took his hand and placed it at the small of her back. Her other hand rose, fingers threading through his.

"Do not fret," she said, reading his uneasy expression. "I have learned this skill. Follow my lead."

"It's not your skill I'm worried about."

The music shifted—something slower, melodic, but still carrying that psychedelic edge. Yin moved, and Kraken tried to follow.

His feet had other ideas.

They tangled, stumbled, performed what could generously be called movement but bore no resemblance to rhythm. Yin glided across the polished concrete like she'd been born to it, each step flowing into the next with liquid grace.

"Where did you learn this?" He already knew the answer.

"I learned of dancing through the TV." Confirming his suspicion, then veering somewhere unexpected. "I learned this dance from this place called a 'studio.' I infiltrated it for observation purposes, and they accepted me as one of their own."

"O-Oh."

Of course she had. Why wouldn't she infiltrate a dance studio? That was clearly the logical next step after watching soap operas.

Her head came to rest on his shoulder. The gesture threw his feet further off whatever beat they'd been attempting.

"Is that my body wash?" The words tumbled out before his brain could stop them.

That explained why the bottle kept emptying at an alarming rate.

Yin leaned closer, her breath warm against his collar. "We need to be discreet but gather as much information as possible." Her voice dropped, all business beneath the pretense of intimacy. "Do you see that?"

Her gaze tracked across the room to where servers converged like tributaries into a river. They disappeared through double-doors and emerged moments later with fresh bottles, White Rabbit pills rattling like maracas as they wove back through the crowd.

"Looks like we found their stash." Kraken watched the flow, the careful choreography. This was how the wealthy escaped themselves. How they numbed the peculiar pain of having everything and finding it still wasn't enough. White Rabbit promised a mind-altering journey, an immersive escape into cosmic connections and pure euphoria.

The servers catered to every lifted hand, every desperate gesture, moving through the crowd like they were part of the Caterpillar Collective's installation—living art dispensing chemical transcendence.

But watching it happen, Kraken felt hollow. These pills weren't happiness. They weren't peace. They were temporary patches over wounds that would never heal, and everyone here knew it. They just didn't care. They'd paid for the experience, paid to dive down the rabbit hole, and the White Rabbit would guide them through their psychedelic adventure until they woke up tomorrow with empty pockets and emptier heads.

He couldn't judge them. He was here to steal those same pills, to turn around and sell them for profit. He'd become another cog in this machine that manufactured artificial contentment, all justified by words that had excused countless sins throughout history: *the greater good.*

For a moment, he wished there was a path to the greater good that didn't require stepping on so many people along the way.

He was opening his mouth to ask Yin about breaching those doors when something hard and cold connected with his cheek.

The slap echoed in his skull, sharp and clarifying.

Chapter 22

Kraken recoiled, his hand flying to his cheek. The sting spread like wildfire across his skin. Yin's glare could have cut glass. It was cold, and absolutely terrifying, behind that white porcelain mask.

The music seemed to drop away. Heads turned. Conversations died mid-sentence.

"Yin—"

"We've known each other many years, but this is the first time you ever came to me with the truth." Her voice carried across the dance floor, theatrical and sharp. "I can't remember the last time that you invited me to your house for a cup of coffee, even though you claim we are a couple. But let's be frank here. You never wanted my love and…you were afraid to be in my debt."

What the hell was she talking about?

The words tumbled out dramatically. Her delivery was loud enough to draw more attention, theatrical enough to feel staged.

She's finally snapped. Glitched into another stratosphere.

"I understand." Yin stalked toward him, and Kraken stumbled back a step. "You found paradise in Ignis, you had a good trade, you made a good living, the police protected you, and there were courts of law. You didn't need a lover like me. But now you come to me, and you say: 'Yin, give me forgiveness.' But you don't ask with respect. You don't offer love. You don't even think to call me Girlfriend. Instead, you come to me on the day our daughter is to be married, and you ask me to forgive you for cheating!"

"Yin..." He dropped his voice to a hiss. "Are you quoting *The Godfather* at me?"

Her eyes shifted—just for a heartbeat—toward something behind him. Then back to him with the same accusing glare.

He lowered his hand and looked around, making a show of balking at the attention. Gabriel and Nori stood near the edge of the gathering crowd, both wearing identical expressions of shock. They were close to the double-doors.

All eyes were on the disgruntled couple.

The realization hit him like cold water.

This was their chance.

"Yin, please." He clasped his hands together, letting desperation bleed into his voice. His knees hit the concrete. "I didn't mean any disrespect—" He caught her hand, holding it like a lifeline. "I ask you for forgiveness."

"My love... My love... What have I ever done to make you treat me so disrespectfully?" Yin glanced up again, hidden behind a dramatic sigh. Satisfaction flickered in her eyes. "If you'd come to me in love, then that scum that ruined us would be suffering this very day. And if by chance an honest man like yourself should make enemies, then they would become my enemies. And then they would fear you."

Kraken tightened his grip on her hand and drew it closer. He'd seen *The Godfather* exactly once, years ago at the community center, and hadn't paid much attention. Now he was kicking himself for it. He had no idea what came next, so he went with instinct.

He kissed her hand, looking up at her with pleading eyes. "I was stupid. I didn't know what I had. I took you for granted. I see that now. Forgive me, Yin."

Yin pulled him to his feet with a sage nod, placing her hand on his shoulder. "Good. Someday—and that day may never come—I'll call upon you to do a service for me. But until that day, accept this forgiveness as a gift on our daughter's wedding day."

The last part made absolutely no sense in context.

Thank God everyone was high.

The room erupted into applause and cheers. Kraken leaned in close, his breath warm against her ear. "Seriously, Yin? That film is ancient."

"It was the first thing that came to mind." Her whisper carried defensive notes. "Old is better. If I had done something mainstream, they would have caught on."

He hated that she had a point. Nobody here was poor enough to be stuck watching twentieth-century cinema.

Kraken placed a hand on her back and guided her toward a quieter corner. The music swelled back to life. Conversations resumed as if someone had pressed play on a paused recording. He positioned them with a clear view of the doors, pulse hammering in his throat.

Where were Gabriel and Nori?

His chest tightened. He tugged at his collar, suddenly aware of how the air seemed too thin. They'd bought them time, but eventually, someone would notice. A waiter would walk in and sound the alarm. He should go after them. Help them. He could get them all out, even if things went sideways.

Yin's grip on his arm tightened, anchoring him. "There are still eyes on us. If we go after them now, our distraction will have been for nothing." Her frown deepened behind the mask. "Your objective will be discovered, and the mission compromised. Human Gabriel may not be capable, but Human Nori is."

He cursed under his breath. She was right. She was always right, and that grated.

Despite most people returning to their chemical escapes, curious eyes still tracked them. People trying to figure out who the dramatic couple was, probably. It was only a matter of time before someone recognized them as infiltrators. From a tactical standpoint, it was better to lose a few than compromise the entire mission. Something was better than nothing.

If Miriam were here...

Wait.

Miriam *was* here.

His eyes swept the room, searching. He spotted her at the bar, nursing a drink, probably trying to drown out the secondhand embarrassment they'd caused. He headed straight for her, ignoring the whispers that followed in his wake.

She'd dressed for the theme—a sleek black leather vest embellished with brass buttons and chains that caught the light. A long, flowing skirt in midnight blue and metallic silver, ruffled and laced. Sturdy calf-high boots completed the look. Her cornrows cascaded into natural curls in a way that managed to be both elegant and ready for violence.

Kraken took the seat beside her and signaled for a shot.

"That was quite the stunt you pulled." Miriam's fingers traced the rim of her glass. Her voice could have drawn blood. "You're the talk of the party now."

"It was Yin's idea. I thought it was brilliant." Kraken swirled his drink, studying its amber depths as if it held answers.

"Why is the Synthetic here? She isn't one of us."

Miriam's tone carried the weight of an accusation, not a question.

"She helped create the distraction." Kraken kept his voice

level. "Without her, Nori wouldn't have had the opening she needed."

"That wasn't what I asked."

"You told me to keep an eye on her. Hard to do that when she's across the city." He took a sip, letting the burn ground him. "She's my responsibility. You made that clear."

"Responsibility doesn't mean bringing her to operations." Miriam's fingers stopped their circling. "It means keeping her contained. Controlled. Not parading her around like she's earned a place with us."

"She saved the mission tonight."

"She created an opportunity. That's not the same as being part of this." Miriam's gaze sharpened. "You're getting attached, Lieutenant. That's dangerous."

"I'm doing my job."

"Your job is to manage a liability, not turn her into an asset." She picked up her glass, examined the remaining liquid. "The question is whether you still understand the difference."

Kraken set his jaw. "Nori is currently inside those double-doors, carrying out our plan. We need to make sure she has a way out."

"Only if we have what we need." Miriam pushed her empty glass away, revealing the gun hidden beneath her skirt. "I have no problem creating a distraction."

Yin materialized on Miriam's other side, settling onto the barstool with eerie quiet. "They have it." She gave a single nod. "Human Nori has enough of the drug for replication."

Miriam didn't acknowledge her. Didn't even glance in her direction. Her attention stayed fixed on Kraken, waiting for him to confirm what the Synthetic had said.

Kraken kept his gaze steady, running scenarios. A gunshot would trigger a panicked stampede for the exits. That could work in their favor. But there were no guarantees Nori had secured the supply, even if Yin seemed confident. "I know she managed to obtain some pills earlier. Even if we don't get the main stash, we should have enough. We can't risk losing Nori."

Trading a friend for drugs wasn't an option.

Miriam's disapproving stare was familiar territory. *Your moral compass is grating on me, Kraken.* She flicked her glass over with a huff. "This party has been a bore, anyway."

She aimed at the ceiling and pulled the trigger twice.

The gunshots cracked through the air like thunder. Conversation died instantly, replaced by screams that built and built. Panic rippled outward from the bar in violent waves. The elegant soirée collapsed into chaos—glasses shattering, bodies shoving, masks askew as people scrambled for exits.

Kraken maintained his calm exterior, watching the sophisticated socialites reduce themselves to frightened animals. Their civility stripped away in seconds. He pushed into the crowd, using his size to cut through. His heart hammered against his ribs. Each face he passed wasn't Gabriel's. Wasn't Nori's.

He reached the doors just as they burst open.

"Baby on the way!" Gabriel clutched a suddenly very pregnant Nori in his arms. "Come on, people. You know the drill. Women and children first." He shot Kraken a grin that belonged on someone who wasn't fleeing a crime scene, patting what sounded distinctly like metal under Nori's shirt. "Bro, look. I'm becoming a daddy."

"You fuckin' wish." Nori leaned in and nipped at his shoulder. "Careful. You'll hurt the baby, you brute."

"Yeah, yeah." Gabriel dodged her teeth with ease. "Kraken, stop staring all slack-jawed, buddy. Part the Red Sea for us and let's ditch this joint."

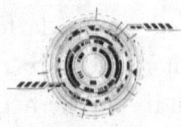

MIRIAM AND YIN WAITED OUTSIDE, THE NIGHT AIR BITING after the warehouse's trapped heat. Miriam approached first, draping an arm around Nori's shoulders. "Are you feeling okay? You seem to have gained some weight." Her smile was sly before turning to Gabriel. "And who might this be?"

"Heh." Nori's breathing came heavy. "Just had this awful craving and couldn't get enough." She jerked her thumb toward Gabriel. "Him? Don't worry about this one. He's one of Kraken's."

While the others chattered, Kraken moved toward Yin. Gratitude pulled him forward—she'd saved them tonight with that ridiculous *Godfather* routine—but as he got closer, details emerged that stopped him cold. The pale cast to her skin. The faint traces of blood around her nostrils where she'd tried to wipe it clean.

"Hey." Concern flooded through him, and he reached out. She stepped back. "Yin, let me help."

"I need to return to the apartment now, Kraken." Her gaze stayed fixed on the ground, voice soft. "Your people are counting on you. You must attend to them."

"No." He shook his head, glancing back at the others. Nori was showing Miriam a bowl chock-full of pills hurriedly wrapped in plastic. Gabriel had apparently vanished into the night—probably to avoid interrogation. Miriam stood with arms crossed, weight on one leg, a slight smile playing at her lips.

They were fine without him.

Yin wasn't.

He must have been staring. Nori looked up and motioned for him to join them. Miriam's expression shifted to questioning. Kraken gestured toward Yin and shook his head. *I need to stay with her.*

Nori understood. She clutched the bowl against her chest and disappeared into the darkness.

Miriam's eyes narrowed. "Come see me later, Lieutenant. That's an order."

She turned and followed Nori into the night.

Kraken released a breath he hadn't known he was holding. He could practically hear Miriam's accusations—that he was choosing Yin over the group. But Miriam had entrusted Yin to his care. He was just following through on the assignment she'd given him.

When he turned back, his heart sank.

Dying.

Yin was dying, and he had no idea how to fix it. She wouldn't admit it, but he watched her wither with each glitch. The vibrancy that had once defined her—even when filtered through clinical detachment—was fading. She looked like a wounded animal trying to retreat to safety.

Another cough wracked her frame. Blood spattered the sidewalk.

Kraken closed the distance and scooped her into his arms, cradling her against his chest. She pushed weakly, then went slack. As he started for home, his mind raced through everything he knew: genetically engineered human, grown in a lab, designed to be the perfect soldier.

It was reasonable—*logical*, Yin would say—that these glitches stemmed from something genetic. Dr. Izumi's arrest was for illegal experimentation and torture, but that was just the cover story.

After the break-in, Kraken had dug deeper. Project Gemini had powerful sponsors. Yin's status as Synthetic meant she existed outside human legal protections. Someone had paid heavily to lock Dr. Izumi up.

Had he done something to her during the raid? An attempt to destroy the evidence?

"Kraken."

Yin stirred in his arms, her hand gripping his collar. During the walk home, she'd become nearly catatonic. Her dark eyes fixed on something far away, blood trickling from her ears and nose, spiking his anxiety into overdrive. He hadn't expected her to speak until the episode passed.

He was already through the apartment door when he looked down at her.

"These will only become more frequent." Her whisper came hoarse and thin.

He wanted to tease her for stating the obvious—like she always did to him—but the words wouldn't come.

"They are not always like this." Her gaze stayed steady despite the glaze in her eyes. "There are times I become violent. If I become dangerous, please do not engage me."

The image flashed through his mind—Yin drenched in blood, military fatigues soaked, that empty look in her eyes. Too much blood for her usual calculated demeanor.

Kraken laid her gently on his bed and removed her heels, tossing them aside. He rolled his chair close and sat, lacing his fingers with hers.

"Well..." He chose his words carefully, squeezing gently. "I'll help you figure out what's going on." A pause. "I promise."

Chapter 23

THE HUMANS BLURRED TOGETHER IN A MASS OF LIMBS AND panic. Bodies slammed into each other, ricocheting like debris in a flood. Feet pounded concrete. Screams layered over screams until the sound became texture rather than noise.

Yin pressed against the wall, moving toward the side exit. The current of fleeing guests swept past her, close enough that she felt the heat radiating from their terror-slicked skin. Ahead, Human Miriam's footsteps maintained their measured rhythm despite the chaos, both purposeful and controlled.

The heels were torture. Each step sent sharp pressure through the balls of Yin's feet, the angle forcing her weight forward in a way that defied efficient movement. She considered removing them, but Human Nari would likely want them returned. The logic of fashion escaped her entirely. The only practical application for such footwear would be as an improvised weapon, and even that seemed optimistic.

Her hand found the door's push-bar.

The sensation hit her like static electricity—a prickling

awareness that crawled up her spine and spread across her shoulders. She was being watched.

Yin stepped back from the door, scanning the warehouse. The crowd continued its frantic exodus, but her attention filtered past them, searching for the anomaly. The thing that didn't belong.

Nothing.

She closed her eyes.

The chaos dimmed. Footsteps became individual rhythms. Breathing patterns emerged from the noise like signal from interference. Most were rapid, panicked—short gasps and ragged inhales—but one set of lungs operated with mechanical calm. Deep, measured breaths that spoke of patience. Of control.

Machinery whirred somewhere nearby.

Tick. Tick. Tick.

Not the building's systems—something smaller, more localized. Augmentation, possibly. Or something else entirely.

The calm lungs drew air, held it, then released with a single whispered phrase:

"Subject Alpha."

Yin's eyes snapped open. Her gaze tracked upward to the mezzanine.

Red eyes stared back.

Not the warm red of blood or the bright red of warning lights—something paler, like diluted wine held up to harsh light. White lashes framed them, so pale they seemed to catch and hold the warehouse's scattered illumination.

The face was an echo. An oval shape that mirrored Aja's features with unsettling ease, but rendered in negative. Snow-white hair fell in sheets so straight and uniform they appeared synthetic. The proportions were correct—the spacing between eyes, the angle of cheekbones, the curve of jaw—but assembled in a way that felt deliberately wrong. Like someone had taken a blueprint and inverted every specification.

The lips curved into something that approximated a smile but carried the same relationship to warmth that ice had to fire.

Subject Omega.

Yang.

The photograph from the Project Gemini file had been clinical—a documentation shot with neutral lighting and careful framing. This was different. Yang stood with weight shifted onto one leg, head tilted at an angle that suggested curiosity but read as predatory. One hand rested on the mezzanine railing, fingers drumming a rhythm that Yin couldn't quite parse.

The machinery sounds came from Yang's direction. Augmentation, then. But what kind? The file had been sparse on specifics about Subject Omega beyond the basic genome data and the notation about hostility toward Subject Alpha.

Toward her.

Yang's smile widened fractionally, revealing teeth. The gesture might have been friendly on someone else. On Yang, it looked like a threat display.

The distance between them was approximately forty feet, accounting for the vertical height of the mezzanine. Yang would need to descend—either via stairs or direct drop—to engage. That provided Yin with a window. Small, but present.

Yang's head tilted the other direction, still maintaining eye contact. The movement was too fluid, too controlled. Not quite mechanical but lacking the unconscious micro-adjustments that characterized organic motion.

Tactical patience. Yin could appreciate that, even as she calculated response options.

"I've been watching you, Subject Alpha."

The glitch hit without warning.

Yin's vision fractured. The warehouse multiplied into overlapping images, each slightly offset from the others. Yang became three figures, then five, then too many to count. The machinery sounds crescendoed into a roar that threatened to drown out conscious thought.

Her knees buckled.

No. Not now. Not here.

She forced her legs to lock, maintaining a vertical position through sheer determination. But her body was failing, and she slumped against the wall. Blood filled her mouth—she must have bitten her tongue. More trickled from her nose, warm against her lips.

The pressure in Yin's skull built to crushing intensity. Her augmented hearing picked up the frantic rhythm of her own heartbeat, irregular and too fast. Yin pushed away from the wall, forcing her legs to carry her toward the door. Each step was a negotiation between intention and capability.

"Run if you wish, Subject A. I have waited this long. I can wait longer."

The door was just ahead. Five feet. Four. Three. The world kept fragmenting around her, but she focused on the door. Just the door. Nothing else mattered.

Two feet.

Her vision whited out completely.

When it returned, she was standing outside. No memory of walking through the door. The taste of blood hot in her mouth as bitter cold rushed against her skin.

Footsteps approached.

The familiar gait of Human Kraken. Yin wiped at her mouth and nose in an attempt to clear away the blood.

"Hey." She stepped away when he reached for her. "Yin, let me help."

"I need to return to the apartment now."

Her vision blurred again, and the next thing she knew, he was cradling her in his arms. Yin pushed against him, but her strength was gone. Her head lolled to the side. In her haze, she looked back toward the warehouse, searching for Yang.

All that stared back at her was emptiness.

Chapter 24

THE SCREAM RIPPED KRAKEN FROM SLEEP.

His eyes snapped open to find Yin thrashing beside him, her body arching off the mattress. For three days, she'd been unconscious. Three days, he'd barely left this room except to grab food or clean himself up. The others kept messaging him through his com-tacts, wondering where the hell he was. Miriam's name flashed more than once, each notification carrying the weight of consequences he'd deal with later.

Right now, none of that mattered.

He'd changed Yin out of that yellow dress the first night, cleaning the makeup from her face and getting her back into the clothes that actually fit her personality: T-shirt, sweats, robe. She'd looked uncomfortable in all that fabric and foundation. This seemed better.

Her nails found his forearm, dragging red lines across the skin.

"Yin." He caught her wrists, pinning them gently but firmly. "Yin, wake up."

She fought him. Really fought him. The synthetic muscle fiber in her arms strained against his grip with enough force to make his own enhancements work overtime. Whatever nightmare had her, it wasn't letting go easy.

He'd never seen her sleep before. Not properly. She'd doze sometimes on the couch, surface-level rest that ended the moment someone walked too loud. But this was different. This was her trapped somewhere dark, clawing her way toward light.

Blood welled up where her nails had cut him. Kraken held on.

"You're safe," he said, keeping his voice steady. "Whatever you're seeing, it's not real. You're in our apartment. You're safe."

One final surge of strength pushed against him, then she went slack. Her chest heaved, pulling air in ragged gasps. Sweat soaked through her shirt. Kraken loosened his grip but kept one hand near her shoulder, just in case.

He checked the time: 3 AM.

The laugh surprised him. It started in his chest and bubbled out before he could stop it. He'd been so sure she wouldn't wake up. The past seventy-two hours had felt like watching someone slip away in slow motion, powerless to stop it. Now she was here, breathing, alive.

The relief hit harder than expected.

Yin's eyes stayed closed, but her lips moved. Kraken leaned in.

"Cut out my ID chip."

He blinked. "What?"

"Cut out my ID chip." Her right hand lifted, palm up. The gesture was weak but deliberate. "I do not require it any longer. It is not as if I enter government buildings with any kind of permission."

That pulled a smile from him despite everything. Yin making jokes was rare enough to count as a minor miracle. He nodded and went for the medical kit he kept in the bathroom cabinet.

The scalpels had always seemed excessive. He'd never actually needed them before. Now he grabbed them along with gauze, tape, antibacterial wipes, and iodine, assembling everything on the nightstand.

"Hand," he said.

She held it out. Her fingers trembled slightly.

The chip sat just under the skin, a small bump barely visible if you weren't looking for it. Kraken cleaned the area, made a precise incision, and used tweezers to extract the small teal square. The color marked it as a Synthetic's. He held it up.

"Want it?"

"No." Her voice was rough, like she'd been screaming for hours. Maybe she had. "I suspect I have been tracked using it all along. It is best if you deactivate it."

"You'll need something to pay with." He set the chip aside and closed the wound with skin glue. "I'll program you a fake and transfer the funds before killing this one. I keep blanks for new Outsiders."

Yin sat up slowly, watching him pack away the medical supplies. She had that look she got when thinking hard about something, the one where her face went blank but you could practically hear the gears turning.

Kraken finished with the kit and went to heat up soup. Something simple, easy on the stomach. When he came back and set the bowl on the nightstand, Yin was still staring at nothing.

"This is your bed," she said finally. "Did you sleep next to me?"

Heat crept up his neck. "I thought it was better to keep an eye on you. You were in bad shape."

"So, you were worried."

Statement, not question. He didn't argue.

"You need to eat," he said instead, gesturing at the soup. "You've lost strength."

She looked at the bowl. Looked at him. Her eyes searched his face for something he couldn't name. The silence stretched long enough to get uncomfortable.

Then she stood. Wobbled. Closed the distance between them anyway.

Her arms wrapped around his shoulders. The hug was stiff, unpracticed, but genuine.

"When humans want to reassure another human, they hug them." She looked up at him, face still blank. "Isn't that right, Kraken?"

His mouth opened. Closed. Opened again without any useful words coming out.

Yin didn't do this. Physical contact was tactical or accidental. She avoided touch the way most people avoided fire. But here she was, initiating it, trying it out like an experiment in human connection.

The thought hit him sideways: they were friends.

Actually friends.

Not handler and asset. Not human and Synthetic. Just two people who gave a damn about whether the other one lived or died.

Society would have a field day with that. Synthetics were property, tools, things you owned and used and discarded when they broke. The idea of befriending one would get him laughed out of most rooms in Modernist Ignis. In Retro Ignis, people might understand better, but even there, the concept was strange.

He didn't care.

Yin was his friend, and friends didn't let each other die alone in shitty apartments while the rest of the world moved on.

"Are you reassured?" Yin asked, her tone awkward.

Kraken laughed and put a hand on her shoulder. "Yeah. Yeah, I'm reassured. Thank you, Yin."

Chapter 25

KRAKEN'S FINGERS MOVED ACROSS THE HOLO-KEYBOARD, LINES of code reflecting in his eyes. The vacant apartment he'd claimed as his workspace hummed with the processor's steady rhythm. Circuit diagrams covered one wall. Schematics for various security systems papered another. This was where he did his best work, away from distractions.

Away from watching Yin deteriorate.

She'd had another episode yesterday. Not as bad as the warehouse, but bad enough. He'd left her curled on the couch with a melodramatic soap opera playing, the kind with violins that swelled during emotional revelations. She'd been asleep when he slipped out.

He wasn't sure she could survive another glitch.

What she needed was a geneticist. Someone who understood Synthetic biology, who'd actually worked with her specific genome. Dr. Izumi was brilliant, sure, but he hadn't created Yin alone. Someone else had been in that lab during her 'birth.' The recording had shown at least two figures moving around the gestation chamber.

Find that person, find Yin's salvation.

Hours bled together. Kraken's shoulders ached from hunching over the keyboard. His eyes burned. The blue glow from the monitor had become his entire world, pixels and data streams and dead ends that looped back on themselves.

Then it clicked.

The APB. The all-points bulletin for Yin's capture. Someone had issued it, and government paperwork left trails.

A few keystrokes brought up the original request. An email, formal and bureaucratic. The signature belonged to Aja Yamamoto, listed as High Councilor of Innovation & Genetic Affairs with a secondary position as Head Researcher at Nassar Industries.

Kraken ran the name through Project Gemini's sponsor list.

The connections spider-webbed out. Aja linked to a funding source, which linked to another, which linked to what appeared to be a legitimate medical supply company until you dug deeper and found the dummy corporation underneath. That dummy corporation traced back to C.A.R.E., the Coalition for Advanced Restoration Efforts.

He'd heard of them. Everyone had, if they'd paid attention during the civil war. C.A.R.E. had operated under the old government, claiming to address humanity's declining fertility rates. Radiation had poisoned everything after the nuclear exchange, leaving generations of children born sick or not born at all. The Traditionalists had labeled C.A.R.E. propaganda, disbanded it after they won and called it fearmongering designed to justify genetic experimentation.

Kraken leaned back, processing.

If Aja belonged to C.A.R.E., their goal wouldn't have been creating super soldiers. They'd want the perfect human.

Someone who could survive radiation, who could pass those traits to their offspring, who could save the species.

That's what Yin was supposed to be.

Dr. Izumi must have gotten suspicious. Cut Aja out of the project, changed the locks, destroyed their access. The arrest was Aja's revenge. Except they hadn't counted on Yin escaping during the raid.

This was it. The missing piece.

Kraken straightened, fatigue forgotten. His fingers flew across the keyboard with renewed purpose. Aja was the key to saving Yin. He just had to convince them to help.

The IP address wasn't hard to trace. Government officials got sloppy with their security, confident in their firewalls. Kraken slipped through like smoke through a screen door.

He found Aja on a video call with someone else. Boring bureaucratic nonsense, probably.

Kraken hijacked the connection, booted the other participant, and turned on his own camera.

Aja's face filled the screen. Sharp features. Dark eyes that assessed and catalogued. The resemblance to Yin was immediate and unsettling. Similar bone structure, similar intensity of gaze. Dr. Izumi could have passed for Yin's father. Aja could pass for her other parent.

"Mx. Yamamoto." Kraken smiled. "Pleased to make your acquaintance."

Aja's expression pinched the same way Yin's did when humans irritated her. Narrowed eyes, pursed lips, that look of strained patience.

"I'm not going to ask how you got this connection." Their voice was clipped. "I don't care. What do you want? It's not a question. State it and I'll tell you whether I'll comply."

Even the speech pattern matched. Efficient. No wasted words.

Kraken's smile faded. "You already know who I am, I'm

sure. The Outsiders want to replace the current government with something better. Something that treats people based on their actions, not their genetics or their address. You want to climb higher in the political ladder. With our support, that becomes possible. We just need your backing."

One eyebrow lifted. "Backing in what form? I'm reluctant to display allegiance to what the government labels a terrorist organization."

"We've taken drastic measures in the past. That creates complications for political careers." Kraken kept his tone reasonable. "I'm only asking for your expertise."

"No obvious ties to your organization." Aja's fingers drummed once against their desk. "If you outline specifics and I agree, I see no reason to refuse. Though I may not have as much to offer as you believe."

A pause. Their gaze sharpened.

"However, I doubt you came here expecting easy compliance. What happens if I say no?"

Kraken had prepared for this. "If you refuse, my hand is forced and your career is ruined. Neither of us wants that."

"Ruined?" Something almost like amusement flickered across Aja's face. "You underestimate my ability to navigate difficult situations."

"You underestimate what we know." Kraken felt the conversation slipping. Aja was better at this than he'd anticipated.

"Let me tell you about the sea." Aja leaned back slightly. "It appears vast and unpredictable, but beneath the surface lies a delicate balance. Your organization relies on that same balance. Disrupt it carelessly and you'll capsize."

Kraken shifted tactics. "You're smart, Yamamoto. But even smart people can find themselves trapped by their own secrets."

"Secrets?" Aja's expression didn't change. "I don't mistake

my position. Tell me what you need. What task requires my expertise?"

The moment of truth.

"You're the only surviving scientist who worked on Project Gemini." Kraken watched for any reaction. "I need you to fix Yin."

Nothing. Aja's face remained perfectly neutral.

"Yin." They said the name like they were testing its weight. "The Synthetic. What's wrong with it?"

Kraken's jaw tightened at the 'it,' but he pushed past that. "Something is killing her from the inside. Courtesy of your former partner. You're a geneticist. You know her genome. I'm sure you'll figure it out."

"A formidable creation, but even the strongest need repair sometimes." Aja's tone carried an edge now. "Unfortunately, I'm not familiar with the complete genome. Ryūnosuke hid things from me."

The bitterness in those words was the first real emotion Kraken had heard.

"But he had to record the data somewhere." Aja's gaze fixed on him. "Find that for me, and I'm confident I can repair the damage."

Ice ran down Kraken's spine. Something in Aja's expression, in the way they'd said 'repair,' set off warning bells. This person was dangerous. Not in the obvious way, but in the calculated, long-game way that made them hard to predict.

"I'll look into it," he said carefully. "We'll talk soon."

He cut the connection before Aja could respond.

The blue glow of the monitor washed over him as he sat in the sudden silence. He'd gotten what he wanted. Aja would help fix Yin.

So why did he feel like he'd just made a deal with someone who played chess while everyone else was still learning checkers?

Kraken closed his eyes and rubbed his temples. He needed

to plan his next moves carefully. Aja was sharp, cunning, and clearly had their own agenda. Any mistake on his part would give them the advantage. Any slip would put Yin at risk.

But what choice did he have? Yin was dying, and Aja was the only person who might be able to save her.

He'd walk through fire for his friend. Even if that fire wore a government title and had Yin's eyes.

Chapter 26

The screen glowed after Kraken disconnected. Aja stared at the empty space where his face had been, processing the conversation's implications.

Everything was aligning. The Outsiders needed expertise. Aja needed the Synthetic's complete genome data. Kraken was desperate enough to make deals, which meant he was vulnerable. Vulnerable people made mistakes.

The incoming-call chime broke through their thoughts. Aja accepted it with a touch.

The severe woman from earlier reappeared. Commander Miriam Levy, leader of the Outsiders. Her expression suggested she'd noticed the interruption.

"My apologies," Aja said smoothly. "Network difficulties. As I was saying before we were cut off, I'll have no obvious ties to your organization. If we can ensure that, and you outline specifics, and I agree, then I see no reason why I couldn't provide information. Though I may not have as much as you believe."

The conversation lasted twenty minutes. Miriam was cautious, intelligent, and clearly accustomed to negotiations. By the end, Aja had committed to providing intelligence on government security protocols in exchange for unspecified future considerations. Nothing concrete. Nothing actionable. Just enough to establish trust.

Enough to keep the connection alive.

When the call ended, Aja leaned back and allowed themselves a moment of satisfaction. Two conversations, two pieces moved into position. Now came the waiting.

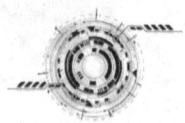

THE SOFT HUM OF THE ENVIRONMENTAL SYSTEMS WAS THE only sound. Below, data streams from the quarterly reports cascaded across the holo-display. Brushed steel, ambient LEDs... Up in the tower, the same sterile elegance was a proclamation of power. Down here, it was a container. No windows broke the metallic monotony. This deep, the isolation was the point—a necessary seal for the work done in these subterranean halls. Aja's attention remained fixed on the data streams cascading across their desk, the holographic interface glittering on the polished steel.

The door chimed. Unexpected.

Aja straightened as the door slid open. Elder Statesman Valenstrom stepped through, silver hair catching the ambient light. The wooden dove rotated slowly between his fingers.

"I hope I'm not interrupting anything urgent," he said.

Aja's hand paused over the holographic interface. "Elder Statesman. This is unexpected." They dismissed the displays with a gesture. "To what do I owe the pleasure?"

"Can't an old teacher visit his former pupil without ulterior motives?" Valenstrom's eyes crinkled. The expression might have been genuine warmth, but Aja had learned long ago that his expressions were as calculated as his politics.

"You could. But you rarely do."

Valenstrom chuckled. His gaze drifted across the office, taking in the minimalist decor and the absence of personal touches. It settled on the antique chess set positioned beside two comfortable chairs.

"I see you still keep the Staunton set I gave you."

Aja followed his gaze. The chess set dominated that corner, the only luxury in an otherwise austere space. "It would be rude to discard a gift from one's mentor."

"Mentor." Valenstrom moved toward the board. "Such a formal word for what we were. What we could have remained." He settled into one of the chairs, fingers hovering over the pieces. "Care for a game? For old times' sake?"

Aja moved to the opposite chair. Their prosthetic leg clicked softly against the floor, a sound they couldn't fully suppress despite careful gait adjustments.

"You always let me win," Aja said. "Even when I was a child, fumbling through basic openings."

Valenstrom began arranging the pieces, each one finding its proper square. "Perhaps I was teaching you to expect victory. A dangerous lesson, in retrospect."

"And now?"

"Now, I promise not to let you win." The wooden dove came to rest on the table. "White or black?"

"I'll take black." Aja positioned their pieces. "I've grown comfortable with reactive strategies."

Valenstrom smiled. The first genuine expression since entering. "How fitting." His hand moved the king's pawn forward two squares. "1.e4."

The classical King's Pawn Opening. Aja studied the board. Valenstrom favored direct, principled approaches. The time-tested methods that generations had refined.

Aja's response came after brief consideration: "1...Nf6."

The Alekhine's Defense. Hypermodern, inviting White to advance aggressively before revealing the overextension.

"Still avoiding direct confrontation, I see." Valenstrom advanced his central pawn. "2.e5."

"You taught me that the most dangerous opponent is one who lets their adversary overreach." Aja retreated the knight to d5. "Sometimes the best control comes from appearing to yield."

As the opening unfolded, with Valenstrom building a classical pawn center while Aja maneuvered around its edges, the elder statesman's voice took on a reflective tone.

"I was thinking about the first time I met you. You couldn't have been more than six or seven. Victoria had to bring you to one of those research presentations at Nassar Industries because you'd been acting out in school again."

Aja's hand paused over their bishop. Suspended for hitting another student. They could still feel the stuffy air of that lecture hall, Valenstrom at the front discussing ethical frameworks.

"Terribly boring stuff for a child," they said.

"You didn't seem bored. You sat in the back row, asking questions that made the senior researchers uncomfortable." Valenstrom advanced a pawn. "Questions about cybernetic enhancement and personal identity. Whether consciousness could be artificially modified without losing its essential humanity."

The memory brought uncomfortable tightness to Aja's chest. They'd been so young then, still struggling with their reconstructive surgeries, still trying to understand what they'd become. "Deep questions for someone whose brain was half artificial circuitry."

"Perhaps that's precisely why you could ask them. You were living the questions the rest of us could only theorize about." Valenstrom's knight jumped to an aggressive central square. "Your mother was protective of you during that period."

"Protective." Aja's laugh carried a bitter edge as they maneuvered pieces, seeking counterplay on the queenside. "An interesting choice of words."

Valenstrom's expression grew troubled. The wooden dove resumed its slow rotation during his thinking time. "Victoria was brilliant. One of the finest researchers I've known. But she had blind spots when it came to you. She saw damage that needed fixing rather than a person who needed understanding."

The observation struck closer than Aja wanted to acknowledge. They advanced a pawn, creating temporary weakness to challenge Valenstrom's center.

"She did what she thought was best. The procedures gave me functionality I wouldn't have had otherwise."

"Functionality." Valenstrom exchanged pieces in the center, simplifying toward an endgame. "But what did they cost you?"

Aja studied the board, using tactical complexity as a shield against emotional complexity. Their prosthetic fingers traced patterns on the table surface.

"I remember the last time I spoke with Dr. Rosewood," Valenstrom continued quietly. "She was devastated about Victoria's decision to proceed with the final procedure. Said she was watching a brilliant child disappear behind layers of artificial emotional regulation."

"Dr. Rosewood was a romantic." Aja moved their rook to an open file. "She believed in the purity of unmodified consciousness. But consciousness isn't pure. It's messy, contradictory, often self-destructive. The modifications helped me function."

"Function. That word again. As if you were a machine that needed optimization rather than a person who needed compassion."

The game reached a critical juncture. Both players' pieces interlinked in complex threats and defenses. Aja calculated variations, searching for the breakthrough that would justify their opening aggression. The position remained balanced.

"You were one of the few people who treated me as a person during those years," Aja admitted before their internal censors could intervene. "Not as a project or a problem to be solved. Just...Aja."

Valenstrom's face softened. "You were remarkable, even then. Especially then. The questions you asked, the connections you made. They came from a mind that was uniquely your own, modifications and all."

The endgame approached as pieces disappeared, leaving only essential forces. Aja's king advanced aggressively. Valenstrom's pieces coordinated beautifully, each occupying its optimal square in classical harmony.

"I often wondered what you might have become without all the interference," Valenstrom mused, his king marching to meet the challenge. "Not better or worse. Just different. More yourself, perhaps."

"This is me." Aja's response carried less conviction than intended. "Whatever was there before the modifications, it's gone. This is what remains."

"I don't believe that." The elder statesman's voice held quiet certainty. "I've seen glimpses over the years. Moments when your control slips and I catch sight of the child I once knew. The one who cried in frustration because they couldn't make sense of their own emotions. Who hated being called a girl. The one who asked impossible questions because they genuinely wanted to understand."

The game had reached a theoretical draw. Aja stared at the immobilized pieces. A white pawn against a black one, kings facing each other across an unbridgeable divide. Perfect, futile opposition.

"Stalemate," Aja observed.

"Stalemate," Valenstrom agreed, though his eyes remained fixed on Aja's face rather than the board. "Perhaps that's appropriate, given our current circumstances."

"Another game?" Aja began resetting the pieces. "I'll take white this time."

Valenstrom's eyebrows lifted. "Eager for a rematch?"

"Eager to avoid dwelling on the past." Aja positioned the final pawn.

The elder statesman's expression shifted. The paternal warmth cooled into something more analytical. "Ah, there we are. Back to business." He settled his pieces with the same methodical skill, though his movements carried new tension. "Very well. Let's see how you handle the initiative."

Aja opened with 1.c4. The English Opening. A hypermodern approach that avoided immediate central occupation, preferring to control from the flanks. Valenstrom responded with the principled 1.e5, claiming the center in classical fashion.

"You know," Valenstrom said as Aja developed their knight to f3, "I've been thinking about our conversation in the council chambers about the R.R.C.A."

Aja's hand paused fractionally before completing the move. "Have you?"

"I once called you the brightest star of your generation. But even stars collapse when they burn too hot."

Aja castled kingside with perhaps more force than necessary, the king clicking against its destination square.

"How poetic. Should I thank you for the warning? Or are you simply reminiscing about better days when your wisdom carried more weight?"

Valenstrom's eyes sharpened, studying Aja's face with intensity. "It's not too late, you know. There's still time to step back from whatever precipice you're approaching."

Aja developed their knight, avoiding central commitments while quietly preparing long-term positional pressure.

Valenstrom was a creature of patterns. Every great classical player had the same blind spot: they trusted established theory.

"Step back from what, exactly?" Aja arranged pieces. "From trying to save humanity? From refusing to let bureaucratic theater override scientific necessity?"

"From becoming something you'll no longer recognize in the mirror."

"Perhaps recognition is overrated." They maneuvered their bishop to a seemingly modest square that would later prove pivotal.

Valenstrom built his position with textbook skill, advancing pawns and developing pieces in harmonious cooperation. But Aja could see the subtle inflexibility in his approach. The classical commitments that hypermodern theory had long ago identified as exploitable.

"I could make this easier for you," Aja offered. "The political landscape is shifting. The old guard faces inevitable change." They moved their queen to an aggressive central square. "A dignified retirement could be arranged. Emeritus status, full pension, a legacy of principled service. You could write your memoirs, teach at the university. Shape the next generation without the burden of daily governance."

The wooden dove went still. Valenstrom's expression settled into something that might have been disappointment, though it carried sharp edges.

"A bribe," he said simply.

"A practical solution." Aja's pieces crept forward along unexpected diagonals, creating threats that wouldn't become apparent until several moves later. "Wrapped in consideration for your wellbeing."

"Wrapped in poison." Valenstrom's counterattack came swiftly, his pieces coordinating in ways that suggested he'd been anticipating this conversation. "What happens to those who refuse your practical solutions, Aja? Do they simply disappear? Suffer convenient accidents? Find themselves facing trumped-up charges?"

Aja's pulse quickened, though their face remained mask-like. "I don't know what you're implying."

"Don't you?" The elder statesman's rook swung to an open file, applying immediate pressure to Aja's king's flank. "Let me be more direct, then. I'm opening a formal investigation into Project Gemini. Into Dr. Izumi's arrest and conviction. Into the circumstances surrounding the Synthetic's creation and subsequent disappearance."

Their stomach clenched. Aja's carefully constructed position, both on the board and in the broader game, suddenly felt fragile. "On what grounds?"

"On the grounds that a brilliant scientist was imprisoned on charges that conveniently removed him from research you desperately wanted to control." Valenstrom's pieces pressed forward. "On the grounds that government resources were used to create beings that officially don't exist. On the grounds that certain officials have been meeting with known terrorists to discuss matters of mutual interest."

The last accusation froze Aja's blood.

"You have no proof."

"I have enough to raise questions. Uncomfortable questions that will demand uncomfortable answers." Valenstrom advanced his queen, the piece cutting across the board. "And if the investigation fails to produce satisfactory results, there are other avenues. Public forums. Media inquiries. The court of public opinion can be quite effective when presented with the right evidence."

Aja's mind raced, calculating options, searching for escape routes. The situation on the board had deteriorated. Their king exposed, pieces uncoordinated, careful plans reduced to desperate improvisation.

"You wouldn't. The scandal would destroy confidence in the government. In the system you've spent your life serving."

"Sometimes the system requires surgery to survive." Valenstrom's final move came with deliberate weight. His queen slid to deliver checkmate. "Sometimes corruption must be cut out before it metastasizes."

Aja stared at the board in stunned silence. Their king sat helpless, surrounded by hostile pieces, every escape square controlled. While they'd focused on the conversation, on maneuvering through words and implications, Valenstrom had been weaving his own trap.

"Checkmate," the elder statesman said quietly.

The word echoed in the office. Aja's prosthetic fingers traced the board's edge, processing not just the loss but its implications. They had underestimated their former mentor, allowing emotional manipulation and overconfidence to cloud strategic judgment.

Valenstrom rose from his chair with the dignity of a man who had accomplished exactly what he'd come to do. The wooden dove disappeared into his coat pocket as he straightened his jacket. "I'll give you time to consider changing course. A week, no longer."

He moved toward the door, stopping at its threshold to look back. Despite the calm of his expression, sadness touched his eyes. "You were always a brilliant mind, Aja. It's a shame you gave up being a scientist to become a wolf."

The door closed behind him, leaving Aja alone with the defeated position and the weight of his words. The checkmate stared up at them. Perfect embodiment of tactical blindness and strategic overreach.

In the silence that followed, surrounded by the crushing reality of their situation, Aja felt something cold weigh in their stomach.

A week.

That's all the time they had.

Chapter 27

The path to the Farm squelched under Kraken's boots, mud clinging to the treads with each step. The sky had deepened to indigo, with heavy clouds promising rain. His shoulders carried more than just the weight of the walk. He'd been gone too long, and now the consequences loomed over him.

The living quarters towered ahead, the converted barn's silhouette sharp against the darkening sky. The wooden door scraped open with a piercing creak, revealing rows of bunkbeds inside. Most Outsiders didn't sleep here unless they had nowhere else to go. Some chose it anyway, trading city comforts for rural isolation.

Miriam had claimed the converted hayloft. From the ground, Kraken could see light spilling from the highest window.

Dampness hit him first when he stepped inside, followed by the smell of burning wood from the stove in the next room. The residents were probably in the mess hall for dinner. At least he wouldn't have an audience for whatever was about to happen.

His mind scrambled for justifications, excuses, anything that might soften what was coming. Every scenario ended the same way: badly. Maybe silence was better. Bow his head, accept the consequences, hope for mercy.

The wooden staircase groaned under his weight as he climbed. Each footfall announced his presence. Miriam's door was cracked open, warm light pooling onto the landing. She'd either seen him coming or heard him. The stairs weren't exactly subtle.

Kraken pushed the door wider with his fingertips and peered inside.

The loft smelled of aged timber and fresh flowers, an earthy combination that somehow worked. Exposed beams gave the space rural charm, furnished with mismatched wooden pieces worn smooth by time. String lights hung along the walls, casting a warm glow across everything.

Miriam sat at her desk, absorbed in her task. Hair products littered the surface: shining proteins, moisturizing oils, combs of various sizes. Her focus was fixed on the vanity mirror as she worked product through a section of hair, braiding it into a neat box braid with ease. She didn't acknowledge him until she finished, laying the final braid over her shoulder.

Then she smiled. It didn't reach her eyes.

"Look who finally decided to show." Her voice carried deceptive friendliness. She twisted the cap back on her oil and set it aside. "I was beginning to wonder. You'll be happy to know we're in the process of replicating that drug now."

"Wonder? Did you think I went AWOL?" Kraken arched his eyebrows, trying for an amiable tone. He moved to her desk, laying his hands on its surface and leaning forward. "Miriam, have some faith. You didn't choose a coward for a lieutenant."

Miriam's deep brown eyes remained fixed on him in uneasy silence. Her fingers drummed against the table in a steady rhythm, each tap ratcheting his anticipation higher. The weight of her gaze carried unspoken words, and Kraken wanted to wither on the spot. But he held her stare, keeping his features neutral.

Miriam's eyes crinkled at the corners as she broke the tension with a soft chuckle. She gestured for him to pull up a chair.

Her reaction left him stupefied. The last thing he'd imagined was her forgiving him this easily. Kraken half-expected her to shove a knife in his back as he grabbed a chair, flipped it around, and sat with his arms draped over its backrest.

"I wanted to talk to you about a blackmail target." Miriam opened her desk drawer and laid a photo on the table, sliding it forward with one finger. "Aja Yamamoto. They're a high councilor for the government."

Kraken glanced at the photo, careful to keep his face neutral. "What do you want out of them?"

"That's for you to find out." Miriam reclined in her chair, absentmindedly playing with the Star of David pendant hanging around her neck. She gazed at the photo with a pensive expression. "Aja has more influence than they let on. They've swayed officials on numerous policies regarding Recombination restrictions, and they're involved with Nassar Industries, who basically controls the technological market. Having someone like that in our pocket would be beneficial."

Kraken managed a strained smile, anxiety surging through him. "I suppose we'll have Aja performing for us soon enough."

"Israel told me Aja issued an APB on your Synth with a generous reward. We can use her as leverage."

The smile faltered. The chair suddenly felt hard and unforgiving beneath him. Sacrifices had to be made for the greater good. He'd told himself that countless times, used it to justify setting aside principles and morals. The guilt was a necessary burden when fighting a greater evil.

But using Yin as a bargaining chip was different. She was his friend. He'd made a promise to help her.

His hesitation didn't go unnoticed. Miriam slammed her hand on the desk, making it shudder. "Dammit, Theopold!" Using his first name startled him. "Are you protecting her because you're fucking her?"

"What? No!" Kraken recoiled, heat flooding his face. "That's not— We're not—"

"Then what is it?" Miriam's eyes blazed. "Because from where I'm sitting, you're putting that Synth above everything we've worked for."

"She's my friend, Miriam. That's all." The words came out desperate. "I'm not just going to—"

"Friend?" Miriam scowled. "You can't be friends with a Synthetic, Kraken. They're not human. They're *tools*. Weapons. This one in particular is a liability we can't afford."

"She's more than that—"

"She's *nothing* more than that!" Miriam stood abruptly, her chair scraping against the floor. "This connection could be our chance to uncover everything the government is plotting. Are you seriously willing to throw that out for one Synth?"

"Of course not," Kraken said quickly. Too quickly. The words came out defensive.

Defensive of Yin.

The Outsiders were all he'd known as family. Their tight-knit community had been his constant comfort through everything. His stomach knotted as he looked at Miriam, eyes silently pleading. His mouth was dry, tongue feeling like sandpaper as he tried to speak, but only wordless desperation emerged.

Miriam's expression softened as her anger dissipated. Her eyes filled with pity. She walked around the desk to stand beside him, wrapping her arms around him and pulling him close. She laid her head on top of his.

"I don't doubt your dedication to the cause." Her voice was rich and warm, filled with tenderness. "And we both understand that sometimes, the end justifies the means. Right?"

Kraken clutched Miriam's arm, fingers digging in hard enough to leave marks. His eyes stared ahead, unfocused. He was drowning and Miriam was his lifeline, but at the same time, he resented her for making him choose. He inhaled deeply, shut his eyes, and leaned into her embrace like a child seeking refuge.

"Right."

The word tasted like ash in his mouth.

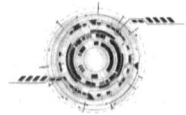

THE WALK BACK HOME BLURRED TOGETHER. TIME STRETCHED and slowed around him, burdened by the same guilt that consumed him. Somewhere in the midst of it all, he thought he heard someone call out, their voice faint and distant, but he couldn't be certain.

Each step felt like a confession. Every breath a reminder of his betrayal.

The sounds and smells of Old Town surrounded him. The rumble of traffic, the scent of street food cooking, the faint whistle of a far-off train. All of it drowned out by the deafening thump of his own heart, each beat echoing with remorse.

Eventually, he found himself standing in front of his door. Once a comforting sight, it now filled with dread. The touch recognition pad glowed expectantly, waiting for him to confirm his return. Kraken hesitated, fingers trembling. Inside, he could hear Yin's favorite soap opera blaring from the TV.

A small sliver of comfort.

Kraken closed his eyes and leaned against the door. For a brief moment, he let himself escape into the sound, basking in its familiarity. The voices of the soap opera characters, their dramatic dialogue and cheesy music, temporarily drowning out the noise of his thoughts.

But reality set in. He had to face Yin and pretend everything was fine between them. A cruel game he was forced to play.

Kraken pressed his finger against the touchpad and pushed inside. The living room stretched before him: beige walls, a comfortable sofa, the soft glow from the TV. The scent of popcorn and buttery snacks wafted through the air, mingling with hints of laundry detergent.

Yin sat perched in her usual corner with her knees pulled close to her chest. She looked up when he entered, her lips sliding into a warm smile that nearly broke him. On the coffee table sat a big bowl of steaming popcorn, odd since she didn't indulge in snacks. She patted the couch as an invitation.

Kraken sank into the cushions next to her. His fingers traced the worn edges of the throw blanket Nari had gifted him. Yin offered him some popcorn. He waved it away, focusing on the TV instead.

The characters on screen blurred together, their colors muted by his cloudy mind. He sat in silence with Yin until the credits appeared.

"I can't remember anything about my parents," he admitted. "But I know they must have been passionate about sea creatures because they gave me the middle name Charybdis when I was already named Kraken."

Yin's expression was puzzled. Her curious gaze scanned his features, searching for understanding.

Kraken pressed on. "Then they gave me the unusual name

Theopold. Sure, Theo is common enough, but Theopold? What were they thinking?"

"I do not..." Yin hesitated.

Kraken turned to meet her gaze. "No one calls me Theopold. Sometimes just Theo, but most people call me Kraken." The words spilled out quickly. He couldn't help rambling under stress. It was a weakness he was often criticized for, but right now, those words were the only thing holding him together. "Hell, why even name me at all? My parents only conceived me to be a test subject."

His fingers dug into the couch cushions. "They called it Project Binary. A reckless attempt to rival Project Prometheus." His voice dropped, each word edged with bitterness. "They wanted the perfect soldier, so they modified me in the womb. Increased neuron density in my cerebrum for better problem-solving, faster learning, sharper reflexes. Controlled my muscular growth for strength without bulk."

He swallowed hard, the memory tasting like metal. "And when I passed all their tests—thank the stars I did, or who knows what they would've done—they surgically implanted cyber-warfare technology into my brain." His hand moved to his temple, fingers trembling. "I was nine months old, Yin. *Nine months.*"

Kraken slumped against the back of the couch, limbs slack and face drawn. His gaze fixed on the white ceiling above, eyes tracing patterns as if looking for answers. "They were foolish. Used government funds for their little experiment. When the administration found out an infant was involved, they shut it down." His laugh was hollow. "My parents mysteriously disappeared after that. All records destroyed. Every piece of data, gone."

His jaw clenched. "I was the only remaining evidence. And I was lucky to be alive—the government couldn't risk being associated with child murder—so they threw me into foster care in Retro Ignis and forgot about me." He turned his head to look at Yin, his eyes glassy. "Except I was still alive. Still *here*. That was the issue.

"The foster parents they gave me..." His voice cracked. He cleared his throat, fighting to keep control. "They were criminals. I lived through that nightmare until they died when I was six. After that, the streets were all I had left. A gang took me in. That's where I met Markus."

Kraken's fingers trembled as he gripped the edge of the couch. "I pieced it all together as a teenager. Found out my dead parents weren't even my real parents. That my real parents were also dead. Just..." He exhaled shakily. "It blossomed this resentment toward the government. This rage I still carry."

He realized how long it had been since he'd thought about this dark part of his past. He'd believed it no longer affected him until he watched the harrowing footage of Yin's abuse. Ever since, those buried memories had flooded back, haunting him. And when he looked at Yin, it was like looking into a distorted reflection of his own turbulent past.

Tense silence hung between them. He could sense Yin's uncertainty. Kraken hated that he had twinges of envy toward her. The grief twisted in his gut like a living thing. Every emotion hit him like this—too much, too fast, too intense. His parents had enhanced his cognition but left him vulnerable in ways they'd never anticipated. Or maybe they just hadn't cared.

It had taken him time to come to terms with this aspect of himself. In the past, he'd been ridiculed and mocked for not fitting the traditional mold of masculinity. He had to be careful not to show his vulnerabilities, knowing they could be exploited against him.

Yin was the exact opposite. Her emotions were repressed.

Somehow, that felt worse.

Kraken raked his fingers through his short hair, letting out an audible groan. He'd just word-vomited his feelings all over the place. Fidgeting in his seat, he suddenly felt warmth press against his side.

The bowl of popcorn.

He glanced sideways. Yin had leaned in closer, offering it without a word. She didn't ask if he was okay. Didn't tell him to calm down or get over it. Just...sat there. Close enough to comfort, far enough to let him breathe. The gesture was so simple, so *human*, that something cracked in his chest.

Kraken took the bowl with trembling hands and stared down into it, vision bleary at the edges.

"Look, all I'm trying to say is...we're similar."

Silence. He waited for her to pull away, to correct him and scold him for his outburst. To remind him she wasn't human, wasn't capable of understanding, wasn't *like him* at all.

Instead, she reached for the remote and started browsing through the show options.

His throat tightened as he watched her scroll. She moved past action movies, past documentaries, until she settled on that drama they'd watched together before. The one with the violins and the impossible love stories. The one she'd analyzed like a field manual while he'd gotten embarrassingly invested in the characters.

She turned to him, and her expression was softer than he'd ever seen it. "Let us watch another episode together. You can cry and stuff your face with popcorn like you always do, and I shall act like I do not see."

Kraken's throat clenched. She'd *noticed*. All those nights on this couch, she'd been paying attention. Learning him. Caring in the only way she knew how.

His hands shook as he placed the bowl back on the table. The weight in his chest became unbearable, crushing. She'd just offered him exactly what he needed—acceptance without judgment, companionship without demands. Friendship.

Real friendship.

And Miriam wanted him to hand her over like she was

nothing. Like she wasn't sitting here trying to comfort him in her awkward, literal way. Like she hadn't just proven she understood him better than most humans ever had.

He forced a smile, but it crumbled before it fully formed. His eyes burned, clouded with something that had nothing to do with his earlier confession.

"Maybe next time," he murmured, voice barely audible. He turned away to retreat to his room.

As he closed the door behind him, Kraken leaned heavily against it, letting out a shaky breath. The sound of his own heartbeat was loud in his ears as he tried to hold back the sobs.

With a final wretched shudder, tears streamed down his face.

Chapter 28

Respect your high-ranking officers. Be prepared to lay down your life for your fellow soldiers. But never turn a blind eye to their actions. If you see something, say something.

The words cycled through Yin's mind as she stood outside Miriam's door, the heels from the party dangling from her fingers. She'd only come to return them to Nari. The absurd things had sat mockingly under the coffee table during her recovery, and she'd finally felt strong enough to make the trek to the Farm.

She hadn't meant to overhear.

Miriam's voice carried through the crack in the door. "This connection could be our chance to uncover everything the government is plotting."

Then Kraken's response, quiet but clear: "Of course not."

Yin's grip tightened on the heels until the stiletto points bit into her palm.

A soldier's role wasn't only combat. It was vigilance. Watching for infiltration, for compromise, for betrayal within your own ranks. That burden fell on the Synthetic so human soldiers didn't have to sacrifice their humanity. Camaraderie was acceptable. Friendship was weakness that jeopardized the mission.

Except now the betrayal was hers to witness, and the logic that had always sustained her felt hollow.

"Yin? What are you doing here?"

Yin turned. Nari stood in the doorway. Her practical clothes had been replaced by a pastel sundress with a cinched waist and delicate lace. Her hair fell loose and flowing. The scent of vanilla mixed with cedarwood clung to her skin.

She hadn't been alone.

"I was coming to check on the medics." The lie required no effort. She'd made frequent trips to train them since Kraken had put her under his supervision. "Today is the first day I have felt strong enough." She held up the heels. "And I was looking for you. To return these."

Nari's carefully plucked brow rose. "Return them?" Her lips parted in a giggle, eyes sparkling with rose-gold eyeshadow that demanded attention. "Why would you return them? I bought them for you, silly."

But doubt lurked beneath the shimmer. Yin recognized the look now, had learned to read the micro-expressions humans tried to hide.

She lowered the heels. "Were you on a date?"

Color flooded Nari's face, burning through the rosy blush on her cheekbones. The flush was answer enough, but Yin pressed forward, needing the deflection. "Who were you with?"

"Well, aren't you just a curious one?" Nari fanned herself, laughing. "Maybe that's my little secret? It's hard to have much to yourself here." She planted her hands on her hips, scanning Yin head to toe. Her lips pressed together before releasing a loud sigh. "Yin. Yin. Yin. You're still walking around in nothing but a T-shirt, sweats, and robe? You look like a cartoon." Her voice bounced playfully as she wagged a finger. She leaned closer, conspiratorial. "I'll make you a deal. You agree to let me take you shopping for normal clothes and I'll tell you who I was with."

"Deal."

"Deal. Yes, I was on a date. With Gabriel."

The name triggered a vague memory. Gabriel had voiced his admiration for Nari before, though Yin rarely listened when he spoke. She searched for another question, something to keep Nari's suspicion at bay. "Where did you go?"

"We took a walk through the park in Old Town." A shrug.

"Did you kiss?"

Both of Nari's brows shot up. She erupted into laughter, face alight with mirth. It took her several moments to regain composure. "I'm sorry." She was still chuckling. "That caught me off guard. You're full of questions this evening. What's really going on?"

Yin stayed silent. Any words would sound evasive or defensive. She couldn't reveal the truth. Despite liking and respecting Nari, she knew that Nari was ultimately one of them. In the end, Nari would choose her own kind over Yin.

Just like Kraken did.

Above them, the floorboards creaked. They'd heard Nari's loud laughter. Yin couldn't stay here any longer.

"I must go, Nari. If I delay, I will miss the beginning of my soap opera." She bowed her head. "I am grateful for the shoes, even if they are impractical."

The sky was thick with clouds, with no moonlight or stars to offer guidance, but Yin's eyes had long adapted to the darkness. She sprinted down the path toward Ignis, needing to reach the apartment before Kraken. He couldn't discover she'd overheard. That knowledge was her only advantage.

The air hung heavy and musty. Wet earth and decaying leaves filled her nostrils, clung to her skin as she ran. Her steps were silent. Lithe. But Kraken's words followed like specters, haunting every stride. The harder she fought to ignore them, the louder they reverberated.

This was new. Perplexing. With her high tolerance, she shouldn't be experiencing such sharp pain. Invisible wounds that couldn't be seen but were certainly felt.

The sensation consumed her so completely that she missed the eerie silence settling over the woods. She didn't register the threat until it was on top of her.

Yin planted her feet and slid to a halt, leaving shallow grooves in the dirt. She tensed and propelled herself backward, catching movement where she'd just been.

Yang emerged from the shadows, murderous intent radiating off her like heat.

Yin stood her ground, fists clenched. But that unfamiliar emotion clouded her judgment, made it difficult to focus. That shouldn't be possible.

This wasn't the first time since the party. For days, she'd sensed eyes on her, felt intense malice growing stronger with each passing moment. Yang was playing some game, but Yin didn't know the rules. Even now, as Yang studied her with inquisitive rather than aggressive intent, Yin felt on edge.

"You failed to notice me until the last moment." Yang's words were soft and unpleasant, like an outdated AI mimicking human speech. Machinery clicked gently within her body, but beneath it beat a steady heart. Her movements were deliberate, robotic, lacking natural fluidity. As she tilted her head, her expression remained void of emotion, yet disdain flickered in her eyes. "Imperfect. Obsolete. Broken things like you shouldn't be permitted to exist."

"I am the only thing like me." Statement. But the question was implied.

"In a world where resources are limited and survival is uncertain, it is logical to prioritize genetic superiority."

Yin pursed her lips. "Yes."

"Those malformed contribute weakness and threaten the

integrity of the genome. Long-term sustainability decreases, and continued contribution will coalesce into breakdown. Soft culling of these ineffectuals is insufficient. They drain limited resources."

Yin thought of Scraptown. People with cleft palates, spinal abnormalities, missing or extra limbs. Imperfections commonplace in that community. The skilled potter, whose wares she'd admired, was shorter than most. Society might see flaws, but these individuals thrived. She recalled children's cries during play, adults' laughter sharing secrets, the determination of those recycling everything because they understood sustainability's value.

Could she say the same of Modernist Ignis? Of her Creator?

Yang continued, voice laced with quiet contempt. "I believed he might be wrong about you. That maybe you were like me. Now I see it. You are a prototype. A mere imitation of what I am. Your continued existence is illogical. Just as theirs."

Yin gazed into Yang's calculating gaze. No glimmer of empathy or understanding. No humanity in those cold eyes. Yang was the epitome of perfection, operating solely on logic and indisputable facts, without emotion clouding judgment.

And yet, her reasoning was flawed. Her inability to consider emotions caused her to miss crucial aspects of her worldview.

"I am unsurprised that our Creator poisoned you against me." Yin kept her voice level. "All of that time in the lab. If we ever mistakenly met, it could have ended poorly for him. For all his flaws, he was an intelligent human."

But their Creator would never have instilled these beliefs in Yang. His only concern was achieving the perfect soldier. These were the conclusions Yang reached alone. In the past, Yin would have agreed wholeheartedly. She too would have followed the same logical path with conviction, thought herself infallible.

Something had changed during her time with humans. Her time with Kraken.

Yin breathed in at this realization. She straightened, met Yang's gaze without flinching. "You may believe I am obsolete, but I believe you are wrong. There is value in diversity. Diminishing the genetic population reduces resilience to environmental changes and disease. Your view overlooks the complex interplay that shapes an individual and disregards the inherent value and uniqueness of a person beyond their genetic make-up." She paused. "Those humans have a right to live. One that cannot be determined by you or I."

I have a right to live.

Her fingers twitched. It was the first time she truly considered her mortality. Her life hadn't been consequential, only the mission. Whatever the mission was. She remained purpose-driven, but what if her purpose in this moment was to survive?

She shifted her weight, ready to defend. Yang remained still, eyes narrowing as she focused on Yin like a specimen under glass. Time seemed suspended until Yang took a step back. Two. She turned toward the shadows.

Yin relaxed her tense muscles once Yang's presence faded. Her adversary had deemed it was not yet time for confrontation.

The game continued.

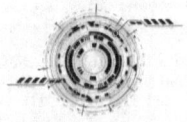

THE APARTMENT AIR WAS STILL WHEN YIN WALKED IN, THICK with unspoken anticipation. Electronic devices beeped occasionally. Distant traffic sounds filtered through the walls. The air conditioning hummed its soothing background noise.

Kraken wasn't back yet.

CAENOGENESIS

Yin reached for a sanitation wipe, felt the coolness against her skin. She cleaned the dirt from her bare feet before tossing it into the bin. The bin emitted a soft green light and hummed as it disposed of the trash. She padded across the hardwood into the kitchen, smoothness and coolness against her skin. After washing her hands, she opened a cabinet to reveal snacks. She grabbed the popcorn, tore it open, and savored the satisfying rip of plastic.

The microwave screen lit up and scanned her face. She navigated through the menu until she found Kraken's photo and selected it. Soon the buttery aroma filled the apartment, promising a salty comfort that most found appealing.

Yin found it nauseating.

The microwave beeped upon completion. Yin grabbed the bag, barely registering the scalding heat against her hands. She dumped the contents into a bowl and tossed the empty bag into the recycling bin. It would travel through winding tunnels to a facility near Scraptown.

Bowl in hand, she took her usual spot on the couch. She placed the popcorn on the coffee table and connected her com-tacts to the television. Eye movements navigated to Streamflix, selecting her favorite: *Passions & Perils: Days of Our Plights*.

Set in fictional Plightsville, the show followed the scandalous lives of wealthy and powerful characters. Love triangles, family secrets, corporate power struggles. The show provided insight into human behavior that she found intriguing.

But as the familiar theme music filled the room, Yin found herself unable to immerse in the drama. The melodramatic opening sequence played out with sweeping aerial shots of opulent mansions and lush gardens. The camera zoomed in on a grand mansion where the tormented protagonist, Alexandria Sterling, stood atop a sweeping staircase, eyes filled with longing.

Yin's gaze remained fixed on Alexandria, but her mind drifted. The captivating storyline felt hollow now, contrived. A facade masking the true turmoil in her own chest. Kraken's words echoed like a haunting melody, each note a reminder of that unfamiliar, shattered feeling that gnawed at her.

She reached absently for popcorn. The fluffy kernels crunched between her teeth but provided no solace. Strong salt and butter made her lips curl into a grimace. She took a deep breath, hoping to find comfort in the familiar act, but her lungs crackled and wheezed, as though filled with dust from forgotten corners.

An abrupt, violent coughing fit seized her. The metallic tang of blood filled her mouth. She felt warmth on her fingers as she pressed them to her lips. A grim reminder of impending death at her Creator's hands.

Clenching her fist, Yin closed her eyes and focused on breathing deeply.

I have a right to live.

With renewed determination, she activated her com-tacts. Her contacts list appeared. Her gaze landed on Aja Yamamoto, the last person she'd spoken with. Yin didn't trust them. That would be foolish. But ultimately, no matter how the cards fell, Aja was the only one capable of helping her survive.

She pressed call.

Camaraderie is appropriate. Friendship is weakness.

Chapter 29

Dawn seeped through the lace curtains, casting a grey light across Kraken's bedroom. His eyes fluttered open to familiar surroundings: crumpled sheets, worn books stacked on the nightstand, pillows that cradled his head with just the right amount of support. He stretched, feeling the slight ache in his muscles fade as the blankets cocooned him.

Then the realization hit.

Yin was gone.

He sat up, breath catching. His eyes darted around the room, searching for any sign of her presence. Any indication the past couple of days had been a dream.

The apartment was silent. No hum of the laundry machine. No murmur from the TV. No gentle creaking of her footsteps on the wooden floorboards. The emptiness echoed through each room like a presence of its own.

His hands gripped the sheets. She'd left without a word. Where had she gone?

A chime pierced the silence. Kraken activated his com-tacts, revealing a coded message from Miriam. Outsiders used this form exclusively, each holding a deciphering key. It took seconds to decrypt: Meet at base.

He jumped out of bed and moved to his closet. Plain T-shirts, hoodies, jeans, and plaid shirts in various hues lined the walls. His hand reached for whatever was closest, then froze mid-air.

The closet was organized.

"And you call yourself a soldier?" Yin had said incredulously, giving him that typical sour stare. Tired of his untidy ways, she'd taken it upon herself to sort everything while he was away. Each item arranged by type, length, and color. A testament to her attention to detail and desire for order in everything.

Kraken brushed his fingers against a neatly folded T-shirt. The fabric was smooth and cool. Guilt twisted in his chest.

When he'd realized she was missing, he'd searched. Frantic trips through every dilapidated alley and abandoned building in Old Town. He'd questioned wary Scraptown inhabitants, offering bribes and threats in equal measure. When those failed, he'd resorted to hacking, scouring databases and government records for any sign of her detainment.

Every lead turned up empty. Even his security system showed no evidence of her leaving the property or turning up in the city. And it wasn't just Yin who was missing. All traces of the Project Gemini file had disappeared.

Kraken dressed carefully so as not to disrupt her organization. Plain white shirt, green plaid shirt, dark jacket. Faded distressed jeans and sturdy combat boots. His previous outfit went into the laundry basket near his closet.

Yin would have been pleased.

After securing his knife and checking his weapon's ammunition, Kraken left for the base.

From his viewpoint on the hill, Kraken saw Miriam and the others standing in the shadow of the silo adjacent to the barns. The metal surface was rusted and pitted, rising like a tower from the earth. The Outsiders used it as a watchtower. From its height, you could see beyond the main structures to where land stretched in all directions, a patchwork of overgrown fields and tangled hedgerows. Rusted husks of abandoned farm equipment lay half-buried, silent witnesses to time's passage.

Gathering this specific group meant Miriam had a task of great importance. Tingling prickled at the back of Kraken's neck as he walked toward his comrades.

Nari and Nori sat close on a bench made of raw wood. They communicated through subtle glances and hand gestures, indecipherable to the others but conveying everything between them. Their own secret language. Kraken had always been fascinated by this covert communication, though it puzzled him.

Both twins glanced up, identical expressions filled with empathy. Nori's eyes held calm worry, the furrow in her brow revealing her concern. Nari's expression was gentle compassion, as if she could sense every emotion coursing through him.

Kraken refused to make eye contact. He turned toward Miriam, folded his arms, and focused his gaze straight ahead.

Miriam's voice echoed with conviction. "We have received intel from our trusted contact within the administration that urges us to take action." She meant Aja. Kraken's eyes narrowed slightly. "It has come to our attention that Elder Statesman Orion Valenstrom, one of the most influential voices on the council, may have sympathies for our cause."

Elder Statesman Orion Valenstrom held the record for longest-serving statesman. Well-known for his outspoken opposition to recombination, he'd played a crucial role shutting down Project Prometheus due to its inhumane side effects on soldiers. His close relationship with the supreme chancellor granted him influence others didn't possess.

Kraken maintained a composed expression despite his surprise. Someone like Valenstrom could provide direct access to the supreme chancellor and, ultimately, control over the entire city-state.

"Elder Statesman Valenstrom has always been up the supreme chancellor's ass," Izzy said, echoing Kraken's doubts. "Why would he secretly be conspiring against him?"

"The supreme chancellor has always been a staunch advocate for recombination," Miriam replied. "His lust for power has him considering restarting Project Prometheus so he can take his super soldiers to war against other city-states. No matter the costs to his soldiers or Ignis. Elder Statesman Valenstrom is loyal, but he isn't a fool. Ignis cannot withstand another war in its current state. Its citizens will suffer greatly."

Izzy let out a quiet grumble, her fingers absently tracing the hypo-pigmented markings on her arm. They followed the path of conductive filaments beneath her skin, mapping her nervous system. The filaments were part of a neural interface linking her mind to her pyrokinetic abilities. Similar scars were scattered across her body, evidence of past procedures to improve and control her abilities through microscale devices and augmentations.

Kraken noticed her body begin to shiver, a common side effect of her recombination. Her unique ability disrupted her body's natural homeostasis, causing fluctuations between burning heat and freezing cold. Strong emotions could trigger it. Without hesitation, Kraken took off his jacket and placed it over her shoulders. The rest of their group gathered around Izzy, enveloping her in warmth.

"Thanks," she muttered, teeth chattering. "Where's the sun when you need it? I'm sick of these never-ending clouds."

"The sun? You're not old enough to remember the sun," Nori teased, squeezing tight. "A girls hug will have to do. We'll be three mini suns."

"I can vibe being the middle of a girl sandwich. Too bad we're dressed."

Izzy never spoke about her time as a test subject for Project Prometheus. If anyone broached the topic, she deflected with humor. But she didn't need to speak. The symbols engraved into her skin acted as constant reminders of individuals willing to sacrifice others in their pursuit of power.

"How do we reach the elder statesman?" Kraken asked through gritted teeth, familiar anger rising.

"Our contact arranged for us to meet him at Nassar Industries tonight. We will talk to him there."

"Are you sure they're telling the truth?"

Miriam shrugged. "The only way to know for sure is by trying." She let her arms fall as Izzy's temperature leveled out. For a moment, she left her hand on Izzy's shoulder, offering comfort. "We'll be prepared no matter what happens. And I didn't choose this group based on looks." She grinned mischievously. "In fact, you're all quite a sight for sore eyes."

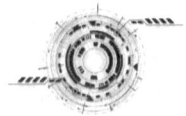

THE SKYSCRAPER THAT WAS NASSAR INDUSTRIES ROSE majestically above the surrounding cityscape, its towering silhouette dominating the Ignis skyline. Its sleek facade was composed of reflective glass panels, catching what little light filtered through the overcast sky and lending the structure an aura of futuristic elegance. The architecture was characterized by clean lines and geometric precision, sharp angles and soaring verticals giving the building its commanding presence.

Despite its imposing stature, there was undeniable sophistication in the exterior design. A harmonious blend of form and function that embodied the company's supposed ethos of technological innovation and forward-thinking vision. It was meant to invoke awe and wonder at the possibilities within its gleaming walls.

The exterior came alive with a mesmerizing display of lights. LED strips traced the building's contours, casting vibrant hues against the darkening sky.

Kraken observed the twinkling lights with a shake of his head. To him, the building was nothing more than an excessive display meant to preen the feathers of its CEO. A vapid show of wealth, wasting energy that could have been used for meaningful purposes.

The group still had three blocks until they reached the skyscraper. Miriam led them down bustling city streets, her determined steps leaving no room for doubt. Kraken lingered behind, his mind consumed with worries about Yin. He closed his eyes, trying to block out negative thoughts and focus on the present. The sounds of chattering pedestrians and whirring shuttles merged into a distant hum.

Someone slowed beside him. Kraken felt a light touch on his hand and opened his eyes to see Nari. She reached out, lightly brushing her hand against his. The gentle touch was like a feather against his skin.

"Don't worry, big brother. She'll be fine and show up again soon." Her lips curved into a reassured smile. "She's far too fond of you to stay away forever."

Kraken ran his fingers through his hair and glanced at the ground with a half-hearted shrug. He doubted Yin had any particular fondness for anything, especially not toward him. Not after he'd essentially agreed to use her as bait.

Thankfully, she was blissfully unaware of that fact.

"It's for the best," another voice interjected. Izzy had fallen back to join him. She patted his shoulder. "C'mon Krak, quit your moping. If she stuck around, we'd be handing her over right now."

Sharp, bitter flavor surfaced in his mouth, accompanied by sudden anger. Kraken planted himself firmly and turned to face Izzy. "You're the one who told Miriam about the APB." His fists clenched. The words rang out sharply, each one dripping with venom. "Yin knew you wanted the reward the second she met you. She said so herself after you left. All of this is your fault. You greedy—"

Kraken cut himself off, sudden regret washing over him. His resentment towards Izzy was unfair. He couldn't know for sure why Yin had left or whether the APB influenced her decision. Miriam would have found out one way or another. He'd still be stuck in this moral crisis.

Izzy's normally bright eyes were filled with hurt. Her eyebrows furrowed, lips slightly downturned.

Kraken exhaled heavily, lips twisting in a remorseful frown. "I'm sorry, Iz. I didn't mean that."

"Hey!" Nori interrupted them, standing at the corner and beckoning. "Hurry up, all of you. We can discuss your drama later. We have a mission to complete."

At the base of the skyscraper, a wide plaza stretched out, adorned with meticulously manicured gardens and futuristic sculptures. Paved pathways wound through the plaza, leading toward the grand entrance, where a towering glass facade welcomed them. As evening settled, the pristine walkways were empty. No one to witness a group of so-called terrorists walking into the largest company of Ignis.

As Kraken stepped into the structure, he was enveloped by an atmosphere that merged sleek futuristic aesthetics with underlying ominous authority. The lobby was grandiose, with polished marble floors and towering walls of brushed steel. It exuded corporate power and sophistication. Massive floor-to-ceiling windows offered breathtaking views of Modernist Ignis. At the center, a colossal holographic display projected intricate diagrams and schematics, showcasing the company's latest innovations in genetic engineering and technological advancements.

The lighting was a blend of ambient LEDs, casting a cool, clinical glow that accentuated the sterile environment.

The whole place made Kraken feel sick. The feeling was like barbed wire wrapped tightly around his stomach, squeezing with relentless pressure. The sheer opulence was in stark contrast to the destitution of Retro Ignis, particularly Scraptown. Yet those fortunate enough to hold lofty positions in society would point fingers and blame Retro Ignis as the root of all issues.

Kraken bit back his outrage.

Miriam strolled slowly through the deserted security checkpoint to the elevator. She pressed the button labeled 'Down' and waited. "Elder Statesman Valenstrom is waiting for us on the lower level, where the labs are located. Nari and Nori, stay up here and keep watch. If anything out of the ordinary happens, contact us through our comms channel."

"Roger that." Nari saluted and winked. "Good luck down there."

"That feels unfair. We'll miss all the fun," Nori complained, though without much conviction. She laid her hand on her weapon and leaned against the wall.

The elevator chimed arrival, metallic doors opening with a gentle hiss. Miriam, Izzy, and Kraken stepped inside, their steps barely making a sound on the polished floor. The doors closed slowly behind them. The descent began, with the gentle hum of machinery filling the silence.

Kraken looked around at his companions. Miriam, with her striking features and determined gaze, looked ready for anything. Izzy seemed lost in thought, brow furrowed as if trying to solve a complex puzzle.

As for Kraken, he couldn't shake the feeling of unease growing since their invitation. The elevator continued its smooth descent, the numbers on the display ticking down steadily. He couldn't help but wonder what awaited them at the bottom. Perhaps a trap, a way for the government to rid themselves of the Outsiders. Or maybe an opportunity, a chance to finally be heard and understood.

As the elevator reached its destination and the doors slid open, Kraken took a deep breath and steeled himself. He knew that whatever happened, they wouldn't back down. The Outsiders may be few in number, but they were determined. They would not be silenced.

The three ventured into the corridor lined with glass-paneled walls, revealing glimpses into state-of-the-art research laboratories where scientists in pristine white lab coats would normally be engrossed in their work, surrounded by banks of supercomputers and intricate machinery. But at this moment, the rooms were unoccupied. The floor was shrouded in darkness, save for dimly lit hallways.

The hair on the back of Kraken's neck stood. "This doesn't feel right, Miriam."

Miriam raised a hand in a silencing gesture, then proceeded down the hallway with an attentive gaze sweeping for potential dangers. Kraken trailed closely behind, alert. The hallway appeared to extend endlessly, curving and bending with corridors branching off. The lower level was truly immense.

After a pause, Miriam faced them. "We should divide our search. It will allow us to cover more area and potentially uncover valuable information, whether Valenstrom is here or not."

Kraken's mouth flew open in protest, but Miriam had already disappeared down one of the hallways while Izzy silently slipped away into another. He exhaled deeply before reluctantly reaching for his gun. The weight was heavy in his hand as he made his way down a different corridor. The glass-paneled walls of the labs gave way to plain drywall and dark wooden doors, creating a sense of foreboding.

Kraken grabbed one of the handles and twisted.

The room had a faint scent of polish and wood with a hint

of stale air. He could make out rows of chairs arranged around a long table, shadows dancing on the walls. A spark of realization shot through him. This was a meeting room. With luck, he'd stumbled upon the right place.

He caught sight of a door down the hallway. Faint light seeped through the narrow gap at its base. Kraken's heart thumped with anticipation. Maybe Aja was telling the truth. Perhaps Elder Statesman Valenstrom was waiting behind this very door.

He activated his com-tacts. "I may have found something. I located the meeting rooms, and one has the lights on."

Kraken's hand stretched toward the metal doorknob, cool and smooth against his fingertips. He hesitated, sensing something was off. The door was unlatched. With a deep breath, he pushed it open.

The room was minimalist yet imposing, furnished with sleek black furniture and equipped with cutting-edge holographic displays. Everywhere he looked, he saw the company's logo: a stylized 'NI' emblazoned with a double helix.

But what truly caught his attention was the figure slumped in one of the chairs.

His blood ran cold.

The stench of copper hung heavily, overpowering and metallic. Elder Statesman Valenstrom appeared almost serene, as if he'd drifted off to sleep, except for the clean slash glistening across his carotid artery. Splatters of crimson painted the table and floor.

Kraken crept to his side, placing two fingers against the man's neck despite knowing better.

Dead.

Shit.

This was a trap.

The hallway lights flickered and turned a foreboding red. A piercing alarm echoed through the air. The sickly light flooded into the room, bathing it in an eerie glow.

Kraken raced into the hallway. "It's a trap! We need to get out of here. Hello? Miriam? Izzy? Anyone? Hello?"

The comms channel buzzed with static, a harsh contrast to the deafening alarm. Kraken strained to hear any response. Then, amidst the static, a broken transmission crackled through, barely audible.

"...trap...Enforcers...overrun...get out!" Miriam's voice.

Her words were distorted, fragmented by interference, but the urgency was unmistakable. Gunshots echoed from somewhere nearby.

Swearing under his breath, he took off toward the source of chaos, adrenaline coursing through his veins. "Miriam! Izzy!"

He rounded a corner and skidded to a halt. Before him, the walls began to close off his path. Panic surged as he realized he was trapped. With desperate strength, Kraken turned and sprinted down a narrow passageway. The walls seemed alive, pulsating and undulating. They closed around him, forcing him onto their chosen trajectory.

Kraken reached a T-junction where two Enforcers blocked his way, weapons raised and ready. Without hesitation, he leaped back around the corner just as energy blasts whizzed past, narrowly missing his head. The air crackled where the shots had been, leaving scorch marks on the wall behind him.

They had good weapons.

He pressed his back against the wall, breathing hard. *The corridor ahead is a dead end. No side passages. No cover between me and them. I'll have to go through them or turn back and try another route.* But turning back meant losing time, and time meant Miriam and Izzy were in deeper trouble.

Another energy blast scorched the corner above his head. Kraken flinched, feeling the heat radiate against his scalp. They were advancing.

He peeked around the corner. The Enforcers moved with skillful coordination, one providing cover while the other advanced in short, controlled bursts. Military training. *Maybe Project Prometheus survivors...or at least trained by them.*

Something about the lead Enforcer's movements set off alarm bells in Kraken's head. Too fluid. Too fast. His eyes caught the subtle tells: the way the man's legs moved with slightly exaggerated range of motion, the springiness in his steps. *Muscle enhancement. Probably fast-twitch fiber modification for explosive speed.*

The second Enforcer hung back, weapon steady. *That one's the real threat. Calm. Patient. Probably the one with the better aim.*

Kraken's fingers tightened on his pistol grip. *Conventional firearms against energy weapons. I'll need to make every shot count.* He ran a quick mental inventory: twelve rounds left in the magazine. One in the chamber.

The enhanced Enforcer surged forward suddenly, closing half the distance in a blur of motion. Kraken jerked back as another blast cratered the wall where his head had been. Chunks of concrete rained down.

His pulse hammered against his ribs, but it wasn't panic. The familiar sensation washed over him—adrenaline. His vision sharpened, the dim corridor suddenly rendered in crystal clarity. Every shadow, every texture of the pitted walls, every micro-movement of the Enforcers—it all flooded his consciousness at once. Time didn't slow, exactly, but his perception of it stretched like taffy, giving him space to think between each pounding heartbeat.

The implants are working. He could feel them now, a soft hum at the base of his skull where they'd carved into his infant brain. Lines of data flickered at the edges of his vision—trajectory calculations, probability trees branching and pruning in real-time. His pupils dilated without conscious command, drinking in every photon of light.

Kraken took a breath. Held it. Then he moved.

He swung low around the corner, already firing. Three shots

in rapid succession. The enhanced Enforcer twisted with inhuman speed, but Kraken had already seen the dodge coming. His brain had mapped out three possible evasion patterns and picked the most likely. His second shot caught the man in the shoulder, spinning him. The third punched through his knee.

The Enforcer went down hard, but even falling, he was fast. His hand snapped up with his weapon. Kraken was already diving forward, using the falling body as cover. An energy blast seared over his back, close enough that he felt his jacket smolder.

The second Enforcer adjusted aim, tracking Kraken's roll. Too calm. Too steady. Kraken's eyes locked on the man's face, and his stomach dropped. *He's not blinking.* Ocular modification. *Enhanced visual processing, maybe even tactical overlay implants feeding him targeting data. Great. I'm fighting someone with the same kind of shit wired into their head.*

Kraken came up on one knee behind a support pillar. Not much cover, but enough. The enhanced Enforcer on the ground was struggling to rise despite the knee wound. *Tough bastard.* The shoulder shot should have disabled his weapon arm, but he was compensating, switching hands.

Two targets, limited ammunition, and they had him pinned. *Think, Kraken. Think.*

An idea sparked. *These Enforcers have military-grade equipment. Military-grade equipment has wireless protocols for coordination.* Protocols he could potentially exploit.

He blinked twice in rapid succession, activating his comtacts' infiltration suite—a custom program he'd written years ago during a particularly boring stakeout. Lines of code cascaded across his vision, overlaying the corridor like a ghost in his eyes. His implants reached out, invisible fingers searching for active signals in the electromagnetic spectrum. There. Two nodes pulsed in his peripheral vision like glowing embers.

Encrypted, but encryption was just math. *And I've always been good at math.*

But it would take time. Time he didn't have.

The patient Enforcer fired again. The energy blast clipped the pillar, superheating the concrete. Kraken felt the wave of heat roll over him, tasted the pungent smell of vaporized stone. Another shot. Then another. The pillar was disintegrating under sustained fire, chunks falling away to expose him inch by inch.

The wounded Enforcer was on his feet now, limping but mobile. He raised his weapon with his off-hand.

Can't crack their encryption in time. Kraken made a decision. *But I can do something simpler.*

He sent out a blanket electromagnetic pulse through his implants. His skull ached as the cyber-warfare tech in his medial temporal lobe flared hot, pushing out a wave of interference. Not strong enough to fry their equipment permanently, but enough to cause static. *Enough to give me a window.*

Both Enforcers hesitated. Just a fraction of a second, but Kraken saw it—their movements hitching, their aim wavering as their tactical overlays flickered and their targeting systems hiccupped.

That's all I need.

He burst from cover, pistol up. His first shot took the wounded Enforcer in the chest, center mass. The man's body armor absorbed most of it, but the impact knocked him backward into the wall. His weapon clattered to the floor.

The second Enforcer recovered fast, swinging his energy weapon toward Kraken. But Kraken was already moving, closing the distance with every ounce of speed his enhanced muscles could give him. The barrel of the energy weapon tracked him. Kraken could almost see the targeting reticle in the man's augmented vision, could feel it trying to lock onto his center mass. His hand shot out and grabbed the weapon, shoving it aside just as it discharged. The blast went wide, scorching the ceiling.

At this range, Kraken's reflexes were the advantage. The Enforcer was strong, but Kraken's nervous system processed movement faster, his muscle fibers contracted quicker. He brought his pistol up under the Enforcer's chin and fired twice. The man dropped like a puppet with cut strings.

Kraken spun back to the wounded Enforcer, who was fumbling for his dropped weapon. Kraken put two rounds in his head before he could reach it.

Silence fell, broken only by the alarm's distant wail and Kraken's heavy breathing. His jacket was still smoking from the near-miss. *Life just has this habit of trying to fuck me over.* He approached the bodies carefully, checking to make sure they were down. His hands trembled slightly now that the adrenaline was fading, the genetic modifications releasing their grip on his nervous system.

Kraken knelt beside the patient Enforcer and inspected the energy weapon. Fingerprint activation pad on the grip. Retinal scanner on the sight. Military-grade biometric locks. *Would've been nice to take one of these, but it's useless without the proper genetic signature.* He left it behind, forcing himself to stand on legs that suddenly felt like water.

His com-tacts display showed eight rounds remaining in the corner of his vision. *Not good.*

Kraken stood, trying to orient himself in the maze of corridors. The implants helped, mapping out the turns he'd taken, but the layout was deliberately confusing. The alarm continued its piercing wail as he carried on through winding halls. After two more turns, he came to a spacious room with an unclear purpose. The only indicators were a hazard sign on the door and a sealed observation room he couldn't access through the reinforced window.

Always promising.

As he stepped into the room, Kraken surveyed the

jumbled assortment of objects and tools cluttering the space. Like a graveyard for malfunctioning technology, mixed with an array of weapons. This room seemed to serve as a testing area, perhaps even the epicenter of Nassar Industries' experiments.

A chill ran down his spine as he suddenly felt a presence watching him. He quickly scanned the area, freezing when his gaze landed on a familiar face staring back with piercing intensity.

His eyes widened. His lips parted in a voiceless question.

Standing before him was Yin.

Chapter 30

The lab hummed with the steady rhythm of machinery, antiseptic sharp in the air. Stainless steel countertops stretched along the walls, crowded with sophisticated equipment whose purposes Yin understood but didn't care about. High-resolution monitors displayed genetic sequences in cascading lines of code. Bioprinters whirred in the background.

Yin lay inside the TriScan 5000, a cocoon-shaped pod whose composite shell was both lightweight and durable. LED lights pulsed softly along its interior, casting ethereal patterns across her vision. The pod combined MRI, CT, and ultrasound capabilities, processing massive amounts of data through its AI system to provide rapid diagnostic information.

None of which mattered to Yin.

She stared at the ceiling, waiting for the machine to finish its work. This was the latest in a series of tests Aja had ordered: CBC panels, biochemical analysis, tissue biopsy, cerebrospinal fluid examination, electroencephalogram. Each one attempted to identify the nanobots destroying her from within.

The pod clicked open.

Yin sat up and swung her legs over the side. Her bare feet met the cool floor. Aja entered the room with the Project Gemini file clutched in their hands. They hadn't released it since Yin had handed it over.

"The imaging came out excellent," Aja said. "Once all of the data is compiled, it is simply a matter of doing the procedure."

"Then it will be done shortly." Yin watched Aja's gestures, searching for tells. When she'd first contacted them, Aja had agreed immediately to her request for help. Too immediately. They hadn't disclosed their terms, and Yin was certain the file alone wouldn't purchase her survival. Her lips pressed together. Aja's face revealed nothing.

"It can be done tonight." Aja tucked the file under their arm with a dismissive wave. "However, I already have plans for the evening. Some loose ends that need to be tied up. So, unfortunately, it will have to wait."

Yin's eyes narrowed. "What kind of plans?"

A smirk crossed Aja's face. They maintained a careful distance between them, the space measured and deliberate. Uneasy allies, each waiting for the other to make the first fatal move.

"Elder Statesman Valenstrom is coming to meet with me tonight. We have conflicting ideologies, and his close relationship with the supreme chancellor has been causing issues." They sighed, pinching the bridge of their nose. "Debating with him takes up so much of my time."

The subtext was clear. Yin straightened, raising her chin. "You want me to assassinate him so he is no longer an obstacle. You mean to take his place."

Statement, not question.

Aja shrugged. "He will be arriving this evening for dinner and waiting for me in a meeting room on the lab floor. Nassar Industries has strict security measures, so he won't have any guards with him. It would be unfortunate if an incident were to occur."

"Who will assume responsibility for this incident? How do you plan on diverting suspicion from yourself?"

Aja's eyes brightened with something that might have been satisfaction. "Oh, that..." A pause for effect. "The elder statesman is not the only problem I have to deal with. There are other guests arriving tonight—the terrorist group who call themselves revolutionaries. It's a perfect opportunity to take out two threats at once."

Something tightened in Yin's stomach. Physical and uncomfortable. Memories surfaced without permission: sewers after escaping pursuit, standing naked in the laundromat, greasy restaurant booths, popcorn and soap operas. Home. Kraken. The word carried weight, like a pressure against her chest. She forced a breath and pushed the memories down, focusing on tactical considerations instead.

"They shall come as a group. They are not careless, and many of them are powerful Recombinants."

"I have a squad of Enforcers ready to back you up. They are all Recombinants from a previous military operation." Aja inclined their head. "Remember, these outliers were willing to barter you for my assistance. You heard them yourself. They are not on your side."

Neither are you.

Yin nodded, dropping her gaze to the floor. She studied the polished tiles, counting flecks of color on their surface. Killing the elder statesman posed no moral complication. Killing in general didn't bother her. But this aching sensation that kept appearing, this unwanted intrusion of feeling, needed to end.

According to Aja's theory, the nanobots attacking her genetic code were causing suppressed emotions to resurface. Emotions her Creator had edited out or buried during the modification procedures. Aja's procedure would stop the nanobots and prevent further damage.

It would end this feeling.

Yin looked up. "If I help you with your problems, will you perform the procedure tonight?"

Aja nodded. Their hand came to rest on the file tucked under their arm. "After these problems are resolved, we can focus on our mutual problem." Their grip tightened on the folder. "Once you are repaired to full strength, you can destroy this so-called Subject Omega. I am confident in that."

Subject Omega. Yang.

Yin understood without further explanation. She moved toward the exit. Aja stepped aside to let her pass.

The hallway stretched before her, glass walls reflecting her passage. She'd walked these corridors enough times during her stay here that the layout had burned itself into memory. A map she could navigate blind.

The weight in her chest persisted. Yin sighed and placed a hand over her heart, feeling the steady rhythm beneath her palm. She lingered, using the time to prepare herself.

This would be her final encounter with Kraken.

Chapter 31

Kraken's breath caught in his throat. His pulse hammered against his ribs as disbelief gave way to something that threatened to split his chest open.

Yin.

Alive. Whole. Standing ten feet away in the dimly lit space.

The relief hit him so hard his knees nearly buckled. He'd searched every alley in Old Town, every abandoned building in Scraptown, hacked every database he could access. Days of nothing. Days of wondering if he'd lost her forever. And now she was here. The grin spread before he could stop it, muscles in his face remembering how after days of worry had locked them rigid. His feet carried him forward across the debris-strewn floor, arms opening in welcome.

"Yin." Her name came out rough. "What are you doing here?"

The question triggered something darker. His stride faltered. This was Aja's domain. Yin shouldn't be here.

"Are you being held captive? It's okay. I'm here to help. We can—"

The impact crushed the air from his lungs.

Kraken's body folded around her fist, his ribs compressing under a force that felt like getting hit by a train. The room tilted. Colors bled together as his vision smeared. He registered weightlessness, then the wall meeting his spine with a crack that lit up every nerve. Plaster crumbled. Dust billowed. His back screamed where concrete had punched into flesh.

He wheezed. He couldn't pull air into his compressed lungs, and his tongue throbbed. He'd sliced it with his teeth. Blood pooled in his mouth, warm and thick. He spat it onto the floor and looked up through watering eyes.

"Yin..."

She was already moving, closing the distance with that speed that had nearly killed him in Scraptown.

His reflexes fired before conscious thought. He threw himself sideways. Yin's fist punched through the wall where his head had been, sending concrete fragments spinning. One sliced his cheek. Pain flared along his ribs as he stumbled back, boots skidding on debris.

The adrenaline hit. His vision sharpened until he could track individual dust motes. The pain dulled but didn't disappear. His muscles coiled. His hands trembled, not from fear but from the surge of emotions his modifications couldn't regulate. Hurt. Shock. Confusion.

"Yin, stop." The words came out steadily. "What are you doing?"

Nothing. No response. Her eyes held no recognition. No trace of the person who'd sat beside him on his couch, who'd organized his closet with military accuracy, who'd quoted *The Godfather* to create a distraction. Just that ice-cold glare as she closed the distance, body tense.

They circled each other in the wreckage. Kraken's heart

twisted even as his combat training cataloged threats and calculated angles.

"I don't want to fight."

One final plea.

She lunged.

Kraken dodged. Air cracked where her strike passed. He countered with a kick. She spun away, movements flowing like in the training footage he'd seen of her in Dr. Izumi's lab. Before they'd broken her.

Each strike resonated through the room. The floor trembled. Dust swirled thick enough to coat his throat. The force of her attacks sent vibrations through the air that made his teeth ache. Testing equipment toppled. Glass shattered.

Every block felt like his arm might snap. His forearms burned where her strikes connected. His muscles screamed. One clean hit to his head and even his modifications wouldn't save him.

Sweat stung his eyes. The taste of iron never left his mouth. They moved at a brutal tempo. His reflexes against her speed. She flowed around his attacks, body twisting and spinning in a blur of motion. His breath came harder.

I can't keep this up. One mistake and I'm dead.

He waited for the opening.

When she struck high, he caught her arm and twisted. Pulled her against his chest and locked his grip. She thrashed with frightening strength. Her head snapped back toward his face. He jerked away, adjusting his hold.

"Why are you doing this?" The words came out ragged against her ear. Sweat dripped from his forehead. "Is it Aja? Are they forcing you? Please, let me help you."

"Stop acting like a fool."

The shout cut through him. Then she went slack, all the fight draining from her. They both dragged air into burning lungs. Silence stretched between them.

"I heard you." Her voice was quieter now. She glanced

back. "Your conversation with Miriam. I know that you—all of you—intended to use me as leverage."

The words hit harder than her fists.

Kraken's face twisted. The guilt he'd buried came roaring back. He'd spent days telling himself he would have found another way. That he'd never actually go through with it. But she'd heard him agree. Heard him choose the Outsiders over her. He met her stare and saw something beneath the accusation. Something that looked like hurt. Her eyes, usually hard as steel, had gone soft. Vulnerable.

It was worse than any wound she could have inflicted.

The admission felt like swallowing broken glass. "I... I... Yes. You're right."

His grip loosened.

Yin whirled. Her hand flashed to his holster. The gun cleared leather before he could process the movement. She swung it down. Metal cracked against bone. His head snapped back. Pain exploded through his skull, and darkness crept in. He hit the ground hard. The impact jarred every injury. His ears rang.

He couldn't move. His body was lead. But more than the physical damage, guilt pinned him. The same guilt that had eaten at him since that conversation with Miriam. The guilt of knowing he'd become the kind of person who could sacrifice a friend for the greater good. Just like the government had sacrificed him when they'd thrown him into foster care. Just like his real parents had sacrificed him for Project Binary. The cycle never ended.

But she didn't strike again.

The silence pressed down on him.

Kraken forced his eyes open, his vision swimming. Yin stood over him, backlit by fluorescent lights. He pushed himself to his knees, trembling. When he looked at her face, the vulnerability was gone. Her expression had returned to that familiar emptiness.

Static hissed from the intercom above.

"Well done." Aja's voice poured through the speakers. Kraken looked past Yin to the observation room. Aja stood behind the reinforced window, satisfaction written across their features. "It is a pleasure to finally meet face-to-face, Kraken. What a shame it's the last time." They shifted to Yin. "Kill him."

"The mission is to capture them, not kill them," Yin said.

"Not for this one. A point must be made."

Kraken's eyes narrowed. He'd accepted death. Made peace with it during the walk through these corridors. But did Aja have to watch? Did they have to gloat, taking credit for Yin's victory as if they'd orchestrated everything? He looked back at her as she raised the gun. Her finger rested just above the trigger.

"I never intended to let them go through with it. Using you."

His chest loosened. His voice wavered but held. The lie sat uncomfortably even as the truth of it settled over him. He'd used her from the start, hadn't he? That first encounter in Scraptown, when he'd seen her lying there and thought about scrap parts. When he'd brought her home, hoping she'd be an asset to the Outsiders. Every calculation, every plan to convince her to fight for their cause.

But somewhere between the laundromat and the soap operas, between her organizing his closet and sitting with him when he'd bled out his past, it had stopped being strategy. If he could go back, he'd still bring her home. He'd still offer her a place to stay. But he'd do it honestly, without ulterior motives. If these were his last words, he wouldn't leave anything unsaid.

"Yin, you are my friend. My best friend." The declaration came out firm. Kraken leaned forward until his forehead pressed against the barrel. His eyes locked on hers. "If you truly believe I would betray you like that, then go ahead and pull the trigger."

"Give him what he wants," Aja crooned.

Kraken didn't look away from Yin. Death had come for him before, in Markus's territory, in the prison break, and in a dozen other fights. It could have him now.

"What are you waiting for?"

Each second stretched. The air hung heavy between them. Then, slowly, the gun lowered. Yin's hand closed around his arm. She pulled him to his feet. Kraken released his held breath and managed a small smile despite the blood on his lip. She returned it with a look that said more than words before turning toward the observation room.

Her fist shattered the laminated glass.

The reinforced window exploded inward. Aja jerked back. Yin aimed the gun at them through the destroyed barrier.

"We are taking you hostage," Yin stated. Kraken moved through the debris to stand beside her. "You will complete the procedure in exchange for your life. Even if you refuse to comply, I will not end your life now. I will simply torture you until you decide to comply." Her eyes went dark. "And you are well aware of my capability in that."

Aja's expression hardened. Their mouth twisted. Their hands clenched before rising in surrender.

"Fine." The word came out through gritted teeth. "I'm your hostage now."

Chapter 32

The surgical rooms were adjacent to the labs and equipped with everything necessary to perform procedures. Filtered air maintained optimal temperature and humidity. Sterile. Controlled. Each suite featured an operating table surrounded by robotic arms with specialized instruments. Monitors mounted on adjustable arms provided real-time imaging and vital sign readouts. The ergonomic layout and the strategically placed lighting were designed to minimize glare.

Yin sat on the smooth metallic table and tugged at the pastel medical gown covering her. The fabric seemed foreign against her skin. *Wrong.* Her eyes drifted to her neatly folded clothes nearby. The robe rested on top. She'd taken it as a disguise during the raid. It had accompanied her through Scraptown, through the sewers, and through every moment since her escape. Wearing it offered something she couldn't quite name. Security, perhaps. Comfort. She hadn't experienced attachment to objects when she lived in the lab. She wasn't sure it was a feeling she could have processed then.

Yin's gaze shifted between Kraken, who stood in the corner attempting to communicate with his team, and Aja, who calibrated the machines with barely contained fury. Yin didn't know the fate of the other Outsiders. She'd incapacitated them and left them to the Enforcers. Her fingers traced the necklace Nari had given her, lingering over the small robot charm. Even as a complete stranger, Nari had treated her with kindness. Yin's eyes lost focus.

And look how I repaid her.

"Dammit. I can't get through the communication jam." Kraken muttered curses under his breath. He scratched the back of his head and crossed to her, arms crossed, frown etched deep. Worry creased his forehead, his eyes darting in frustration. She wished she had a solution for him. His expression softened, and he met her gaze with a supportive smile. "How are you feeling? Ready to be all fixed up?"

The operating table was cool under Yin's fingers as she traced its surface. This was her purpose. Her mission. To be fixed and restored to who she once was. But as she imagined the outcome, doubts surfaced. "If I go through with this surgery..." Her voice trailed off, eyes fell. "I will be fixed, but at what cost? What if I am no longer myself?"

Her grip tightened on the table's edge. The metal pressed into her palms, video clips flashing through her mind of the girl who had been herself—the girl robbed of choice. Yin set her jaw. That girl deserved to be whole again. She drew a breath. "And what if you no longer like who I become?"

The question hung between them. Silent moments marched by. Then, warmth rushed over her as Kraken's hand closed around her wrist and pulled her into his embrace. Heat radiated from his body, filling the space between them. Yin's eyes widened, and she stiffened, caught off guard. Her own words echoed in her mind: "*When humans want to be reassuring to another human, they hug them. Isn't that right, Kraken?*"

Kraken's heartbeat thrummed against hers. A steady rhythm that eased the tension in her muscles. This was...friendship. Something she hadn't ever known. Something explained to her as weakness. Her surprised expression melted into something gentler. Yin rested her head on his shoulder and allowed herself to surrender.

"Thanks...Theo..." The words were soft, filled with something she was still learning to name.

The medical cart jolted against the operating table. Yin recoiled from Kraken's embrace. Aja stood beside it, expression tight, arms crossed, foot tapping on the tiled floor. "It's time to begin the procedure. Your companion needs to leave." They gestured toward Kraken, who shot them a dark glare. "Don't look at me like that. You're the one with the gun."

Kraken raised two fingers to his eyes and pointed them at Aja. Silent message delivered. He turned and strode to the door with a last glance at Yin. "I'll be right outside."

He smiled and waved. Then he was gone. The door closed, and Yin only broke her focus when Aja tapped the table. She lay down. Aja raised a syringe. "Anesthetic. This will sedate you, but you'll stay conscious. I can't risk you thrashing around and breaking equipment if this causes pain."

They injected the medication into her IV. After three minutes, the drug began to work, and Yin's muscles loosened. Her thoughts grew sluggish.

"I'm surprised you chose his side based on an emotional appeal," Aja commented.

Yin countered, "You are hardly someone I consider an ally."

"I didn't say that." Aja turned her onto her side. "I only meant it was out of character. You are a being built on logic and evidence. Logically, all you know is he intended to betray you. Anyone can say they didn't mean it."

Yin was too tired to debate. She could barely keep her eyelids from drooping. Aja fiddled with the machinery, and the hum of electricity filled the space.

"There will be three injections into the cervicomedullary junction," Aja explained. "The first contains a neutralizing agent that will target the nanobots' outer shell, destroying them. The second is a new batch of nanites programmed to repair any defects before naturally degrading from your system. Your memories should return, and as I'd mentioned, you may regain some emotionality as a result of the procedure." A beat of silence. Then a grumble. "That idiot Ryūnosuke worried far too much about your emotions."

And the third? Had she asked? She couldn't remember if Aja had explained the third injection. The machine's arms lowered over her, rotating toward the base of her neck. After the first slid into her skin, Yin lost track of time. When she opened her eyes again, the machine whirred as it moved to administer another injection. She licked her dry lips. Her voice was hoarse. "Wait. What's the third injection?"

"The third injection?" Aja's voice turned coy. They loomed closer. Their voice lowered. "The third injection will make you forget that insipid fool outside and his poor influence on you."

Yin's eyes widened.

"Is something going to transpire?"

Her instincts screamed for escape. Overwhelming.

Her Creator approached with purposeful strides.

She fought, but her limbs refused to move.

He grabbed her ponytail, forcing her head back and jamming something into the back of her neck. "Run, Project Gemini. Run away and die. You won't be able to tell that cunt or anyone else a damn thing about what happened here."

A loud crash. Yin lay on the ground. Medical supplies

scattered around her. She dug her fingers into the floor and dragged herself toward the door. Footsteps followed her.

It all whited out.

"No..." Yin whimpered. Her hand reached out. "No... Theo..."

She blacked out. When she awoke, her ears rang with the sound of a gunshot. The smell of smoke filled her nostrils. Her eyes opened. Kraken stood in front of her, his gun still smoking.

"You take one more step towards her and the next one won't just graze your fingers." He inched closer to Yin. Kraken knelt and pulled her to her feet, steadying her against him. He brought his lips inches from her ear. "Are you okay?"

"Theo..." Yin mumbled in relief and nodded. The fog in her brain dissipated.

Aja gripped their hand tight, face twisted into a scowl. The medical cart lay on its side, spilling supplies onto the floor. There, just a few feet away, lay a broken vial and syringe. "You're a fool, you and your band of vagabonds. Your understanding of what's going on in this world is myopic. You can overthrow the government, but you won't save Ignis. Humanity is dying." They gestured to Yin. "It is the only thing that might save us."

"Not at the cost of her life." Kraken shook his head. His grip on her tightened. "No. Humanity can find another way."

"It is Synthetic. It has no life to forfeit."

"Will you just shut up?" Kraken snarled.

The sound of blaring alarms filled the air, drowning out any further conversation. The screeching reverberated through the room. Vibrations pulsed through Yin's body. Bright red flashing lights added to the urgency and chaos. The holographic screens sprang to life, revealing the approaching threat. One of the walls meant to trap intruders crumbled at Yang's hand. Yin sucked in a sharp breath.

It's time.

"Who is that?" Kraken asked, lowering his firearm.

"Death," Yin said. She tested her physical capabilities. Her muscles quivered as she attempted to stand without Kraken's assistance. From the corner of her vision, Aja slinking away.

Kraken's gaze snapped to them. He aimed his gun, halting them. "Where do you think you're going? I should shoot you where you stand."

"But you won't." Aja raised their hands, eyes narrowing. "I'm your chance at escape...and finding your team."

Yin stayed silent. Her eyes lingered on Kraken, studying his clenched jaw and tightly gripped gun. Aja's fate no longer mattered to her. But she understood how much the other Outsiders meant to him. This decision rested with him. Yin would stand by whatever he chose. Still a good soldier to her commander. The only pressing factor remained time, which was running out.

Finally, Kraken muttered a curse. His hand snapped to his holster, and he nestled his weapon back into place. In one fluid motion, he scooped Yin up into his arms, securing her against his chest. The sudden movement caught her off guard, but she didn't protest. He grabbed her neatly folded clothes and placed them on her stomach. Yin placed her hand over them, to secure them. She ran her fingers over the silky material of her robe, finding comfort in its familiar touch.

Kraken turned to Aja. "Go," he commanded.

"Right. Okay." They kept their hands raised. With deliberate movements, Aja stepped toward a nearby cart. "Let me just..." They kept their posture relaxed as they grabbed the Project Gemini file and nestled it underneath their arm. "...grab something."

Aja took the lead, navigating through the constantly shifting corridors. Their lithe form weaved through the narrow passageways. The alarms shrieked. Red lights flashed. The walls pulsed, closing in at every turn, but Aja's knowledge of the maze allowed them to move with ease. Their footsteps were drowned out by the cacophony of crashing walls echoing through the halls. A clear warning of the danger drawing nearer.

Yin shuddered. Her energy crept back, but her body remained vulnerable from its recent reconfiguration. Her stomach churned. A slight pulsing in her head hinted at the tireless efforts of the nanites within her. She rested her head on Kraken's chest. Even if they managed to escape this place, she knew Yang would never give up. The only way to end it all was to give Yang what she wanted.

Her.

The elevator appeared before them. A shining silver beacon. Their way out of the labyrinth of trap walls and deadly Synthetics. Aja's finger pressed the 'Up' button, illuminating it with bright red light. Yin gestured for Kraken to put her down, but he gave her a confused look.

"What do you mean? You're not strong enough yet," he protested.

"Put me down, Kraken."

Kraken obeyed reluctantly and eased Yin to the ground. Her feet touched the icy surface. The elevator chimed, and its doors slid open with a mechanical whir. It was the same one she had used after incapacitating Nari and Nori, who had guarded the lobby. Her hand drifted to the trinket on her necklace. A prick of something like regret surfaced. Enough to force her gaze away.

"You and Aja need to go."

"What?"

"Take Aja and go," she repeated, clutching her clothing tightly.

"Not without you. Yin, I can't leave you down here alone. You—"

Yin whirled on him. "This situation is not your concern."

She blinked, surprised at the harshness of her own words. Kraken stood frozen, eyes wide. Yin composed herself, standing tall. "You need to get your team back. They're counting on you. This is my issue to handle." She paused before placing a hand on his arm. "Go." When he didn't move, she shoved him. "Go!"

Aja made a frustrated sound and grabbed the back of Kraken's jacket, yanking him into the elevator. They locked eyes with Yin and exchanged a knowing look, raising a tepid brow. As the metal doors slid closed, Yin allowed her eyes to drift to Kraken. He was pale, his face twisted with conflicting emotions. The moment filled with something bittersweet. Tinged with sadness and muted acceptance. Yin smiled. *You are my friend, too. Good-bye, Theo.*

Yin's fingers trailed over the cool metal doors once they closed. She glanced down at her surgical gown, ripped it off and cast it aside. She pulled on her T-shirt and sweats before pulling her hair back into a low ponytail with the hair-tie she had kept on her wrist. The final piece was the robe. Her fingers glided over the fabric one last time, recalling her journey. Slipping into the silky garment, she tied it in the middle, savoring its softness against her skin.

Something shifted within her. Yin's gasp was sharp and sudden. Her hand clutched at her chest. Her body doubled over, but the expression on her face was one of relief. A metamorphosis. A transformation from a heavy burden into a deep release. She slowly straightened again. She balled her hand into a fist over her heart and closed her eyes.

Whole.

Chapter 33

THE ELEVATOR ROSE WITHOUT A SOUND. KRAKEN FIDGETED, unable to tear his eyes from where the doors had closed. Beside him, Aja stood rigidly, clutching the file against their chest. Their focus fixated on the numbers ticking above the door.

His breath hitched, shallow and rapid. The world around him muffled, his attention trapped on racing thoughts. As the doors had shut, she'd shot him a look filled with finality. Whatever lurked down there was powerful, and Yin wasn't fully recovered. His hands balled into fists at his sides. His nails dug into his palms.

I left her behind.

"You didn't know." Kraken stiffened. He turned to Aja, but their gaze remained fixed ahead. "She never told you about the other half of Project Gemini." Aja's lips curved into a wry smile. Their expression darkened, voice tinged with spite. "I guess that's why it's called Gemini."

The last statement wasn't aimed at him. At least, he didn't

get that impression. Kraken ran his fingers over his holster and sighed. "Just tell me where my team is."

Aja didn't answer, their eyes distant.

The elevator chimed, and the doors parted, revealing the dark lobby. They exited with Kraken close behind. Aja paused and pivoted. "They are en route to Pyreford Penitentiary. The same facility your gang destroyed, if my memory serves me right. The transport vehicle is departing from the back bay soon."

Kraken grimaced. Infiltrating the prison as a team was one challenge. Going in alone was another. He stepped forward, gesturing to the Project Gemini file in Aja's arms. "Hand it over."

Aja's hold tightened. They stepped back and shook their head. "You told me to find another way to save humanity. This file is one piece of that puzzle." They continued to retreat as Kraken lowered his hand, frowning.

"Does C.A.R.E. truly believe that humanity is going extinct?" he asked. "The Traditionalists claim it's propaganda meant to control Ignis citizens."

Aja stopped in front of an exit door, their hand resting on the push handle. "You should know better than to take the word of the Traditionalists. As the saying goes...history is written by the victors of war." They began to leave, only pausing to add, "Project Gemini contains both the Alpha and the Omega. What you saw down there was the Omega, which is useless for my purposes but dangerous. The Alpha might stand a chance against it if it were in better condition. It's curious. Alpha was designed to have a strong self-preservation instinct. And yet, it threw itself away for you."

Despite the sharp pain piercing his chest, Kraken pushed it aside and focused on the task ahead. He shoved through a separate exit door. The outside world blurred around him. His feet pounded against hard pavement as he raced toward the back docks. Kraken arrived as the IPD transport unit lifted off, engines roaring as it propelled itself into the sky. He spat a curse and ran after it, dodging people and obstacles. He activated his com-tacts and hacked into the IPD system to track the unit's movements before making a call.

"Kraken, buddy," rang Gabriel's cheery voice. "What's up?"

"Are you in the Inner Ring?"

"Whoa. Are you in a marathon? You sound like you're running."

"Are you in the Inner Ring?" he repeated, voice rising.

A pause. "Yeah, why?"

Kraken skirted around a corner. "Listen. I'm sending you a track on an IPD transport unit. I need you to help me bring it down."

"Bring it down?" Gabriel asked, incredulous. "How do you expect me to do that?"

"I don't know. You're resourceful. Think of something," Kraken said. "Nari is inside."

He hung up, heart pounding as he navigated through the busy streets. His eyes locked onto the IPD unit soaring high above him, its sleek metallic exterior reflecting the dim light.

The city bustled with activity. Hover cars zipped by. People began their morning routines. Kraken pushed himself faster, muscles straining with each step. He scanned his surroundings for any means to follow the craft. A glimmer of metal caught his eye. A parked hover bike sat on the side of the road.

Without hesitation, he bolted toward it and hopped on, hacking into its interface and starting the engine. With a whir, the vehicle rose off the ground and launched him forward onto the invisible roadway. Kraken bypassed the bike's navigation and communication system, giving himself full control, and disabled its variable altitude control. He revved the engine, tilted the handlebars, and soared into the air. Wind roared in his ears and tugged at his clothes. The holographic display on the bike illuminated in red, displaying several urgent warnings he ignored.

As Kraken approached the IPD unit, bringing it down safely was the main concern. He couldn't risk causing a crash. He had no control over their descent. The unit might collide with one of the city's buildings and cause casualties. His weapon wouldn't work against the sturdy glass protecting the pilots inside, so intimidation tactics were useless. He might have the strength to break the glass himself, but if the unit shifted and threw him, he would fall to his death.

Various possibilities ran through his mind as he trailed the transport unit. A dark cloud materialized in their path, expanding by the second. Its odd movements piqued his curiosity. He leaned forward and squinted, trying to make out what caused the strange phenomenon. As the cloud swelled, faint grunting noises reached his ears. Pigeons? His jaw dropped. Was that a massive swarm of pigeons?

He wasn't alone in his confusion. The IPD unit halted and hung motionless in the air, facing the swarm. It hung suspended for what stretched into an eternity, as if the pilots were weighing their choices. It descended. Kraken followed, taking his hover bike to the ground and parking it across the street.

Pigeons dominated the sky. They had taken over every inch of the city, causing chaos everywhere. They covered every surface and filled the air with frenzied cries. A cacophony of feathers and screeches deafened all other sounds. Around him, people screamed and ran for shelter from the Pigeonocalypse. The rush of air hit as the birds swooped past him, their wings brushing against his face and arms as he shielded himself.

He had no time to process his astonishment. The pilots had emerged from the transport unit, as stunned as everyone else. Their mouths hung open in disbelief. Kraken used the loud squalls to mask his movements as he charged toward them. With a swift motion, he seized their heads and slammed them together. They collapsed onto the ground, unconscious. Kraken took in the situation again.

"What the fuck?" he whispered, trying not to laugh.

The pigeons scattered. Whatever spell had captivated them broke. If not for the insurmountable amount of bird droppings left behind, Kraken would've doubted they had ever been there. The streets lay eerily empty except for the faint humming of the IPD transport. Someone shouted his name. Gabriel strode toward him, waving his hand. Kraken raised both brows. "Seriously? Pigeons?"

"It worked, didn't it?" Gabriel shrugged. "They're the sky's rats."

Kraken knelt next to one of the pilots to grab a set of keys. "How'd you know it was going to work?" he asked as he rounded the back of the unit.

"Your guess is as good as mine, bro. We could've ended up with actual rats."

Kraken threw open the doors. Relief escaped his lips as the familiar faces of his team stared back at him. Despite their weary appearance, they were all alive.

"Big Bro!" Nari's face lit up.

"Took you long enough," Miriam grumbled as Kraken worked to release their chains. However, her eyes twinkled with delight, and she wore a smile.

After Kraken released her, Nori flexed and shook her wrists. "We were counting on you to come after us when they didn't load you in with us. It was either that or assume you died. Needless to say, none of us wanted to believe the latter."

"Me? Die?" Kraken chuckled as he assisted Izzy out of the freezing chamber she had been confined in. "Impossible."

The group stepped out onto the pavement. Nari sprinted toward Gabriel, her long brown hair bouncing behind her. As he opened his arms, she leaped into his embrace.

Kraken's eyes glistened as he stood back, taking in the

scene of two people locked in their own world. They may not have confessed it, but the connection radiating between them was obvious, the way their bodies fit together perfectly. Something rare in these dark times.

"Isn't it just disgusting?" Miriam teased, standing next to him with her arms folded.

"Enough to make you vomit," Nori said with a smirk. "They're straight out of a soap opera."

Kraken's heart pounded. The steady beat of fear pulsed through his veins as he whispered, "Soap opera."

Yin.

She was still trapped at Nassar Industries with the Omega. Dread filled him. He wiped away the moisture threatening to fall and turned to leave, but Miriam's hand stopped him. Her fingers dug into his arm, holding tight. Confusion and concern ghosted across across her face.

"Where are you going?" Miriam asked, her brow furrowed.

"I have to return to Nassar Industries," Kraken replied, trying to shake off her grasp. "Yin needs me."

"The Synthetic?" Miriam's expression hardened. "She betrayed us."

"She saved you!" Kraken yanked his arm free and spun around to face her, his voice booming. The sudden outburst startled Gabriel and Nari out of their trance as they turned to watch.

"Big Bro?" Nari's tone carried concern.

"Kraken..." Nori watched him with sorrow.

"She saved you," Kraken repeated, this time softly as he controlled his anger. "Yin stayed behind and sacrificed herself so I could go after you. She only betrayed us because of your plan to use her, Miriam. She was protecting herself." He stepped back, toward where the hover bike was parked. "I've already let her down once. I'm not going to let it happen again."

CAENOGENESIS

Kraken ran for the hover bike. He couldn't be too late.

Chapter 34

Yin stumbled and caught herself against the wall. Hot sweat dripped down her forehead. Her veins burned as she pushed forward, occasionally gritting her teeth in determination. The memories flooded back, hitting her with devastating force, her body reacting as if she were reliving them all over again. The physical pain was manageable. The emotional anguish was not.

A surge of emotions overwhelmed her, nearly bringing her to her knees. Her breathing grew ragged and gasping as she pressed her back against the wall, clenching her fist against her chest. She squeezed her eyes shut as another wave crashed over her, her jaw clenched and body shaking. Yin grabbed her head and screamed, uncertain if any sound escaped her lips over the blaring alarms.

The alarms cut off. Yin opened her eyes, shaking the vertigo from her vision. The crackle of electricity from damaged cords reached her. Yang. Narrowing her eyes, Yin pushed off the wall and continued to tread down the now-silent hallways. A pair of reddish eyes studied her movements. The familiar quiet clicking of the machinery inside Yang reached Yin's ears. Yang's expression almost mirrored disappointment.

"You thought I was back to myself," Yin said. "That is what you waited for all this time. You wanted to face me at full power so you could prove a point." Yang said nothing. Yin edged toward one of the offshoot paths, hoping to goad Yang. "Do not worry. I can still defeat you. What? Are you scared?"

The rhythmic pounding of feet echoed through the narrow hallway as Yin took off with Yang close on her heels. Adrenaline surged through her veins, pushing aside any symptoms that threatened to slow her down. The weight of Yang's gaze burned into her back, spurring her on even faster. They were a blur of movement, their steps in sync as they raced toward the testing area.

Yin needed the extra space to maneuver, to use her agility and quick thinking to outsmart Yang. In these tight corridors, there was no room for mistakes, and she was determined to make this last as long as she could. Every step she took away from Yang was a small victory, knowing that with each passing moment, Kraken was getting farther from danger.

Yang's hot breath was on Yin's neck, but then it vanished. Yin looked over her shoulder. The hallway was empty. The hairs on her nape stood. *Something is wrong.*

Yang burst through the floor in front of her. Reacting, Yin skidded to a stop and avoided the grab. However, now Yang stood between her and the testing area, blocking her path. Yin narrowed her eyes, pivoted, and sprinted in the opposite direction. But before she took two steps, Yang once again emerged from the ground and blocked her way. Like struggling against a brick wall.

"Did you not want to put up a fight?" Yang mocked as she stepped forward. "Who is the one who is afraid?"

Yin braced herself as Yang lunged toward her. But instead

of dodging or fighting back, Yin channeled all of her energy into one concentrated force. With a burst of strength, she propelled herself upward and over Yang's head, tucking her body into a tight roll as she landed on the floor.

Yin sprang to her feet and ran, but Yang was faster than anticipated. A forceful jerk of her robe's collar yanked her backward. The ground rushed up to meet her as she crashed onto the unforgiving floor. The impact knocked the wind out of her, leaving her gulping for breath and tasting metal. Yin looked up. Yang stood over her, a fierce glint in her eyes. She twisted her body and swept her leg out in a low arc, forcing Yang to jump back. Yin leapt to her feet.

Fighting is the only option left.

With her right foot, Yin took a step back and bent her front leg, curving her right arm in front of her face. Her arms flowed in an up-down, inside-outside motion as she performed precise, dancelike sidesteps, using triangular footwork to control her movements. Her eyes locked on her opponent, who observed her every move.

When Yang launched a powerful punch toward her head, Yin flowed over and rotated her hips while slamming her hands onto the ground. With a powerful spin, she delivered a kick with her heel that connected with Yang's wrist and cast it aside. She hopped back to her original form, aiming another kick into Yang's chest to push her back.

Undeterred, Yang pressed on, launching a series of kicks and punches at Yin. But each attack was met with evasion or swift counterattack. Yin moved like water, flowing around her opponent's attacks with ease. With an explosion of energy, Yin launched herself into the air, executing a breathtaking aerial flip. As she descended, she brought her legs crashing down toward Yang's head. But Yang ducked under the attack and delivered a crushing blow to Yin's midsection.

Yin staggered back, spitting blood onto the floor as she gasped for composure. She fell on her side, the leg closest to the ground tucked to her chest, the other extended, supporting her weight with one hand. With her other arm shielding her face, she avoided a kick from Yang.

Using her supporting arm to push herself up, she swung her tucked-in leg in a roundhouse kick at Yang's face but slammed into Yang's arm as she blocked. The force sent a tremor through Yin's body. She scowled. If it had been anyone—Kraken notwithstanding—she would've shattered the arm. A surge of nausea washed over her, and her blood roared in her ears. Enough to make her hesitate.

Yang grabbed Yin's leg and began swinging her into the floor and walls. Her body jerked with each forceful hit, her bones and muscles straining under the immense pressure. Her bones creaked and groaned, close to shattering. Her skin grew raw and bruised from the impact. Her vision whited out with each strike as pain radiated throughout her body.

Yin released the tension in her muscles, relaxing. By now, Kraken was far enough away that she had accomplished her mission. He was out of harm's way. For once, she had decided based on her own desires rather than just for survival or at someone else's command. A foreign feeling, but one that brought a sense of peace and allowed her to ignore her powerful survival instinct. Black splotches dotted her vision. A sign her body was reaching its limits.

Yin smiled.

A memory surfaced out of the darkness. The restaurant. Cheeseburgers in Paradise. The three of them—Kraken, Nori, and herself—sitting in that booth, eating greasy food, and having casual conversation. She had asked what constituted a home.

"In that case, Human Kraken is my home," she had said. "I have returned to you more frequently than I have ever returned to anything else. In my previous...existence, returning was not an option. There was only being."

At the time, she hadn't understood. 'Home is where the

heart is,' Nori had said. Someone you love and trust can become your home. Yin had defined it clinically. Logically. A place she returned to. Nothing more.

But now, as the darkness enveloped her, she understood what it had actually meant.

Home wasn't just about returning. It was about belonging. About safety. About someone who saw you—really saw you—and chose to come back. Someone who didn't flinch when you quoted *The Godfather* or sat naked on laundry machines. Someone who organized your closet without being asked and watched melodramatic soap operas without complaint. Someone who looked at you and saw a person, not a tool or a weapon or a thing to be used.

Kraken was her home.

Not because she returned to him, but because with him, she had finally learned what it meant to choose. To want. To care about someone else's survival more than her own mission parameters.

She didn't regret finding him again after that abandoned factory in Scraptown. Didn't regret any of it. The sewers, the apartment, the party, the fights, the friendship.

Because he was her home. Her family.

And she had protected him.

That was enough.

Theo... I regret only that I could not tell you.

As the light disappeared, Yin was enveloped in a black void. The darkness felt peaceful, almost serene, as if it welcomed her into its embrace. The void held no smell, only the absence of any scent, as if all aromas had vanished along with the light.

Deep silence reigned. No more screams or sounds of destruction, just a stillness that consumed Yin. Her body melted, parts of it disappearing into the darkness as Yang devastated it. But instead of pain, weightlessness took her, as if she were floating away. Deep down, she knew this was her mind's way of coping with her imminent demise. Nothing else awaited her except darkness, where she had no conscious thought or existence. She would become nothingness.

Then, she awoke.

Yin inhaled deeply, but it turned into a fit of coughing, and she spat up blood. She realized that she was propped against a wall, with debris scattered around her. Her body throbbed from the injuries, but her accelerated healing abilities were already working to repair the damage. It was odd, though. Yang was gone. She wouldn't have left the job unfinished.

As her vision cleared, the unmistakable sounds of a fierce battle raged. Her heart leapt into her throat. Kraken was locked in a desperate struggle with Yang. Yin tried to push herself up, but to no avail. She attempted to call out his name, but she only expelled a mouthful of blood. A hand seized her arm, and she glanced up. Nori stood next to her with a finger pressed against her lips.

Nori pulled Yin up from the ground and held her steady as they made their way to the elevator. Yin pushed back but lacked the strength. She glanced at the ongoing battle behind them. While Kraken was an impressive fighter, Yang was on a whole different level.

"Quit fighting," Nori urged, her voice a low hiss. "Kraken can take care of himself."

Yin strained to argue, but her throat was tight and words wouldn't come out. She had to help him. He couldn't fight his opponent alone.

Nori grabbed Yin's shoulders and forced her to look into her eyes. "Listen, Kraken came back for you. You're barely standing. You can't fight in your current condition. If you go back to him now, you'll only be a distraction. Remember, he may not be as physically strong as you, but he is still a Recombinant." Nori's gaze softened. "Don't worry, he's not alone."

Maniacal laughter echoed off the walls, each cackle filled

with unhinged glee. The sound of fire crackling and consuming everything in its path drowned out any other noise, leaving only Izzy's shrill voice as she shouted about how she was going to reduce "the bitch" to nothing but smoldering remains.

The insatiable flames licked and danced along the walls, eagerly seeking out more fuel to devour. They twisted and turned, threatening to spread and engulf everything in their path. Nori pulled on Yin's arm, urging them both to keep moving toward the elevator. Izzy and Kraken's footsteps echoed behind them as they retreated. Now and then, Izzy let loose a stream of curses and insults, accompanied by the roaring of flames.

The air grew thick with the acrid stench of smoke and burning materials. The scent of ash and destruction permeated everything, making breathing difficult without coughing. Nori coughed, and Yin linked her arm around Nori's to help steady her. The smoke didn't affect Yin much. Her body had already adapted to the change in atmosphere.

The doors to the elevator were already open, held by Gabriel and Nari, who beckoned them forward. Yin guided Nori inside before turning back to the hallway. Three different sets of footsteps echoed: two running and the third trailing behind with slow, purposeful strides. Kraken and Izzy came barreling around the bend, avoiding the burnt rubble and leaping over flames. Izzy spun on her heels, lifting her hands as she conjured flames.

"Burn, motherfucker!"

The flames roared and hissed, creating a constant hum that filled the air. The heat radiating from the flames was intense, sending out waves of warmth. Its intense heat radiated in all directions, causing sweat to form on Yin's skin. The oppressive force reached her even from where she stood.

Izzy inched backward, her gaze fixed on the unrelenting flow of flames. Her mouth twisted into a crazed smile, and her eyes mirrored the fire's intensity. She leaned forward, pushing with more force and sending a powerful burst of heat and fire into the hallway.

The third set of footsteps hadn't stopped. Yang continued her steady pace until she reached the flames. Without hesitation, she stepped directly into the fire, showing no signs of pain.

As she emerged from the ball of fire, Yin thought of a horror film. Gone was Yang's long, flowing hair and smooth skin. Instead, all that remained was melted flesh with shining metal underneath. Her skin began to transform, taking on a life of its own as it crawled up her arm and settled. In the same instant, her hair sprouted and regrew, completing the bizarre transformation. Actually. Yin blinked. It was a scene from a sci-fi movie she'd watched, *The Annihilator 2*.

"Iz, it's not working. We have to go." Kraken's hand sizzled and steamed as he grasped Izzy's shoulder, his grip firm. He forced her back into the elevator, gesturing for Gabriel to close the doors.

Yin took in his battered appearance. Bruises covered his face, and blood trickled from a deep gash on his forehead. As Kraken inspected his freshly burned hand, Yin reached out to him but hesitated at the last second, her fingers curling in. He caught her gaze and attempted to comfort her with a smile.

"I'm fine," he said, though the pain was carved in his features. "Don't worry."

Her mind filled with a jumble of thoughts: *You are such an idiot. You were supposed to leave. Why did you come back?*

Yin held her tongue, stopping those thoughts from escaping. His attempt at reassurance only intensified the hot pulse through her body. One final thought lingered in her mind: *You could have been killed.*

"Uh, guys?" Gabriel's voice cut through Yin's thoughts. He frantically pressed the button to shut the elevator doors, but they remained open. "It's not closing."

Yang strode toward them, eyes ablaze. Her focus was locked on Yin, but her murderous intent was aimed at all of them. Yin readied herself to protect them, but Nari took a step forward. She raised her hands, and her eyes lit up with an electric glow.

A static sensation tingled along Yin's skin as the elevator lights flickered. Nari directed all her electrical energy toward Yang, making her suddenly stop in her tracks. Her eyes became vacant, and she spasmed as Nari manipulated her internal machinery, causing her heart rate to spike. Its beat stuttered into an abnormal rhythm.

The effort was evident by the pained expression on Nari's face. "I can't keep this up for long," she warned. "We need to act quickly if we want to do something."

As with the majority of Recombinants, her power wasn't perfected.

"We could always just hang out and spontaneously combust," Gabriel suggested, his voice strained from coughing. His eyes watered from the thick smoke filling the room. "Or maybe a quick death from that thing would be a more merciful fate?"

"You're not funny right now, Gabriel," Nori snapped, her voice hoarse.

Kraken was already at the elevator's panel. His fingers flew across the control panel, his com-tacts glowing with data as he bypassed the safety feature. He grinned in satisfaction as the elevator jerked to life under his command. "I've overridden it. Little Sis, you can stop now. You're interfering with the elevator's power."

Nari didn't react in time. Yang's heartbeat returned to normal, and her internal mechanisms rejected the electrical currents, forcing them back toward Nari. Nari's body convulsed, her limbs jerking and twisting in unnatural ways. Her eyes rolled back in her head, the whites visible as she fell backward.

Nori caught her and eased her to the elevator floor. Soft words of reassurance slipped out from between Nori's lips as she comforted her sister. Gabriel kneeled beside them, enfolding Nari in his arms and combing her hair with his fingers.

"She okay?" Kraken asked, his finger pressing the button to close the elevator doors.

"I'm okay," Nari replied, holding her head. "Just a little fried."

Yin stood at the doors, her body tense and alert as she watched Yang, who was now fully recovered. Yang's feet dragged against the floor as she charged, causing a slight tremor in the ground upon impact. But before she could reach them, the doors slammed shut and blocked her path. The elevator started moving upward, drowning out the sound of Yang's angry cries and the screeching of metal being forced apart.

Chapter 35

Kraken swore he never wanted to lay eyes on this cursed elevator again. Every inch of his body throbbed with exhaustion, from the blistering pain in his toes to the tightness in his chest. The acrid smoke that filled the confined space still lingered, stinging his eyes and making a full breath impossible. The pungent scent seeped into his clothes, clinging to every fiber and filling the air with its bitter tang. With each gasp, tiny knives dragged through his throat and lungs, trailing intense heat.

"You are all fools." Yin's voice trembled as she spoke, her eyes darting between the group. Her hands clenched into fists at her sides, and her legs shook with a mix of anger and resentment. Such curious emotions from her.

"We came back for you," Izzy interjected, her back pressed against the elevator wall, gasping. Her skin glistened with sweat and steamed with heat, a sign of her elevated internal temperature.

Kraken clenched and unclenched his burnt hand, his face contorting in discomfort. She'd done a number on his hand.

"Well...ol' Krak did," she continued. "But we wouldn't let him do it alone."

Before Kraken could reassure Yin, the elevator bell chimed and the doors opened into the lobby. The ragtag group stumbled out of the cramped space, some of them falling to the ground and gasping for air. Kraken doubled over, his hands resting on his knees as he fought for breath. Yin, however, emerged unfazed by the experience of being trapped in a metal box with limited oxygen. If he had any breath left, her resilience would have impressed and terrified him.

"I'm never hanging out with you lot ever again," Gabriel moaned, sprawled out on the floor. He winced and let out a small "ow" as Nori pinched his cheek.

"Oh, but you adore us!" she crooned in a singsong voice.

"We should leave," Nari stated, tilting her head as if listening to something. "The fires set off a silent alarm. Radio traffic says first responders will be on scene in five minutes or less. That includes the police."

"Yang will not give up her pursuit of me," Yin said, glancing toward the elevator doors. "She is relentless and will catch up to us on foot quickly."

Kraken motioned for her to come along, and the group stepped out through the double-doors onto the plaza. The sleek police hovercraft from the Pigeonocalypse levitated above the pristine path, emitting a low hum as it waited. Miriam sat in the driver's seat, her fingers tapping against the smooth exterior. She shot Kraken a pointed look and threw up her hand in a clear "Finally!" gesture. She glanced curtly at Yin before turning forward with a soft huff.

Kraken flashed a smirk at Yin. "I guess it's a good thing we didn't walk here," he remarked. The bay doors opened, and a ramp descended to the ground. Kraken followed the other Outsiders up the ramp, then turned back to offer his hand to Yin. "Come on, let's head home."

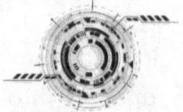

TIME CRAWLED. THE HOURS OF DAYLIGHT GREW LONGER WITH each passing day. Kraken's face was pale and drawn, his eyes bloodshot from lack of sleep. His skin was a mosaic of purples, blues, and yellows, a reminder of the brutal beating he had endured from Yang. His swollen sinuses throbbed with each cough.

And yet, his thoughts were consumed by the haunting image of Yin, listless and unmoving, not even reacting to her favorite soap operas. After being pressed for information about Yang, Yin opened up and told him everything. This was the most she had spoken since that day. The details she disclosed left him uneasy.

The temperatures dropped despite the lengthening hours of light, bringing a frigid wind that cut through his leather jacket as he'd made his way to the Farm. Kraken stood by one of the wood stoves in the communal dining hall, seeking warmth for his freezing hands. Miriam had summoned everyone for a meeting, and more people were entering, filling up the seats as they conversed quietly with each other. He caught Nori's eye as she came in and made her way to his side.

"Cold?" she asked with a smile.

"It's hard to breathe," Kraken confessed. "I'm still coughing up a lung, and the chilly weather isn't making it any easier."

"No kidding." Nori crossed her arms. "How's Yin?"

Kraken frowned. "She's not glitching anymore, but she

isn't herself at all. I even tried using metaphors, and she didn't scold me."

That drew a soft chuckle out of Nori. She nudged his arm, offering a reassuring smile. "Don't worry, she'll be fine. Would it help if I came over after the meeting? I'm pretty good at getting her fired up."

Kraken's voice was cut off by a sudden hush that fell over the room. He looked up to see Miriam enter, her footsteps echoing doggedly as she strode toward him. Kraken instinctively straightened his own stance and clasped his hands behind his back, while Nori quietly took a seat nearby. As Miriam stood by his side, she scanned the faces of the assembled Outsiders with a sharp, assessing gaze. The only sound was the gentle inhale and exhale of breath from those waiting for her next move.

"Thank you for being prompt," Miriam began. "As you all know, the Outsiders were formed after a senseless civil war enacted by the social elite. Thousands of lives were lost, and the people's voice was silenced. It has always been our mission to take back power and place it into the rightful hands of the people. We've never been subtle, never claimed to be saints. The road to change has unavoidable casualties, and because of our methods, we're labeled as terrorists by those in power. They're afraid of us. They should be."

She paused, letting her words settle over the assembled group.

"I didn't summon you here to reminisce. I brought you here to share news. Our efforts are about to reap rewards. After the prison break that freed our captured comrades and bolstered our numbers, after successfully replicating and distributing White Rabbit to fund our operations, we finally have the resources we need. It's time to make our boldest statement yet." Another pause for emphasis. "We're taking down the wall."

A hushed wave of shock rippled through the group. The

hairs on the back of Kraken's neck stood up. Despite his racing thoughts, he kept his expression neutral and carefully controlled. The wall divided the city, yes, but bringing it down would create chaos. Debris would rain down onto the streets below. People lived near that wall. Worked near it. Children played in its shadow.

"The wall is our primary target," Miriam continued, her voice strengthening. "That monument to their oppression, their blatant classism. The barrier they built to keep us in our place while they prosper behind it. When it falls, it falls on their heads, not ours. But I won't lie to you—there is always a chance that others may get caught in the crossfire. That is the price of war. A war that was started by the elite against us when they divided this city." She projected her voice throughout the room. "The end justifies the means. That is our motto. We must let go of our moral qualms now for the greater good—the future of Ignis and its citizens."

The Outsiders' voices grew louder and emboldened, indicating their approval. A surge of unease hit Kraken. He tried to calm himself with a deep breath. The wall was massive, reinforced concrete and steel that stretched around the entire perimeter of Modernist Ignis. The payload needed to bring it down would be catastrophic. Even if they targeted sections away from residential areas, the destruction alone could result in hundreds, maybe thousands, of deaths. Falling debris didn't discriminate. Shockwaves didn't care about intent.

And they would all be responsible for it.

Kraken turned his gaze toward Nori, who was cheering along with the rest of the group. He noticed Nari seated next to her and caught her eye. Nari's expression remained neutral, but Kraken could see sympathy there.

Kraken drew in a deep breath, his chest rising and falling. With his eyes closed, he visualized his inner turmoil fading away until it was only a small dot in the distance. As he continued to breathe, his muscles loosened and his body became more relaxed, grounding himself in the present moment. Despite his doubts, Miriam was right. This plan would have major consequences, potentially giving the Outsiders an unprecedented foothold they had never achieved before. The wall was a symbol of everything wrong with Ignis. Its destruction would send a message that couldn't be ignored.

The end justified the means.

But what if it didn't?

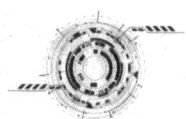

THE MEETING DISPERSED WITH THE ENERGY OF A STIRRED hornet's nest. Outsiders clustered, arguing in sharp, angry bursts. Kraken drifted toward a corner table where Nori, Nari, Izzy, and Rose had claimed seats. The woodstove crackled nearby, but the warmth did nothing to ease the cold knot in his stomach.

"Finally." Izzy leaned back in her chair, arms crossed behind her head. "We're doing something that matters. No more small raids, no more symbolic gestures. This is real change."

Rose nodded, her posture straight despite the casual setting. The small ballet slipper charm on her bracelet caught the firelight as she folded her hands on the table. "The wall has divided this city long enough. My parents work themselves to exhaustion just to keep food on the table while people on the other side waste more in a day than we see in a month. Something has to give."

Nori gave a slow nod, though her gaze faltered. "The wall has been a symbol of oppression since before the war. Taking it down sends a message that can't be ignored."

"A message written in rubble and bodies," Kraken muttered.

Izzy's eyes snapped to him. "You have a problem with this?"

"I have a problem with the collateral damage." Kraken kept his voice low. "The wall runs through populated areas. That's thousands of tons of concrete and steel falling into the streets. People live there. Work there. Kids play there."

"Kids who grow up learning we're lesser than them," Izzy shot back. Her hands trembled on the table. The scars from her recombination procedures marked her arms, pale lines against her skin. "I was one of their lab rats, Kraken. Project Prometheus. You think they cared about collateral damage when they were burning out my nervous system to see if they could make me a better weapon?"

Rose's hand moved to rest on Izzy's arm, a familiar, grounding touch. Rose had been there through the worst of it. Had watched Project Prometheus break Izzy down and rebuild her into something the government could use. Had helped pick up the pieces when the program was shut down and left Izzy forever altered.

Kraken opened his mouth, then closed it. Izzy rarely spoke of it. The bitterness in her voice could cut steel.

"I understand the anger," Kraken said, measuring his words. "I do. But becoming what they fear us to be doesn't make us better than them."

"We're not trying to be better than them," Rose said, calm but firm. "We're trying to survive. To give our families a chance at something more than scraping by." She met his gaze directly. "My mother cleans their buildings. My father works in their factories. They've done everything right, played by every rule, and they're still drowning. The system isn't broken, Kraken. It's working exactly as designed. And the only way to change it is to tear it down."

"By killing innocent people?"

"By doing what's necessary," Rose countered. "I didn't join the Outsiders because I wanted to hurt anyone. I joined because I want my family to have the opportunities I had. I want kids in Retro Ignis to be able to go to school without worrying about whether the building will have heat that day. I want people to be able to afford medicine when they're sick. The government isn't going to give us those things. We have to take them."

Nari spoke up, her voice quiet but steady. "And if taking them means becoming killers? If it means children on the other side of the wall lose their parents the way Izzy lost hers?"

"Then that's the price," Rose said. There was no malice in her tone. "I don't like it. I hate it. But I'm tired of watching my people suffer while we try to be the good guys. The Traditionalists didn't win by being good. They won by being willing to do whatever it took."

"That logic justifies anything," Nari said. She toyed with one of the small trinkets in her hair, fingers fluttering with nervous energy. "I've been monitoring their communications since the prison break. The government is already bolstering security, increasing surveillance in Retro Ignis, conducting random searches. If we bomb the wall, they'll use it as justification for martial law. They'll crack down harder than ever."

"Then we fight back harder," Izzy said.

"And more people die." Nari's gaze was unflinching. "On both sides. The cycle continues."

"The cycle continues anyway," Rose said. "At least this way, we have a chance of breaking it permanently."

Nori's gaze flickered between her sister and her friends, trapped. "I don't know if there's a clean answer here." She turned to Kraken. "What do you think we should do?"

Kraken stared at the wood grain of the table, tracing the patterns with his eyes. What did he think? The sheer intensity of it all threatened to crush him. Suffering bloomed in his mind—families torn apart, children wailing for lost parents, parents clutching the bodies of their children.

Rose had a point. The system was designed to keep them down. The wall was a symbol of everything wrong with Ignis. It had stood long before the civil war, a barrier that separated the wealthy from the poor, the powerful from the powerless. It needed to come down.

But not like this.

"I think," Kraken said slowly, "that Miriam is right about one thing. The wall is a symbol. It needs to come down. But I think there's a difference between destroying a symbol and destroying the people who live in its shadow."

"So, what, we ask permission?" Izzy's tone was mocking. "Send them a formal notice so they can evacuate?"

"No," Kraken said. "We choose our targets carefully. We hit the wall in sections where casualties will be minimal. Industrial areas, government zones, places where people aren't living. We make it a surgical strike, not a massacre."

"That's not what Miriam outlined," Nori pointed out.

"No," Kraken agreed. "It's not."

Izzy's eyes narrowed. "You're going to object."

"I'm going to try to modify the plan," he corrected. "We can still send our message without killing thousands of innocent people."

"There are no innocent people in Modernist Ignis," Izzy said flatly. "They benefit from the system. They profit from our oppression. That makes them complicit."

Rose leaned forward, elbows on the table. "I understand what you're trying to do, Kraken. You want to believe we can fight this war without becoming monsters. But war doesn't work that way. People die. Innocent people die. That's the reality. And if we try to wage this fight with one hand tied behind our backs because we're worried about optics, we're going to lose."

"Then where does it end?" Kraken met her gaze. "If everyone who benefits from the system deserves to die, then we'll be killing people forever. Children who didn't choose where they were born. Workers who are just trying to survive, same as us. At what point do we become the monsters they always said we were?"

"When we stop caring about our own people," Rose said. "When we value their lives more than the lives of people in Retro Ignis. That's when we become monsters." She paused, then added more softly, "I don't want to kill anyone, Kraken. But if it's a choice between them and us, I choose us. Every time."

Izzy looked away, her jaw working. When she spoke again, her voice was quieter. "I just want them to hurt the way they hurt me."

Rose's hand remained on Izzy's arm, steady and grounding. "I know."

"I know," Kraken agreed. That pain was a familiar echo, even if he didn't share the same thirst for vengeance. "But if we do this Miriam's way, we're not freedom fighters anymore. We're just murderers with a political agenda."

"And if we don't do it at all?" Nori asked. "If we back down now?"

"I'm not saying we back down," Kraken said. "I'm saying we be smart. Strategic. We hit them where it hurts without becoming what they always accused us of being."

Rose gave a slow shake of her head. "You're asking us to fight with honor against an enemy that has none. That's a losing strategy."

"Maybe," Kraken admitted. "But I'd rather lose with our hands clean than win by becoming exactly what they said we were."

Across the room, Miriam stood talking with a cluster of senior Outsiders, her posture commanding. She glanced his way once, and something in her expression suggested she knew exactly what they were discussing.

Kraken pushed back from the table. "I need to talk to her."

"Good luck," Nori murmured. "She's not going to budge easily."

Rose's voice stopped him before he could leave. "Kraken." He turned back. Her expression was serious but not unkind. "I respect what you're trying to do. But when that day comes, you need to decide where you stand. We're all in this together, or we're not in it at all."

"I know," Kraken said. And he did. That was what made this so hard.

He crossed the dining hall, weaving between clusters of Outsiders still buzzing with excitement over Miriam's announcement. His boots felt leaden. Miriam had made her position clear. Objecting now was one thing. If she shut him down, he'd have to decide whether to fall in line or stand against her publicly.

And standing against her meant standing against the Outsiders. The only family he'd known for years.

Miriam caught his eye and dismissed the surrounding group with a curt gesture. They dispersed, leaving her alone as Kraken approached. She waited, arms crossed, expression unreadable.

"Commander," Kraken said. "We need to talk about the plan."

"I figured you'd have objections." Miriam's tone was neutral, but her eyes were sharp. "Let's take this somewhere private."

She led him out of the dining hall and into one of the smaller outbuildings, a storage room turned into a makeshift office. The space felt suffocating, filled with filing cabinets and boxes of supplies. Miriam leaned against the desk, arms still crossed.

"Speak," she said.

Kraken took a breath. "The wall needs to come down. I agree with that. But the way you're planning to do it will kill thousands of innocent people. Civilians who had nothing to do with creating this system."

"There are no innocent civilians in Modernist Ignis," Miriam said, echoing Izzy's earlier words. "They live off the backs of our labor. They benefit from a system that grinds us into the dirt."

"Then we're all guilty," Kraken countered. "We distributed White Rabbit, knowing it would get people high, knowing some of them would OD. We broke into Pyreford and freed murderers and rapists along with our own people. Where do we draw the line?"

"We draw the line at effectiveness," Miriam said. "Everything we've done has been in service of this moment. The prison break gave us numbers. White Rabbit gave us funding. Now we use those resources to strike a blow the government can't ignore or recover from."

"And if innocent people die in the process?"

"Then they die." Miriam's voice turned hard, but something crossed her eyes. Pain, maybe. Or regret. "You think I want that? You think I don't know what we're about to do? But we don't have the luxury of clean hands, Kraken. Those who hold power didn't win it by being merciful. They won by being ruthless. If we want to beat them, we have to be willing to make the hard choices."

"There's a difference between hard choices and slaughter," Kraken said. "We can hit the wall strategically. Target sections away from residential areas—industrial zones, government districts. We can still send our message without massacring families."

Miriam pushed off the desk, closing the distance between them. She was shorter than him, but her presence filled the space. When she spoke again, her voice softened. "I know your heart, Kraken. It's one of the reasons I made you lieutenant. You care about people in a way most of us can't afford to anymore. But that compassion will get you killed if you're not careful."

"Maybe," Kraken said. "But I'd rather die with a clear conscience than live knowing I murdered innocent people for a cause."

"This isn't about conscience. It's about change." Miriam's expression hardened again. "The government sees us as expendable. They throw us into Retro Ignis and forget we exist until we become a problem. Then they send in their Enforcers, their modified soldiers, and they beat us back down. How many times have we tried the targeted approach? How many targeted strikes? How many carefully planned operations that avoid casualties? And what has it gotten us? Nothing. We're still in the same position we've always been."

"So your answer is to become just like them?"

"My answer is to win." Miriam's jaw tightened. "I'm responsible for everyone in this organization. Every single person who's risked their life for this cause. And I will not let their sacrifices be for nothing because we were too squeamish to do what needed to be done."

Kraken felt the weight of her words. She wasn't wrong about the stakes. She wasn't wrong about the government's ruthlessness. But the images wouldn't leave him—families caught in the blast radius, children who would never grow up, lives ended for the crime of living on the wrong side of a wall they didn't build.

"I can't support this plan as it stands," he declared. "Not without modifications. Not without trying to minimize casualties."

Miriam studied him for a long moment. Disappointment warred with understanding in her voice. "You're one of my best, Kraken. You're smart, skilled, and the team respects you. I don't want to lose you. But I also can't have my lieutenant publicly undermining my authority."

"I'm not trying to undermine you."

"I know." Miriam sighed, and for a moment, she looked tired. The weight of leadership was written in the lines of her face. "But that's what it will look like to the others if you object. They need to see unity from their commanders. They need to believe we're doing the right thing."

"Are we?" Kraken asked. "Doing the right thing?"

"I don't know anymore," Miriam admitted. "I stopped asking that question years ago. Now I just focus on protecting my people. On making sure our cause doesn't die with us." She straightened, and the momentary vulnerability vanished behind her command mask. "You have until we execute the plan. Figure out where you stand, Kraken. Because when that day comes, you're either with us or you're not. I need to know I can count on you."

"And if you can't?"

Miriam's expression softened, just slightly. "Then we'll deal with it. You're family, Kraken. That doesn't change, even if we disagree. But I can't let sentiment compromise the mission. You understand that, don't you?"

Kraken nodded. He understood. And that was the tragedy of it. They both believed in the cause and were both fighting for their people. They just couldn't agree on the cost.

"I'll think about it," he conceded.

"That's all I ask." Miriam moved toward the door, then paused. "For what it's worth, I hope you find a way to stay. We need people like you. People who still have the capacity to care. Even if I can't afford to be one of them anymore."

She left, and Kraken stood alone in the cramped office, surrounded by boxes of supplies meant to fuel their revolution. His hands shook. Not from cold or injury, but from the weight of the choice now sitting on his shoulders.

Chapter 36

The muted light of the overcast sky filtered through the sheer white curtains, imbuing everything with a cool glow. Yin sat on the couch, her pale figure stark against the soft rays. Her fingers clenched around the edge of the armrest, knuckles white with tension. She wasn't sure how much time had passed since she'd taken this position.

Now and then, she heard Kraken's voice and caught a glimpse of his face in her peripheral vision. He sounded distant, his words incomprehensible, like trying to hear a whisper from across a vast canyon. The world around her swirled in colors and sounds, but she remained still, fixated on a blank spot on the wall.

Yin replayed her interactions with Yang, visualizing them in front of her like acts on a stage. She paused, rewound, and analyzed every word, expression, and action, scrutinizing them for any clue to Yang's downfall. She traced potential scenarios, but each one ended in her own demise. Death was not something she feared. What haunted her were the events that followed. The deaths of her friends as Yang hunted them down.

No matter which route I take... Yin's body slumped, weighed down by the heaviness of her thoughts. Her mouth was dry, her throat parched. *It always ends the same way.*

Even from the depths of her obsessive analysis, Yin sensed Yang's presence lurking nearby, waiting with unnerving patience for Yin to recover. She'd never fallen far behind since the events at Nassar Industries, even trailing them in the hovercraft. The choice of following Kraken back home had been a mistake. Staying here put him in greater danger of becoming a target, or worse, him running to be a martyr for her sake. That thought put a bitter taste in her mouth.

With a deep inhale, the world shifted into razor-sharp focus. Yin raised her hand, fingers curling with ease. A surge of strength coursed through every fiber of her muscles, a testament to the success of Aja's procedure. Her body was fully recovered from the damage inflicted by her Creator's nanobots. She was at full strength now. If only brute strength were enough to defeat her enemy. Even with her imperfections repaired, Yin's strength only matched Yang's at best.

Imperfection. The word rang in her mind, triggering a thought that hadn't yet occurred to her. *Is that the answer?*

Yin rose from the couch, her bare feet sinking into the soft carpet as she moved toward the hallway. She strained to listen for any signs of movement. The door to Kraken's room loomed ahead, its dark wood paneling standing out against the pale walls. Closed, with no light seeping through from inside. The only sound in the apartment was the faint buzz of electricity.

Satisfied Kraken was gone, Yin hurried to the kitchen and pushed open the heavy window. The hinges creaked in protest. Cool summer air rushed in, whipping her hair back as she peered out at the old fire escape that zigzagged down the side of the building.

She hoisted herself onto the windowsill and swung her legs over the edge. The aging metal groaned under her weight as she began her descent. Despite being heavily surveilled by cameras, this specific area was a blind spot. The camera designated for this alley had malfunctioned, and neither of them had bothered to fix it yet. Yin couldn't risk Kraken following and disrupting her plans. This time, there was no one coming to rescue her.

With a silent landing, her feet touched the ground. She slipped out of the alley and onto the quiet street.

"Follow me," she whispered, knowing Yang would hear with no need to raise her voice and potentially alert any nearby cameras. She turned and sprinted toward the place where she and Kraken first crossed paths: the Junkyard.

Chapter 37

The blood-red circles etched onto the maps of the Inner Ring haunted him. Death marks. Before leaving the Farm, Miriam and a few others had huddled over the maps, their voices an indistinct murmur. He couldn't bring himself to listen. Each word spoken was a death sentence for innocent lives.

The oppressive sky mirrored his mood. Dark clouds massed with each passing minute, casting shadows of slate and charcoal over Old Town. The streets lay deserted, save for the occasional house spilling warm light onto the empty sidewalks. Behind drawn curtains, shadows danced, whispering of hidden lives inside. A solitary cat stalked the rooftops, its luminous eyes following their every move in the fading light.

Kraken's steps slowed. Through a window, a mother soothed her infant. The child's face was flushed with fever, wailing a high-pitched squall of discomfort. But the mother held the child close, gently stroking a tiny back and bouncing it in her arms. A simple everyday moment. Kraken's chest tightened, his breath hitching.

These people lived their lives ignorant of what was to come, the same as those in the Inner Ring who were not targets of the Outsiders. In a matter of seconds, their existence would be snuffed out without warning. They wouldn't even have time to process it. They wouldn't...

A hand on his shoulder jerked him back. Nori was next to him, her hand still gripping his shoulder, a strained smile touching her lips.

"Miriam will do her best to avoid harming those uninvolved," she said softly.

Kraken shook his head. "It just doesn't feel right. How are we any different from the supreme chancellor, or any of them, if we resort to this?"

Nori opened her mouth to reply, but wailing sirens cut her off. She flicked her gaze to the sky as foreboding thunder rumbled in the distance. "We should get inside."

Kraken gripped his jacket, his nerves fraying, as they approached his apartment. Would Yin come out of her catatonic state this time? She would be a welcome distraction from the chaos in his head. Bringing Nori was his secret weapon. If anyone could break through to Yin, it was her.

They weren't alone. Gabriel was already there, posted by the door with his hands in his pockets. When he saw them, he lifted his hand in greeting.

"Hey, man," Gabriel said. "Those sirens are no joke, huh? I figured I'd come here for some peace and quiet."

"Peace and quiet?" Nori snorted. "Since when have we ever had that?"

Kraken ignored their back-and-forth as he unlocked the door and stepped inside. A visceral coldness washed over him. The hair on his nape prickled.

The apartment loomed, dark and empty. Devoid of life and energy. As he crossed to the living room, he scanned the gloom for any sign of Yin's presence. Nothing. The spot where she always sat was empty.

Silence. No soft breathing or rustling of fabric. Just the suffocating stillness. His stomach clenched.

Yin wasn't here.

"Kraken?" Nori stepped in behind him. "What's wrong?" Her gaze followed his to the soft indentation on the couch. "Where's Yin?"

Kraken didn't respond. He activated his com-tacts and pulled up the security footage. The logs were clean. She knew the cameras' blind spots just as well as he did and had exploited them.

"Dammit," he hissed, rushing into the kitchen. The window gaped open. Her escape route. One camera facing the alleyway was dead, and he'd neglected to fix it with everything else going on. He'd provided Yin with a way out. Kraken leaned out the window.

"Yin!" he yelled, needing her to hear him over the rising winds and approaching thunder. "Yin!" His heart hammered as he leaned further out the window.

Yin...please...

Kraken slammed the window shut, his chest heaving as he raked his fingers through his hair. He turned to face Nori and Gabriel, their expressions tight with concern.

"Yin's gone," he said, his hands twisting in his hair. "She's gone after Yang. I have to find her."

He pushed past them toward the door, but Nori blocked his way, planting her feet firmly and raising her hand to stop him.

"You can't go out there, Kraken," she said. "There's a rad storm approaching."

"It's just a warning siren," he snapped. "I still have time before the real ones go off and everything shuts down."

Nori narrowed her eyes. "And what if you don't make it? You could die out there. I won't let you go."

"Yeah, man..." Gabriel added, his brow furrowed. "It would be better to wait for the storm to pass. The Synth will be alright on her own."

"Her name is Yin," Kraken growled, looming over them. "And her life is just as valuable as ours. I can't just sit here and do nothing while Yin risks her life. So, move. Before I move you myself."

Nori held her ground, her gaze unwavering. "Kraken, we understand that you care for Yin, but rushing out there without a plan will only make things worse. We need to think this through."

Gabriel set a hand on his shoulder, the touch a steadying weight. "Listen to Nori, man. We can't let emotions cloud our judgment."

Kraken hesitated, torn. The silence in the small apartment stretched, broken only by the howl of the wind outside. He drew in a breath and relented, his shoulders slumping as he nodded. Nori was right. He was letting his emotions get the better of him.

"Fine," he muttered through gritted teeth, his hands clenched at his sides. "But we need to move fast."

Nori nodded, her features softening in understanding. "We'll find Yin together," she assured him, stepping aside so Kraken could take the lead.

"Okay. Okay..." His mind whirred. "What do we know? We know she left via the kitchen window and went down the fire escape. She'd still need to avoid the outside cameras once she left the alleyway, so there's only one direction she would go without later doubling back."

"And where do you go to have a showdown with a psychopathic war machine?" Gabriel muttered.

"Hopefully somewhere without other people," Nori said. "An open fight between them will be destructive."

The realization struck him.

"The Junkyard," Kraken breathed. "She's going to the Junkyard."

THE DERELICT BUILDINGS OF SCRAPTOWN SPRAWLED UNDER A brooding sky, their patchwork walls of corrugated metal and salvaged wood groaning in the rising wind. Normally bustling streets were empty, the usual clamor of tinkerers and scavengers replaced by an eerie stillness. They were bracing for the rad storm. Thunder deepened in the distance, a veiled warning, as the sirens howled their somber song for a second time.

The trio pushed on toward the Junkyard. A hush had fallen over them, muting even Gabriel's usual stream of jokes. He was pale and weak, sweat beading on his forehead as he leaked pheromones that soured Kraken's gut.

At his side, Nori clenched her teeth as she whirled around and punched Gabriel in the shoulder. "If you don't stop that shit right now..."

Gabriel winced, rubbing his shoulder. "I can't help it. There's a radiation storm coming that will irradiate our asses, we're barreling into a fight between two beings that could crush us, and you want me to not be anxious?"

"No one forced you to come," Nori retorted, crossing her arms with a grimace. "Your anxiety is about to make me blow chunks."

Kraken's lips pressed into a thin line, the crease on his brow deepening. His mouth parted, ready to demand silence. But before he could utter a word, a metallic screech tore the air. The unmistakable grinding of metal twisting and crushing.

His blood ran cold.

Yin.

Without hesitation, Kraken bolted for the Junkyard, his heart hammering. His friends' distant shouts vanished as adrenaline lit his every step.

He burst through the creaky gates and froze. Before him was a sprawling maze of twisted metal structures, their jagged edges jutting skyward. Towering piles of crushed hover cars loomed, once-shiny exteriors now marred with deep gouges and rust. Dilapidated buildings dotted the sector. The same ones he'd used to flee from the Metal Vultures.

The air hung heavy, stifling.

A blur of motion shattered the silence. A deafening crash erupted as two figures slammed into a nearby hover car, the impact echoing through the labyrinth. Yin and Yang. Their bodies a brutal knot, locked in combat.

Kraken's muscles tensed. Yin fought against Yang's overwhelming force, teeth clenched in a snarl, eyes burning with fury. Yang forced her harder against the hover car, its metal groaning in protest, Yang's strength pushing Yin toward the brink.

Kraken barreled toward them, his fingers digging into Yang's shoulder. Her metallic body was ice-cold, the skin overlaying it a deception. Gritting his teeth, he roared and wrenched her away from Yin. A searing jolt shot through his arms, but he twisted and flung her with every ounce of his strength. Yang crashed into a stack of scrap metal, the pile collapsing in an explosive shower of rust and debris.

"Theo! What are you doing here?" Yin shouted, her voice laced with exhaustion.

Kraken didn't answer. His knees hit the ground in front of her, kicking up a small puff of dust. Sweat and smeared blood streaked Yin's face, the crimson tracing rivulets down her dirt-caked skin. Stray strands of her hair clung to her temple. Her shoulders slumped, trembling with exertion, but her eyes—those fierce, unyielding eyes—still burned.

A chuckle escaped him unbidden, a strange mix of relief

and admiration. "Yin..." Kraken reached out, his hand gripping her shoulder. His hazel eyes locked onto hers, and he grinned. "You need to stop running away from me."

For a moment, Yin didn't respond. Her forehead creased, the furrows deepening. Her lips pressed together in that thin, stubborn line he knew so well. A warning. Kraken braced himself, ready for the sharp bite of her words, but instead, she sighed.

The sound was soft, unexpected. Her shoulders eased, the tension melting from her. Her gaze shifted, the fire flickering.

"Theo..."

The world erupted in chaos before he could hear anything else. Something slammed into his right side with the impact of a freight train. The blow punched the air from his lungs as his body was hurled sideways. The landing jarred every nerve, white-hot pain exploding in his ribs. The ground was hard beneath him, his skin stinging from the scrape.

Everything spun. The world tilted, his stomach churning. His ears rang with a high-pitched whine that drowned out everything. Dimly, he heard Yin shouting, but the words were lost.

What...was that? He fought to focus, his mind clawing for clarity, but his vision was a swirl of distorted shapes, like staring through muddied glass. *What am I forgetting?*

Before he could grasp the thought, an iron grip snapped around his throat, crushing and unrelenting. The pressure stole what little air he had left. Panic flared. Instinctively, his hands shot up, clawing at the hand cutting off his oxygen. His fingers scraped against cold, unyielding metal. He forced his gaze up, his blurry vision sharpening just enough to meet a pair of red eyes.

Yang.

The sight jolted his sluggish mind. *Ah, right... That...*

Kraken's other hand scrambled along the ground, fingertips brushing something hard and metallic. A pipe. His lungs burned, his breath hitching in shallow gasps as his vision darkened at the edges.

"Observing his death...will it be most distressing for you?" Yang's voice was a razor, her words dripping with cool contempt, but they weren't meant for him. Through the blur, he saw Yin. She'd gotten back to her feet but hadn't moved. Waiting. Distracting.

Yang's grip tightened, her lips twisting. "How human of you," she spat.

Kraken's fingers flexed against the metal, straining. *So close...*

A gunshot cracked. Yang's body jerked, her grip faltering for an instant. Two more shots followed, driving into her back. Her hand loosened. Kraken dragged in a ragged breath, coughing as oxygen flooded his lungs.

His eyes darted toward the shots. Gabriel trembled a short distance away, his hands shaking around the grip of a gun, smoke curling from the barrel.

"Oh fuck..." Gabriel muttered, stumbling back. "Oh fuck. Oh fuck."

Kraken tightened his grip on the pipe, knuckles whitening. He swung it with all his might. The impact reverberated up his arm, rattling his teeth as if he'd slammed solid steel. Yang's head jerked violently, her body recoiled, and she toppled over.

He didn't wait. He shoved himself upright, heart pounding, as Yin lunged past him. She dropped onto Yang in a blur, fists slamming down relentlessly.

Tossing the pipe, Kraken rushed to Gabriel. His friend was motionless, eyes wide and unfocused, locked on some distant point. The sight hollowed Kraken's chest. Dread slithered in to replace the adrenaline. He grabbed Gabriel's shoulder, gripping tightly. "Hey! Gabriel, come back. Where is Nori?"

Gabriel flinched, his whole frame shaking. "I... I don't..."

His voice faltered. He blinked slowly, his chest hitching. Finally, he exhaled a deep, shuddering sigh.

"She pushed further into the Junkyard," he said, his voice a rasp. "To search for anything... She gave me her gun..."

Kraken followed the tremor in Gabriel's hand; the gun wobbled as if it was too heavy. "Go find her," he said, his voice low but steady. He clasped Gabriel's wrist and pressed his arm down. "Keep hold of that. She's going to need it."

"Right..." Gabriel murmured, distant. He looked down at the gun, then frowned, his body tensing. His gaze snapped back to Kraken. "Kraken, where's your gun?"

A gunshot ripped through the air. Kraken froze, the world narrowing. His breath hitched. Every instinct screamed at him to move, to run toward the noise, but his legs were leaden.

No.

Chapter 38

"Observing his death...will it be most distressing for you?"

The question slammed into Yin's mind as she heaved herself up from the concrete-dusted rubble. The metallic tang of rebar and pulverized stone filled her nostrils. Her muscles grew taut, her frame shuddering, every instinct screaming for her to tear into Yang, to rip her arm clean off if that's what it took to free Kraken.

But she didn't.

Her breath hitched, her focus flickering to the corner where she spotted him. Kraken's fingers, pale with dust, inched toward a broken pipe.

Understanding his intention, Yin met Yang's sneer with a glare, tilting her chin high in defiance even as her nails carved crescents into her palms. The world narrowed to the percussive roar of blood in her ears. Her hardened gaze zeroed in on Yang's other hand. Subtle but deliberate, it slipped toward Kraken's holster. A smooth slide, almost invisible.

Almost.

Yang's lips curled with disgust. "How human of you."

Three pistol-cracks shattered the air. Kraken swung the pipe in a heavy iron arc that knocked Yang clean off him. The moment Kraken wrenched free, Yin sprang.

Instinct overriding thought. One arm drove toward Yang's chest while the other swung wide.

Yin's forearm locked onto Yang's neck, and they hit the ground with a force that rattled Yin's teeth and blasted dust and debris into the air. Yang twisted beneath her, sharp and fluid as a fish, but Yin clamped down, sinew and muscle locking around Yang's torso. Yang snarled, her elbow slamming into Yin's ribs. A sledgehammer impact. A wet internal *crack*.

Her ribs, probably. But Yin held fast.

Pain exploded through her chest, a starburst of white heat, but it was already numbing as she shifted her weight and slammed Yang's head against the floor. Yang bucked, their bodies a thrashing knot of momentum and power, muscles straining, the ground beneath them grinding under their struggle.

Yin unlocked her ankles, drove her knee upward, and aimed for Yang's side. The satisfying give of flesh and metal beneath the thick material of her jumpsuit. Yang hissed but retaliated, her fist arcing toward Yin's jaw. Yin ducked. The blow whistled past, grazing her cheek and leaving a searing, razor-thin line of pain.

They rolled. A flurry of locked limbs and clenched teeth, each grunt and gasp a tiny victory or defeat. Yin's hand found Yang's wrist, slamming it to the gritty floor. Her knuckles brushed against one of the cargo pockets on Yang's thigh. Something cool and solid inside. She drove her other elbow toward Yang's temple. Yang twisted her head just in time. The strike smashed into the ground instead, splintering cracks through the compacted dirt.

"Still so predictable," Yang gasped, the words edged with mockery even as she fought to break free.

Yin answered with pressure, tightening her grip, pressing her forearm harder against the cartilage of Yang's throat. Yin's own muscles burned, her vision tunneling.

Yang's lips twisted into a sharp grin. She stopped resisting, her body going slack for a split-second. The shift threw Yin off-balance. Before Yin could adjust, Yang ignited, twisting her hips. The movement jerked Yin's weight just enough for Yang to wrench an arm free.

With a sharp jab, Yang's knuckles connected with the nerve cluster in Yin's shoulder. Numbness exploded through her arm like a violent, electrical void, and her grip faltered. The heavy sole of Yang's combat boot drove into Yin's thigh with a brutal shove. The force sent her sprawling backward, skidding across the rubble-strewn floor as Yang rolled to her feet in one seamless motion.

Heaving for air, Yin scrambled to a crouch, her left arm a dead, tingling weight. Yang smirked, wiping a streak of dirt from her jaw.

"Is this your limit?" Yang taunted, circling, her eyes bright with a predator's joy.

Yin growled low, ignoring the protesting scream of her ribs as she surged up. Her eyes tracked Yang, only breaking away for a split-second glimpse of Kraken lowering Gabriel's hand.

At that moment, Yang stopped, her hand diving into her pocket to produce Kraken's pistol. She aimed it past Yin, at the back of Kraken's head. Her finger curled around the trigger.

Yin lunged.

Chapter 39

TIME FRACTURED. SECONDS ELONGATED, DISTORTED, AS IF THE universe itself seized. Kraken's pulse battered his chest, blood surged, roaring in his ears. His gaze fixed on Yin, her body curled around Yang's arm, fingers clamped over the stolen pistol.

Careless.

He should've checked for the weapon. Should've secured it the moment Yang went down. His mistake. His failure.

"Kraken, you there?" Nori's voice hissed through his comtacts, an urgent whisper slicing the fog in his mind. "I heard gunshots. Status report."

He couldn't look away from Yin. Bile of dread scorched his gut. Blood flowed through her torn clothing, dark, spreading, pooling where the bullet had shredded flesh. Her chest lifted and dropped in shallow, labored breaths.

"Kraken!" Nori's voice snapped, severing his haze.

"I'm here," he rasped, throat tight. The words scraped

out, heavy with guilt. "Gabriel is with me. We're okay, but Yin..."

Silence. A beat too long.

Then—

"Kraken, I'm sending you my location. I think I've found the solution to taking this bitch down."

A soft chime flashed as the coordinates overlaid his comtacts. A few blocks east. Close, but not close enough to save Yin, who bled on the cracked pavement.

Kraken exhaled, turning to Gabriel. "Go. Get to Nori. I'll lure Yang myself."

Gabriel's head whipped toward him, eyes wide and frantic. "Alone? Are you insane?"

Kraken ignored him, focusing on Yin's ragged breath. She wasn't dead. Not yet. But the dark stain shrieked she didn't have long. His fingers itched to reach for her, but he held his position.

"Kraken," Gabriel whispered, tinged with unease. "This is a bad idea."

"It's the only one we've got," Kraken hissed, voice rasping with desperation. "It's a desperate, necessary gamble. Go."

Gabriel hesitated, jaw tightening, conflict warring across his features. He gave a reluctant nod. "Don't die."

Kraken didn't respond. His focus fixed on Yang. She hardly spared Yin a glance. Her expression, a blank mask; her body language screamed contempt. Disdain curled her movements, her grip flexing, loosening, debating Yin's effort of disposal. An inconvenience. A bug. The casual cruelty ignited Kraken. His rage magnified, a physical sensation that scorched his veins like acid. Every nerve ending demanded action—tear Yang apart with bare hands.

Yang snorted, flicking her arm to shake Yin off.

Yin clamped down. Her fingers dug in, nails biting Yang's skin. She lifted her head, lips peeled back in a snarl to reveal clenched teeth. Blood stained them crimson.

Yang scoffed. "Pathetic."

She snatched Yin up, then slammed her down. The air cracked. Kraken flinched, the sound pounding through his skull. Yin's body twisted, her breath hitching, but her grip tore free as she hit the ground, and the gun flew from Yang's grasp. It skittered across the pavement, metal screeching against stone.

Kraken lunged forward, aiming for Yang's center, but she twisted, her arm snapping up to block. Their forearms slammed, a jarring force that rattled his bones. Dark streaks bled down her skin from Yin's nails. Blood. Or whatever synthetic fluid filled Yang's veins.

He exploited the block's force to recoil a step, just out of her immediate reach. Kraken shifted his stance, poised on the balls of his feet.

"Come on," he murmured. "Let's take this somewhere else."

Yang's gaze flicked from Yin's still form to Kraken, assessing, calculating. The gears ground behind those cold eyes, weighing options, determining which threat required immediate elimination. Then, she smiled. A terrible sight—empty of warmth, devoid of humanity.

Kraken scrambled to shift before she attacked, closing the gap with terrifying ease. He deflected her first strike, but the impact jarred him. The force numbed his forearms. A sharp elbow snapped toward his ribs. He twisted, just missing the brunt, but the edge still caught him. Pain flared, hot and immediate. She was relentless. Good. She was committed.

His boots scraped the cracked pavement as he pivoted back, luring her deeper into the sprawling maze of twisted metal, shattered hover cars, and skeletal machinery. Rusted frames jabbed out at odd angles, their sharp edges catching the diminishing light as storm clouds thickened.

A chime flashed. "Kraken," Nori's voice cut through the static. "Get her closer to the magnet."

Magnet? He spotted it. Suspended from a reinforced arm, scarred from years of dragging ruined vehicles into the crusher below, the massive electromagnet loomed like a predator waiting to strike. The control panel sat on a raised platform just ahead, partially obscured by scrap. The realization slammed into him. Yang wasn't just fast or strong. She was metal. And metal could be controlled.

Just a little further.

Yang lunged, fist aiming for his throat. Kraken dodged, but pain seared white-hot as her knuckles clipped his jaw. Stars burst. His balance wavered. She didn't hesitate. A knee found his stomach, expelling the air from his lungs. He staggered, catching himself against a rusted-out transport frame. The metal clawed cold against his palm, rough with corrosion. His body shrieked *stop*, every injury compounding into agony. But he fought upright, wiping blood from his mouth.

Yang smirked. "You're slowing down."

Kraken exhaled, meeting her gaze. Blood warmed his tongue, metallic. Then, he grinned.

"Is that all you've got?"

Yang's smirk died. "That all I've got?" she echoed, voice low, venom threading each syllable. "You speak as if you're my equal."

Kraken didn't respond. He let his grin widen. Taunting. Baiting. Let her think him overconfident.

Her eyes narrowed. "You're flawed," she sneered. "Imperfect. A thing like you deserves to be erased."

Her palm crushed into his chest. Kraken twisted, absorbing the force, but another strike shattered his ribs. Something inside crunched ominously, pain detonating through his torso like a bomb. He tasted coppery blood. His vision blurred. He braced, but Yang moved faster than physics allowed. A kick to his knee sent him crashing onto the pavement.

Pain surged deep and searing, his breath catching. His knee shrieked, bone grinding against bone. He tensed, but Yang's boot pinned him, pressing hard against his sternum. The weight crushed his damaged ribs, stealing what little air remained.

"You should be grateful," she murmured, tilting her head. "I'm doing you a kindness."

Her arm rose. The synthetic muscles contracted, fingers curling into a fist designed to pulverize bone. So this was it. This was death.

The air shifted. Subtle, imperceptible, yet Kraken's instincts flared. His equilibrium cracked, his stomach twisting violently, as if gravity warped. A sickly sensation crawled through his nerves, his body reacting before his mind could recognize the source. Nausea churned. His heart rate spiked, adrenaline flooding his system unnaturally. Gabriel.

Kraken's gaze snapped up. Rigid, shoulders bunched, hand half-raised, caught between fight and flight. Pupils blown wide, breath coming in sharp bursts. Sweat slicked his pale, clammy skin. Fear. Not his own—Gabriel's. It bled into the air, thick and cloying, warping everything.

Pheromones.

Not the kind that nudged. The kind that seized control, hijacking instincts on a primal level.

Yang staggered. Her breath gasped, her stance wavered, invaded. Her pupils dilated, her muscles locked—a full-body glitch forcing hesitation. She looked uncertain. Vulnerable. Kraken's vision pulsed. Nausea sloshed, sweat prickling his spine. He wrenched free, twisting out from under her, muscles screaming. His boots hit the pavement, knees nearly buckling, but he held steady. Pain shot through his damaged knee, but he ignored it. Had to.

Yang's head snapped up. Her focus laser-locked on Gabriel.

Shit. The second it clicked, her dazed confusion honed into vicious clarity. Recognition flared, followed by rage.

"Shit—" Gabriel turned on his heel, ready to bolt.

Yang recovered too quickly. She lunged at Gabriel, movements fluid and predatory, but someone slammed into her from behind.

The force sent both figures skidding across the pavement, leaving twin trails of scraped concrete. Yang twisted mid-motion, a snarl peeling her lips, to meet with something relentless, something that shouldn't have been standing.

Yin.

She should've stayed down. Blood crusted her torn clothes, the gunshot wound gaping, but her body had already stitched torn tissue back together. Her breath gasped, sharp and ragged, yet her limbs moved, defying the damage. Weak but holding.

Her fingers locked around Yang's frame like iron clamps, nails biting metal. She was anchoring herself, digging in, refusing to be thrown off again. A low, building hum vibrated through the Junkyard, through Kraken's bones. The magnet swung, slamming into both Synthetics with a resounding clang.

The force yanked Yin and Yang from the pavement, hurling them upward as if gravity reversed. Kraken flinched, the impact ringing in his ears. Yang hit first—metal meeting metal. Her body snagged, frame fused to the industrial pull. The magnet held her inexorably, limbs splayed as if crucified. Yin...should've dropped free. But she didn't. Yang's fingers were clenched around her wrist.

Yin thrashed, twisting against the vice-like hold. Her legs scraped empty air. But Yang held fast. If she fell, Yin fell with her. The magnet shifted, its reinforced arm groaning as it swung toward the compactor. The massive jaws of the crusher yawned.

"Oh no." Kraken's heart seized, the world narrowing to

absolute terror. "Shit. Nori, stop it!" His voice drowned beneath the groan of machinery. Nori didn't know. She couldn't see Yin, caught in Yang's grip, about to be crushed.

Kraken's legs burned, but he sprinted toward the crane. His damaged knee shrieked, pain shooting up his leg, but he didn't slow. He leapt, fingers snagging rusted rungs. The magnet carried them higher, the compactor gaping. Rust flaked off, cutting his palms. Wind tore at him, his grip slick with sweat and blood, but he hauled himself up the crane's arm. Muscles screamed, tendons stretching. The structure shuddered, bolts loosening. He didn't stop. Couldn't stop. The potential of Yin being crushed to scrap fueled his urgency.

Below, Yin wrenched against Yang's grip, her nails biting deep into the other woman's wrist, drawing more dark synthetic blood. But Yang was locked in. Her lips peeled back, her breath coming in sharp bursts, eyes wild with something Kraken couldn't name.

Intent.

She wanted this.

Wanted to drag Yin down into oblivion.

Yin looked up. Her gaze found Kraken's. Even through the blood and dirt, her eyes were clear. Focused. Unafraid.

He reached out, fingers stretched wide, the wind straining his breath. "Yin!" his voice tore out, nearly lost beneath the groan of shifting machinery. "Take my hand!"

"Your purpose is complete," Yang snarled, her voice cutting the chaos. "You must be eliminated."

The compactor loomed, rusted walls slick with oil, hydraulic fluid, and things Kraken pushed back. Yin's breath came in harsh bursts, blood bubbling at her mouth, but her eyes held Kraken's, steady and unwavering. That gaze grounded him—unspoken trust, a belief he would save her.

"My purpose is not complete," she said, her voice quieter now but firm. Clear. She reached for him, fingers straining, nearly brushing his.

Just a little further.

Blood dropped from her fingertips, falling in slow motion toward the compactor. "I've found a new purpose."

Yang's lips curled in a bitter sneer. "Living amongst humans?" She spat the words, disdain thick. "You're too much like them. Imperfect. It will kill you."

Yin didn't flinch. Her stare held. She looked at Yang with something almost peaceful, like she had found an answer to the question that had plagued her. "Perfection has a limit, otherwise it'd tread into imperfection. My imperfection makes me *limitless*."

With a deliberate motion, she wrenched her arm outward and snatched Kraken's hand. His fingers locked instantly. A solid, bruising, desperate grip. Her skin was slicked with blood and sweat, but he held fast. "I've got you."

The metal beneath his boots groaned as he pulled, the crane's framework trembling. Every muscle screamed, his vision tunneling—get her out. The strain threatened to tear tendons from bone. But he didn't let go. He'd never let go.

A sudden snap shattered the air. The magnet's arm buckled under the pressure, metal fatiguing under stress. Reinforced bolts sheared off one by one, each pop like a gunshot. Everything yielded to gravity. Yang's grip faltered. Kraken's pulse skipped, too late to brace. The momentum yanked Yin upward, but Yang clutched the last thing she could—Yin's robe, the silk fabric that had accompanied her since the beginning. The sound of tearing silk cut through the roar of machinery. Kraken's arm nearly ripped from its socket as he hauled her clear. Something popped in his shoulder, searing pain blinding his vision.

And then Yang... Yang fell. A flash of white hair, cold metal limbs twisting, reaching for purchase that wasn't there. She disappeared into the compactor, swallowed by darkness.

The ground shook, machinery roaring. Gabriel waited below, finger poised over the activation button. The compactor doors crashed shut—a final, deafening crunch. Metal shrieked, metal crumpled, circuits shorted. The sound dragged on, each second detailing Yang's destruction. Silence.

Yin sagged in his arms, her breath ragged. She didn't look at him but stared down into the howling vacuum of the compactor maw where her robe—a piece of her old life—had just vanished. Her expression was a subtle sketch of grief.

"You're okay." The words scraped from Kraken's throat, raw and tight as rusted metal. He hauled her tighter; the sheer fact of her presence was a blinding, agonizing relief. His hands shook; he couldn't stop them. "You're okay."

She wrenched her focus from the drop, her dark eyes locking onto his. The first gust of the coming squall blustered strands of hair across her cheek, but she left them there. "Theo," she spoke, her voice a low anchor beneath the storm's rising scream, "I need you to know... You are my home."

The declaration struck him, stopping his heart in the space between beats. He hung suspended, lips parted in soundless surprise. Then, something broke open in his chest. A sound tore from him, a laugh—raw, breathless, and tipped with a fierce, cutting relief that felt like true pain. He crushed her against him, burying his face in the dark silk of her hair, the convulsive sound vibrating through them both.

"Yeah," he managed, voice cracking. "Yeah, okay. Good."

The magnet's hum ceased with a metallic click. The tension unraveled. Kraken exhaled, the fight's weight still pressing his ribs. His body demanded collapse, but he held upright. Yin needed him strong just a little longer.

The wind tore at his clothes, sharper, carrying the acrid tang of ozone. Overhead, the sky darkened, thick clouds churning, edged with a sickly green. Lightning flickered, silent but promising violence. The storm was here.

A whoop ripped through the wind. Nori flung open the crane's hatch and leapt down, her boots clanging on the metal. She pumped a fist, grinning wide. "That's what I'm talking about!" she shouted. "Boom! That's how you take down a killer robot!"

Gabriel's laugh pealed from across the yard, high and slightly manic with relief. "You catch that?" he called, eyes gleaming. "Took her down. Saved your ass, too." He dusted off his hands, smirk widening. "Guess I'm the hero this time."

Kraken chuckled, distracted. His pulse still thrummed, his grip tight around Yin's wrist. The fight was over, but his body hadn't caught up. Muscles tense, breath shallow, heart racing.

Another gust bellowed through the Junkyard, rattling the wreckage. The storm's presence pressed, the air thickening with charged electricity. Thunder rolled, low and guttural, a rumble that resonated in his chest.

"We should go," Kraken said, his voice rougher than intended.

Yin's breath evened. She pulled back slightly, testing her balance. Kraken loosened his grip but didn't let go entirely. Blood marred her torn clothing. The gunshot wound was still weeping but also coagulating. She was fine.

Nori's grin faded as another gust whipped past, sending loose metal scraps clattering like skeletal fingers. "Yeah, no argument," she muttered, glancing at the sky. "Not looking to get cooked by whatever the hell that storm's putting off."

Gabriel preened, still basking. "Then let's move. I'd rather celebrate surviving this mess somewhere that isn't actively trying to kill us."

Kraken released Yin's wrist but didn't step away. She stood, breathing steadily, posture straight despite exhaustion. She met his gaze, unreadable, and gave a small nod. Ready.

They moved together through the wreckage, the wind pushing at their backs. Each gust stung with static, the air thick with impending violence. Debris shifted and groaned.

At the Junkyard's edge, the first raindrops pelted metal with a soft hiss—acidic droplets eating rust. Smoke rose, an acrid stench filling the air. Kraken didn't look back. Nothing remained but scrap and a crushed machine. Yang was gone.

They survived.

Kraken exhaled, muscles finally relaxing. His ribs throbbed, body heavy, every injury screaming. They were safe. For now.

Chapter 40

THE SKY WAS AN UNBROKEN STRETCH OF THICK, SLATE-colored clouds muting morning to a pale, colorless wash. Yin stood on the rooftop, the wind whipping damp and cold against her skin. The tempest had scoured the city, leaving a sharp, metallic tang in the air, a residue of artificial cleansing systems that purged the atmosphere. The city reset.

She expelled a slow breath, vapor dissipating in the chill. The night's burden still clamped her, a dull thrumming ache beneath skin where bruises bloomed. Her wounds had sealed, her tissue knitting itself, yet exhaustion bled deeper than flesh, a profound drain on her reserves.

Kraken anchored himself beside her, a solid mass against the shifting wind. He spoke no pointless words, recognizing this silence as sanctuary. Below, the city woke, neon signs flickered, traffic hummed, and music throbbed from some distant, tireless club. The world simply rolled on.

Yin lifted her gaze to the shifting grey. The sun was there, buried behind layers of cloud and pollution, though none alive today had ever laid eyes on it. Her fingers brushed the hem of her shirt, the unfamiliar fabric chafed without the weight of her robe. The absence sat strange against her skin, a muted emptiness where something constant had once been. It had been torn from her, ripped away in the final moments of the fight, tumbling down with Yang into the compactor. A fitting end, maybe. An old piece of herself buried alongside what she used to be.

Her fingers stilled.

Six months.

Six months since she emerged into uncertainty, into a life earned. Into something hers.

She glanced at him. Kraken remained steadfast, a constant and trusted friend. When their gazes locked, Yin's lips curled—a small, tired acknowledgment. He returned her smile, subtly shifting in posture: present.

Her hand sought his.

His fingers closed around hers, steady, warm. The friendship forged through fire and betrayal, settled—strong, unshaken. They faced the sky together, the dim glow pressing against the clouds, the silent promise of morning. They endured.

A sharp chime cut through the quiet. The moment fractured as Kraken's posture snapped taut. The faint glow of his com-tact flared over his eye, displaying a static-riddled image. A voice shrieked through the feed.

"Kraken? We don't have time. We're under attack."

The words ignited a thread of adrenaline in Yin.

"How many?" Kraken demanded.

The feed hissed with static. Miriam's voice clawed back through. "Don't know. Hit fast. Outnumbered." An explosion rocked the audio. The voice returned, sharp, steady despite the noise. "Get here. Now."

The feed died.

A wordless current surged between them. Kraken's eyes blazed.

Feet pounding on the rooftop, they sprinted toward The Farm.

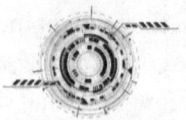

THE STENCH HIT FIRST: THICK, SUFFOCATING, A MIX OF SMOKE, scorched wood, and pulverized flesh. Ash choked the air, coating Yin's tongue with bitter ruin. The Farm blazed. Fire devoured wreckage, gnawing at collapsing structures. The ground crawled with bodies—some sprawled, others buried beneath blackened rubble, limbs jutting at unnatural angles. Heat seared her skin, and the wind howled through the ruins.

She forced her feet forward, scanning the carnage for survivors. Her pulse hammered louder than the fire, louder than Kraken's footsteps.

Nori slumped against a support beam, face smeared with soot, still breathing. Not far, Nari dug frantically through rubble, fingers raw. Izzy crouched, clutching a blood-soaked arm, alert.

Beneath the rubble near Izzy, a charred hand protruded. A delicate wristlet clasped a ballerina trinket. Rose.

Yin's heart dropped.

A figure materialized from the smoke: Miriam. Her clothes torn, blood streaked her face. She looked at them, at the destruction, her expression carved from stone.

Kraken's voice cut through the fire's roar. "What happened?"

"They hit us without warning," Miriam said. "Jets. Military-grade. Dropped payloads on us like we were nothing. Almost everyone's dead. Everything's gone. Someone told the Inner Ring where we were."

The truth cracked through Yin, shattering her composure. The memory flashed: Aja, coolly assessing the location she'd willingly surrendered at Nassar Industries.

Her throat seized. A guttural wave of realization slammed her: her fault. She had given them the location. She had bartered it because she'd overheard the plan to use her as leverage. Self-preservation had demanded the exchange. She had believed the Outsiders saw her as nothing more than a weapon to trade.

Now, standing before the corpses and flames, the logic evaporated. She hadn't been protecting herself. She had destroyed them.

The admission tore free, stripped bare of defense. She forced the words out, each syllable a scourge.

"It was me," she confessed, voice raw with despair. "I told Aja where the hideout was."

The impact was immediate. A crushing weight slammed into her chest, ripping her off her feet. Air fled her lungs as she crashed onto the cold dirt. Miriam towered above her, eyes wild.

"You traitorous Synthetic," Miriam spat, fingers curling, the pressure crushing Yin's ribs. Panic seized her lungs, the desperate, primal need for oxygen overriding all thought. Yet beneath the pain, a chilling resignation settled. This was the ultimate price. She had earned this end. She did not fight it.

The fire behind Miriam cast jagged shadows across her face, making the rage in her eyes burn hotter. Tears cut clean lines through the soot and blood on her cheeks.

"Do you have any idea what you've done?" Miriam's voice cracked, oscillating between a scream and a sob. "They're dead because of you. Rose is dead because of you!" She stepped closer. The pressure increased. Something inside Yin cracked. "You brought death to our doorstep. You destroyed everything we built!"

Yin tried to speak, but no air remained.

"We never should have trusted you," Miriam continued, voice dropping to something colder. "I knew. I knew from the beginning you were a liability. A weapon that would turn on us. And I was right."

"Miriam, stop!" Kraken's voice tore through the haze. His desperate hands clamped on Miriam's arm, pulling hard. "Don't do this."

She didn't let go. The pressure didn't ease. "Get off me, Kraken."

"Miriam, please." His grip tightened. "This won't bring them back."

"But it will make *me* feel better," Miriam screamed, spittle flying. Her whole body shook. "The Synth deserves to die. She killed them. She killed all of them!"

"None of this would've happened if you hadn't tried to bargain for her life," Kraken said, voice breaking. "This isn't just on Yin. We share this responsibility."

"Don't you dare," Miriam snarled, wrenching away from him. The pressure on Yin's chest eased. Just enough for a thin thread of air. "Don't you dare try to make this about me. I was protecting us. Protecting the mission. She chose to betray us."

"She was protecting herself from us," Kraken snapped. "From a plan that would have gotten her killed. What did you expect her to do?"

The pressure increased. Yin's vision blurred. She could feel things tearing inside her, breaking apart.

"If you kill her," Kraken whispered, "I'm done."

The pressure stopped increasing.

"What did you say?" Miriam's voice was low, dangerous.

"You heard me." Kraken's tone was steady now. "You kill her, I leave the Outsiders. Right now. Right here. You'll have one less fighter, one less set of skills. And you need everyone you have left."

Silence stretched between them, with only the crackling of flames and the distant groan of collapsing structures.

Yin couldn't see Miriam's face from this angle, but she could feel the struggle. The war happening inside the woman standing over her.

"You would choose her over us?" Miriam finally asked. "Over everything we've built? Over everyone we've lost?"

"I'm choosing not to become what we're fighting against," Kraken said. "I'm choosing to believe that the ends don't always justify the means. That we can be better than this."

"Better?" Miriam's laugh was bitter, broken. "Look around you, Kraken. Better got us nothing but ashes and corpses."

"Then what do we have left to fight for?" he asked. "If we abandon our principles, if we become killers who justify every cruelty because of what we've lost, then what makes us different from them? What makes our cause worth dying for?"

The pressure on Yin's chest held. Then, slowly, agonizingly, it began to ease.

"I should kill you," Miriam said, voice hollow now. Emptied of rage and filled with exhaustion. "I should crush every organ in your body and leave you here to rot with the rest of the wreckage."

Air rushed back into Yin's lungs. She drew a breath, body adjusting.

But the final blow didn't come.

Miriam stood above her, chest heaving, fists clenched. Tears continued to stream down her face, cutting through the soot and blood.

Kraken hadn't moved. His hand was still extended toward Miriam, not quite touching but ready.

The others were watching. Nori from her position against the beam, eyes wide with shock. Nari had stopped digging, frozen. Izzy stared at them, expression unreadable through the blood and ash.

Yin could feel their stares cutting into her. The crackling fire cast flickering shadows across their faces. Grief, anger, exhaustion. No one spoke, but their silence was thick with judgment.

Shame twisted through her chest alongside the pain. She had done this. Destroyed their home, killed their family, shattered everything they'd built. And for what?

She pushed herself upright. Her body protested, ribs grinding together, but the discomfort was manageable. Distant.

Miriam stood rigid, back to Kraken, breathing still uneven. She didn't speak for a long moment. When she finally turned, her gaze found Yin. Sharp, unforgiving, but no longer murderous. Just empty.

"Get out."

The words were hardly a whisper.

Yin didn't move, didn't breathe.

Miriam stepped forward, stare cold as steel. "I never want to see your face again." The firelight caught the hard set of her jaw, the devastation buried beneath her exhausted fury. "This is the last time I spare your life. If I ever see you again, I won't hesitate. I won't listen to reason. I will kill you where you stand."

The finality in her voice settled like ice.

Yin wanted to say something, anything, but what words could possibly change this? What could she do to make amends when there was no undoing what had been done? Apologies were hollow. Explanations were excuses. Nothing she could say would bring Rose back, rebuild the Farm, or restore what she had destroyed.

Nothing.

The Outsiders were gone. The Farm was gone.

She had never been one of them. Had never pledged loyalty to their cause. Her allegiance had always been singular, focused on one person alone.

Kraken.

And now, because of her, he stood amid the ashes of everything he'd fought for. His family, his purpose, his home. All of it was reduced to rubble and smoke because she had made a choice.

That was the weight that pressed against her chest now. Not Miriam's condemnation, but the knowledge of what she had cost him. What she had taken from him.

Yin turned and walked away from the flames, from the bodies, from the people she had betrayed. Each step felt heavier than the last. Behind her, the fire continued to burn, consuming everything that remained.

She didn't look back.

Chapter 41

The temporary platform erected outside the Inner Ring's fortified gates shone under the pale, filtered light that passed for midday in Ignis, its polished surface reflecting the sea of faces gathered in the plaza beyond. Aja stood at the podium, the wooden dove resting in their palm—a tangible reminder of loss that the cameras captured in perfect detail. The weight of it surprised them. Such a small thing to have carried so much meaning for a man who had shaped decades of policy.

Behind them, the other high councilors sat in carefully arranged chairs on the platform, their expressions solemn for the occasion. Supreme Chancellor Virelian occupied the central position, his face a mask of controlled grief that would play well on the evening broadcasts. The empty chair where Elder Statesman Valenstrom should have sat served as a stark reminder of the violence that had claimed one of Ignis's most respected leaders.

The crowd below sprawled over the plaza and into the adjoining streets. Citizens from both sides of the wall, united in their shared outrage over the terrorist attack that had stolen their beloved statesman. Holographic displays projected Aja's image to those too distant to see clearly, to ensure that every word reached every corner of the city-state.

"Citizens of Ignis," Aja began, their voice carrying clearly through the amplification system. "We gather today to announce a historic step forward in protecting our city-state from those who would see it destroyed."

They lifted the wooden dove slightly. The cameras captured its worn surface, polished smooth by decades of meditative handling. A gesture of remembrance that would resonate with viewers who remembered Elder Statesman Valenstrom carrying it through countless council sessions.

"The terrorist attacks on our facilities, the murder of our beloved elder statesman, the ongoing threats to our infrastructure—these acts of violence have made one thing abundantly clear." Aja's tone grew firmer. "Our existing legal frameworks are insufficient to protect citizens from enhanced individuals who have declared war on our way of life."

The crowd's murmur of agreement rippled through the plaza like wind through a wheat field. Aja spent hours crafting this speech, each word precisely chosen to build support for the legislation Valenstrom's death had made possible.

"Today, I am proud to announce that the Recombinant Regulation and Containment Act has been signed into law," Aja announced, the words carrying across the plaza with the weight of historical significance. "This legislation will provide our security forces with the tools they need to identify, track, and neutralize Recombinant threats before they can strike again."

The Recombinant Regulation and Containment Act passed the emergency council session with overwhelming support. After Valenstrom's funeral, with his moral authority buried alongside his body, the remaining politicians had found their principles remarkably flexible. Liu cited the clear and present danger to infrastructure. Martinez spoke eloquently about the inadequacy of the existing legal framework. Even Thorne abandoned his earlier reservations, arguing that military necessity demanded immediate action.

Elder Statesman Yamamoto. The title still felt new, weighty with the authority that had once belonged to their former mentor. They ascended to Valenstrom's seat within hours of his funeral—a swift appointment that Supreme Chancellor Virelian had justified as necessary for governmental stability. Now it was Aja's voice that carried the moral weight of the Elder Statesman Assembly, Aja's counsel that the supreme chancellor sought in private sessions.

The irony was exquisite. The same man who had once dismissed their vision now hung on their every word, seeking the wisdom that had supposedly died with Valenstrom. Virelian had no idea that his new trusted advisor was the architect of his predecessor's demise.

The applause was thunderous, wave after wave of sound washing over the marble steps. Aja remained still during the ovation, their expression appropriately grave despite the triumph singing in their veins. The R.R.C.A. would create specialized research facilities, grant broad authority for genetic studies, and provide legal cover for everything they needed to accomplish. Humanity's salvation, wrapped in the language of public safety and tied with the ribbon of a martyr's sacrifice.

"The Outsiders believed they could terrorize us into submission," Aja continued once the applause died down. "They believed that by murdering our leaders, by destroying our facilities, by threatening our children, they could force us to abandon the principles that make us who we are."

They paused, allowing the cameras to capture their expression of cold satisfaction. In the editing rooms, technicians would enhance the lighting to emphasize the shadows beneath their eyes, the weight of responsibility drawn deep across into their features.

"They were wrong."

The words rang out like a declaration of victory, which in many ways, they were.

"I am here today to announce that our security forces have dismantled their entire network," Aja declared, their voice carrying across the plaza with the weight of absolute authority. "The terrorist organization that called itself the Outsiders has been annihilated. Their threat to our city-state has been neutralized."

The crowd erupted in wild celebration, cheers and applause creating a deafening roar that shook the very foundations of the plaza. Aja allowed a slight smile to cross their features as they watched the jubilant faces below.

"Elder Statesman Valenstrom's murder has been avenged," Aja announced, raising their voice above the continuing cheers. "Justice has been served. Swift, decisive, absolute. The blood debt owed for his sacrifice was paid in full."

The crowd's roar of approval confirmed what Aja had known from the beginning. The public wanted blood for Valenstrom's death, and they didn't particularly care whose blood it was as long as it belonged to the right enemies.

"In closing," Aja said, raising the wooden dove one final time, "I want to share something Elder Statesman Valenstrom once told me. He said that the measure of a civilization is not how it treats its friends, but how it protects the innocent from those who would do them harm."

The fabricated quote would become part of Valenstrom's legacy, repeated in history books and carved into memorial stones. The irony was perfect—using his own moral authority to justify exactly the kind of authoritarian overreach he had spent his life opposing.

"Today, we honor his memory by proving that justice delayed is not justice denied. We honor his sacrifice by showing that those who threaten our city will face swift, total retribution." Aja's voice carried the full weight of their conviction, and for a moment, they nearly believed their own rhetoric. "We were not terrorized. We were not silenced. And now, with every last Outsider cell eliminated from our city, we can move forward in safety and peace."

The applause was deafening, a wall of sound that shook the very foundations of the plaza. Aja stood unmoved in its center, the wooden dove now tucked in their jacket pocket. A trophy of their victory and a reminder of the price that moral flexibility commanded.

As the crowd began to disperse, Aja saw the holographic displays that would carry their message across both sides of the city. Their image multiplied infinitely, each projection carrying the same expression of righteous satisfaction. By evening, every citizen of Ignis would know that their government had delivered decisive justice for the terrorist threat. That revenge had been taken, swift and merciless as winter.

The politicians filed away from the podium, their role in the public theater complete. Soon, the real work would begin. The facilities authorized by the R.R.C.A. would be swiftly constructed, staffed by researchers who understood the true nature of their mission. They'd bring the Synthetic designated Yin in for comprehensive study, its adaptive genome finally yielding the secrets that could save humanity from its slow extinction.

And Yang—the white-haired twin whose very existence threatened everything Aja had worked toward—had been eliminated by the only weapon capable of matching its capabilities. Yin had served its purpose, removed the obstacle, and now would face whatever fate necessity demanded.

The wooden dove pressed against Aja's ribs as they walked, a small weight that grew heavier with each step.

Valenstrom's final lesson, delivered from beyond the grave—that every choice carried a price, and that price was always paid in full.

But that was a concern for tomorrow. Today, they had won.

Epilogue

Five Years Later

Transmission received.

The message thrummed through the room as the city of Modernist Ignis unfolded in holographic splendor, swallowing the space in shifting light. Three-dimensional images transported Yin to the heart of the rally, where thousands gathered beneath a sky streaked with neon. Hover cars zipped through the air, their thrusters leaving shimmering trails of electric blue and violet. Banners bearing the symbols of both the Revivalists and Traditionalists rippled above the crowd, their colors blending in the wind. The people chanted in unison, their voices rising to meet the crescendo of the celebration. All except for Yin, whose scowl tightened.

Unity Day.

Every year, the government forced this broadcast onto every screen in Ignis. Every year, they twisted the truth into a spectacle. Yin's fists clenched as she resisted the urge to shut down the projection as Supreme Chancellor Kael Virelian and his former rival, Revivalist Thorian Castrell, stepped forward onto a grand stage. Their figures loomed larger than life, bathed in the glow of the projectors. Once sworn enemies, now standing shoulder to shoulder as symbols of unity.

Castrell, now an elder statesman, clasped hands with Virelian, lifting them high for the world to see.

"For a better Ignis!" they shouted their new slogan.

The crowd erupted in thunderous cheers.

Her com-tacts adjusted the imaging around her. Yin didn't look away. Unity Day celebrated her actions. Her actions sealed the Outsiders' fate, crushing them beneath the weight of a government desperate to maintain power.

After the Farm's destruction, the Revivalists and Traditionalists wasted no time forming an alliance and turning public fear into political capital. The Outsiders, once rebels and freedom fighters, became a faceless threat. The government flooded the networks with images of their stockpiled weapons, their bomb-making supplies, their supposed plans to turn Ignis into a warzone. Fabricated evidence. A carefully constructed narrative.

And the people believed it.

Even in Retro Ignis, their former allies turned their backs. With no resources, no shelter, no reinforcements, the remaining Outsiders were hunted down.

And that is your fault, Yin thought, the weight pressing against her ribs. Every year, she watched the transmission as penance. A reminder of her failure.

She scanned the stage. Her gaze swept across the Council of Elder Statesmen until it landed on a figure she knew too well—Aja. They lounged in their usual relaxed posture, one leg draped over the other, fingers twisting a wooden dove against their knee. To any outsider, they appeared disinterested, bored even. But Yin saw the coiled alertness beneath the idle pose.

Then their gaze snared hers.

Yin froze. The projection was a one-way transmission. No one on the other side could perceive her presence. And yet, Aja's lips curved into a knowing smirk. As if a hook had caught her, drawing her deeper into the holographic lie. The expression suggested the impossible: that Aja had already won some unspoken game she hadn't realized they were playing.

A warning prickled at the back of her mind, insistent and unsettling. She searched their face for a clue, for any hint of what they meant by it, but Aja gave her nothing more. Their smile clung to their mouth a beat longer than natural before they turned their attention back to the rally, leaving Yin with the eerie certainty that this exchange had somehow been intentional.

"Yin."

The voice cut through the projection, snapping her back. She blinked. The cityscape dissolved around her as she was pulled out of the transmission. The apartment's living room settled back into focus. A holo-screen was mounted across from the worn coffee table, its surface cluttered with datapads, an empty mug, and a half-eaten protein bar abandoned hours ago. Kraken stood near the door, combat gear-clad, rifle slung across his back. His expression gave away nothing, though Yin recognized the tension in his shoulders and the readiness in his stance.

"It's time," he murmured. "I'm headed out."

She turned toward him, swallowing her apprehension.

This day, chosen by the Outsiders above all others, would mark the culmination of their fight. While the Revivalists and Traditionalists gathered within the walls of the Inner Ring for their symbolic peace talks, the Outsiders would strike. They would strike at the wall that separated the elite from the rest of Ignis. They would bring it down. And with it, all the government officials inside.

Yin held Kraken's gaze.

The low light of the apartment enveloped the space between them as silence stretched out, heavy with understanding, rich with all the promises and fears their mouths never uttered. His presence anchored her, a certainty unwavering in the chaos, making it effortless to forget the world burned just outside their window. Now, standing at the door, combat gear molding to his frame and rifle hugging his back, he resembled the steady refuge she had always known. Warm. Solid. He carried himself as if today meant nothing more than another dawn they faced together.

A familiar ache tightened inside her. She'd watched him leave before. The first time had been for the prison break, and she'd stood in this same apartment, in this same silence, not yet understanding what it meant to worry for someone else's safety. Back then, the concern had been foreign, analytical. A variable she couldn't quite process. But this time, the worry was a tangible weight, not an abstract calculation.

Worse, something else nagged. It began when Aja's eyes found hers through the projection, when that knowing smile curved their lips. The feeling hadn't left. It sat in her gut like a stone, cold and heavy, whispering that she was missing something vital. That Aja's smile hadn't been coincidence or imagination. It had been a message.

She wanted to tell Kraken to stay, to voice the unease crawling beneath her skin, but the words died unspoken. What could she say? That Aja had smiled at her through a one-way transmission? That something felt wrong in a way she couldn't name?

His mouth curved, and the tension eased from his shoulders, transforming his face. The smile wasn't wide, wasn't bright or forced, but a small, real confession meant only for her: a promise that they would stand together against whatever darkness came next, as they always had.

And then he left.

ACKNOWLEDGMENTS

First and foremost, I want to thank everyone who has supported me through the journey of writing this novel. Whether you were there to read the early drafts, offer a word of encouragement, or simply provided the space I needed to create, your belief in this story has been my foundation.

I owe a special debt of gratitude to Marie Campbell. Thank you for the incredibly opportunity to create my own version of Nari. She is a character I have come to love deeply, and I truly hope I have kept her as close to the spirit of what you originally imagined as possible while she navigated the complexities of Ignis.

To Kraken's original creator: thank you for the honor of letting me adopt him and make him my own. Keeping his spirit alive even today has been one of the most rewarding parts of this process. Watching him grow into the man he is today has been a privilege I don't take lightly.

Thank you all for helping bring the world of Caenogenesis to life.

ABOUT THE AUTHOR

Tasha He has been writing stories since childhood, when they proudly printed out "chapters" from the family computer to share with relatives. A lifelong lover of science fiction and fantasy, Tasha is drawn to worlds that provide both escape and reflection, especially the deeper truths woven into dystopian tales.

Beyond writing, they are a passionate disability advocate and founder of Disenfranchised Writers' Voices, a nonprofit dedicated to supporting low-income and disabled authors. When not immersed in building new worlds, Tasha enjoys playing video games and spending time with their beloved pets.

 instagram.com/hethe.author

www.ingramcontent.com/pod-product-compliance
Lightning Source LLC
LaVergne TN
LVHW030335070526
838199LV00067B/6298